SNIPER

A FRANK RENZI CRIME THRILLER

"You live by the gun … you die by the gun …"
– Joe Valachi, member of a New York-based crime family

SUSAN FLEET

Music and Mayhem Press

Sniper is a work of fiction. Although certain world figures are named in the book, the events depicted herein are entirely fictional. All other names, characters and events are products of the author's imagination or used fictitiously. Any resemblance to actual persons living or dead is entirely coincidental.

ISBN-10 1-7321301-0-8
ISBN-13 978-1-7321301-0-4

Cover photographs used with permission from Fotalia:
 Crosshair on paper © pilotl39
 Silhouette of businessman talking on the phone © Prazis Images

Back cover author photo by Pete Wolbrette

Printed in the United States of America

Praise for Susan Fleet's Frank Renzi crime thrillers

ABSOLUTION

Best Mystery-Suspense-Thriller of 2009 — Premier Book Awards

"Relentless tempo . . . sharp writing." — Kirkus Reviews

"Creole-flavored suspense." — *Attleboro Sun Chronicle*

"A serial killer is on the loose in New Orleans [and] detective Frank Renzi [must catch him] before he claims his next victim. A whole-hearted Bravo!" — *Florida Times-Union*

DIVA

"Fleet subtitles *Diva* a novel of psychological suspense. That's an understatement." — Jan Herman, *Arts Journal*

"... an obsessed stalker lusts after his victim." — Tom Bryson, *Too Smart To Die*

"A jazzy, classical thriller ... left me wanting an encore." — Amazon reader

NATALIE'S REVENGE

Best Mystery-Thriller of 2014 — Feathered Quill Book Awards

"Fast paced, well written and extremely challenging to put down."
    — Rebecca's Reads

"Natalie is a truly intelligent and seductive character. A tremendously great series. This is one great author!" — Feathered Quill Book Reviews

"Superb. The plot was riveting. This book could easily be made into a movie." — Amazon reader

JACKPOT

"Thrilling and gripping. The writing is tight and builds to a tense climax." — Readers' Favorite

"A page-turning thriller. Frank Renzi hunts a disturbed serial killer."
    — Tom Bryson, author of *Sarcophagus*

"The coolest detective in literature at the moment [is] Frank Renzi."
    — Feathered Quill Book Reviews

NATALIE'S ART

"Compelling characterization and a surprising conclusion. That's fine art, indeed." — Midwest Book Reviews

"Non-stop twists begin on page one. A fast-paced, action-packed read!" — Feathered Quill Book Reviews

"Buy your ticket for this roller coaster ride! [The] action continues until the very end!" — Amazon reader

MISSING

"Fleet opens with a bang … fast-paced and hard-hitting with satisfying twists. An emotional roller-coaster ride far above the usual whodunit."
    — Midwest Book Reviews

"[The] action never stops ... the suspense is palpable." — Feathered Quill Book Reviews

"Surprise read of the year. I could hardly put it down."
    — Amazon reader

NATALIE'S DILEMMA

"There is no better place to begin a suspense/thriller than on the gritty streets of New Orleans, and no better person to begin with than Homicide Detective Frank Renzi." — Feathered Quill Book Reviews.

"The gritty atmosphere comes vividly to life [with] characters who face difficult choices. *Natalie's Dilemma* will delight fans of intrigue and thrillers." — D. Donovan, senior reviewer, Midwest Book Reviews

"From Italy to New Orleans, this intense thriller will take you on the ride of your life!"— Amazon reader

DEDICATION: For VB, whose Armenian parents fled Turkey
during the Armenian genocide

CHAPTER 1

FRIDAY June 24, 2011 – New Orleans

He felt no animosity toward her. She was merely a convenient target.

Rain or shine, four mornings in a row she had jogged around the corner at 7:20, her blonde ponytail bouncing, elbows bent, hands curled into fists, legs pumping. No rain today, but no sun either, the sky overcast with thick gray clouds.

Lying prone on the roof of a four-story building across the street, he nestled the rifle stock against his cheek, inhaling the faint odor of gun oil, the polished-walnut stock caressing his skin.

The final moments before the kill were always the same, an ache in his groin and a pre-combat hard-on.

An image of his former lover flashed into his mind, her sullen expression during their final quarrel. She wouldn't give in, nor would he. But to hell with her. Focus on the assignment.

The runner was almost in position.

Sighting on her through the scope, he centered the cross-hairs on her head.

Snipers obsessed about weapons, but the powerful Schmidt & Bender scope and the bolt-action L39A1 Enfield rifle had served him well during the war. He had already done the calculations, the distance and the wind speed, currently null, the air dead calm.

He breathed deep to steady his heart rate.

Set his finger on the trigger. Gently squeezed.

Her head exploded, spewing brain matter and a mist of blood into the air. She staggered, her legs wobbling, and fell to the ground.

Excellent. A perfect shot. She was probably dead before she hit the sidewalk.

A normal round would have made a loud crack as it left the muzzle faster than the speed of sound, but he used subsonic ammo, and the suppressor attached to the rifle barrel reduced the report to a quick *pop*, like a balloon breaking.

He retrieved the casing, put it in his pocket, disassembled the rifle and carefully placed the components into his knapsack. The runner had her routine and he had his.

Snipers lived to shoot again by getting into and out of position without being seen. He scanned the windows across the street, then the sidewalk below. No sign of witnesses, but soon there would be.

Crouched low, he scrambled to the access door to the roof, which he'd propped open with a plastic wedge. He shoved the wedge in his knapsack and raced downstairs.

His getaway vehicle was in an alley one block away. The runner was not his first hit in New Orleans, and she wouldn't be his last.

———

7:45 AM

Homicide Detective Frank Renzi stood on Prytania Street outside the crime-scene tape. The body lay on the sidewalk, a woman in running shorts, her blonde hair matted with blood.

NOPD cruisers with flashing blues prevented access to this block, and two patrol officers on the opposite sidewalk urged curious onlookers to move along.

Prytania Street was in the Garden District, not Frank's jurisdiction, but after the 9-11 call, his friend, patrol officer Tony Coppola, got here first. Tony took one look at the woman's head and called Frank on his cellphone to alert him about another possible sniper victim.

He hoped to hell it wasn't. One was plenty.

But Tony had questioned the man who'd called 9-11. While leaving his building across the street, the man saw the woman fall, ran to her, saw the blood and called 9-11. He hadn't heard a gunshot, hadn't seen anyone else on the street, with or without a gun.

Which led Frank to believe the woman might, in fact, be another sniper victim.

Ten days ago someone had shot a cab driver in the French Quarter —his jurisdiction—and as lead investigator he was under enormous pressure. The NOPD brass—berated by business owners, irate politicians, and the New Orleans Tourist Bureau—wanted the killer found pronto. New Orleans was a tourist destination, and a murder in the French Quarter was bad for business.

But ten days later he had no leads, no witnesses, no suspects. The ballistics report said the slug that killed the cab driver had come from a high-powered rifle, likely one commonly used by military snipers. The grieving widow claimed her husband had no enemies, no quarrel with anyone. So much for motive.

If the woman on the sidewalk turned out to be another sniper victim, he had to consider the nightmare scenario: a sick-o with a rifle was using New Orleans residents for target practice.

If the national media got wind of it, they'd be here in a New York minute, trumpeting garish headlines nationwide: There's a sniper on the loose in New Orleans!

Calculating the possible trajectory of the bullet, he crossed the street and entered an alley between two four-story brick buildings. One step past a smelly dumpster, he felt a creepy-crawly sensation on his neck. His gut tightened, his mouth suddenly dry. He'd been shot at a few times, though not by rifle fire. He looked upward.

Was the sniper up there, drawing a bead on him?

No, that was his lizard-brain, messing with his mind. The sniper was long gone by now.

He ran across the street and raced upstairs to the victim's apartment. Tony stood outside a door, six-foot-four and barrel-chested, a twenty year NOPD veteran savvy enough to call him on a cellphone, not the police radio, to keep things quiet.

"I think we've got another one," Frank said.

"Sure as hell looked like it to me." Tony nodded at the door. "Take a look, but make it fast. A District-Six homicide detective could get here any minute."

Frank put on blue latex gloves and went inside.

When investigating a homicide, he always did a victim profile. The more he knew about the victim, the better his chances of finding the killer. But that might not help if she was a random victim. Maybe this was a copycat. The sicker the crime, the more media attention it drew. Plenty of nut-jobs out there, eager for the spotlight. He'd seen it happen more than once.

The kitchen was nothing fancy, a black-and-white linoleum floor, white appliances, a high-speed blender on the counter. No dishwasher, no dirty dishes in the sink, the drying rack beside it empty. An ordinary kitchen where a woman cooked her meals.

Until someone shot her in the head.

A straw purse sat on the counter beside a cellphone. He opened the phone and skimmed the contact list. The first one that jumped out: Mom. A daughter who called her mother often. But today, instead of a call from her daughter, Mom would get devastating news. The next contact was labeled Jim, a boyfriend, maybe.

He couldn't retrieve the voice or text messages without the password, but the D-6 detective could get them from the cellphone company. Providers retained copies of all messages, even deleted ones, in its database, handy for cops who needed them. The company could also tell them which cell towers her most recent calls pinged off, to track her movements in the days before she was shot.

Inside the wallet he found forty dollars cash, two credit cards, and a Louisiana driver's license. The woman was twenty-three, born the same year as his daughter. The coincidence unnerved him. If someone shot Maureen, he would be devastated.

In the purse, a small notepad yielded a grocery list, errands to run, appointments. That might be helpful. A key ring beside the purse held four door keys. No car keys.

In the living room he found a laptop computer, another avenue to explore—emails and social media accounts. On the table beside it, a *Times-Picayune* and *Computer World* magazine. A woman who followed the news and appeared to work with computers. He'd better interview her co-workers.

In the bathroom, eyebrow pencils, eye shadow, hairspray and skin lotion stood on the vanity. Inside the medicine cabinet: tweezers, a nail clipper, over-the-counter pain remedies, and a packet of birth control pills.

Across the hall in her bedroom, a double bed was neatly made. A slim black skirt and a maroon blouse lay atop the sky-blue comforter. Her work clothes, Frank assumed, ready to put on once she took a shower after her run.

He massaged his eyes and stifled a yawn. Ever since the cab driver homicide, he'd been sleeping four hours a night at best. Forget sleeping tonight. The first twenty-four hours of a homicide investigation were crucial.

His cellphone rang. He checked the ID and frowned. Juliana, his boss's wife.

"Hi Juliana, what's up?"

"Nothing good, Frank. Last night Morgan was throwing up and having chest pains. I called an ambulance and they rushed him to Ochsner Hospital."

"Jesus! How is he? Is he okay?"

"No. They ran some tests and said he needed open heart surgery right away."

Stunned, Frank couldn't speak. Homicide Detective Lieutenant Morgan Vobitch was his boss, but also a cherished friend. Open heart surgery was risky. Some people survived, some didn't. Today a young woman had gone out for a morning run and now she was dead.

Vivid memories of Vobitch flashed in his mind. Nine years ago when he'd moved here from Boston to work in the Homicide unit, Vobitch had taken him under his wing, saying they were kindred spirits. Vobitch had spent twenty years working homicides for NYPD. "We're a couple of scalawags," he said. "Damn Yankees, and I'm not talking about the baseball team!" Whereupon they had both cracked up, roaring with laughter.

Now, they often met at a pub near Vobitch's house for a burger and beer after an aggravating day at work, sometimes to kibitz on troublesome cases, sometimes just to bitch about life in general.

The possibility that they might never do that again crushed him.

"Juliana, where are you now? At the hospital?"

"Yes. He's still in surgery ...." Normally low pitched and musical, Juliana's voice wavered.

"I'll be there in ten minutes."

CHAPTER 2

11:20 AM – New Orleans

Her heart thumped her ribs, fueled by a rush of adrenaline. The familiar zing of excitement.

She put on her designer sunglasses—the tinted over-sized Avatars she'd swiped from Saks Fifth Avenue in Canal Place—and turned onto Royal Street. The street with the ritzy stores and overpriced boutiques. She pulled down the brim of her floppy straw hat. No way to tell if the security cameras on the light poles were working. No sense taking chances.

Merging with other pedestrians, she sauntered along in her skinny black skirt and loose-fitting hip-length tunic. Just another Gen-X rich-bitch tourist. That brought a smile to her face.

This Gen-X bitch was packing. A snub-nosed .22 was inside her padded shoplifter pocket. Not that she intended to use it, but feeling the weight of it was comforting. In case she got in a jam.

One block later she stopped at a window display. Royale Gifts put their most enticing items in the window. Colorful paintings of local landmarks. Historic black-and-white photos of Louis Armstrong, Billy Holiday and Jelly Roll Morton. But she wasn't looking to score any art today.

Twice last week, disguised in her funky-casual outfits, she had cased the shop. Only two clerks were working, even in the late-morning when traffic was heavy. No sign of a security guard, but there were security cameras mounted near the ceiling in each corner. Wandering through the store, she'd chosen the item she wanted. Not the jewelry locked in the glass case beside the register. Not the ritzy designer purses that decorated metal trees along the right wall. Not the glitzy designer shirts hanging from the wood carousels.

No, a bottle of expensive French perfume would do nicely, thank you. In 2005, Thierry Mugler had created a special fragrance called Alien. Perfect. *Alien* was one of her favorite movies.

Too bad she didn't have a boyfriend. Dab some on her neck, seduce him and hit the sack. Then again, boyfriends could cause problems, always wanting to move in with you. She liked living alone.

Alone with her loot. Free to admire it, enjoy her triumph, and plan her next score.

To support herself, she sold the crappy stuff: candy, steaks and chicken from grocery stores, vitamins, toiletries and disposable razors from pharmacies. She kept the special treats for herself.

A bell dinged as she entered Royale Gifts. Ahead on her left, a female clerk at the register looked over and smiled at her. She didn't smile back. Maintaining a haughty air, she glided past the register toward the rear of the store.

Where was the other clerk? There had to be one.

Her heart rate ratcheted up a notch. The thrill of the hunt. Almost as good as sex. Better, if your partner was a dolt.

Ah, there he was. Men were so easy to manipulate, and he was young enough to appreciate her charm, fake though it might be. She allowed herself a faint smile as he approached her, playing the cool seductress. She wasn't a knockout, but this had nothing to do with physical beauty. It was all about attitude. She'd been perfecting it for years. A careless toss of the head, the appearance of confidence, the faux indifference. That drove men wild, made them try harder.

"Hi," he said, his bright blue eyes welcoming her. "Can I help you find something?"

She pursed her lips, frowning. "Zhees French Quarter you call it," she said, feigning a French accent. "I hunt for zee magnifique French parfum, but ..." She stopped, feigning helplessness.

"Hunt no more, madame. We have some fine French perfume. Follow me."

He took her to a small glass case near the front of the store. Lined up inside were sleek bottles of Givenchy and Yves Saint Laurent and her target, Thierry Mugler.

"How about a bottle of Givenchy?" the clerk said as he unlocked the case. Smiling at her, he set the bottle on the counter and gave her a small square sample to sniff.

She held it to her nose. Tilted her head back and forth. "*Merci, mais non*, I think not."

"The Yves Saint Laurent is very popular." He took out a bottle of Parisienne.

She sniffed the sample and shook her head. "Non. This eez gift for my leetle sister." She shrugged. "A teenager, yes? Tres difficile!"

"I hear you," he said, grinning now. "I've got one of my own. I know just the one to please her. Alien, one of our best sellers, by Thierry Mugler."

7

He bent down to retrieve it from the case and set the sleek bottle of Alien beside the other two bottles.

Another adrenaline rush sent her pulse racing. Now her coveted prize wasn't locked up, it was on top of the case. She glanced at the other clerk. The woman was ringing up an order, chatting with the customer, an older woman in a prim gray pantsuit. A quick peek at the door. No one about to enter. No other customers in the store. Perfect.

"Your sister will adore it!" the clerk said, smiling at her.

She sniffed the sample and picked up the bottle of Alien.

"Magnifique!" she exclaimed.

With a sweep of her arm, she knocked the other two bottles to the floor, and they shattered, sending fragments of glass and perfume across the floor, expelling a sweet aroma into the air.

The clerk stood there, frozen in shock. She ran like hell.

Three strides got her out the door. She shoved the bottle of Alien into the pocket of her shoplifter tunic and dashed across the street, headed for the next corner. Oddly, no one took any notice, as if it were perfectly normal to see a short girl in a slinky black skirt and a straw hat racing along the sidewalk.

But then she saw an NOPD patrol cop up ahead. Damn! Before he could spot her, she bolted around the corner past a coffee shop and took off, heading north.

"Stop!" yelled a male voice behind her.

She glanced over her shoulder. She couldn't believe her eyes.

Damn! The clerk was chasing her! Worse, he was gaining on her, his long legs eating up the distance between them.

Shit, shit, shit. Without breaking stride, she reached in her pocket and pulled out the gun.

Another shout from behind her. "Stop, thief!"

Her heart pounded her chest, not with excitement this time. Panic was more like it. She'd been caught once before, not in New Orleans, but the memory was vivid in her mind. An ugly and degrading experience. Damned if she'd go through that again.

Skidding to an abrupt halt, she turned and raised the gun.

The clerk stopped, his face a study in shock and amazement.

He raised his hands.

She pulled the trigger. The loud report hurt her ears.

The clerk dived to the pavement. A gray-haired older man on the sidewalk stared at her, his mouth open.

She turned and sprinted away, rounded a corner and ran for her life, turning one corner after another. At last, she stopped at a lamp post, panting, gasping for air, her chest heaving.

No footsteps pursuing her.

She ducked into a narrow alley and climbed the wire-mesh fence at the end. Home free.

———

1:35 PM

Frank stood beside the hospital bed, gazing at his boss. Swaddled in white sheets, Vobitch lay deathly still, eyes closed, his normally ruddy cheeks as pale as the sheets. Tubes in his nose and attached to his arm were hooked up to machines, beeping and whooshing.

A pale shadow of his obstreperous, trash-talking self. But at least he was alive.

After a difficult six-hour operation to replace a valve in his heart, the surgeon had come to the waiting room to tell Juliana that her husband had survived and was in the recovery room. After they settled him into a private room, Frank and Juliana had gone to see him.

Relieved but still anxious, Juliana bent over the bed and kissed her husband's cheek. Vobitch opened his eyes, looked at her and said in a weak raspy voice, "I guess I'm alive."

"Thank goodness for that," Juliana said.

"Yeah," Frank said. "I can't get rid of you." A wise-ass remark to cheer him up. Vobitch looked at him, shut his slate-gray eyes, and conked out again. A half hour later, Frank had told Juliana to go home and get some rest.

Now the machines beeped and whooshed as he stood by the bed, recalling other visits to other hospitals. Maintaining a vigil in his mother's room, right before she died. The saddest day of his life.

Visiting Kelly after she'd been shot, not knowing if his lover, another NOPD detective, would live or die. To his everlasting relief, she had survived.

He hadn't called to tell her about Vobitch yet. The doctor said his prognosis was good, but Frank wouldn't believe it until Vobitch showed a glimmer of his usual feisty self. Dropped an F-bomb or two, maybe.

He felt a sudden urge to call his father. Two o'clock in New Orleans, an hour later in Boston, Judge Salvatore Renzi was probably sitting in his courtroom, dispensing justice. Seventy-six years old and still working. Frank hadn't seen him since Christmas, six months ago, he realized. He should call him more often, but work kept him so busy—

"Frank." A soft croak.

Startled, he looked at Vobitch. His eyes were open, more alert this time. "Glad you decided to quit loafing," Frank said, using sarcasm, their frequent mode of communication, to avoid blurting: *I'm glad you're alive but you look awful.*

Vobitch slid his right arm—the one not tethered to machines—out from under the sheet and touched the tube in his nose with one finger. "Fucking tube. I'd like to rip it out."

"Bad idea, Morgan. The nurses might arrest you."

"Arrest me," Vobitch muttered. "What time is it?"

"Almost two in the afternoon. You had a long snooze on the operating table."

"So the doc said. Jesus, they put a fucking pig valve into me."

Frank smiled. "It could be worse. They put in a donkey valve, we could call you a jackass."

"Plenty of people already do. Who's minding the store?"

"Relax, Morgan. Believe it or not, NOPD will survive a day or two without you."

"Day or two, my ass. More like a week. Christ, the fucking criminals will take over the city."

More like two months, Frank thought, but didn't dare say.

He wasn't going to tell Vobitch about the second sniper victim, either. Two victims in ten days, the top brass would be screaming at the district commanders and hounding the homicide detective supervisors, like Vobitch.

"Juliana gave you a big kiss about an hour ago, remember that?"

A faint smile. "Yeah. She's a peach. I'm a lucky man."

At first glance Morgan and Juliana seemed like an odd couple. Morgan was a fireplug, squat and muscular, silvery hair, slate-gray eyes and a foul mouth. A former ballerina, Juliana was six-feet-tall, with smooth ebony skin, expressive dark eyes and enough smarts and charm to tame her irascible-cop husband.

Their mutual love of classical music and opera, discovered more than twenty years ago in New York City, had deepened into an abiding love.

"Hey, you'd do the same for her. I sent her home an hour ago, told her to get some rest. Now that you've decided to rejoin the living, I'm leaving, too. I got phone calls to make."

Vobitch gave him a knowing look. "Kelly?"

"Yes." Vobitch was well aware of his relationship with NOPD Detective Kelly O'Neil. "Sleep tight," he said. "I'll see you later." But not tonight. Not with a second sniper victim.

He left the room and rode the elevator downstairs. As he entered the parking garage his cellphone rang. He checked the ID. Jesus, why was his daughter calling him? Unnerved by seeing Vobitch so weak and vulnerable and the dead runner, born the same year as his daughter, he thought: *Please let Maureen be okay.*

His mind flooded with images. Maureen in her bassinet, clamping her tiny hand around his finger, gurgling as she smiled at him. Watching her play basketball in third grade. Driving her to riding lessons and a few years later, watching her face glow with excitement as she guided her horse over a difficult jump. Maureen was all grown up now, an orthopedic surgeon with a practice in a Baltimore suburb.

But that didn't stop him from worrying about her.

When he answered, she said, "Hey Dad, what's going on down there? I just saw a news alert on the Internet, a Fox News report about another sniper victim in New Orleans."

Damn! Already it was on the national news.

Get ready for a media circus.

"It's not confirmed yet, but the gist of it's true."

"He shoots at random victims, they said. Why would anyone do that?"

"Good question. I'd love to talk to you, Mo, but it's hectic."

He seldom discussed the sleazebag criminals he was hunting. Or their evil crimes.

"No problem, Dad. Keep me posted. Love you."

"Love you too," he said, and got in his car. On the way to the office he'd call Kelly. Then he'd start hunting for the Sniper.

CHAPTER 3

12:15 PM

Slouched in an easy chair in a secluded corner of the lobby, he put down the magazine he was pretending to read and took out his disposable cellphone, playing Spy-gate in a cheap New Orleans hotel.

Twelve-fifteen on the dot it vibrated in his hand. He answered and said, "Hi, how's it going?"

"The sun finally came out. It was nasty this morning." The correct response.

"I wouldn't know. I was sleeping." His coded answer.

"Lucky you." Confirmation. And after a pause, "The project went pretty well."

The sniper clenched his jaw. *Pretty* well? It was perfect! After the hit, he had collected any telltale evidence and sped away with no one the wiser.

"The Foxhounds are already sniffing at it."

His heart surged with excitement. Fox News was reporting the story. His sniper skills were drawing international attention. "When does The Package arrive?"

"Not for a bit," Control said, in his supercilious-Brit voice.

His excitement fizzled like a leaky balloon. Christ, how long did he have to wait? He'd been here for six weeks. All expenses paid including a hotel room, but he wanted to wrap this up, collect the rest of his loot and fly home. His most lucrative assignment ever. Fifty grand already in his bank account, twice that when he completed the job.

"Can you be more specific?" *Stop dicking me around, you putz.*

"No."

"Tell me more about The Package." *Who the hell is he? Or she. Plenty of powerful women around these days. And plenty of people who wanted them dead.*

"Sorry, I've got another call coming in."

Fury rose up inside him. Control was blowing him off. The prissy little paper-pusher told him who, where and when, but never got his hands dirty. *Have you ever seen a person die?* he wanted to scream. *Up close and personal through a sniper scope? Their head exploding? Their blood and brains spilling out?*

"George wants to have a beer with Harry," he said. "*Soon.*"

George was his code name. Control was Harry. Not their real names, but George sure as hell did want a face-to-face with Harry. Coded phone calls were too fucking tedious.

"That might work. I'll ask him." Sticking to protocol with the proper coded response.

"Remind him about that tune he heard in Chicago." Saturday in the Park, recorded by the rock band Chicago. The park was one of their designated meeting points. Tomorrow was Saturday.

"I will. Two to one he'll go for it. As long as it's sunny." Two minutes to one. PM not AM.

"Beaver," he said, indicating which protocols to use on their next call. He rose to his feet. Tomorrow he'd rip his obnoxious self-important minder a new asshole if he didn't give up some Intel. In the meantime, he'd go up to his room and watch Fox News. Check out the local stations, too.

He spotted a crumpled newspaper on a nearby sofa, discarded by another guest. Strolling past the sofa, he swiped the *Times-Picayune* and headed for the elevator.

———

12:25 PM

Gasping for breath, her heart racing, she locked her apartment door and went in the kitchen. Her mouth was so dry she could barely swallow. Jesus! What if the clerk had caught her?

She filled a glass with cold water and gulped it down. But he didn't catch her. She was too focused. Determined.

And she had a gun. She'd never had to use it before, but it sure was handy, stopped the damn clerk in his tracks just as she had intended. She took the snub-nosed revolver out of the padded pocket in her tunic and set it on the counter. She hadn't hit him, but she could have if she'd wanted to. She played paintball every weekend and hardly ever missed her targets.

To hell with the clerk. Time for her reward. She took out the bottle of Alien, smooth purple glass with gold trim, a hundred bucks for three ounces. She loved the lettering. Alien

Jagged and mysterious, like the monster in the movie.

Just holding it in her hand got her excited.

13

She took the bottle in the living room and placed it on her coffee table. Her apartment was no palace, but it had the usual appliances and a shower, and the rent was cheap. Iron bars covered the window overlooking the alley, courtesy of her landlord. A second floor apartment didn't discourage the monkey-robbers in New Orleans. She never left the window open when she left the apartment.

Now it was stifling, and she was already hot and sweaty.

She closed the curtains, pulled off her black skirt, then the tunic and sniffed the armpits. Yuck. Time to ditch this one. Three more shoplifter outfits were in her closet.

Clad in her bra and panties, she sat on her futon, five-foot-four and 118 pounds according to her primary care physician last week. The doctor had renewed her birth control pill prescription and said she was in fine shape. The doctor thought she worked out at the gym, knew nothing of her other strenuous activities: paintball, rollerblading, shoplifting.

She stretched out on the futon, contemplating her narrow escape. The only time she'd ever been caught was in California when she was sixteen. She'd been shoplifting for a year and figured she had it down. Wrong. In a mall department store she'd stuffed a pricey pair of Tommy Hilfiger jeans into her pocket-pouch and waltzed out the door, but a store security guard outside the door nabbed her.

The memory made her skin crawl. She'd cried and pleaded with him to let her go. No dice. The fat pig grabbed her arm and dragged her into the store security office. And made her give him a blow-job. Disgusting. Then he'd zipped up his pants and let her go.

But that was then and this was now. Antique photos and colorful posters decorated the walls of her living room. Recalling where she'd swiped them, she smiled. A bookcase opposite the futon held a dozen paperbacks, all stolen, crime thrillers by Patricia Cornwell, Lisa Gardner and Lee Child—she hated romance novels—and one hardcover, a book about astrology.

Her prize trophies were on the top of the bookcase. Energized, she got up and admired them. Her favorite lay inside a velvet case: a pendant with her astrological totem in the center. She was a Scorpio, like Mother, but unlike her in every other way. They'd never gotten along, not even when she was a toddler. Later, it got worse.

She despised her mother, but she loved the pendant, a two-inch circle edged in gold. Inside it on a blue background were symbols of the twelve signs. In the center on a pale gold background was a black scorpion. She only wore the pendant on special occasions.

Or when she was depressed and needed to get out of a funk.

Beside it were her diamond stud earrings. Boosting them had been risky but exciting. At the jewelry store she got a clerk to unlock the case and take out several pairs of earrings. Then she distracted her, slipped the diamond studs in her pocket and left the store.

Orgasmic. The more difficult the get, the greater the thrill.

She picked up the bottle of Alien. A difficult get and a close call, but she had escaped. She ran her fingers over the bottle, smooth as silk beneath her touch. She pressed the button, emitting a mist of Alien into the air, inhaling the scent. A feminine fragrance, as promised on the Thierry website. Rich and bewitching, designed to bring out the goddess in every woman,

Enthralled, she walked through the mist. Felt it kiss her shoulders and neck. Bliss.

———

11:30 PM

Frank set his bottle of Sam Adams on Kelly's kitchen table, watching his lover put a plate in the microwave and punch some buttons. She had a nice living room, but they almost always wound up talking in her kitchen. Or in bed.

Tonight she had on a scoop-necked teal top and white shorts. Five years together and she still turned him on. If he wasn't so tired he'd jump her. Maybe not living together was the answer. He had a small condo in the French Quarter. At a dead run he could get to the District-8 station in six minutes if he had to. But no frolic in bed tonight.

No rest for the weary with a fresh homicide. After a quick visit with Kelly, he would go back to the office, see if anything new had surfaced.

"I can't believe Vobitch had open heart surgery," Kelly said, tugging at a lock of her dark curly hair, what she did when she was worried about something. "He can be a grouch sometimes, but he was always nice to me when I was working Homicide."

"He didn't look so hot, but he dropped a couple of F-bombs."

Kelly laughed. He loved her laugh. Straight from the gut, it lit up her sea-green eyes.

"That's a good sign," she said.

15

"True, but he's already worried about work. Said he'd be back in a week, but I doubt it. Needless to say, I didn't mention we had another sniper victim."

"You're sure it was the sniper?"

"A single entry wound in the forehead blew the back of her head off. The coroner said it came from a high-powered rifle. We'll know more after we get the autopsy report."

Kelly sipped her beer, gazing at him, her eyes somber. "You get an ID?"

"Linda Seeling, twenty-three, mother lives in California, father's deceased. It already made the national news. Maureen called to ask me about it."

"In Baltimore?" Kelly hadn't met his daughter, but knew she lived in Baltimore.

"She saw it on the Internet. Nancy Grace will probably show up here tomorrow, which I need like a hole in the head. I got no leads on the first one."

"You know what Vobitch says. Means, motive and opportunity."

He raised his beer bottle in mock-salute. "Thank you for reminding me, Detective O'Neil."

Kelly was a great detective, had a drawer full of commendations. Another turn-on. When he'd met her, she was working Homicide in District-5, an ugly case that drew plenty of media attention, mostly directed at him, none of it good. Until they solved the case.

"There's no mystery about means," he said. "He's got a high-powered rifle."

"So who uses high-powered rifles? Hunters and people in the military."

"And snipers. Like the Texas Tower guy at the University of Texas in Austin back in the sixties. I looked it up online. Charles Whitman was a hunter *and* a Marine."

"We had a sniper in New Orleans too," Kelly said. "Terry used to talk about it."

Terry O'Neil was her husband, an NOPD cop until he stopped to help a disabled motorist on the I-10 seven years ago and a drunk driver hit him. The drunk survived. Terry did not.

The microwave dinged. Kelly got up, took a plate out of the microwave and brought it to him. "Mama Leone's, a chicken Parmesan sub with eggplant. Eat up, Frank. Knowing you, it will be black coffee and potato chips all night, and more black coffee and doughnuts for breakfast."

"Got me all figured out, huh?"

She arched an eyebrow. "Not completely, but don't try to fool me."

He grinned. "Only a crazy man would do that. Thanks, it smells great." He took a bite and realized how hungry he was. "Tell me what Terry said about the New Orleans sniper, in seventy-three." He'd read about it, but he wanted to hear Terry's take on it.

"Terry knew a patrol cop who survived it. A black guy had a grudge against cops, started targeting policemen on New Year's Eve. They chased him but he got away. A week later he got up on the roof of the Howard Johnson's Hotel near City Hall and shot nineteen people, including ten police. It was awful. Nine people died, four of them were cops. "

"Let's hope this guy doesn't start shooting cops."

"Jesus, Frank. Don't even think it."

"The Howard Johnson's sniper was military, right?"

"Yes. A Navy veteran."

"And don't forget the Beltway Snipers in 2002." He yawned and massaged his eyes. His eyelids felt like sandpaper. He needed some serious shut-eye.

"But that was two guys. A former veteran and his teen protégé."

"Exactly," Frank said, working on his chicken Parmesan sub. "I got a bad feeling about our sniper. This isn't like those cases where the snipers kill a lot of people during a single incident. Our guy shoots them one at a time. He seems more like a serial killer, except he kills from a distance, not up close and personal. No sexual component, unless he gets off on shooting a gun. No emotional frenzy."

"An organized killer," Kelly said, using FBI terminology. "He plans them."

Years ago when Frank was a homicide detective in Boston, he'd taken an FBI profiling course at Quantico on serial killers. Kelly hadn't, but he'd told her about it. She knew the terms.

"Not exactly. Maybe he just goes to his sniper perch and waits for a good target. A male cab driver in the French Quarter, a female runner in the Garden District."

"Different parts of the city," Kelly said. "At least five miles apart."

"That's what scares me. One place we could isolate him, but he roams around. No shortage of tall buildings and roof tops here." He swigged some beer. "I think this guy is ex-military. Could be a hunter too, but hunters don't operate in urban environments."

Kelly pursed her lips and arched an eyebrow. "What makes you so sure it's a man? Women can shoot too. That shoplifter is raising hell in the French Quarter, shot at a clerk."

"Jesus, don't remind me. All the politicians and business owners are calling the NOPD bigwigs. But I think the sniper is a man." He grinned at her. "I also think I better go. You're looking way too delectable. What's up tomorrow? You on call?"

Kelly worked in the Domestic Violence unit now, another high-risk job. Investigate a domestic call, you never knew what you'd find, could be nothing, could be a guy with a gun. Or a machete.

"No, I'm off this weekend. Frank, we know he's got a rifle, but why is he shooting people?"

"The million-dollar question. No communications to the media."

"Not yet."

"Damn! Wouldn't that be a kicker? Son of Sam on a roof."

Kelly grinned. "BTK with a sniper rifle."

Referencing two notorious serial killers who'd sent letters to journalists or the police. Black humor to soothe frazzled nerves. Civilians might consider it shocking, but sometimes humor was the only therapy on a job that forced them to confront the worst crimes imaginable on a daily basis.

"Be careful, Frank. Your name is out there as lead detective on the French Quarter murder."

"Yeah, yeah. I better get into Wit-Sec program, have the FBI protect me."

"Don't joke. What if he's killing them to piss off cops? Get their attention."

Frank rose from his chair, cupped her face in his hands and kissed her. "You've got my attention at the moment."

"At the moment, but I know that look in your eye. *I'm gonna get the fucker.*"

Recalling the lifeless young woman on the sidewalk, born the same year as his daughter, he said, "You can take that to the bank. I am going to *get* that motherfucker."

CHAPTER 4

SATURDAY – June 25, 2011 – 8:30 AM

Damn! Nothing new about the New Orleans Sniper on Fox News.

Disappointed, he raised the clicker and switched to a local station. Surely they'd have something. He shifted his butt on the crappy easy chair in his room. The bed was okay, but the chair was lumpy, like some 300 pound gorilla had rented the room and sat on it for a week.

Located two blocks north of the French Quarter, the hotel was a bit seedy, but he'd slept in worse places. At least it had cable TV and a mini-fridge he could stock with a beer or two.

A news jingle sounded and there it was, a stark headline topping the news. **ANOTHER SNIPER VICTIM**

He listened intently as the newswoman said, "New Orleans police have identified the latest sniper victim, twenty-three-year-old Linda Seeling." A photograph flashed on the screen: a closeup of a smiling young woman with a blonde ponytail and sky-blue eyes.

Studying her face, he felt a pang of regret. Another reason he didn't like this job. Already two non-combatants had died. Back when he was fighting a war, he'd only ever shot men wielding guns, looking to shoot him. Kill or be killed. That was his motto, then and now.

"A talented computer programmer and a graduate of UCLA-Berkeley, Linda came here four years ago to work at Software Unlimited. The company issued a statement saying Linda was a fine worker and their thoughts and prayers go out to her family and friends. Her grieving co-workers say she was a special person, easy to work with, always cheerful and smiling."

Fine, but what are the police saying?

Linda's photo disappeared, replaced by another, an older black man, also smiling.

"The first victim was shot ten days ago on Canal Street in the French Quarter. A longtime driver for Metro Cab, Hector Alvarez was about to go off duty when he was shot." Another photo, a sobbing black woman leaving a church, comforted by other mourners. "His grieving widow wants to know why police haven't caught the man who shot him."

The sniper waved a hand like he was swatting away a fly.

Because I'm too smart for them. Pick your spot, leave no evidence, and get out fast.

19

"New Orleans police have scheduled a press conference for Monday morning, but this is unlikely to calm New Orleans residents. They fear they might be next. And who can blame them?"

He raked his fingers through his thick dark hair. He hoped there wouldn't be a next one. He wanted to complete his assignment, collect his loot and go home. But The Package wasn't here yet.

His fucking minder wouldn't even tell him who it was. But five hours from now he would.

Meet Control in Lafayette Park and scare the bat-piss out of the prissy little man with the wire-rim glasses, flabby belly and fidgety hands, obsessing over the city's high murder rate, so terrified of the gangs that roamed the city, he never ventured out after dark.

He didn't know where Control was staying, at a safe house or some posh hotel maybe. They worked for the same outfit, a firm with offices all over the world, including the one he and Control worked for in London. But he was certain Control had never worked in the field, had probably never fired a gun, not at a human target anyway.

What should he say to him?

Tell me who it is or I'll blow your fucking brains out. No that wouldn't do. Control might tell the Boss. Then there'd be hell to pay.

A grainy black-and-white photo on the television screen caught his eye, a still from a security video, a woman wearing a floppy hat and over-sized sunglasses.

"The Shoplifter managed to hide her face during her most recent crime," the newswoman said. "Yesterday morning she stole an expensive bottle of French perfume at Royale Gifts."

He smiled. The woman had balls. And smarts, hiding her face from the security cameras.

"But this time the store clerk chased her. Police released a clip from a surveillance camera outside the store." More grainy footage, the woman running, and a man chasing her.

He studied her legs, slim but muscular beneath her short skirt. Sexy. But the man's legs were longer, he was gaining on her ...

Hurry up or he'll catch you!

"Then she pulled out a gun and shot at him. Fortunately she missed. Unfortunately, this wasn't caught on a surveillance camera. If you recognize this woman, New Orleans police ask you to call Crimestoppers. Tipsters can remain anonymous and may be eligible for a reward. Take another look at the photo and video."

The still photo flashed on the screen, then the video.

Damn! Look at her go!

A woman after his own heart right here in New Orleans.

A risk taker like him, packing a gun, and the cops couldn't find her.

He laughed aloud. The cops couldn't find her, but maybe he could.

Give him something to occupy his time until The Package arrived.

———

11:00 AM

She raced down the corridor, hearing shouts behind her.

"She went down there!"

"No, over here, Carlos. This way!"

Breathing hard, she burst through a doorway into the courtyard, the door long since stolen by looters. The school had been abandoned after Katrina, perfect for paintball games, Carlos had said, chatting her up as he drove down a narrow street overgrown with weeds and lined with trash bags full of rotting garbage. She'd rolled up her window to avoid the smell.

Here, the stench was worse. Three brick walls enclosed the courtyard, tagged with graffiti. **POO-BAH** in huge white letters outlined in black. Underneath it **COOCH** and **ALLY CAT**.

Her heart pounded as she sprinted past a five-foot stack of abandoned tires to a burned out car, no telling what make it was, some kind of sedan, both doors missing on one side. She crouched beside the trunk and shoved a 10-shot pod-pack—high-grade gelatin caps with thin shells, guaranteed to break on impact—into her compressed-air paintball gun.

She and Carlos were the last ones standing on their three-man teams. She was the only woman. Quick and agile, Carlos made it competitive, which was fun. He played to win and so did she. She'd worn her nose-ring and her purple goth wig, short and spiky. Four months ago, her goth getup and marksmanship had convinced Carlos and his pals to let her play with them.

One corner of the trunk faced the wall with the open doorway. The trunk's hinges were sprung so it didn't close completely. She pulled her goggles down over her eyes, climbed inside and peeked through the opening, watching the doorway.

Her camo shirt was soaked with sweat. New Orleans was a great

21

city, but sweltering in the summer. Holding her weapon in her right hand, she wiped sweat off her forehead.

"Hurry up, Carlos. Get her!" His teammates urging him on.

Carlos stuck his head around the doorway.

She waited.

He eased into the courtyard, his eyes darting this way and that. Quick as an ally cat, he ran to the stack of tires, crouched behind them and stared at the roof. Did the idiot think she was on the roof? How would she get there? The lowest section of the roof was ten feet high.

He rose from his hiding place. "Times up! Olly-olly in free!"

She shot him in the back, and an orange pellet exploded. "Bang-bang, Carlos is dead!"

He whirled as she climbed out of the trunk. "No fair, Jaybird! You cheated! Time's up! "

As if she cared about rules. Whatever it took to beat her opponent and claim victory.

He walked toward her, a scrawny pimple-faced kid, scowling at her.

"Come on, Carlos. You got me last week."

"Did not. That was two weeks ago."

She took off her goggles. "Time flies when you're having fun. Got any weed?"

Carlos grinned. "Got some in my car. You looking to score?"

"Yup. Got a twenty with me. Let's go get it."

"The guys will be mad."

"Fuck 'em."

He cocked his head, leering at her. "What you gonna do for me?"

Ick. He wants a blow job. Fat chance. She'd told him she was nineteen, and he believed it because she was short and had big brown eyes like her idol, Winona. Nineteen? Hell, she was twenty-four.

"Gonna give you a twenty. Period. If you don't want it, I'll score someplace else."

Clearly disheartened, he frowned at her and said, "Aw-right. You're a tough babe, Jaybird."

Tougher than you know. "So are you," she said. Make him feel important. Guys were easy to manipulate, always worried about status and respect, worried most of all about impressing women.

She'd left home at fifteen and never looked back. Well, now and then she called her dad when she needed money. Other than the fat-pig security guard who caught her, she'd always managed to get her way with guys. But she had no interest in Carlos.

Too bad. It had been a while since she'd had sex and she was horny. But someone would turn up sooner or later.

"Let's go, Carlos. Take me to your car." Get the weed, go home and take a shower, have a cold beer and smoke some weed.

Then get on the Internet and scope out her next score.

———

12:35 PM

Frank left the hotel and got in his car, picturing the victim's mother, Nancy Seeling, slumped on a chair, hollow-eyed, recalling her parting shot. "I want you to get the bastard who killed her!"

He wanted to get him, but he wasn't lead detective on this case. Fine by him. He had enough on his plate with the first sniper kill. District-Six Homicide Detective Roger Vance had caught the brass ring on this one. Well liked by his colleagues, Vance was a solid detective with twelve years experience and happy to share the load. They had split up the list of people to interview—friends, co-workers and nearby residents—and agreed to swap any pertinent details. When Frank said he wanted to talk to Mom and the boyfriend, see if their stories lined up, Vance readily agreed. Frank didn't think Mom or the boyfriend had ordered the hit, but stranger things had happened.

Twenty-nine hours after the murder, they had no leads. They were still waiting for the autopsy report. No one had seen the shooter, no forensics at the scene other than blood and the spent round. Just like the first one. The sniper was a phantom. Choose the target, take a deadly head-shot and split.

He started the car and headed for the boyfriend's condo. Jim Lortzing, age twenty-six. He hadn't called to say he was coming. Forewarning people gave them time to get their stories down pat. Better to just show up. He'd run Lortzing's name through the system and found no criminal activity. A Google search yielded the usual social websites: Facebook, Twitter, MySpace. Judging by the photographs, Jim was a good-looking guy, in a masculine sort of way. Strong chin, straight nose, smiling eyes. But Frank doubted they'd be smiling today.

Ten minutes later he rang the doorbell at a two-story condo complex, well-maintained, nice landscaping, glossy white paint on the window and door frames. Lortzing opened the door, his eyes blood-shot, his face haggard, looked like he hadn't slept for days. Frank showed his badge, introduced himself and asked if he could come in.

Lortzing's mouth quirked in annoyance. "I already talked to the other detective."

"I know. But I'm investigating the other sniper case, the one in the French Quarter. Detective Vance thought it might help us solve both cases if I talked to you, too."

Without a word, Lortzing took him into the living room. The place was a mess, clothes strewn over the floor, a pizza box open on the coffee table beside a bottle of Jack Daniels and an empty highball glass. Lortzing closed the pizza box, tucked the liquor bottle under his arm and said, "Can I get you something? Bottled water? A beer?"

"No, thanks. I'm good."

"Have a seat. I'll be right back." Dressed in shorts and a T-shirt, no shoes, Lortzing went in the kitchen, visible through a cutout in the living room wall. He opened the refrigerator, took out a beer, came back and sat on the couch.

"I'm very sorry for your loss, Jim. I know this is a bad time for you."

"Who the hell would want to kill Linda? Jesus, everyone loved her. We were going to get married." Lortzing slumped back on the couch, barely holding it together. A handsome guy, dark curly hair, even fea-tures, chapped lips and bloodshot eyes.

"How did you meet Linda?" He knew Lortzing wasn't from around here, born and raised in Detroit, attended college there, moved to New Orleans three years ago.

"We met at a computer conference three years ago and hit off right away. She writes software, I sell the hardware. She's smart as hell, the smartest woman I ever met."

"Always great to hit it off with someone. Any disagreements lately?"

"No." Lortzing frowned. "We were going to get married. I told you that."

"Had you set the date?" He knew they hadn't. Linda's mother had told him.

"No. We were thinking about next year. In the spring maybe. Linda wanted everything to be perfect. She's fanatical about being organized. Not OCD, but close. She had flowcharts for everything. I'm more of a wing-it kind of guy."

Frank nodded. *A toss-your-dirty-clothes-on-the-floor kind of guy.* "What's a flowchart?"

"Oh. Sorry. That's a computer programming term. A chart with little boxes that shows which data goes where, how it flows." He shrugged. "Programming was never my long suit."

"So Linda was an organized person."

"Beyond organized. She kept a schedule of her daily routine. Monday through Friday she'd get up at 6:45, drink some OJ, take her vitamins and do her stretching exercises. Go for a run at 7:05. Get home and take a shower at 7:35. Get dressed and head for work at 8:15."

"What about weekends?"

"Weekends? Weekends were different." Lortzing's face took on a haunted expression. Frank knew it well, had seen it many times, the moment when the deceased's loved one realized things were never going to be the same.

"On Friday Linda would come here after work. We'd go out for dinner or maybe cook here. Linda always stayed here Friday and Saturday nights. Like clockwork."

Like clockwork. Frank rose to his feet. "Thanks for speaking with me, Jim. I appreciate it."

"I watch the news," Lortzing said, his eyes flinty. "Some nutcase is shooting people. Ten days ago he shot a man in the French Quarter, and now Linda's dead. Why can't you catch this guy?" His unspoken words being: *If you'd caught him, Linda would still be alive.*

"We'll get him, Jim. I can't promise when, but we'll get him."

He left the condo and got in his car, Lortzing's words buzzing his mind like a mantra. *Like clockwork.* Compulsively organized, Linda kept a minute by minute schedule, ran the same route at the same time every day before work.

Maybe that's what got the Sniper's attention.

Plenty of targets on Canal Street in the French Quarter where he shot the cab driver, but why choose a quiet residential street in the Garden District, to kill his next victim?

Frank had no idea, but he intended to find out.

CHAPTER 5

Hidden in shadow like a Bengal tiger hunting its prey, he waited behind a live oak tree in Lafayette Park. He had arrived an hour ago. Leave nothing to chance. Monitor any suspicious individuals. Know your escape route. Any nasty surprises, he'd be gone in five seconds.

Planning and preparation. Stalking and concealment. Skills he had mastered in the military.

Control was late, a pathetic attempt to exert his power.

Pathetic and annoying.

Ever vigilant, he surveyed Lafayette Park, a vast open space with gravel paths weaving through green grass, bushes and trees. He could smell the sweetness of nearby wildflowers, heard birds chirping in the tree above his head. Fifty yards away, an imposing statue stood in the center of the park, Henry Clay, an influential politician during the Civil War era, according to the metal plaque on its base. Near the statue, a young mother tossed a ball to her toddler, feeling safe and secure. Oblivious to the man who'd already shot two people in her city.

And many others, during the war.

These days, killing the enemy was an impersonal act. Most died from missiles fired from great distances, or 500-pound bombs dropped from airplanes, or computer-guided explosives from an unmanned drone, whirring quietly overhead. Some chased the enemy in helicopters, firing machine guns at them as they ran, closer targets, but still too far away to look like real humans.

Snipers never got near the people they killed, but high-magnification scopes allowed them to see their targets with great clarity, up close and personal. Like his last hit, in Bonn.

Lying in total silence, utterly still, he had acquired his target, a bald German in a pricey suit, yawning as he got out of his limousine. The bald man was over a mile away, 2,100 yards on his range finder, but thanks to his high-powered scope, he could see the hairs sprouting from the man's ears. He exhaled longer breaths, willing his heart rate down, seeking the sweet spot for a trigger pull that ensured a kill. He took a slow, calm breath, held it and squeezed the trigger. The bald man had died instantly.

Like the female runner. And the taxi driver.

So would The Package, if his fucking minder ever told him who it was, walking toward him now, furtive and fearful, his eyes darting here and there, terrified some thug might jump him.

The sniper stepped out of the shadows and sat on the wooden bench four feet ahead of him, their designated meeting spot. Control joined him, a small foppish man wearing a powder blue shirt beneath his dark business suit, his shoes spit-and-polished to a shine.

"Nice day," Control said, regarding him through the thick glass of his spectacles.

"Like hell it is! Six weeks I've been here. How can I plan a hit if I don't know who the target is or where it will be?"

"Bloody hell, keep your voice down."

"Shut up and listen. The first two hits went well because I planned them. With no help from you, I might add. When does The Package arrive in New Orleans? Who is it?"

Control's hands fluttered to his weak receding chin, then his beak of a nose. "Don't blame me. I'm waiting for word from the man up-stairs. The Boss calls the shots."

His anger deepened, driven by disgust. Control feared the Boss even more than the New Orleans thugs. A pathetic excuse-for-a-man, Control would never dare question his superior. The sniper had never met the Boss, but he'd heard rumors about him, whispered in de-serted corridors at the London office of Zenith Intelligence, LLC.

Shrieks came from the toddler fifty yards away. Control jumped as if they were rifle shots, clutching his chest. Pitiful. "Calm down," he said. "It's only a kid. How long must I wait?"

"He'll be here in a couple of weeks."

He'll be here. A man then, but still. "Two fucking weeks? What do I do in the meantime? Wank off while I'm watching porn flicks on TV in my room?"

Aghast, Control stared at him. "Surely you don't do that. It will turn up on the hotel bill!"

"Where do you wank off? Go to some strip bar on Bourbon street for a lap dance?"

Control turned on him, his cheeks mottled with anger. "Don't fuck with me. I'm all you've got here. London doesn't want to deal with you."

He gritted his teeth. Damn right they didn't. The managers were a bunch of asswipes. There were layers upon layers of protection at

Zenith Intelligence. No paper trails. No sordid charges on hotel bills. No bitchy snipers. Plenty of lucrative clients.

"Do some target practice," Control said, rising from the bench.

"Don't tell me how to do my fucking job!"

"Don't tell me how to do mine," Control said coldly. "No more face-to-face meetings. Check in with me every day by phone. I'll tell you where and when your next hit will be."

"What do you mean, next hit?"

But Control was already hurrying away.

Rage rose up inside him, his heart pounding so hard he feared it might crack his ribs. Simulating a gun with his right forefinger, he aimed it at Control and pulled the imaginary trigger. Evil thoughts crept into his mind. Next time the gun might be real. After he finished this job and made sure the money had been wired into his account, he would take great pleasure in offing his asshole minder.

1:45 PM

Dressed in gray running shorts and a black T-shirt, Frank did his daily five-mile run on Prytania Street in the Garden District. Not his usual route, but he was trying to figure out why the sniper shot Linda Seeling here, a vibrant young woman the same age as his daughter. Earlier Maureen had called to ask how his weekend was going. What could he say? He was glad she was alive? "Not too well. I'm working a homicide. The second sniper victim. She was a talented software programmer. It made me think of you."

"How awful," Maureen had said. "But if anyone can catch the bastard, you can Dad." His daughter, the perpetual optimist.

"Thanks for the vote of confidence. I better get back to work."

"Okay, Dad. Love you. Be careful!"

Recalling their conversation, however brief, brought a smile to his face as he pounded along Prytania Street, an east-west thoroughfare in District-Six. Shaped like a narrow wedge of pie, D-6 covered acres of territory, a maze of streets and hundreds of businesses.

The wide end at the bottom bordered the Mississippi River. To the east, D-6 bordered District-Eight, and north of D-8, District-One. The western side bordered District-Two. *Location, location, location.* The real estate mantra echoed the thump of his feet on the sidewalk.

But he wasn't selling real estate, he was hunting a serial sniper, no telling where he'd strike next. He'd shot his first victim in the French Quarter. Plenty of targets there. Lots of rock stars played the Sanger Theater, and the Louisiana Philharmonic played concerts at the Mahalia Jackson Theater in nearby Louis Armstrong Park. Hell, the sniper could sit on a roof ten blocks away and pick people off as they left a concert.

New Orleans hosted dozens of music festivals. This year, Jazz Fest alone had drawn a half-million people, and that didn't include the sporting events: NFL football at the Superdome, plus college teams in the Sugar Bowl, and NBA basketball games at the New Orleans Arena beside it.

Plenty of concerts at other venues, too. On his way here, he'd driven past Lafayette Park. Last night there had been a concert, but today hardly anyone was there. The park was named after a local Revolutionary War hero with a long complicated name. Otherwise known as Marquis de Lafayette. Oddly, his statue wasn't in the park, but there was a statue of Henry Clay, an American statesman and United States Senator, known for his efforts to mediate the battles between northern and southern states over slavery. Clay had lost that battle, also lost when he ran for president, three times.

A terrifying thought brought Frank to a sudden stop. This was an election year. What if the Sniper was gunning for President Obama? Lee Harvey Oswald had assassinated JFK when he was campaigning in Dallas. But the Secret Service would notify the NOPD Intelligence Unit if Obama was coming to New Orleans, and Frank hadn't heard about any impending presidential visits.

He mopped his sweaty face on his T-shirt, started jogging again and refocused on his goal: Figure out where the Sniper might strike next. And stop him.

The National World War II Museum drew millions of visitors. On the sixth of June, there had been a huge event there, commemorating the anniversary of D-Day. NOPD provided security for such events, but that wouldn't deter a determined sniper. Bottom line, there were plenty of places in New Orleans for the sniper to shoot a history buff, music lovers, sports fans, convention goers. And tourists, the lifeblood of the city's economy.

The sniper wasn't a mass murderer like Charles Whitman or the New Orleans sniper back in the seventies. This guy shot them one at a time. Frank had no idea what had drawn him to Prytania Street in District-Six, but he knew someone who might.

With a burst of speed, he sprinted to his car parked in front of Linda Seeling's apartment building, picturing the photo of Linda in the apartment, a pretty woman with a blonde ponytail and a pixie-like smile, looked like she belonged in the pages of *Town and Country*. Now, remnants of yellow crime scene tape littered the sidewalk in front of her building.

Inside the car, he mopped sweat off his face with a hand towel, staring at the rooftops of two buildings across the street. D-6 Homicide Detective Roger Vance had gone up there to look for signs that the sniper had been there, but he had found nothing. The Sniper was a phantom who made sure he left no evidence of his evil presence.

Frank got on his cellphone and called Tony Coppola.

"Yo, Frank, how's it going?"

"No leads on the latest sniper hit, but I need a consultation. How about I treat you to a burger and beer?"

Tony chuckled. "You don't have to ask me twice. Where and when?"

"Six o'clock, the usual place."

3:25 PM

Lying prone on the roof, he took out his Nikon binoculars, not as powerful as his sniper scope, but he wasn't going to shoot anyone today. He zoomed in on the French Quarter streets, fourteen blocks laid out in a grid. Beneath a cloudless blue sky, the relentless rays of the sun beat down on him. He was sweating like a racehorse, but in the army during the war he had endured worse conditions.

Eleven days ago, he had shot his first target from this very roof. He replayed it in his mind, unreeling it like a Technicolor movie, the orange sun sinking low in the sky, the light dimming to dusk, the air thick with humidity. Sounds drifted upward from Canal Street, horns honking, hotel doormen hailing taxicabs, other men in tuxedos and top hats calling out to tourists from mule-drawn carriages, the mules pawing the pavement. But he was no tourist. He was on assignment, six floors above them, cloaked in his Army-veteran disguise: a fake beard, worn jeans and a denim jacket decorated with an American flag. Five-foot-eleven and built for speed.

In his business, preparation and accuracy were essential, but foot-speed was equally important for a clean escape.

The setting sun glinted in his eyes, but he seldom operated in perfect conditions. Find a target, take the shot and get out. Some on the sidewalk below were workers headed out for a beer with their mates or a date with a hot babe maybe. In combat one of his mates would have acted as a spotter. But this wasn't Iraq. Here, he was flying solo.

If he screwed up, this assignment might be his last.

The suppressor would reduce the muzzle blast and sonic signature, confusing any witnesses questioned by police. He sighted through the scope and set his finger inside the trigger guard. Scopes were great, but they could be finicky. Lose the target and precious seconds could elapse before it was reacquired. Guaranteed failure.

And he never failed. He was one of the best snipers in the world.

Below him, a black man in a navy-blue uniform with brass buttons got out of his taxi and stood there, savoring the last rays of the setting sun perhaps, or contemplating the dinner his wife had prepared for him. The cross-hairs settled on the man's head. His finger squeezed the trigger. And the cab driver had died.

But that was days ago. He wasn't working today. After his meeting with Control he'd calmed down. Now he knew The Package was a man, one who would come here in two weeks. Was he a businessman like the German in Bonn? A politician on the campaign trail? Earlier he'd researched the current presidential candidates. Republicans Mitt Romney and Newt Gingrich hoped to defeat the incumbent, Barack Obama. Could it be a foreign official, a diplomat perhaps?

In the course of his research, he had discovered there were fifty foreign consulates in New Orleans. Some were tiny countries like Haiti and Monaco, others larger and more important: France, Germany and the UK, countries he knew well. He was fluent in all three languages, a major asset when they paid him to do jobs there.

But why obsess over that now? Today he had a different goal.

Today he had positioned himself on the side of the roof overlooking the French Quarter and the many stores that catered to wealthy tourists, selling expensive designer clothes and accessories, shops with glittery window displays that screamed *buy, buy, buy*.

Stores that attracted the Shoplifter. He was certain she lived nearby. None of the news articles mentioned a getaway vehicle. He was dying to meet her. He wanted talk to her.

Hell, he wanted to fuck her.

Bourbon Street was jammed with tourists. He zoomed in with his binoculars. An older woman in a sleeveless dress, her flabby arms pink with sunburn. A fat man with a bushy mustache in baggy shorts. Whoa! How about the woman with long red hair, sauntering along in a short black skirt and a white tank top, holding a drink in her hand, a fancy concoction with an umbrella sprouting from it.

Should he shoot the drink out of her hand, like the American sharpshooter Annie Oakley? Or pop her in the head? It would be an easy shot, three blocks away. *Bang bang, you're dead.*

Sometimes evil thoughts entered his mind, unbidden. Like the old women in that Dickens novel his mum had read to him when he was just a boy. *It was the best of times, and the worst of times.* Even now he could hear Mum's voice, reading about the old women in the square with the guillotine, knitting as they waited for the bastards who'd committed crimes against the poor to march to the scaffold, eagerly awaiting the moment when their severed heads fell to the ground.

By then they'd been living in London. Mum read to him every night before bed, practicing to eliminate traces of her foreign accent. But why did she choose such dark stories? *The Strange Case of Dr. Jekyll and Mr. Hyde,* by Robert Louis Stevenson, Dr. Jekyll creating the demonic Mr. Hyde, believing he could control the monster. Wrong.

The sniper smiled. Everyone had a dark side, but his was darker than most. Was this due to Mum's literary choices? Only later on her deathbed had she told him about the nightmare she and his dad had endured, fleeing those who wanted to kill them.

He blew a kiss to the red-haired woman and whispered, "Today's your lucky day." His rifle was locked in his storage unit.

He resumed his search, focusing on the streets at the far end of the French Quarter. Burgundy. Dauphine. Bourbon. Royal.

Where was his risk-taker soulmate?

The Shoplifter with the sexy legs who carried a gun.

And wasn't afraid to use it.

CHAPTER 6

Frank speared one of the French fries beside his half-eaten barbecued chicken sub, ignoring the chatter of other diners. The Poorhouse Pub was always busy, a local joint three blocks from Vobitch's house where they often met. Barring any medical complications, it looked like they'd do that again, but not anytime soon.

Tonight Tony Coppola was seated opposite him in a corner booth, chowing down a cheeseburger. No uniform tonight, wearing a short-sleeved shirt that displayed his muscular arms and brawny shoulders.

Twenty years ago after serving in the Gulf War, Tony had returned to New Orleans and joined NOPD. In his early fifties, he was still in good shape, worked out at the gym every day, a husky Italian, proud of his heritage. His prominent Roman nose was crooked, a testament to his youthful boxing days. Last year Tony had helped him solve a tough case. He wasn't a detective, but Frank valued his opinions.

"How's Vobitch doing?" Tony said, mopping the last of his burger in some ketchup. "Man, I can't picture him in a hospital bed. He's a force of nature. A tough son-of-a-bitch."

"That he is. He didn't look too good when I saw him yesterday, but I talked to Juliana an hour ago. She said he's better. He's being his usual obstreperous, she said."

Tony grinned, his mug of draft beer halfway to his mouth. "Forget the fifty-cent words. He's dropping F-bombs, right?"

"Right. He knows about the second sniper victim, saw it on TV." Frank took a long swallow of Sam Adams. "He's pissed at the doctors. He wants to get back to work."

"Jesus, open heart surgery and he wants to go to work?"

"Juliana brought him a disk player with his favorite operas. To calm him down."

"Good luck with that. My old man was wild about opera. You ever see *Prizzi's Honor?* Jack Nicholson plays a mob hitter. In one scene the mob boss, this little old man, is sitting in a big chair with his eyes closed, listening to opera. It cracked me up, reminded me of my father." Tony chugged some beer. "He loved Italian operas, especially that composer, I forget his name, rhymes with zucchini."

Frank burst out laughing. "Puccini. One of Vobitch's favorites."

33

"Yeah, that's it. Frank, you gotta see that movie. Kathleen Turner plays another hitter, packs a gun, goes at it with Nicholson. Man, she's something." Tony grinned, his dark eyes mischievous. "Maybe your French Quarter shoplifter thinks she's Kathleen Turner."

"Forget the shoplifter. I've got a sniper to worry about." Frank pushed his plate aside. Great barbecued chicken but acid was eating the lining of his stomach. He had too much on his mind, the most important being: how to find the Sniper before he shot someone else.

"Sorry," Tony said. "I know you got a lot on your plate right now. How you getting along with Roger Vance? He's a solid detective, what I hear."

"Vance is fine, but we don't have much to go on. No witnesses, no forensics. No ballistics report yet, but I'm willing to bet the slug came from the same rifle as the one that killed the first victim. I checked the federal data bases for crimes with a similar MO and got nothing."

"Check with the big city police departments near here," Tony said. "Could be they got a current case, haven't had time to put it in the federal data bases."

"Kenyon and David have already called some of them. Atlanta's got some asshole shooting at cars from a highway overpass. That doesn't feel like the same MO as our sniper, but we'll stay on top of it. And we've still got more calls to make. New York, Boston, LA."

"You get anything from the runner's family?"

"Her mother told me to catch the bastard who killed her." He smiled tightly. "That's a direct quote."

"I don't blame her." Tony shook his head. "Seriously. Her daughter's twenty-three, goes out for a run and bam. Lights out. Who the hell does something like that?"

"I wish I knew. I talked to her boss and her co-workers and got nothing. According to them, everyone loved her. I crossed her boyfriend off the suspect list, but something he said got me thinking. Linda was super-organized, kept to a strict schedule, did her run every weekday at the same time."

"Okay," Tony said. "So?"

"So I'm thinking maybe the sniper was watching her ahead of time."

"Stalking her?"

"Not exactly. Not her, specifically, but what if he was up on a roof, saw Linda do her run at the same time every morning and picked her off? Like she was a convenient target."

Tony leaned back against the padded booth, frowning now, processing the idea. "Like he was up on a roof in the French Quarter, saw the driver get out of his cab on Canal Street and shot him. The cab driver and the runner happened to be in those locations at the wrong time."

Frank shrugged. "It's just a theory. You got a better one?"

"Maybe they were practice runs, you know? Like they do in the movies. They just did a remake of *Day of the Jackal*, you see it?"

Frank shook his head. Tony was a movie buff, saw all the mob flicks, spy movies and thrillers.

"No, but I saw the original. Great flick."

Tony leaned forward, his dark eyes serious, and whispered, "What about the Big Enchilada?"

"Obama?"

"Yeah. You know how it is, politician runs for re-election, travels the country sweet-talking people, looking for votes."

"Well, he's not coming here anytime soon. I would have heard about it. You know the deal. A president comes to town, advance men get here three or four weeks ahead of time and notify the NOPD Intelligence Unit. Besides, why would he come here? He won't get many votes in Louisiana. Too many people hate him."

"So? Lots of people in Dallas hated JFK but he went there anyway, remember? "

"Hell, yes. I'm from Boston." Even now, recalling that fateful day sent chills down his neck. It happened before he was born, but he'd seen the Zapruder film and the television documentaries about the assassination. "Okay," he said. "For the sake of argument, let's say our sniper's getting ready to assassinate some big-shot. There's plenty of places in the French Quarter where a VIP might go. But what's near the runner's apartment on Prytania Street?"

Tony thought for a moment, scratching his chin, then said, "The Swedish Embassy is right down the street."

"Huh. I didn't know there was a Swedish Embassy here."

"But I haven't heard any rumors about any VIP Swedes coming here." Tony grinned. "How about that singing group, ABBA? Back in the day they were hot. Gorgeous blondes."

Frank drank some beer, thinking. "What about Bjorn Borg, that tennis champion? But I guess he's retired now, right?"

"Beats me. Tennis isn't my game. Play whack-a-moley with a ball."

"Is there a King of Sweden?"

Tony gave him a look. "Frank, you're talking to a former boxer, not a history professor. And what if we're wrong? What if the Sniper's just some nutcase with a rifle?"

"Worse case scenario? Ten days between the first two victims, I figure he'll do another one soon. I'd give him a week, maybe less. Do me a favor, okay? Stop by the Swedish Embassy and see if anyone important is coming here within the next couple of weeks."

"No problem. But there must be fifty embassies in New Orleans."

"Fifty?" Frank stared at him. "Jesus, just what I need. Fifty more locations to worry about, in addition to all the others in this town."

Tony nodded, somber-faced. "Yeah. And more VIP targets."

––––––

7:25 PM

Control stood by the desk in his office, gripping the phone, too nervous to sit down, waiting for the Boss to speak. The Boss ran the Special Ops Unit, which conducted certain activities the firm's directors considered sensitive enough to merit plausible deniability to themselves and others.

A sinister voice, briefly delayed by encryption, spoke in his ear. "The Buyer wants us to eliminate the problem. There must be no mistakes. You have made this clear to your operative?"

Control pictured him, a brute with muscles galore and killer eyes. The last time they'd met in his London office, a gruesome photo of a man's severed hand lay on the desk. Following his gaze, the Boss had skewered him with a look, ready to squash him like a bug.

"I made that clear to him, but—"

"Shut up! Must I remind you of the consequences of failure? Termination. Or worse."

Or worse. Control shuddered. Corporate espionage was a spider's web of half-truths, layers of misdirection, deception and outright lies. Corporate executions were far worse. He'd heard the rumors. A sudden death, made to look like an accident. He imagined himself sinking into the Thames, his skull fractured like an eggshell. He had no idea who the Buyer was, only that the Buyer was paying an enormous sum of money to have The Package terminated.

"My helper has performed well, don't you think?" No need to tell the Boss about his insufferable attitude at this morning's meeting.

"The proof of this will come when he completes the job."

A brittle cough pierced his ear. *Ack-ack-ack.* The Boss was a heavy smoker. The momentary respite gave him time to conjure up something positive. "He gets away without a trace. The cops are stymied. No leads, no witnesses."

"That's his job. We can have no failures. None. Have you made this clear to him?"

"I have, but he wants more Intel on The Package. He says he needs to prepare—"

"He will get this information when he needs to have it. You are his minder! That is why I sent you there. No fuckups. Your helper is disposable, understand?"

Jesus, did they expect him to kill ... ?

"I will call with more instructions soon."

A loud click pierced his ear like a rifle shot. Control clutched his chest and sank into his chair. His hands trembled as he pulled out a handkerchief and mopped sweat from his face.

———

9:35 PM

Positioned on the roof overlooking the French Quarter with his night-vision field glasses, he waited. Now that it was dark the air was cooler but still humid, not a hint of a breeze. Perfect sniper weather.

But he wasn't going to shoot anyone tonight.

This afternoon he had maintained his vigil for three hours. No sign of his sexy little shoplifter, so he got a take-away dinner and ate it in his hotel room. As he waited for darkness to fall, he had listened to music on his MP3 player, a device no bigger than a cigarette pack. Shostakovitch's *Symphony #5*, forty-five minutes of stirring music with a triumphant conclusion.

No music allowed on recon missions. Maintain situational awareness and be patient. He'd watched the runner four mornings in a row. Then, a perfect hit and a fast getaway. Sooner or later the shoplifter would show herself. Already he felt a deep connection to her.

He'd seen plenty of films about star-crossed lovers, but they were Hollywood fantasies. Never in his thirty-one years had he felt like this about a woman. He tried to analyze it. Was it her risk-taking behavior? Her desperate flight from the man who chased her? Her willingness to use the gun?

Unlike his former lover in Amsterdam, a tall blonde with big tits. She didn't know what he did for a living, only that he made enough money to pay half her rent. But she wanted him to play daddy to her six-year-old son. Her severely disabled son, confined to a wheelchair. He felt bad for the kid, but how could he relate to him? He would never take him in the woods to stalk deer. Never teach him how to shoot a rifle. Never take him for a ride on his motorcycle.

A sudden thought hit him. That's what he'd do! Take his sexy little shoplifter for a ride on his big black Ducati, zoom down the I-10 at 100 mph and give her a thrill.

A flash of motion caught his eye. Adjusting the field glasses, he zoomed in on a woman zipping along the sidewalk on a skateboard seven blocks away. Was it the shoplifter? She was the right size, wearing a Saints ball cap, the bill tugged down over her forehead, pushing off the sidewalk with one foot, making the board go faster and faster.

He studied her legs. Slender but muscular. It was her! He was certain of it. Not only was his shoplifter sexy, she was clever. She didn't use a car or a bike for her getaways, probably hid the skateboard somewhere to facilitate her escape.

He watched her glide to a stop outside a convenience store. She hopped off the skateboard, grabbed it with one hand and entered the store. Was she going to shoplift something? He waited, his hands sweaty on the field glasses, his heart racing with anticipation.

Five minutes later she emerged with a plastic bag, a rectangular package, a six-pack of beer perhaps. Gripping the bag in one hand, she mounted the skateboard and zipped away, reversing her route. She was going home! Three blocks later she stopped at a four-story building, hopped off the skateboard and went inside, taking the skateboard and the package with her.

He wanted to shout for joy. Now he knew where she lived!

Dauphine Street, # 1321 in black metal numbers on the door.

Perfect. Tomorrow he'd pay her a visit.

Maybe they'd have a beer.

CHAPTER 7

SUNDAY – June 26 – 10:15 AM

The minute Frank walked into the hospital room, Vobitch sat bolt upright in bed, his steel-gray eyes focused him like laser-beams. "Tell me about the shooting in D-6. Was it the Sniper?"

Frank had intended to avoid this topic, but Vobitch was loaded for bear. He looked better today, no tubes in his nose, no wires hooked up to beeping machines, faint color in his cheeks.

He pulled up a chair and said, "We got the ballistics report this morning. The technician compared the slugs that killed the cab driver and the woman in D-6 and got a match."

All rifle barrels differ from one another in minute respects. When a weapon is fired, the barrel's rifling leaves definitive scratches, called lands, on the bullet. The marks were like fingerprints.

"Who's lead investigator on the D-6 homicide?"

"Roger Vance. We're already collaborating. Seems like a good guy. You know him?"

"Only by reputation, but I hear he's good. What have you got so far?"

"No leads, no witnesses. I checked the national data bases for crimes with a similar MO and got zip. And as you already know, the reporters are all over it."

"Fucking vultures. I convinced the doc to let me go home on Thursday. Juliana didn't like it, but I told her I'd sign myself out if the doc wouldn't do it."

"Go home that soon, after major surgery? Why don't you rest up a few days—"

"Fuck resting." Vobitch's cheeks flamed red. "Can't go back to work for two months, the doc says. Christ on a crutch, what am I gonna do? Sit home and twiddle my thumbs?"

"Morgan, we're on it. Kenyon and David are working overtime, same as me. They were in the office this morning. They send their regards."

Homicide Detectives Kenyon Miller and David Lee were his District-Eight colleagues. Kenyon was his oldest friend on the force and a great detective. David was a recent addition to Homicide, but equally competent, smart, determined and a big NBA fan, like Frank.

"Tell 'em I said thank you. But who's gonna ride herd on my homicide detectives in D-1, D-5 and D-8? The Super won't let me do it from home." A big frown. "I already asked him."

"How about Orville Wilkes? He's been working Homicide the longest."

Vobitch gave him a Darth-Vader stare. "How about Frank Renzi? You've got the experience, twenty years with Boston PD before you came here."

"But not as a supervisor. Besides, I hate paperwork and I don't need the hassles. IAD cleared me after the King Rock incident last year. No charges, but the Deputy Super wasn't happy."

King Rock, a known drug dealer and gang leader, had murdered his girlfriend, the mother of his son. Frank eventually captured him, but during a shootout he'd wounded King Rock.

"Hicks is an asshole. It was a righteous shoot, Frank. Thanks to you the bastard went away for a long time. Hicks should have given you a commendation."

"Fat chance. He's still got it in for me." Like King Rock, Deputy Superintendent Wendell Hicks was black. Unlike King Rock, Hicks bent over backwards to accommodate the black community, ultra-sensitive to any criticism from black leaders and ministers.

"Just for two months, Frank. Until I get back on my feet."

Unwilling to commit himself, but knowing Vobitch hated being out of the loop, he said, "I'll call you every day, fill you in on what's going on, maybe hold a meeting with your detectives. Right now I'm focused on the Sniper. Last night Tony Coppola and I met at the Poorhouse Pub and tossed around some ideas."

He summarized their discussion. When he finished, Vobitch said, "I hear you on on the locations, but he could do another one tomorrow somewhere else. And I'm not sold on the VIP theory. If the sniper's gunning for a VIP, why hasn't he shot one already?"

Knowing Vobitch didn't expect an answer, Frank said nothing.

Vobitch grimaced. "You know how many celebrities we've got running around town. Musicians, movie stars, pro athletes, and that's just the ones that live here. Plenty of others come here to party."

"Tony says there are fifty foreign consulates here."

"True, but protecting them isn't our responsibility." Vobitch smiled faintly. "What, you think the Queen of England is coming here for vacation and the sniper's gonna pop her?"

"Probably not. I don't think she's into brass bands and second line parades, but how about the King of Sweden? The Swedish Embassy is on Prytania Street near where the runner got shot."

"Get out. Are you serious?" Vobitch gazed at him, dismay written large on his face.

"I am. Tony said he'd talk to them, find out if any VIPs are scheduled for a visit."

"Check with the NOPD Intelligence Unit. They get notified weeks in advance if some bigwig is scheduled to come here." Vobitch pursed his lips, frowning. "Presidential election year, you better find out if Obama is coming here to campaign."

"I already did. No visits to New Orleans anytime soon. After you get home on Thursday, I'll come over and give you the latest on the investigation." Frank rose to his feet. "I better get back to work."

But he had other things on his mind besides the Sniper. Kelly O'Neil, for instance. He hadn't seen her since Friday, an all-too-brief visit. He needed some serious R&R.

He went out to his car and dialed her number. This time on a Sunday morning, she was probably home, eating breakfast. Hit her with his favorite fantasy line, see what she said.

When she answered, he murmured, caressing her with his voice, "What have you got on?"

"Mmmm," she said, going with it. "Not a stitch. It's so hot in here, I took my clothes off."

He grinned. "Perfect. I'll be there in ten minutes. Want me to bring anything?"

After a low chuckle, Kelly said, "Just your always-exciting self."

Energized, he started the car. Have an intense reunion in the sack, then some pillow-talk, go for round-two, then get back to work.

———

10:35 AM

Lurking in the recessed doorway of a building on the corner, he watched the sunny side of Dauphine Street. His sexy little shoplifter's apartment was diagonally across the street. Earlier, he had soaped himself in the shower, shampooed his hair and shaved to eliminate any trace of dark stubble. Then he'd put on his best pair of jeans and his emerald-green polo shirt to emphasize the green in his hazel eyes.

During the war, he and his mates prided themselves on looking scruffy. In the barracks they walked around with their shirts hanging out, scraggly hair and long sideburns. Scruffy for a reason. Snipers had to operate behind their own lines, in no man's land, even behind enemy troops. Hide out in long grass stinking of Suave shampoo, they wouldn't last long. Regimental Sergeant Majors loathed snipers. RSMs wanted everyone to look smart, shiny buttons and spit-and-polished boots. But snipers didn't give a shit about that. It didn't make you shoot any better.

But that was then and this was now.

He wasn't looking for the enemy. He was waiting for the shoplifter.

No one had left # 1321 for the past two hours. The only door to the four-story apartment building opened onto the street in front. He'd circled the place to make sure, then checked to see how many flats there were. Eight mailboxes and buzzers in the foyer, two flats on each floor probably, no lights in any windows, but it was a sunny day, shaping up to be another scorcher.

What were the other occupants doing, he wondered. Watching TV? Sleeping in after partying last night? Did they know his sexy little shoplifter lived in their building? Probably not. She was too cagey for that. He shifted his feet and leaned against the wall beside the door.

He was dying to talk to her. If she didn't come out by eleven, he'd have to go inside and find her. At noon, he had to make his daily call to Control: a major annoyance.

But he'd prefer to wait until she came out. Patience. Patience.

In wartime snipers had two primary functions. Both required patience. First up, reconnaissance, obtained either by covert action or long-distance observation through a sniper scope. Sometimes Intel was just as important as bullets. Snipers could report on enemy tank or troop positions and have them destroyed by artillery without ever giving their own position away.

Their second job, equally critical, was taking out priority targets to disrupt enemy battle plans. Top targets were enemy commanders and senior officers. Rank-and-file soldiers were low priority. Losing one or two would have little effect on an enemy attack. But if they were the only targets that popped up, kill them all the same.

A taxi stopped at the corner, then drove past him without a glance.

What was she doing, he wondered. What if she had a boyfriend?

What if they were lying in bed together right now?

42

A hollow pit formed in his stomach.

He couldn't bear the thought of someone else touching her.

No, he reassured himself. She was a loner like him. A dare-devil who took chances.

And there she was, stepping out the door in a sleeveless pais-ley-print top, white shorts and running shoes. He thought his heart would stop. No skateboard this morning. No hat either, just a pair of large Raybans, walking down the street with a purposeful stride.

He didn't know where she was going, but she clearly had a destina-tion in mind.

Employing his surveillance skills, he tailed her, lurking a half block behind as she made several turns, heading toward the commercial section of the French Quarter. Soon there were other pedestrians, some of them tourists, others locals. The shoplifter spoke to no one.

Ten minutes later, she entered a grocery store on Royal Street.

He waited a minute, then followed two tourists with cameras slung 'round their necks into a small shop cooled by wood-bladed overhead fans. Mouthwatering aromas filled the air: ripe bananas, coffee, and fresh strawberries. Watermelons and cantaloupes sat in crates along one wall. Even at this hour, the shop was busy; cramped aisles jammed together left barely enough space for shoppers to pass one another between the well-stocked shelves. He picked up a small shop-ping basket and began a methodical aisle-by-aisle search.

Two minutes later he found her near the back of the store, stand-ing by herself at the refrigerated cheese section, holding a basket with a carton of OJ. He drew closer and pretended to examine a container of yogurt, studying her.

She was short—five-foot-four by his estimate—small-boned, but athletic-looking, well-toned arms, muscular legs. Her face was gor-geous, short dark hair curling around her ears, a pert nose and a strong jaw. No lipstick on her luscious lips. He was dying to kiss them. She'd pushed the Raybans over the top of her head, but he wasn't close enough to see the color of her eyes.

He side-stepped closer. She didn't look up, examining a plas-tic-wrapped block of Wisconsin cheddar cheese.

"I like your style," he said, smiling at her.

She turned and looked at him. No smile. Her eyes were huge. Liq-uid-brown pools of mystery.

"Do I know you?" she said.

"No," he said, speaking softly. "But I know you. You're the shoplifter."

Clearly startled, she blinked but recovered quickly. "Buzz off buddy." She turned to leave.

He took hold of her arm, firmly, but not squeezing. "Don't worry. I'm not a cop. I've got no interest in turning you in. But I know what you do. You're a risk-taker, like me."

She glanced down the aisle at another customer, then gazed at him, anxiously licking her lips.

"I just want to talk to you," he said. *And kiss your luscious lips and take you to bed.*

Annoyance flashed in her liquid-brown eyes. "Let go of my arm."

He squeezed it gently, enjoying the smooth feel of her skin beneath his hand, and let go. "How about if I take you for a ride on my motorcycle and give you a thrill?"

She stared at him. Said nothing.

"Come on," he said, giving her his most persuasive smile. "What have you got to lose?"

Her jaw muscles clenched. "Go away. Leave me alone."

"No," he said quietly. "I'm not going away. I know who you are. You're the woman on the security videos they've been playing on the news."

Frowning at him now, she put the shopping basket on the floor and rubbed her arms.

"Be nice and I'll take you for a ride on my motorcycle."

"Why should I?" she said, her voice rising in panic.

"I'll pick you up at your place this afternoon, one o'clock. I know where you live."

She gasped, staring at him, aghast.

"One o'clock outside your place on Dauphine Street." Regarding her sternly, he said, "Don't even think about leaving town. If you do, I'll come and find you."

Rigid with fear, she gazed at him, her liquid brown eyes fearful.

"We'll have fun," he said. "You'll see."

CHAPTER 8

2:15 PM

She clung to him, her arms around his waist, a laugh bubbling up in her throat. Never in her life had she felt like this. Thrilled and terrified at the same time. The speed and the sound, and the certainty that if she let go of him and fell off, she'd be dead.

Light stanchions alongside the highway flying by at a dizzying speed, the wind whipping her cheeks, the deafening roar of the engine piercing her ears. Delicious vibrations diddled her crotch, jammed against the seat. Terrified and thrilled and happy.

But what would happen next? He was slowing down, approaching the Esplanade Avenue exit, having passed the ramp that would have taken them past the police station. Smart. A lot of cops hated bikers.

He chugged the bike sedately down Esplanade, a Ducati Monster, he'd told her an hour ago as he strapped on her helmet, saying the 696-cubic-centimeter V2 engine could take them up to 140 mph if he pushed it. Smiling at her as he'd said this.

She loved his big black Ducati. Sleek and powerful and sexy. Like him.

Two blocks from her apartment, he rolled to a stop on Dauphine Street beside a black-painted hitching post with iron rings, helped her off the bike and took off his goggles.

"Fun?" he said, gazing at her with his penetrating hazel eyes.

She looked at him, her body thrumming with adrenaline. "Fucking fantastic!"

An amused smile. "I knew you'd like it. We'll walk from here. Take off the helmet, but bring it with you." He took a padlock out of a saddlebag and secured the bike to a ring on the hitching post. Satisfied no one could steal it, he brushed strands of dark hair off his face.

No helmet for him. Maybe he liked living dangerously. Her stomach lurched, every nerve in her body quivering with tension.

What would happen when they got to her apartment? Jesus, she didn't even know his name! He said he wasn't a cop, but he was several inches taller than she was, almost six feet. His chest and shoulders looked hard as cement, and ropy veins and wiry black hairs lined his muscular arms.

What if he was some kind of nutcase?

If he was, she might shoot him.

He took her hand and hurried toward her apartment building, extending his long-legged stride. She had to hurry to keep up. His face was tanned beneath his thick dark hair, but his eyes were the big draw. Intense and scary. Hazel with green flecks, gazing at her like she was a new toy and he was deciding what to do with her. Terrifying and thrilling, like riding on his Ducati.

"So," he said. "What do you think of my magnificent machine?"

She laughed. "It's a lot faster than my skateboard. How fast were we going?"

He squeezed her hand. "If you give me a beer, I might take you out again."

Her heart thudded inside her chest. Yesterday she had lamented her lack of a boyfriend, but consoled herself, thinking, *Someone will come along, sooner or later.*

Maybe the man with the bike was that someone. And maybe he wasn't.

Five minutes later she took him into her apartment. She'd neatened up the living room, no dust balls in the corners, no day-old newspapers on the coffee table. Just her bottle of Alien.

He wandered around the room, admiring her posters, and stopped at the bookcase. He picked up her favorite diamond earrings. "One of your shoplifting acquisitions?"

"Yes."

He approached her, his eyes fixed on hers. "Why do you do it?"

"It excites me, gives me a rush. That's why you ride your bike, right? Go fast and feel the wind whip your face."

"That's part of it."

"What's the other part?"

"I'm thirsty. Got any beer?"

"Sure. Hold on while I get some."

She went in the kitchen and took out two bottles of Becks, smiling as she took them to the living room, thinking, *Now he'll have to take me for another ride.*

He was sitting on the futon, with one arm stretched along the top, holding her bottle of Alien in his other hand. "Is this the perfume you're wearing?"

She handed him the beer. "Yes. My latest acquisition."

"I like it. And I like Becks. Nice to know we have similar tastes."

He set the bottle of Alien on the coffee table and twisted the cap off the bottle of Becks. But he didn't drink any. He waited until she took the cap off her bottle, then clinked his bottle against hers.

"Here's to a fine relationship," he said, gazing into her eyes.

The intensity of his gaze unnerved her, excitement and fear competing for her attention like red warning flags. "Okay. But if we're going to have a relationship, you need to tell me your name."

He hesitated, frowning. After a moment he said, "Peter. What's yours?"

She smiled. "Win."

"Hmm. I like it. Is that short for Winifred?"

"No. Just Win. W-I-N. It's not the name on my birth certificate. I changed it."

He seemed amused, muttered something under his breath, then "What's your real name?"

She curled one leg underneath her and turned to face him. "Janis. J-A-N-I-S. My mother chose it. She loved Janis Joplin. She saw her at Woodstock. That's how my parents met."

"What's Woodstock?"

Astounded, she studied him. His English was good, but at times he spoke with an odd cadence, and his features looked foreign somehow. "You're not from here, right?"

He seemed taken aback. "From New Orleans? No."

"Peter. Forget New Orleans. You're not from America. Everyone knows about Woodstock. The summer of sixty-nine? Peace, free love and rock-n-roll? Jimi Hendrix, Joan Baez and Janis Joplin. Not to mention acid and LSD."

Expressionless, he drank some Becks. "Summer of sixty-nine. I guess I missed it. Were your parents into drugs?"

"Pot, maybe, not acid or LSD. They were teenagers, just out of high school. Dad said it was love at first sight. For him, maybe. I don't know about Mother." She drank some beer. She didn't want to think about her mother. "Woodstock was huge, four-hundred-thousand people listening to music in the pouring rain on some little farm in upstate New York."

"You don't care much for your mother," he said, studying her.

Careful. He's trying to psych you out. "So? My mother was an anti-war freak. Ban the Bomb, cops are pigs and the government's crooked.

47

Still is, as far as I know. I left home when I was fifteen. What's your mother like?"

He set his beer bottle on the table. "Show me your gun."

Flustered, she said, "What makes you think I've got a gun?"

"Everyone knows you've got one. It's all over the news. I want to see it."

She thought about telling him to take a hike. But he hadn't made any fuck-me-type moves. Not yet anyway. She got up and went into her bedroom. He followed her, standing by the bed while she opened the bottom drawer of her bureau and took out the snub-nosed .22-caliber revolver. He took it out of her hand and checked to see if it was loaded. It wasn't. He frowned. "Why is it not loaded? What good is it to have a weapon if it is not loaded?" He handed it back to her and said, "Show me your stance when you're going to shoot."

She looked at him uncertainly. "What do you mean?"

Seemingly annoyed, he said, "How you hold the weapon. Two hands? One? Show me."

She grasped the gun with her right hand, inserted her finger into the trigger guard and braced the gun butt against her left forearm.

"No." He came closer and nudged her feet apart. "You must adjust your feet, so."

Moving behind her, he squared her shoulders and told her to pretend the Louis Armstrong photograph on the wall was the target. "If you are serious about shooting someone, two hands are best, especially with a small weapon like this. A .22 is a fine gun for close range, quite accurate. I will show you." He placed her left hand below the trigger guard. "Extend your arms straight at the target. Support the gun with your left hand. The right hand must remain loose, not tense. Sight along the top of the barrel. Your finger does not go onto the trigger until you are ready to shoot."

She tried to relax. Felt his body against hers. Warm and intimate. A major distraction.

"When you are ready, take a deep breath, hold it and gently squeeze the trigger."

She took a deep breath. Held it. Squeezed the trigger.

Click. The hammer fell on an empty chamber.

"Very good," he murmured into her ear. He slid his hands down her ribs and nuzzled her neck, easing her toward the bed.

Not so fast, Romeo. "Thanks for the lesson, but I'm still thirsty. Let's have another beer."

He released her and stepped back, his face expressionless.

Annoyed, she put the gun back in the drawer and left the room. Peter thought she needed a gun lesson because on the news it said she shot at the clerk and missed. But she could have hit him easily enough. She'd missed him on purpose.

She went in the kitchen and took two Becks out of the refrigerator. Maybe she'd tell him about paintball, how she hardly ever missed her target. No, bad idea. She didn't know enough about him. But he was hot to trot. She was horny too, but better to make him wait.

Don't be too eager. Get him talking about himself. Make him feel important. Guys liked that.

When she went in the living room, he was sitting on the futon, looking morose. Was he sulking because she didn't hop into bed with him right away? Too bad. She handed him a beer and said, "You sure do know a lot about guns. How did you learn how to shoot?"

He popped the cap on the Becks and drank some. "I was in the UK Army. My unit fought in the Gulf War, not the first one in 1990, the one in 2003. Ugly place, Iraq."

She nodded, feigning interest. She didn't give a shit about Iraq. "Did you ride a motorcycle?"

"No. Trucks or Range Rovers got us where we had to go. It's a shithole, Iraq. A sand-blown, hot-as-hell wasteland. Along the border with Iran there are still wrecked tanks and artillery from the Iran-Iraq war back in the 1980s." He drank some beer. "The smell was the worst part. Even the big cities are filthy, three-hundred-thousand residents and no sewage system, piles of uncollected garbage everywhere. Shit and piss and dirty bathwater running along the gutters."

I don't give a damn about garbage. Tell me something interesting. "Did anyone shoot at you?"

"Plenty of times. Little boys played in the shit-filled gutters, but hard-eyed men stood outside their houses giving us the evil eye. These blokes are religious fanatics. Holy nutcases, we called them. Violence is a way of life for them. Human life has no value. They'd as soon kill you as look at you."

"Were you ever wounded? Did you have any close calls?"

He stared into space, somber-faced, like he was remembering something sad. "One day someone in the truck ahead of us screamed

Grenade! Some bastard had thrown one at our convoy. Grenades are little oval-shaped pieces of shit, no bigger than a large peach, but deadly. Release the handle and an internal hammer rams a percussion cap that ignites the gunpowder fuse. Seconds later the fuse is hot enough to ignite the explosives. The grenade missed the truck I was riding in and hit one of my mates in the chest. Bounced off his body armor and rolled along the road."

He massaged his eyes, clenched his jaw and drank some Becks. "When that happens everyone ducks. Then, *BOOM.* A blinding flash of light, a deafening bang and a huge shock wave, shrapnel flying in all directions, tiny red-hot pieces of metal whizzing through the air, pinging off metal and stone walls. Not to mention whirlwinds of dust and debris whipped up by the blast."

"Jesus! Were you hurt?"

He looked at her, his eyes somber. "No, I was lucky. For weeks I couldn't hear properly, had this ringing in my ears, could barely listen to music. But my best mate died. Chest wound."

She didn't know what to say. *That's why Mother was against the war?* No. *I'm sorry your friend died?* No, that would sound sappy. *War is hell?* Jesus, even worse.

"Did you kill people?"

He gazed at her silently for several seconds, expressionless. "Many."

"What kind of gun did you use?"

"A rifle. Or a handgun in close combat. Urban warfare is extremely dangerous."

"But that was a long time ago. What do you do for a living now?"

"I kill people."

"Get out. You do not."

He raised one of his bushy black eyebrows. "You doubt me? It's true."

She drank some beer. This was getting weird. Was he serious? Her heart jittered inside her chest. "Why do you kill people?"

"For money. That beautiful bike you like so much costs a shitload of money."

"I don't believe it."

"You asked what kind of gun I used during the war. It was a sniper rifle."

"Yeah? So?"

He leaned closer to her. "You are the Shoplifter. I am the Sniper."

She stared at him, goosebumps dancing over her arms like an army of ants. "You are not."

He appeared hurt. "It's true. Why would I lie to you? I hunted for you from a roof with my night-vision field glasses. Last night you put on a ball cap and got on your skateboard and went to a store to buy this beer." He raised the bottle of Becks and took several swallows.

But his eyes never left her face.

Jesus! He was the Sniper? Her thoughts disintegrated into jumbled chaotic fragments, red warning flags waving at full force. To buy time to think, she drank some beer and picked at the label on the bottle. He said his name was Peter. No last name. And he killed people. Or so he said. If she didn't give him what he wanted, would he kill her? Her gun was in the bedroom. Unloaded.

She realized he was smiling at her, not the smile of a killer. A friendly smile. "You and I make a fine pair, Win. We are both risk takers. Thrill-seekers. I am the Sniper. You are the Shoplifter. The main difference being, there is a security video of you fleeing the crime. But none of me."

Risk-takers and thrill-seekers. She had to admit he was right. The tougher the get, the bigger the thrill. "Okay," she said. "Take me with you when you do the next one."

He frowned. "No."

"Why should I believe you then?"

"This I cannot do."

"Show me how you do it then. Show me where you shoot from."

"No. That would be too dangerous."

"Why? You got away without anyone seeing you, right?"

He rolled his lips together, gazing at her silently. Was that a flicker of anxiety in his eyes?

She went in for the kill. "You said we're a pair. Risk-takers, you said. Thrill-seekers. So here's the deal. You want me to believe you're the Sniper? Prove it. Show me your sniper perch."

He massaged his eyes, then his temples, frowning at her.

She leaned closer, kissed his lips and drew back. "Peter. You want to take me to bed? *Show me.* Otherwise, Hit the Road Jack."

CHAPTER 9

MONDAY June 27 8:30 AM

He lay beside her on the roof, close enough to feel the warmth of her body. Close enough to inhale her perfume. Almost close enough to kiss her. Intoxicating. He'd barely slept last night, imagining how her bare skin would feel beneath his hands. Her breasts, her thighs and the slick wetness when he plunged inside her.

He could hardly wait. Already he had an erection.

Five stories below them, workers were headed for jobs and tourists were exploring the French Quarter. But up here he was alone with Win in their own magical world. Nothing else mattered.

Hit the Road Jack? Not if he could help it.

He wanted this to last forever.

He had on his sniper outfit, faded jeans and a long-sleeved Army jacket. Win was dressed in a pair of frayed blue jeans and a long-sleeved cotton shirt as he had instructed. But they wouldn't be here long. Give his sexy little Shoplifter the thrill of a lifetime, then hustle her back to her apartment and take her to bed.

It was another sunny day, the temperature already in the 80s, the air soggy with humidity. When they got to the roof, he'd wedged the access door shut, removed his equipment from the gym bag, assembled the rifle and set them up facing the French Quarter, not the Canal Street side where he'd shot the cab driver. The glare of the morning sun would make it difficult for her to see much.

But she wasn't going to shoot anyone.

"When do I get to hold it?" she asked, giving him a seductive smile.

"You don't," he said sternly. The rifle was loaded: nine .300 Winchester Magnum cartridges in the magazine, one in the chamber. She wanted him to prove it? Push came to shove, he might. He didn't want any lingering doubts in her mind. Send a message to Control too, his insufferable minder withholding information about The Package, having him shoot civilians for no apparent reason.

"Come on, Peter," she said, pouting at him. "Why can't I hold it?"

She ran her fingers over the walnut stock.

"Nice," she said, smiling seductively. "Smooth and sexy ... like you."

He gazed into her eyes, aching with desire. "You can't hold it, but if you behave yourself, I might show you how to use the scope."

"You gonna shoot someone?" she said, challenging him with her eyes. Daring him to do it.

"Maybe." He inched forward on his belly, gripped the rifle and sighted through the scope. Even at this hour Bourbon Street was jammed with tourists. He adjusted the reticle and peered through the scope. *Who's it gonna be?* The hefty Italian with the bald head, the sweaty face and curly black chest hair? The bottle-blonde in the mini-skirt, sleeveless top and sparkly eye-shadow to the max? The white-haired man in a Saint's T-shirt standing outside the porn-parlor with neon lights flashing **Naked Dancing Girls!**

He flicked the safety lever and gathered himself, feeling the famil-iar rush of adrenaline.

"You're no fun. Come on, Peter. Let me hold the damn gun!"

Jolted out of his concentration, he took his finger off the trigger, practical considerations overriding any desire for a vicarious thrill.

I'll tell you where and when your next hit will be, Control had said. If he shot someone today, it could screw up the assignment. Hell, Control might even fire him. Kiss the big bucks goodbye. Kiss Win goodbye, too. He'd be back in London tomorrow.

"Let me show you how to use the scope," he said. "This one's a Schmidt & Bender, with a magnification of twenty-five, meaning it gets you twenty-five times closer to your target. Close enough to see if they've got any pimples."

Win wrinkled her nose at him. "Yuck."

"Okay, forget the pimples. The best feature is the illuminated reti-cle."

"What's that?" she said, gazing at him with her big brown eyes.

"Think of it as the cross-hairs, only more sophisticated. It has a range-finder, tiny colored dots to measure the distance to your target and adjust for windage and drop. But no need for you to worry about that." He tapped the slide-focus knob. "You can adjust it with this."

He rose to knees and set his right knee on the asphalt on the other side of her body, straddling her, his thighs hugging her rib cage. He bent closer, inhaling her intoxicating scent, aware of the throbbing ache in his groin. Supporting the rifle with his left hand, he cupped her right hand and placed it under the trigger guard.

"Keep your hand right there," he said. "Below the trigger guard. And keep your finger away from the trigger."

"Okay." Braced on her elbows, she lay on her belly, put one eye to the scope and squinted, then adjusted the slide-focus knob with her left hand.

To his surprise, she seemed quite comfortable with the weapon.

"Wow! This is great! I can see my apartment from here."

"Correct. That's how I spotted you. Not with the sniper scope, with my field glasses. I wasn't planning on shooting you."

She turned and looked at him, her liquid brown eyes wide and enticing and full of mystery. "That's good."

"I already knew we'd be friends." He smiled. "Soon we'll be more than friends."

She raised an eyebrow, gave him a seductive look and put her left hand on his crotch. To his embarrassment, she discovered his erection and gently squeezed his cock.

"Ooooh," she murmured in a low throaty voice. "Sexy."

Was it his imagination, or did she want him as much as he wanted her?

She turned her head and put her eye to the scope.

Enthralled, he watched her, his groin aflame with desire. Luscious lips, sexy legs and a great ass. Soon he would kiss those lips and caress that ass. For the past three weeks this assignment had been a royal pain in the butt. He'd worked with other minders, but this was his first go-round with Control, who wanted to micro-manage every bloody detail, treating him like a rookie who'd never successfully completed an assignment.

But if he hadn't come to New Orleans, he would never have met Win, the girl of his dreams. With his previous lovers he'd always felt like an invisible screen came between them. They didn't understand him, but Win did. They were so much alike. Soulmates.

"The tourists are already out on Bourbon Street," she said.

"Toting their bloody cameras, I'll wager."

"Some of them." She adjusted the focus knob. "Whoa, look at that! A pig on a horse."

"What?"

"A pig on a horse. And I've got the solution."

Pop. The shot erupted, muffled by the suppressor but loud enough to be heard.

He yanked the rifle away from her. "Bloody hell! What did you do?"

"I shot the pig on the horse. On Bourbon Street."

He zeroed in on it immediately. Jesus-fucking-Christ! A mounted police officer and a horse. But the cop wasn't on the horse, he was lying in the street, and a crowd was gathering.

"You bloody idiot!"

She stared at him, a stricken look on her face. Too bad. Ignoring her, he hurriedly broke down his equipment and put it in the gym bag. They had to get out of here fast. Every second was precious.

He snatched the spent shell and stowed it in the bag with the rifle components. "Keep your mouth shut and follow me."

He grabbed her arm and ran for the access door.

8:45 AM

"Belize," Frank said. "Where the hell is that? I've never heard of half the countries on this list."

Seated opposite him at his desk in the homicide office, Kenyon Miller gave him a mischievous look. "Best brush up on your geography, Frank. Big quiz next week."

Despite his frustration, he had to smile. Kenyon was his closest friend on the force, a husky African-American, six-foot-six, 240 pounds, an experienced homicide detective and a great partner. Frank loved his droll sense of humor. Last year, Kenyon had been shot while serving an arrest warrant and almost bled out. Thankfully, he survived, but he'd been out on medical leave for several weeks. Frank was glad to have him back. He needed all the help he could get.

On his way to work this morning he'd tuned in the local AM-radio talk show. No wonder people were terrified, listening to border-line-hysterical comments from the radio host like, "No one is safe, You could be next!"

From his desk in the corner, David Lee said, "I think Belize is in South America."

"Thanks," he said. It figured that David would know. He was the scholarly type, always tops in his class. At 33, David was the youngest man in the Homicide unit, and the only Asian-American. Last year he'd transferred into D-8 Homicide from Vice and Narcotics. Both of them were basketball fans, so they bonded immediately. David loved Yao Ming and rooted for the Houston Rockets. Frank was a Celtics fan. When the workload allowed, they alternated as point guards on the NOPD basketball team. David was shorter than Frank, only five-nine, but he was fast and a great ball-handler.

"Hold on," David said, "I just looked it up. It's on the east coast of Central America, bordered by Mexico and Guatemala, and the Caribbean."

"How about Saint Vincent and the Grenadines?" Frank said.

"Sounds like a rock group," Kenyon said.

"Yeah," Frank said, "like Saint Francis and the Ten Inch Nails."

"Forget the small embassies," David said. "Check the big ones, Germany, France and the UK."

"Kelly and I talked about it last last night," Frank said. "She thinks the VIP might be a presidential candidate like Mitt Romney, maybe."

Kenyon beamed him a sly look. "Good to know you consulted another one of our fine NOPD detectives. Was your consultation satisfactory?" Jiving him.

"Indeed it was," he said, recalling their exquisite love session last night, followed by their usual pillow talk. It had cost him some sleep but he wasn't complaining.

Kenyon rumbled a laugh. "Glad to know it's not all work and no play."

"But foreign VIPs are only one possibility," Frank said. "Plenty of celebrities live here. Musicians, movie stars, sports figures."

"Maybe he's got the hots for Angelina Jolie," Kenyon said. "Gonna hit Brad Pitt so he can snuggle up with Angelina."

"Maybe he'll shoot the shoplifter," David said. "Take the pressure off me. The Deputy Super called me yesterday and told me to forget everything else and catch the French Quarter Shoplifter. I told him we worked homicides, but he said the French Quarter business owners are crawling up his ass and he wants results not excuses."

"Man," Kenyon said, "I can't believe Hicks wants you to waste time on the shoplifter. Only shoplifter I can recall is the movie star that played the nutcase in *Girl Interrupted*. I forget her name."

"Winona Ryder," Frank said. "But she got busted for shoplifting years ago. I think she paid her dues and went straight."

"Come check out these security videos," David said, "and tell me what you think."

They gathered around David's desk and he played the videos on his computer.

Frank studied the grainy black-and-white images. No clear shot of her face. He didn't think this was an accident. Inside the store the woman appeared calm and professional, casually touching an item of clothing, then a handbag, displaying the relaxed-but-alert posture he'd seen many times. An experienced criminal plying her trade.

But her demeanor piqued his interest. Fire in the belly, for sure. Intent on her mission, no doubt. But she also appeared to have a fuck-you attitude bordering on defiance.

"She must live in the Quarter," Kenyon said. "Took off running like that."

"I agree," Frank said. "No getaway car, she hightails it back to her bolt hole."

"She must come out sometimes," Kenyon said. "A girl's gotta eat."

"I've watched security videos from the previous heists," David said. "She wears a different disguise each time."

Kenyon nodded sagely. "Wears a casual outfit for her everyday activities."

David elbowed him. "Don't joke, Kenyon. How do I find her and her bolt hole?"

Frank's phone rang. He hustled back to his desk and answered. He listened for a moment, then opened the bottom drawer of his desk and took out his SIG Sauer. "I'll be there in two minutes."

Knowing something serious was up, David and Kenyon regarded him with dismay.

"The Sniper just shot a mounted policewoman," he said, securing the holstered SIG to his belt. "Bourbon Street, corner of Orleans Avenue."

"Jesus!" Kenyon said. "Be hell to pay on this one."

CHAPTER 10

9:45 AM

"What the hell kind of stunt was that?" he snarled, unable to contain his fury. The first words he'd spoken to her since he'd left the roof twenty minutes ago, intent on evading the cops and any witnesses.

Seated on the futon, she hugged her knees to her chest, gazing at him like a scolded puppy. Her enormous brown eyes reminded him of the sad-eyed Cocker Spaniel in one of his mum's velvet paintings.

"I take you to the roof like you wanted and you shoot someone, a cop in uniform, for crissake! My employer will be furious." Furious? Bloody hell, they'd haul his ass back to London and put him on a short leash, might even make him go through the training exercises again.

"All cops are pigs," she said, waving a hand dismissively. "That's what my mother says."

"Mom says all cops are pigs," he said, mocking her in a sing-song voice as he paced the room. "Jesus! You sound like a ten-year-old."

Her eyes narrowed to angry slits. She sat forward and planted her feet on the floor. "What about the cab driver? And that woman in the Garden District? You shot them, didn't you?"

"Not my choice."

"Just following orders?" she said with a sardonic smile.

"Yes, unlike you. I told you to keep your finger off the trigger."

"I wanted to prove that I can shoot. Every weekend I play paintball games. I hardly ever—"

"People don't die playing paintball," he snapped.

"When you were fighting in the war, were there any women snipers?"

He'd heard stories about a Russian female sniper who'd killed at least 300 German soldiers during WW II, but he wasn't going to tell Win about it. These days men were the best snipers.

"No," he said. "Women don't have the temperament for it."

"I do," she said, raising her chin. "I just proved it. We could be a team."

Stunned, he stopped pacing and stared at her. Be a team?

He rolled the idea around in his mind, like he did playing pinball, hit the flippers and watch the little steel ball bounce around.

Be sniper partners as well as lovers? Share the work? The preparations and the planning? Plot their moves after they made love. Hell, she could even lure the target to the proper location ....

No, that would never work. That was a dick-brain fantasy. These days he worked solo.

His cellphone vibrated against his thigh. Control calling him. Blast! Was the cop-shooting already on the news? He pulled out the phone, turned away from the futon and punched on.

"What the fuck are you doing?" Control screamed, so angry he didn't bother using the code.

"Not now. Call you in ten," he said and ended the call before Control could reply.

Fuck all! Ten minutes to figure out what he'd say. He turned back to the woman who wanted to be his partner in crime.

"That was my employer. Now I have to explain why I shot a cop on Bourbon Street in the French Quarter. I can't tell him you did it. That would only get me in more trouble."

"I'm sorry" she said, hunching her shoulders, looking solemn and contrite now. "I didn't mean to get you in trouble."

"I'm leaving now, but I'll be back. Do not leave the apartment, understand?"

"Yes," she said, gazing at him with her big brown eyes.

Eyes full of mystery.

Eyes that had tempted him into doing something stupid.

And now he was going to pay for it.

———

Frank sprinted to the blue-and-white NOPD cruiser parked sideways across Bourbon Street, lights flashing, blocking the intersection of Bourbon and Orleans Avenue. The cop stationed beside it recognized him and waved him through. Standing behind waist-high metal police barriers on the sidewalk were local residents, tourists and the inevitable ambulance-chaser ghouls who feasted on violent deaths.

It had only taken him four minutes to get here, but already word had spread. At the far end of the block a mob of reporters, photographers and TV cameramen jockeyed for position behind more police barriers, and the whump whump of news choppers filled the air.

Midway down the block, the policewoman lay on her back in the street, her head resting on a folded towel. Nearby, a patrol officer in a short-sleeved blue shirt tried to calm her mount, a chestnut-brown mare with white forelegs, shying sideways, nostrils flared, eyes wide with panic. Blood pooled on the pavement beneath the wounded cop, a black woman with close-cropped hair and dark skin. Frank couldn't tell if her eyes were open or not, nor did he recognize her. A female patrol officer and a woman in civilian clothes were tending to her.

He trotted over to a patrol cop standing in the shade of a balcony behind yellow crime-scene tape, writing an incident report. "Hey, Norm, how is she? How bad is it?"

A veteran cop with graying hair, Norm said, "She's alive, that's all I know. The fucker shot her in the back." As a wailing siren signaled the arrival of an ambulance, he added, "The EMTs get her to the hospital fast she might make it."

"Any idea where the shot came from?"

"Couple of people thought the shot came from that way," Norm said, pointing west toward Canal Street. Indicating the female officer tending to the wounded woman, he said, "Me and Dawn were around the corner. Didn't hear the shot, just heard Kimba scream and the horse whinnying, hightailed it over here. I tell you, Frank, this gives me the creeps. Go to work, you gotta worry this motherfucker's gonna shoot you. You think he's gunning for cops?"

Frank didn't answer, his thoughts in turmoil. The sniper had claimed his third victim, no doubt in his mind. A serial killer with a sniper rifle was targeting people in New Orleans, terrorizing the city's 350,000 residents. But this time he'd shot a cop.

"What's her name? You know her?"

"Kimba Davis, got a seven-year-old daughter, so she works the day shift. First woman to join the mounted unit, just started two months ago." Visibly angry, his face ominous as a thundercloud, Norm said, "She gets on her horse, does her job like she does every day and the fucker shoots her. We gotta get this guy, Frank."

"Don't worry, the NOPD brass will pull out all the stops after this one." Hell, ten minutes from now they'd be crawling up his ass like an army of fire ants. Now they had a dead cab driver, a dead runner and a wounded policewoman. And no leads. He envisioned the sniper on a roof somewhere, pumped with adrenaline, hunting his target, every nerve in his body pulsing with anticipation.

This guy got off on killing people.

Every single day, somewhere within the fifty states, there were two or three murders. Some were domestic homicides; others were robberies gone bad or impulsive crimes of passion. But on any given day, several serial killers were roaming the country, seeking their next victim. When three homicides were linked to one killer, the FBI classified it as a serial killer case.

Now the New Orleans Sniper had shot three people. Two of them were dead, but Kimba Davis was alive, and Frank dearly hoped she stayed that way. Technically speaking, the Sniper wasn't a serial killer, but Frank considered him one nevertheless.

All murders were horrible. But there was horrible, and there was horrific. The Sniper lay in wait for his victims. Killed them from afar.

Frank fingered the jagged scar on his chin as he often did when his emotions threatened to boil over, his frustration and anger escalating to a red-hot fury as he strode toward the mob of reporters at the far end of the block.

Their voices rose to shouts, clamoring for a comment. He waited until they positioned their microphones and cameras.

"My name is Homicide Detective Frank Renzi. I'm lead investigator on the cab driver murder on Canal Street, and I'm collaborating with the lead investigator on the Garden District runner homicide. Now a mounted policewoman is fighting for her life, shot by a sniper." He waited a beat, then said, "Snipers are long-distance killers. They never go near their victims. They lie in wait where they can't be hurt. Snipers are cowards."

Gazing into the nearest TV camera, he spoke in a firm voice. But he wasn't talking to the TV audience, he was talking to the killer. "The New Orleans Sniper is a coward. And we're going to get him."

———

She paced around her living room, swigging from a bottle of Becks, too jittery to sit down. She could hardly believe she'd shot the cop. Would Mother be proud or what?

Peter was pissed at her, but what she'd said was true.

When she was a kid, her mother would come home from protest rallies, sit down to the dinner Dad had prepared and rant about the police, saying, "All cops are pigs."

Dad wouldn't say anything, but he didn't look happy.

Dad was the one that took care of her. Fine by her. One day when she was six, he took her for a ride on the roller coaster at an amusement park. The biggest thrill of her life at that point. She'd coaxed him into taking her for two more roller coaster rides. Then he'd said, "That's it, Janis. Let's get a Snow-Cone."

Back then her name was Janis. Getting her kicks from shoplifting was still years away. But boosting expensive items didn't give her half the rush she got when she shot the cop.

Dad wouldn't be happy if he knew she'd done it. Peter sure wasn't.

She sipped some beer, recalling their frantic escape. On a Vesper, not the Ducati Monster. Peter had parked it beside the Ducati inside a storage unit at XTRA Storage on Canal Street above the French Quarter, and dragged her back to the apartment. Then he'd given her a lecture, gazing at her with murder in his eyes. Scary, but thrilling. More thrilling than riding on the Ducati even.

None of her previous boyfriends made her feel like this. She pictured the fury in Peter's eyes, glaring at her like he wanted to strangle her. Oddly, it gave her an incredible rush. She'd have to make up a new word for it. Blitz-thrill, maybe.

Then he'd told her to stay in the apartment and rushed off to talk to his employer, who was furious. In the beginning, she didn't believe him when he said he was the Sniper. She did now.

He said shooting the cab driver and the runner wasn't his choice. So whose choice was it? His mystery employer? How much did he pay Peter to shoot them? Plenty, probably.

She looked around her living room. In November she'd be twenty-five. She didn't want to live in a dump like this forever. It might not be smart to stay in New Orleans much longer, either. She'd already boosted swag from the most expensive stores on Royal street, and the cops had video of her. Not her face, but still.

Maybe she could be a sniper too. When she'd said this to Peter, he brushed her off, but if she played her cards right, she was certain she could convince him. Peter wanted to screw her. That was the deal when he agreed to take her on the roof: He expected to have sex with her when they came back to her apartment.

But shooting the cop changed that.

Peter had said he'd be back. But when? She hated being cooped up in her apartment.

She grabbed the clicker and tuned in a local station on the TV.

SNIPER

A news reporter was doing her report from Bourbon Street. "The wounded policewoman, twenty-eight-year-old Kimba Davis, joined the mounted police unit just two months ago."

Wow! That's a stunner. The cop was a woman?

When she looked through the sniper scope, the cop had his back to her, but he had short dark hair, like the fat-pig security guard in California who'd forced her to give him a blow job.

So she shot him in the back. But the cop was a woman.

She drank some Becks as the TV reporter said, "Kimba Davis has a seven-year-old daughter."

Like that was a big fucking deal. The cop probably put her in day care, or hired a sitter like Mother. Why did women have babies if they didn't want to take care of them?

Wait. The reporter had said *wounded* policewoman. Which meant she was still alive. Would that screw up her plan? Maybe not. Maybe Peter's employer wouldn't be mad at him if the woman lived.

She couldn't wait for him to come back, but she had to play this carefully, reel him in like a fish.

Feign indifference. That drove guys wild.

No question he was smitten with her. Reel him in, convince him to let her be his sniper partner and make the big bucks.

CHAPTER 11

The moment he entered his hotel room, he tuned in a local channel on the television set. Bloody hell! They were already covering the cop-shooting, **Breaking News** emblazoned across the screen.

He muted the sound and studied the chaos: a half-dozen patrol cars, two dozen cops, a mob of reporters and TV cameras, and two news choppers flying over the scene to give viewers a Sky-Eye view. They weren't showing the cop or the horse, but an ambulance was edging around the crowd. He wiped sweat off his face. Christ, what a fuck-up!

Now he had to call Control. He'd given this considerable thought as he raced back to his hotel. Control would be furious, but down deep the asshole was a wimp. Don't explain, don't make excuses, attack.

He punched in a number, heard it ring. "Red Flag," Control said, an emergency code to tell him he was on an encrypted phone, no need for subterfuge and coded messages.

"Understood," he said, and waited. Let the games begin.

"You have done something very stupid. What the bloody hell were you *thinking*?"

"Thinking a lot of things. Thinking I've been here six weeks, waiting for information about the final assignment. You tell me to shoot two innocent civilians ...." Control drew a sharp breath, but he kept going before Control could interrupt. "Assignments I executed perfectly, but when I ask for Intel on The Package, you tell me nothing."

"I can't tell you—"

"Be quiet! I'm not done!" Weeks of pent-up anger and frustration exploded inside him like a hand grenade. "At our last meeting you said you'd call and tell me when and where to execute the next hit, like a bloody school teacher handing out a fucking homework assignment."

"I didn't call and tell you to shoot a fucking cop!"

"I'm tired of your bullshit. Tired of waiting. I need to stay sharp."

"By shooting a cop? Jesus! Are you crazy?"

"I'll tell you what else I think. The Package is the real target, some VIP pooh-bah, but you want to make the cops think some nutcase is running around the city shooting people at random. These other hits are just a smokescreen."

Silence on the other end.

Then, "Listen carefully because I'm not going to say this twice. If you pull a stunt like this again there will be serious consequences. No more action until I say so. Wait for my instructions. Is that clear?"

Relieved that Control wasn't going to fire him and send him back to London, he said, "Yes."

"Good," Control said. "Call me tomorrow, usual time, usual code."

He closed his phone and looked at the TV as reporters crowded around a tall rugged man in dark trousers and a polo shirt open at the neck. Not in uniform, but he looked like a cop.

He upped the volume.

"... Homicide Detective Frank Renzi. I'm lead investigator on the cab driver murder on Canal Street, and I'm collaborating with the lead detective on the Garden District runner homicide. Now a mounted policewoman is fighting for her life, shot by a sniper."

A female cop? Fighting for her life? He felt a momentary surge of relief, until he studied the cop: black hair, a prominent Roman nose and dark eyes. He'd seen eyes like that before. Motherfucker eyes, gazing into the camera as he said, "The Sniper is a coward. And we're going to get him."

"Not if I get you first, asshole." He aimed an imaginary gun at the screen and pulled the trigger.

Incensed that the cop-motherfucker had called him a coward, he shut off the TV. Did Renzi know what it took to be a hero? Had he ever come under fire in combat? Had he ever watched his best mate die, bleeding out from a gaping chest wound?

To calm himself, he put on his headset and started the Shostakovitch *Waltz* from the *Jazz Suite* on his mini-MP3 player, three minutes of gorgeous music.

Stanley Kubrick had used it in *Eyes Wide Shut*.

He shut his eyes and pictured Nicole Kidman dancing with the Count. Imagined himself dancing to the music, naked—not with Nicole Kidman, with Win—and got an instant hard-on.

He felt bad that he'd yelled at her this morning—albeit with good reason—recalling how her luminous brown eyes brimmed with tears.

Still, he couldn't allow himself to be distracted.

Now that he'd placated Control, he still had a job to do, and he in-tended to execute it perfectly.

———

1:30 PM

When Frank walked into the room, Vobitch was seated in a chair beside his hospital bed, the mother of all frowns on his face.

"The motherfucker's shooting cops now?" Vobitch said.

"That's what it looks like," Frank said. "She's only been with the mounted unit for two months. I called the hospital an hour ago. She's out of surgery. In critical condition, but barring any unforeseen complications, they think she's going to make it."

"That's good news," Vobitch said. "Gimme the details. The damn TV reporters told me jackshit. They just want to stir up trouble, yammering about the New Orleans Sniper."

"The first officer on the scene didn't hear the shot, just heard the policewoman scream. The sniper could have been anywhere, on a roof probably. But we can't post officers on every roof—"

He broke off as a stocky dark-haired nurse entered the room with a clipboard and a small paper cup, frowning at Vobitch. "Sounds like *Law and Order* in here, Mr. Vobitch. Time for your meds."

"Okay, but don't take my blood pressure. It's off the chart."

The nurse skewered Frank with a look, then said to Vobitch, "Open heart surgery is nothing to joke about. The doctor doesn't want you getting riled up. This is a hospital room, not your office."

"No kidding. I can't wait to get out of here." Vobitch beamed her a delighted smile. "I'm going home on Thursday."

She smiled grimly. "Yes, and I know a few people who are rather happy about that."

Frank laughed. "You and the rest of the nurses, right?"

Amused, she nodded and handed Vobitch the paper cup. "Take you meds, Mr. Vobitch."

Vobitch tossed them back and washed them down with a gulp of water from a paper cup. The nurse jotted a note on her clipboard, gave him a sardonic smile and said, "I'm off at three. Try and behave yourself until then."

After she left, Frank said, "Man, she's got your number."

"Yeah. Take your meds. Get up and take a walk. No ice cream for dessert, no pancakes for breakfast. Christ, a guy could starve in here." Vobitch opened the front of his johnny, exposing a ten-inch long scar from his sternum to his gut.

"See this? I had Juliana bring me my iPad and looked up open heart surgery. They use a saw to carve open your chest, stop your heart and hook you up to a fucking machine." His slate-gray eyes widened. "Five hours, I got no heart! And then they take out the bad valve and replace it—"

"With a pig valve," Frank said. "But hey, look at it this way. Pigs are smart. Maybe it'll rub off on—"

"Don't be a wise ass." Vobitch closed the johnny and got down to business. "Forget your other cases, Frank. The sniper goes to the top of the list."

"He already is, but I need help. Obama isn't planning any trips to New Orleans, but we've got fifty foreign embassies, no telling when some bigwig might decide to pay us a visit. I want Kelly to transfer back in Homicide. Just until we catch the sniper."

"District Eight? I don't know—"

"No, District Six. Vance is good, but I want eyes and ears over there. Kelly knows that district. She's worked with a lot of Dom-V clients in that area, and she's a great detective."

"I'll drink to that." A tight smile. "Well, I would if I could. If I ask Nurse Ratched for a beer, she'll flip out. Okay, I'll call the NOPD Super back and ask him to approve the transfer. This morning I told him I want you to act as temporary supervisor of my detectives."

Shocked, Frank fingered the jagged scar on his chin. He felt gratified that Vobitch respected him enough to recommend him for the job, but he didn't want to sit at a desk, doing paperwork and filing reports. He prowled the mean streets and caught bad-ass killers.

"The Super nixed the idea." Vobitch grimaced. "He's focused on the Sniper, wants to set up a task force. Unfortunately, he's putting Deputy Superintendent Wendell Hicks in charge of it. Hicks wants to see you in his office first thing tomorrow."

———

Control braced himself for an explosion, the phone clamped to his ear, terrified that the Boss had heard about the cop shooting.

"We have a problem," the Boss said in his deep sinister voice. "The Buyer just called me. The Yipper in Ankara is leaning on him."

In addition to his two-pack-a-day cigarette habit, the Boss was addicted to nicknames. The Yipper in Ankara was Turkish Prime Minister Recep Tayyip Erdogan.

Control shuddered. If The Buyer was Turkish, it was bad news. The Turks were ruthless. Many Turkish citizens who opposed the Erdogan regime disappeared, never to be seen again. Turkey was a pulsating glob of pus, geographically situated between Europe to the north and the Middle East to the south. And Erdogan was the pustule who ran it with an iron fist.

"Someone who opposes The Buyer has damaging information about an important Turkish official, not The Buyer, a government official."

Control breathed a sigh of relief. The Boss was worried about Operation Smokescreen, not the cop shooting. Eventually the Boss would hear about it, but he'd worry about that later.

He waited, heard the Boss puff his cigarette.

"The man who threatens to ruin our operation is Aram Takvorian, an Armenian. They hate the Turks. In 1915, the Ottoman Turks killed millions of Armenians. They claim it was genocide, but Erdogan will never admit this."

Control said nothing, thinking: *The Buyer has to be a Turk.*

"Erdogan has many enemies. The Dry-Fart in London, the Poodle in Paris, the Bitch in Berlin," the Boss said. "To name only three."

He rapidly decoded the Boss's idiotic nicknames. The Dry-Fart in London was the British prime minister. The Poodle in Paris was French President Nicholas Sarkozy. The Bitch in Berlin was Angela Merkel. Was one of them The Package?

"The Armenians want to prevent Turkey from joining the European Union. To that end, Takvorian has put incriminating information about a Turkish official on a flash drive. This morning he took it to the FBI office in New York City, but they blew him off. The Ape in Washington wants to get Turkey *into* the EU, not keep them out."

Control grimaced. The Ape in Washington was Obama. Un-PC, of course, but the Boss cared little for such niceties. However, it now seemed absolutely clear: The Buyer was Turkish.

"The Armenian has booked a flight to New Orleans. We believe he will contact the FBI office there. This we must prevent." The Boss coughed, *ack-ack-ack.* Then he said, "The Armenian and his wife will arrive tomorrow night and stay in a French Quarter hotel. Have your Helper go to his hotel room first thing Wednesday morning, kill the Armenian, acquire the flash drive with the incriminating information and deliver it to you."

Control mopped sweat off his face with a handkerchief. As if he didn't have enough problems …

"If your Helper fails to do this, there will be dire consequences, understand?"

"Of course. I'll make that clear."

"Good. Because any failure will have consequences for you. I will fax you the details about this Armenian, including photographs. Call me immediately when you have the flash drive."

"Yes, sir," he said, and ended the call.

He took a bottle of Valium out of his desk drawer, shook three into his hand and dry-swallowed them.

His employers handled many clients. The vast majority involved business or politics. Business clients were straightforward enough. Company X wanted the CEO of Company Y eliminated, to cement their hold on a particular market. Political hits were far more complicated. Some clients wanted these assassinations to look like accidents. A politician was in the wrong place at the wrong time.

The Russians were the worst. Critics of the Kremlin often wound up dead. In 2006, Alexander Litvinenko had died of polonium-210 poisoning in London. Last year another man's body was found inside a duffel bag in an empty bathtub, so badly decomposed pathologists could not determine what killed him. The man's family claimed the Russian secret service or espionage agents had poisoned him.

Control massaged his aching temples. Now he had to meet with the Sniper, and face another grilling about The Package.

But the Boss still hadn't told him who it would be.

Was it the Dry-Fart? The Poodle? The Bitch in Berlin?

This Armenian assignment might be a blessing in disguise. The Sniper was getting anxious, his finger itchy on the trigger, shooting a bloody policewoman for crissake! Maybe a new assignment would improve his disposition, and keep him out of trouble.

CHAPTER 12

Imagining himself dancing naked with Win to the music from *Eyes Wide Shut* failed to erase his dark mood. Today had been an unmitigated disaster. Win shooting the cop. Their harrowing escape. Their nasty argument. So he escaped to his usual fantasy-land: a movie theater.

Years ago after his mum died, he'd felt … not lonely exactly, just alone. No family, no friends, not even his army mates. Yearning for some sort of emotional connection, he began going to "girly" movies.

Clint Eastwood was great in *The Bridges of Madison County*, but Meryl Streep left him cold. *Pretty Woman* was better, Julia Roberts had gorgeous brown eyes. *Ghost* was the first movie that made him weep. He'd sat there, staring at the screen, thinking: *If I died, would anyone care?*

By then he was hooked, sitting in the darkness, engrossed in the action, moved by the emotional power. In Paris, he'd seen *The Deer Hunter* at a theater rerunning blockbuster war movies. He still didn't care for Meryl Streep, but he loved the hunting scenes, and Christopher Walken was amazing. When Walken cried in the hospital scene, he'd wept right along with him. The next day he saw *Full Metal Jacket* directed by Stanley Kubrick. When he found out Kubrick used classical music in some of his films he'd made a point to see them.

His favorites were *2001, Clockwork Orange* and *Eyes Wide Shut.*

But the movie he'd seen today left him restless and unsatisfied, a horror flick with Nick Cage. Afterwards, he returned to his hotel room, a battle raging in his mind worse than any firefight in Iraq. Should he go and see Win? He had a job to do, and she'd damn near screwed it up. But he couldn't get her out of his mind, especially her luscious brown eyes, sucking him in with promises of things to come.

At four o'clock, he took a shower, shaved and got dressed. At four-thirty, he rang her bell, his head throbbing with a dull ache. On the way, he'd stopped to buy a six-pack of beer.

Her voice came over the intercom, "Who is it?"

"You know who it is. Buzz me in."

The buzzer sounded and he opened the door. Carrying a plastic bag with the beer, he climbed the stairs. A thrill of anticipation made his heart soar as he approached her door. Before he could knock, she opened it. The sight of her took his breath away.

Dressed in a pair of white shorts and a red halter-top, she gazed at him solemnly, no smile, her big brown eyes as mysterious as ever.

"I brought us a six-pack of Becks," he said, handing it to her.

"Thanks. Would you like one now?" No hint of a smile.

"Yes. We need to talk."

Without a word, she took the six-pack into the kitchen. Too anxious to sit down, he paced the room until she came back. She handed him a beer, sat on the futon and drank some beer, gazing up at him, her face unreadable. "Was your employer pissed?"

"Pissed? In the UK, pissed means *pissed as a lord*, meaning drunk, and I assure you, my employer wasn't drunk, he was fucking furious!"

She blinked when he yelled at her, shrinking back against the futon. "What do you want, Peter? I told you I was sorry. And the cop didn't die. She's in the hospital."

"Which makes it even worse. It makes me look incompetent. During the war, me and my sniper mates had a motto. One shot, one kill. If we missed, it gave the enemy a chance to kill us the next time. Missing a target is not acceptable in my business."

"But I didn't miss her. Mother would be proud if she knew."

Stunned, he popped the cap on his beer and took a gulp. What sort of mother would be proud of her kid for shooting a cop? His mum wouldn't. She didn't care much for cops, but if he killed one, she wouldn't like it. Wouldn't like it if she knew he was killing people for money either.

"Why would your mother be proud?"

"I told you before. Mother says all cops are pigs. After Woodstock, she turned into a Peacenik. She'd go to anti-war protests with a bunch of other Peaceniks and the cops would harass them."

"The Vietnam War? During the seventies?"

"Yes. She and Dad lived in a hippie commune in Vermont for a while, but Dad got sick of it. He wanted to go to college." She smiled at him. "Like my teeth? No cavities, thanks to Dad. He's the one who took me to the dentist."

"The policewoman has a seven-year-old daughter. Dad wouldn't think much of that, right?"

"No." She drank some Becks. "After a while he didn't think much of Mother, either. He got accepted at Ithaca College, but she gave him grief about living in Ithaca. What a joke! He's learning to be a pharmacist, she's smoking pot and listening to Janis Joplin records. By then she was a professional protester."

"What's that?" Part of him wanted to take her to bed and make love to her. Another part wanted to find out how his sexy little shoplifter had turned into a woman able to shoot someone in the back, intending to kill them, and remain untroubled by it.

"She worked for a non-profit protest group, used their van to drive protesters to rallies and back home afterwards. All over New England and parts of New York."

"Did she take you with her?"

Win threw back her head and laughed. "Are you kidding? Not bloody likely as you Brits are fond of saying. I wasn't even a twinkle in her eye back then. When they moved to Ithaca they weren't even married. That happened later, after Mother got pregnant. With me."

He evaluated her expression as she sipped her beer and stared into space. Win clearly had a problem with her mother. Loved her dad though. "And then Win arrived," he said. "What year was that?"

"Not Win, Janis. Nineteen-eighty-six. I'll be twenty-five in November."

"You're too young to be shooting people, cops or anyone else."

Anger flared in her eyes. "What the hell do you know? I left home when I was fifteen. Been on my own ever since."

He sat beside her on the futon and drank some beer. This wasn't going the way he'd planned. Now she was angry. He didn't want to take her to bed angry. "My mum used to take me to concerts when we lived in London, plenty of concerts there. Mum loved Russian composers, Tchaikovsky, especially. Pyotr Ilyich Tchaikovsky. Better known as Peter. She named me after him."

He couldn't believe he'd told her this. What was he thinking?

Clearly unimpressed, Win said, "That's nice. I don't listen to classical music much."

"Mum was a classical flutist. She gave lessons to kids who'd come to our flat. She wanted me to play flute, too. I had no aptitude for it, but I loved the instrument." He waggled his fingers. "All those complicated mechanical parts. When I got older, I used to repair it for her. Got my mechanical skills from my dad. He owned a bicycle repair shop."

He never told women about his family or his early life. But Win was different. Win was his soulmate.

"That's what got you interested in motorcycles," she said. "I want to be a sniper. I know I'd be good at it."

He shook his head. "Pulling the trigger and hitting a target is only part of it. A sniper has to be a hunter. First, you have to track down the target. Surveillance means lying on a roof in pouring rain for hours being wet, tired, miserable and dirty, or sitting inside a sweltering attic. It takes discipline to put up with shitty conditions like that. Plus, you need to learn how to get in and out of places without being seen. How to evaluate the possible consequences of a kill. And there's a lot of math involved, calculations to judge distance and wind speed. Above all, you need a shitload of patience."

Throughout his recitation, she gazed at him, rapt. When he finished, she said, "I can be patient, and I always do surveillance before I boost stuff from ritzy shops. I'm good at math, too."

"Okay, but here's the most important thing. You'll see the target's face when you kill him. Up close and personal because you've been studying him for days. When that moment comes, you can't teach people how to feel. That's why choosing the right person is so important. A sniper needs mental toughness."

She drew a breath, about to speak, but he silenced her with his hand. "You asked why I shot the cab driver and the runner. Not my choice, but I did my job. When you pull trigger, you have to compartmentalize. Ignore the fact that you're taking a life. You can't think about his wife and kids. He might be father of three, but tough shit. At that moment, he's the enemy."

She grabbed his face and kissed him on the lips.

Stunned, he put his arms around her and pulled her close. Her mouth opened, yielding and moist, sucking his tongue.

He thought his chest would explode, his heart pumping like a firetruck at a three-alarm blaze. She released him, gazing at him with her entrancing eyes. "I love hearing you talk about it."

He pulled her to her feet, put his hands inside the waistband of her shorts, slid his hands inside her underpants and ran them over her butt, feeling her smooth skin. Already his cock was as hard as granite. He unhooked her bra, took her breasts in his palms, fondled her nipples with his fingers.

Moaning with pleasure, she pulled up his shirt, a frantic motion. She stepped out of her sandals and pushed down her shorts. Her legs were beautiful, slender but muscular. He ripped off his clothes and she grabbed him around the waist, hugging him to her with both hands. The feel of her bare skin against him was like a shock of electricity. He closed his eyes as she caressed his face. Aching to be inside her, he nuzzled her neck, inhaling her musky perfume.

She wrapped her arms around his neck and he picked her up and carried her to the bed and fell upon her. Within seconds he was inside her and she was moaning, calling out his name. She hooked her legs around his hips and brought him deeper inside her. For a while their gasps and irregular breathing were the only sounds in the room, in the whole world, the whole universe.

All the ugliness of the day melted away.

No bloody corpses, no screaming spectators, no desperate flight to escape the police. Only pleasure to numb the pain in his heart. He felt her climax, her muscles shuddering uncontrollably. Seconds later he exploded inside her, trembling and breathing hard.

After a moment he pulled out of her, and they lay side by side.

She kissed his forehead, then his cheek. He brushed hair from her forehead and kissed her neck.

He didn't want this moment to end.

———

8:35 PM

Relaxed and happy, Frank lay on his side, snuggled against Kelly, his fingers roaming over her bare skin. Kenyon was his best friend in the department, a smart detective with a sly sense of humor. David was a basketball player like him, so they thought alike: Go with the flow, see how the play develops. Tony was another good friend, a no-nonsense cop to whom loyalty was everything.

Kelly was all that and more, a passionate partner in bed, no holding back. What would he do without her? Immerse himself in his work, growing more and more cynical as the years passed, a worn-out homicide dick who'd seen too many corpses and too many grieving relatives? Sure, he could find another attractive woman, take her to bed and make love to her. That part was easy enough. He knew how to please women in bed and loved doing it.

But with Kelly, the sexual aspect—fantastic as it was—was only part of it. Kelly was a cop. He could discuss cases with her, get her take on them. When he got discouraged about solving a homicide, she would tease him, make some wisecrack to get him out of his funk. He loved her sense of humor. Bottom line, Kelly understood him. Far better than his ex-wife ever had.

She propped herself on an elbow and said, "Did Vobitch give you a hard time about me transferring back into Homicide?"

"I figured he might. That's why I suggested putting you in the D-6 unit." He traced a finger down her cheek. "I told him you were a great detective."

"Uh-huh. Flattery will get you ..." Kelly gave him a sly look. "Another beer. What happens after that is up to you."

He pulled her closer and kissed her lips. "We'll see about that."

Another sly look. "I'm sure we will. How's Vobitch doing? I haven't had time to go see him."

"Going home on Thursday. The nurses are thrilled."

Kelly laughed. "He's being pig-headed as usual, right?"

"Right, but dig this. He showed me the scar, said he googled open heart surgery online. I was shocked. He actually seemed ... I don't know, not frightened. More like he was contemplating his mortality. Five hours, his heart was disconnected, he said."

"Mmm. That's heavy. I better call Juliana and ask if I can do anything to help her."

"That'd be good. Vobitch is bullshit about the sniper shooting the policewoman."

Kelly gazed at him, her sea-green eyes somber. "How is she?"

"Last I heard she was doing okay. I've been too busy to visit her."

"Too busy giving comments to the reporters. Calling the sniper a coward."

"So? He is a coward. Sits on a fucking roof and shoots a policewoman. And now we got British Prime Minister David Cameron coming here to speak during the Fourth of July celebrations. A guy from the NOPD Intelligence Unit called this afternoon to tell me."

She stared at him. "Whoa! Just when you think things can't get any worse."

"Oh, but they can. The NOPD Super set up a task force to catch the Sniper and put Wendell Hicks in charge. Hicks wants to see me in his office tomorrow. And you know what an asshole he can be."

Kelly grimaced. "Indeed I do. Good luck with that."

CHAPTER 13

She waddled down Royal Street in her old lady disguise, two bath towels strapped around her middle under a dowdy blue dress to make her look plump. To go with her frumpy gray wig.

But she didn't feel like an old lady. She felt like a million bucks, still on cloud-nine after last night's orgy with Peter. So much for playing it cool. She couldn't get him out of her mind. What a sexy bod, lean and muscular, slim hips and broad shoulders. Thinking about his bare skin pressed against hers gave her goosebumps.

She'd never had sex like that in her life. Not only that, he didn't roll over and fall asleep afterwards like most guys. "Stay here while I get us a beer," he'd said. When he came back, he had her put on his headphones and listen to music. "A waltz by Shostakovitch," he'd said. "Kubrick used it in *Eyes Wide Shut*. Did you see it? Nicole Kidman dancing with the Count? It makes me think of you."

That made her uneasy. Nicole Kidman was six feet tall and gorgeous. To her disgust, she was short like Mother. But Peter loved her eyes. They were dark brown like Dad's.

And Winona's. She hadn't told him about Winona yet.

She stifled a yawn. She never got up this early. Never let guys stay overnight either, but Peter was different. She had a feeling her plan was going to work out. His employer hadn't fired him after all. Peter said he'd be here for a couple more weeks, to finish the job he'd been sent here to do. Plenty of time for her to convince him to let her be his sniper partner. This morning he said he had work to do, but they could have dinner together. She could hardly wait.

To take her mind off Peter, she'd put on her old-lady disguise and walked over to Royal Street to plan her next con game.

She stopped at Rau Antiques and studied the items in the window, recalling her first big score here, months ago. Rau Antiques sold the most expensive items on Royal Street. They weren't in the window, of course. They were locked in a safe. To see them, you had to make an appointment. According to an article she'd seen on the Internet, Whoopi Goldberg had paid a small fortune for twelve place settings from a Civil War-era set of dinnerware that had once belonged to the King of Hanover. Wherever that was.

Her neck prickled, the uneasy feeling she got when someone was watching her. Angling her body, she checked her reflection in the window glass. Twenty feet behind her, a young Asian man stood on the sidewalk, leaning against a light post. Jesus! Was he a cop?

Her heart jolted and her palms grew sweaty. Damn! She should have worn her big floppy hat. A dowdy dress and a gray wig didn't hide her smooth, unwrinkled skin. The skin of a young woman.

She hadn't even worn her Raybans because it was a dreary day, the sky overcast with clouds. She turned ever so slightly, glancing at him out of the corner of her eye.

No doubt about it, he was watching her. No cop uniform, but that meant nothing. Early thirties, a few inches taller than her, his glossy black hair neatly trimmed, gazing at her with his dark Asian eyes.

She went into survival mode. Be cool. Act like an old-lady tourist. Check the store hours posted on the door, feign disappointment and get the hell out of here. But slowly.

Easing to her left, she stepped closer to the door of Rau Antiques, pretend-studied the hours and shook her head, feigning disappointment. Recalling a character in a movie she'd seen, she limped back to the sidewalk. Favoring her left leg, she turned her face away from the cop, her heart pounding her chest, slowly limping along the sidewalk, when every instinct told her to *run!*

She passed one store, stopped at another one that sold Mardi Gras masks, pretended to look at them in the window and checked the cop. He wasn't following her, but he was still leaning against the light post, watching her.

Her heart slammed her chest, beating like a wild thing.

If she could get to the next corner ... She turned and slowly limped off, playing the part. Just a gimpy old-lady tourist looking for souvenirs. The next cross street was two stores away.

Digging her nails into her palms, she paused at the next shop, looked in the window, kept going and limped past the next store.

The instant she turned the corner she broke into a dead run, heading toward the river, not her apartment, but she'd worry about that later. She raced around the next corner, dodged two older women and kept running, ripped the wig off her head and ran faster.

Two minutes later, panting for breath, she paused outside a coffee shop. No cops chasing her. With a triumphant smile, she mopped her sweaty face on her sleeve and headed home.

———

9:30 AM

Located on the top floor at NOPD Headquarters, the Deputy Superintendent's office had a large window with an expansive view of downtown New Orleans. When Frank entered the office, Wendell Hicks, seated behind his desk facing the door, looked up and smiled.

He had a certain phony charm, but Frank knew better than to fall for it. Hicks never forgot a slight, no matter how insignificant. Not a man to cross if you could help it.

"Have a seat, Detective." An African-American in his mid-fifties, Hicks was strikingly handsome, smooth dark skin and high cheekbones, his head shaved to mask a receding hairline. In his starched-and-pressed police uniform Hicks made a great impression when speaking to the media with the cameras rolling, but he hadn't worked the streets for twenty years.

Lining up the pink message slips on his desk to show how busy he was, Hicks said, "I understand you attended Boston College for a while. Why did you drop out?"

Annoyed, Frank said, "What is this, a job interview?"

Hicks smiled, though his eyes remained cold. "I like to get to know the detectives who work for me." Reminding him who was in charge.

"I decided to join Boston PD."

"So I see." Hicks tapped a folder. "Did your father help you?"

Frank gritted his teeth. *No. I had the second highest score on the police exam, unlike you.*

Aloud he said, "My father wanted me to go to law school. He started out as a prosecutor. Now he's a federal judge in Boston. I wanted to get the criminals off the street."

Expressionless, Hicks said, "So you joined Boston PD, got your detective shield in record time it seems. Your supervisor sent you to Quantico to take an FBI profiling course. How was it?"

"Very enlightening. It helped me solve a couple of serial murder cases."

Hicks smiled tightly. "A fine record until you shot the girl."

He clenched his jaw, trying to stay calm. Hicks was baiting him, trying to get a rise out of him.

"Nobody felt worse about it than me and my partner."

For months after the shooting, images of the girl's face had jolted him awake every night. Even now he still had nightmares about it. His partner had never recovered, had retired to Florida, a broken man. "IAD investigated and cleared us of any charges."

"Two white officers shot a nine-year-old black girl," Hicks said, his eyes glinting with anger.

"She got mixed-up with a drug dealer. We had a murder warrant for him. I've got no problem with law-abiding black folks, Wendell, but I've got a problem with black thugs running around with guns, pushing drugs and killing innocent people. Most of whom are black."

A muscle worked in Hicks' jaw. "Last year you shot King Rock."

"A *drug dealer* who murdered the mother of his son. He shot at me first. After I shot him, taking care not to *kill* him, he told his girl-friend to kill me. She shot at me and missed. I could have shot her, too, but I didn't. It was a righteous shoot. Even IAD said so."

"A lot of people think otherwise."

"What did you do? Contact King Rock's asshole defense attorney to dig up dirt on me?"

"No," Hicks snapped. "Your reputation speaks for itself."

"My reputation with black folks in this town is fine. You sit up here in your office, away from the blood and gore. I'm the one who has to tell the grieving parents their son or daughter is dead. I'm the one who works my ass off to find the killer. Let's stop screwing around and talk about important things. We got a sniper killing people with a high-powered rifle, not just in the French Quarter, in the Garden District, too. We need help. Vobitch wants Detective Kelly O'Neil to transfer into D-6 Homicide from Domestic Violence." His idea, but he'd let Hicks think Vobitch suggested it. "She used to work for him in the D-5 Homicide unit."

Hicks ran a hand over his shaven head. "Fine with me. Right now I've got eighteen homicide detectives to cover the whole city, and the homicide rate is off the chart. Over a hundred, halfway through the year, the highest rate of any city with two-hundred-thousand resi-dents. Sixty percent of whom are African-American." Hicks clenched his jaw, glaring at him.

If looks could kill, I'd be dead, Frank thought.

"Your comments to the media at the crime scene on Bourbon Street were *totally* out of line. Calling the sniper a coward. Practically *begging* him to shoot someone else. No more loose-cannon comments to the media. From now on, you refer all calls from the media to *me*."

"Suit yourself, but no matter what anyone says, he'll shoot someone else."

"Not if I can help it," Hicks snapped. "That's why the Superintendent set up a task force."

But Hicks didn't look too happy about it, a big scowl on his face now. Why was that? Frank wondered.

Hicks supplied the answer. "All well and good, but that means working with the FBI, ATF and Homeland Security, not to mention the State Police Major Crimes Unit."

"Good. The more help we get, the better. We don't have the troops to cover every roof in the city, but if the State Police helped us, we could cover the Quarter and the Garden District near where he shot the runner." Seeing the angry look on Hicks's face, he knew he should have kept quiet. *Go along to get along. For now anyway.*

"I don't see it that way," Hicks said. "The feds won't share their information with us, but they expect us to give them whatever we've got. And anytime the Major Crimes Unit gets involved they want to take over. I've seen it happen, time and again."

Frank said nothing. Let Hicks do the talking.

"We need to calm the residents and quiet the media. I'll hold a presser tomorrow on the steps of the Federal Court House on Royal Street. Every NOPD homicide detective will be there in uniform. I'll announce a hotline number for people to call."

Hicks wagged a finger at him. "Stay away from the media, Renzi. No more loose-cannon comments."

He fought down another surge of anger. Picturing the wounded policewoman, he said, "Fine, but hold the presser on Bourbon Street where the motherfucker shot the policewoman."

Hicks stared at him, expressionless. "Let me be crystal clear, Renzi. *I'm* in charge of the task force. *You* are not. Get to work."

———

12:35 PM

He waited as Control sat down beside him on the bench, took out a handkerchief and mopped sweat from his face. Wearing his usual pin-striped suit today but no tie, his white shirt unbuttoned at the throat. Lafayette Park was relatively quiet today, young couples in shorts meandering along the gravel paths, a few mothers playing with tiny tots in swimsuits. But he got the feeling Control wasn't sweating because of the heat and humidity. Was the Boss giving him grief about the policewoman? If so, he'd hear about it soon enough.

"I have a new assignment for you," Control said, gazing at him through his spectacles. "A man will fly here from New York City with his wife tonight." He opened a folder and took out a sheaf of papers. "Aram Takvorian. Here is copy of his passport photo."

He studied the photo. Aram Takvorian, age 53, thick white hair, a pock-marked face and an Armenian name. Interesting. Was this related to The Package?

"Takvorian has gathered incriminating Intel about a friend of the Buyer and put it on a flash drive. The Boss wants you to terminate him and take the flash drive."

"How do I know where he'll be?"

"He and his wife will land at Louis Armstrong Airport tonight at seven-thirty. Here is a photo of her passport." Control handed him a sheet of paper.

He took a quick look. Nicole Takvorian, age 33, an attractive woman with dark eyes and wavy brown hair falling to her shoulders.

"They will stay in the French Quarter at the Hotel Cavendish on Canal Street." Control gave him another sheet of paper. "Here are the details. His wife intends to go shopping tomorrow."

"How do you know this?"

"Our New York operative had eyes and ears in their hotel room."

That didn't surprise him. Zenith Intelligence had high-tech operatives all over the world.

"Tomorrow morning after she leaves the hotel, have Takvorian meet you in the hotel tea room. He'll be expecting your call." Control handed him a Federal ID badge with his photo on it. "You are FBI Agent Joseph Macklin. Your FBI colleague in New York called and told you Takvorian has information to give you. Take him to his room and kill him. Quickly and quietly. Leave no trace of yourself. Take the flash drive and leave the hotel immediately."

Incredulous, he said, "They land here tonight and you expect me to take him out tomorrow? That's crazy. There's no time to prepare. I need to—"

"Just do it!" Control hissed. "Or the Boss will get someone else."

He considered his options. If he refused would they cancel his other assignment? "What's on the flash drive?"

"You don't need to know this. What you need to *understand* is this. If you fail, there will be serious consequences. Time is of the essence. The Package will arrive soon."

"When?"

"Soon. Two weeks at most."

"What's on the flash drive?" He didn't like the sound of this. Too many unknowns.

Control iced him with a look. "Just do your job. And no fuckups, understand? Call me immediately when you have the flash drive so we can set up a meet for the exchange."

Shaking with anger, he watched Control walk away. Control expected him to work miracles on short notice. The Armenian would arrive tonight and less than 24 hours later he had to kill him.

When Control passed the big statue in the center of the park, he hurried after him. He needed Intel and there was only one way to get it. Following him wasn't difficult. Control hadn't worked in the field for years. He worried about black thugs, not an experienced operative tailing him.

Ten minutes later, he watched Control open a gate and walk up a driveway paved with crushed white stone. Spaced at six foot intervals, security cameras and spotlights topped an eight-foot wall surrounding a two-story Victorian. What good was a safe-house without high--tech goodies to keep unwanted visitors out?

Unwanted visitors like an experienced killer such as himself.

Breaking into the safe-house would be difficult but not impossible. An olive-green Saab was parked out front, Control's rental car, he assumed. Sooner or later Control would leave the house in his car. There were no restaurants nearby, and he couldn't picture Control cooking for himself.

Unbidden, an image of Win entered his mind, her sexy brown eyes and her luscious lips. He banished the image. *Focus on the job.* He had a lot of work to do. The scraps Control had given him were only a starting point.

Maybe he'd let Win help him. That would make her happy. And two sets of eyes were always better than one.

CHAPTER 14

12:30 PM

After his meeting with Wendell Hicks, Frank took a power walk around the French Quarter to calm himself down, didn't get back to the District-8 homicide office until twelve-thirty. Kenyon Miller and David Lee had just finished take-out sandwiches, Kenyon seated at his desk, David sitting beside him in a visitor chair.

"Hey, Frank, where you been?" Kenyon said, with a broad smile. "Kelly stopped by a few minutes ago. As of tomorrow she'll be back in homicide, working out of the District-6 office."

"Excellent," he said. "Vobitch probably pushed for the transfer. The docs won't clear him to go back to work, but he's got his cellphone, acts like his hospital room is his office. Last I heard he's going home on Thursday. That'll make the nurses happy."

"He giving them a hard time?" David said with a faint smile.

"What else?" Frank said. "I've been keeping him up to speed on the Sniper. He's bullshit about Kimba Davis."

"Shoot a policewoman in the back," Kenyon said, squinty-eyed, his jaw clenched, "enough to piss off every cop on the force."

"Exactly," Frank said, "so let's talk about how we catch the bastard. I had a meeting with Wendell Hicks this morning."

"You don't look too thrilled about it," David said.

"It wasn't a fun meeting. First he dumped on me for the King Rock shooting. Then he called me a loose cannon for calling the Sniper a coward. Bottom line, talking to the media is off-limits for Frank Renzi. If any reporters call me, I have to refer them to Hicks."

"What an asshole!" Kenyon exclaimed. "You're the lead investigator!"

Frank smiled tightly. "Nothing new there, and it will only get worse. Hicks is in charge of the task force to catch the Sniper, but he's got no clue how to do it." He sat down at his desk and said, "Let's brainstorm for a while, figure out our own plan to nail the Sniper."

"Two shootings in the French Quarter," David said, running his fingers through his glossy black hair. "He must be sleeping somewhere. How about we check the hotels in and around the Quarter, find out if any male guests have been staying there since the first shooting in June?"

"Good idea," Frank said. "Maybe Kelly can check the hotels in the Garden District."

"That's a shitload of hotels," Kenyon said. "Can we get the other D-6 detectives in on it? Maybe have a meeting and split up the load?"

"I like it," Frank said. "Vance is lead on the female runner case. He's been very cooperative, but we better not meet in the station. I don't want Hicks to get wind of it."

"Speaking of Hicks," David said, "this isn't Sniper related, but I think I might have spotted the shoplifter this morning. Hicks is leaning on me to get her."

"Where did you you spot her?" Frank said.

"I was in the 600-block of Royal Street and saw a short dumpy woman in a blue dress and a frizzy gray wig outside the window at Rau's Antiques. The shoplifter hit them for a big item a few months ago. Anyway, it seemed like she spotted me, started limping away. But she wasn't limping when I first saw her. She ducked around a corner onto a side street. I chased her, but when I got to the side street, she was gone. No sign of her."

"Maybe that's her new disguise," Kenyon said, wagging his head at David. "Disabled old lady. I thought you were the track star, but the disabled old lady gave you the slip."

"Right," David said. "So maybe she wasn't disabled. But that's not why I mentioned it. Half the security cameras don't work. If they were working, maybe we could spot the Sniper after he leaves whatever perch he's shooting from."

"We know why they're not working," Frank said, doodling dollar signs on his notepad. "No money in the budget to fix them."

"They might spend the money if they think it will help catch the Sniper," David said.

"Maybe," Frank said, "but we don't know what he looks like. Maybe he uses a disguise like the shoplifter."

"How about we put a bounty on his head?" Kenyon drawled, his deep voice oozing sarcasm. "You know, give folks an incentive to look for the guy. See some motherfucker with a rifle in his hand, take his picture with your cellphone and make some bucks!"

"Don't knock it," Frank said. "Everybody's got a smartphone these days. And I got a bad-news call from the Intelligence Unit. British Prime Minister David Cameron is coming here to speak at an Independence Day event. He's flying in on the first of July."

"Holy shit!" Kenyon said. "This Friday, three days from now? Does Hicks know about our VIP theory?"

"Not yet," Frank said. He had intended to tell Hicks about it at their meeting but when Hicks attacked him, he abandoned the idea. He had no evidence to back up the theory, just a hunch and a gut feeling. Hicks would have shot him down in a New York minute.

"Be hell to pay if the sniper shot the Brit PM," David said. "Almost as bad as JFK in Dallas."

"Exactly," Frank said. "NOPD security for the July Fourth celebrations is always tight, but the clock is ticking, so let's get to work. We need to find the Sniper ASAP and get him off the street."

6:25 PM Louis Armstrong Airport

He squeezed a gob of mayonnaise onto his plate, dipped two French fries into it and ate them.

Win wrinkled her nose. "That is so weird. Why do you put mayo on your French fries?"

Amused, he said, "Will that be the cause of our first fight?"

They were perched on stools at the counter of a seafood joint, overlooking the tarmac. He didn't want to sit at the bar. No booze tonight, both of them drinking ice water, plus he wanted privacy. Piped-in jazz filled the air, competing with the chatter of travelers seated at the bar behind them.

"No," Win said, dragging one of her fries through a glob of ketchup. "But I don't know anyone who eats mayo on French fries."

Through the plate-glass window he watched a plane descend to a runway. The Armenian and his wife wouldn't arrive until seven-thirty, but he'd brought Win here early to prep her for her assignment.

"Before my family moved to London, we lived in Brussels for a while. Everyone there eats mayo on their fries. But it's better than this crap. Spicier."

"Did you live there long?"

"Only until I was three." Since then he'd been back many times, but Win didn't need to know that. "Before we left Mum took me to see the Manneken Pis."

"What's that?" Win said, gazing at him with her luminous brown eyes.

"A bronze statue of a naked little boy peeing into a fountain. It's not real piss, of course. The fountain pumps water through the pipes. Mum said I'd love it, and I did." He grinned at her. "At one time or another every guy gets into a pissing contest with his mates. See who can pee the farthest."

"Pissing contests." Win made a face. "That's a guy thing."

He stared out the window, thinking of his Army mates. As a child, he'd never had any friends. In Brussels he was the foreign kid with the odd name. Same thing in London, despite the British name. The other kids shunned him because his dad repaired bicycles and his mum spoke with a foreign accent.

But that changed when he joined the Army. For the first time ever in his life he felt like he belonged, relishing the camaraderie with his mates: pissing contests, bitching about orders, griping about keeping their gear spotless. His mates accepted him, admired him for his abilities. In combat, the danger was intense, but fighting alongside his mates, knowing any one of them could die, brought an incredible feeling of solidarity and brotherhood.

"How come we're at the airport?" Win said. "Are you going somewhere?"

"Not yet." Pushing his fish and chips aside, he put Win's plate on top of his, wiped the counter with a paper napkin and took some documents out of his gym bag. Time to get to work. But no Army veteran disguise tonight. He was wearing his best black jeans and a leather jacket. As instructed, Win had dressed up for the occasion, a knee-length black skirt, a filmy white blouse and shiny white sandals with three inch heels. Her dark glasses were in her jean jacket on the stool beside her.

"I'm expecting a man and his wife to land here at seven-thirty." He took out their passport photos and showed them to Win. "I need better photographs. That's why I brought you with me."

"Who are they?"

"We'll check the arrivals board to make sure their flight lands on time. I don't know if they will have checked any luggage or not. That's where you come in." He took out a disposable cellphone and gave it to her. "Your job is to go downstairs to baggage claim. A PA announcement will tell us which carousel their bags will go to."

"Where will you be?"

"Upstairs near the ramp where the passengers with carry-on bags come up to the concourse. I want you to study the pictures to make sure you'll recognize them."

"No problem. The man has distinctive white hair. And the woman has a pretty face."

He gave her a stern look. "But we don't know how tall they are, and there might be other men with white hair. You need to memorize their faces. Can you do that?"

"Yes. But what if they decided to wear wigs?"

He stifled a smile. "Very good. Now you're thinking. But I doubt that they'll be wearing wigs. They're not expecting anyone to be looking for them at the airport."

Win gazed at him, her dark eyes somber. "Are they your next targets?"

Unwilling to say, he kept silent, thinking: *My sexy little shoplifter is smart. Maybe too smart.*

"If you spot them at the baggage claim," he said, "call me right away and I'll come down there. If they come up the ramp and stay in the concourse, I'll call you. Get up here as fast as you can, okay?"

"Got it," she said, smiling at him now.

"Either way, I need to photograph them." He gestured at his gym bag. "My camera's in the bag, but I need you to distract them when I take the photos. Just for a few seconds. Pretend you're a visitor. Ask them where the taxi stand is, something like that."

"I can do that," she said. "To make sure they stand still so you get a good picture."

"Exactly," he said, watching as she bent over the passport photos, studying them, like a good soldier.

After a minute, he said, "Let's go. I'll buy you an ice cream cone. Then we'll hit the rest rooms and check the arrivals board."

———

7:31 PM

Win leaned against an outer wall opposite the #2 baggage carousel, nervous but excited. Feeling a buzz, sort of like when she took off a sweater and static electricity crackled over her skin.

Peter was counting on her. She couldn't afford to screw up, but damn! Was this fun or what? Another Blitz thrill.

More exciting than the toughest get she'd ever pulled.

Visualizing the man's photo, then the woman's, she fixed her eyes on the escalator. She assumed they'd be together, but maybe not. She'd only flown a few times, but the first thing she did when she got off the plane was hit the nearest restroom. Maybe the woman would, too.

What was Peter doing, she wondered. He looked so handsome in his leather jacket, his dark hair neatly combed, licking his coffee ice cream cone, her favorite flavor. He'd bought her a single scoop. His was larger, two scoops for the big guy.

Her lips spread in a smile, quickly suppressed. *Stop mooning about your new boyfriend. Be cool. Focus on the job. Prepare your acting skills.*

Tonight she wasn't a disabled old lady, she was a first time visitor to New Orleans. A damsel in distress who needed help finding a cab.

A minute later she saw them, descending the escalator side by side. The man was only a couple of inches taller than his wife, five-seven at most. No wigs. His hair was silvery white. Hers was long and wavy, but not dark brown like the passport photo. Now it was lighter, almost blonde.

But lots of women dyed their hair these days. Aram was fifty-three. Nicole was thirty-three, twenty years younger. What did she see in him? Maybe he had money. Maybe she was a trophy wife.

As they walked toward the #2 carousel, she took out the cellphone Peter had given her, dialed him up, and said, "They're approaching baggage carousel number two."

"Good job!" Peter said. "I'll be down in a minute. Keep your eye on them."

Her heart surged. Peter was happy with her. Now all she had to do was make sure he got the pictures he wanted.

———

He closed the phone and hurried downstairs. The metal conveyor belt on the #1 baggage carousel wasn't moving, no passengers around it. Near the outer wall, Win was leaning against a concrete staircase opposite the #2 carousel. That conveyor belt wasn't moving either, but a crowd of passengers had gathered around it, the Armenian and his wife among them.

He took out his camera as he approached Win and said, without looking at her., "Get them to look this way if you can."

After she left, he adjusted the camera settings. The lighting down here was fairly bright so he wouldn't need a flash. He stood beneath the cement stairwell and waited, watching Win as she sidled up to his targets. Flashing her winsome smile, she leaned closer to the Armenian and said something. Then she turned and pointed, not toward him, toward the roadway outside.

The Armenian and his wife turned to look.

He ripped off two quick shots, then quickly zoomed in for two closeups. Perfect. Just what he needed.

Win had executed her assignment perfectly.

It was almost as good as working with his Army mates.

Maybe he really should think about making her his partner.

In New Orleans, anyway. No telling where he might wind up next.

CHAPTER 15

The relentless rays of the morning sun beat down on the intersection of Bourbon Street and Orleans Avenue. Frank was glad Hicks had taken his suggestion to hold the presser here, but not happy to be serving as one of his props. Every NOPD homicide detective in the city—nineteen now that Kelly had joined District Six—stood on a hastily-assembled platform, wearing dress blues, their shields gleaming in the sunlight.

But no feds. Frank didn't know how Hicks had managed to exclude agents from the FBI, ATF and Homeland Security, but it didn't surprise him. With a serial sniper on the loose, two dead citizens, and a policewoman clinging to life in the hospital, the presser would draw national attention, and Hicks didn't want any feds grabbing the spotlight.

Local politicians stood at the front of a huge crowd of spectators, eager to go on camera, demanding that the NOPD find the Sniper when reporters in feeding-frenzy mode shouted questions.

If Hicks allowed any questions. Ramrod stiff in his dress blues, Hicks stood with the NOPD Superintendent and the New Orleans Mayor, ten feet behind a podium thick with microphones.

Standing to their left—as far away from Hicks as possible—Frank glanced at Kelly, who ran a middle finger up and down her nose vertically, a surreptitious *Fuck You*. Knowing it was intended for Hicks, he suppressed a smile. Two minutes ago, he'd told her about his meeting with Hicks.

Mayor Ethan Brown stepped to the podium. A light-skinned African-American, Brown had just been re-elected to a second term. "We gather here today to reassure the public. Not just New Orleans residents, but visitors to our great city as well." Gesturing at the array of uniformed officers behind him, he said, "These are New Orleans finest homicide detectives. They work tirelessly, day and night, to keep our city safe. Thanks to their efforts, law and order will prevail in our great city. We are fortunate to have an outstanding police department, led by NOPD Superintendent Sanders, who would like to say a few words."

A formidable six-foot-six black man, Raul Sanders approached the podium. Appointed Superintendent earlier this year, Sanders had been with NOPD for thirty years, fifteen as a homicide detective with a high clearance rate. Most NOPD cops—whatever their skin color—considered him a tough but fair leader. Born and raised in the city, Sanders knew the trouble spots.

"I second your statement, Mr. Mayor. Law and order *will* prevail in our great city. The Sniper will be caught and prosecuted for his crimes. A fifty-thousand-dollar reward has been offered for information leading to his arrest. The Better Business Bureau and the Auto Dealers Association of New Orleans put up the money." Saunders smiled, his eyes roving over the crowd. "I urge other businesses in the area to donate whatever they can to increase the reward. I have organized a task force specifically dedicated to apprehending the Sniper.. Deputy Superintendent Wendell Hicks will lead the task force, and I have asked him to say a few words."

Hicks strode to the podium, grim-faced. "My remarks will be brief, because my homicide detectives are eager to get back to work. I asked them to be here to show my unconditional support for them. As the mayor said, they are New Orleans' finest. Collectively they have more than two hundred years of experience investigating homicides. They work every case tirelessly, around the clock, but they carry a heavy caseload. Right now, they're focused on the Sniper, but other homicides also require their attention. We need more homicide detectives, and that will only happen when the City Council appropriates more money to fund the police department."

In a dramatic gesture, Hicks flung out his arms. "Two days ago at this very intersection, the Sniper shot a policewoman. We pray for her swift recovery. Any attack on an NOPD officer is an assault on each and every one of us. *This must not continue!*"

Spontaneous applause rippled through the crowd of spectators.

"But unlike sixty-minute TV shows, crimes like this aren't solved overnight. I cannot go into specifics about our efforts to capture the Sniper. That might jeopardize our investigation. The third victim was one of our own. Officer Kimba Davis was devoted to her job. She worked hard to earn a position in the NOPD mounted police unit. Her seven-year-old daughter wants to know why Mom can't come home. But Kimba remains in the hospital."

One spectator shouted, "The bastard doesn't deserve to live!"

"Amen!" said another.

Working the crowd, Hicks thundered, "There's a fifty-thousand-dollar bounty on his head! It isn't just NOPD detectives looking for the Sniper. Everyone is after him. And *we will find him!*"

A chant arose from the spectators. "Lock him up! Lock him up!"

Hicks held up his hands to quiet the crowd. "We will take no questions today, but I ask members of the news media to publicize the reward far and wide. *Everyone* needs to help, residents and visitors alike. If you see something, say something. Call the NOPD Tipline or Crimestoppers."

But not Frank Renzi, Frank thought, *the lead detective on two of the shootings.*

Almost as if Hicks had read his thoughts, he stepped away from the podium and looked at Frank, sending a message with his eyes. *Don't fuck with me, Renzi or you'll regret it.*

Great, Frank thought. Those task force meetings are going to be tons of fun.

9:15 AM

Seated with his back to the wall, the Sniper waited at a marble-topped table for two in the tea room. *Always protect your flank.* He glanced to his right, checking the elevators visible at the end of a short hallway. No sign of the man he was waiting for.

Known for its exceptional amenities and deluxe suites, the Hotel Cavendish, a British-owned chain of boutique hotels, had expanded to several American tourist destination cities, like New Orleans.

Ahead of him, a waist-high partition decorated with English ivy separated the tea room from the lobby, where crystal chandeliers dangling from a twenty-foot ceiling cast light upon a gleaming ceramic tile floor, plush sofas and sweet-smelling exotic plants. Two guests stood at the check-in desk along the far wall. Twenty yards to their left, two uniformed doormen stood outside the entry doors.

He pretended to sip his tea. No caffeine today. Nothing to jangle his nerves or increase his heart-rate. For his FBI agent disguise, he'd worn a white shirt and a muted tie under a dark business suit. He could fake the lingo. He had an ear for accents and made a point of listening to American newsreaders on TV. Another task added to his comprehensive regimen: workouts at a gym, a daily ten-mile run and, most importantly, target practice with his rifle and handgun.

Last night when he dropped Win off at her apartment after their airport recon, she had asked him to stay. Lord knows he wanted to, but he had work to do. When he declined, she seemed disappointed, but he would make it up to her tonight. Focused on the assignment, he had sped off on his Vespa to the Hotel Cavendish.

Never enter a building without knowing how to walk out of it. That task accomplished, he cased the Armenian's room on the seventh floor. He'd been sorely tempted to finish the job then, but judging by the voices seeping under the door, the man's wife was in the room with him. In the end, he had decided it was better to wait and avoid unnecessary collateral damage.

Ten minutes ago a waitress with a frilly white apron tied over her black skirt had served his tea and gave him a menu, smilingly informing him that breakfast was served until ten o'clock.

But he wouldn't be needing the menu.

His pulse ratcheted up a notch as he saw the Armenian emerge from one of the elevators. Eager to meet the FBI agent who'd called him ten minutes ago, Aram Takvorian came directly to the tea room.

Clutching an attache case in one hand, Takvorian sank onto the chair opposite his. He looked older than the photographs. The cheery lighting exposed deep lines etched around his dark eyes and a sickly pallor on his pock-marked cheeks. He wore a white dress shirt under an elegant Savile Row suit, but his tie was askew, as though he'd dressed in a hurry, and his thick white hair was disheveled.

He surreptitiously flashed his FBI badge. "Thanks for meeting me on such short notice. I'm Special Agent Joe Macklin."

"To be honest, your call surprised me," Takvorian said in perfect Brit English, no trace of a foreign accent. "I told your colleague in New York I had important information, but he had no interest in it." The Armenian half-turned in his chair and glanced over his shoulder.

The Sniper suppressed a smile. Fearful people often worried about who was behind them, instead of worrying about the man seated across the table who was there to kill him.

"What sort of information?" Control wouldn't tell him, but maybe the Armenian would.

"Incriminating information about the Turkish Finance Minister. The miserable swine."

Interesting. "If you want attention, why not take it to a reporter at the *New York Times?*"

Takvorian frowned. "You don't understand. This information will inflict serious damage on the Turkish government. When it becomes public, I will need protection. That is why I contacted the FBI. I have put everything on a flash drive." Takvorian set his attache case on the marble-topped table and flipped open the catches.

"Not *here*," the Sniper said urgently. "Too many witnesses. We need to do the exchange in your room."

Takvorian shook his head, his dark eyebrows knit in a frown. "Not in my room."

Did he suspect what was about to happen? Too bad. His fate was sealed.

"My wife is there," Takvorian added.

Lying to him. A half hour ago he had seen Nicole Takvorian leave the hotel. Was someone else in the room?

Blank-faced, he said, "Don't worry. It will only take a minute."

Takvorian removed a handkerchief from his suit pocket and mopped his sweaty face.

Alert to any unusual movement, the Sniper spotted the two men the instant they entered the foyer and thought, *Muscle.* Guests at the Hotel Cavendish were wealthy tourists who wore designer clothes or business executives in expensive suits. In a cut-rate hotel, two large men in cheap suits, loose-fitting to conceal their weapons, might blend in. But not in a classy hotel like this.

And they had spotted him—no, not him, the Armenian.

Others might not have noticed, but he was trained to spot such behavior, a sudden stillness that lasted a fraction of second. Then the men walked over to a wooden stand that held pamphlets about things to do in New Orleans.

Maybe the Armenian had reason to worry. Reasons that had nothing to do with him. He rose to his feet. "I have to get back to my office. We need to do this now."

Clearly reluctant, the Armenian rose, and he hustled him to the elevators. When he pressed the call button, the doors on one car opened immediately. He entered the car, hit the Door Close button and smiled pleasantly at Aram Takvorian.

"What floor?" As if he didn't know.

"Seven."

He pressed the button and said, "What do you do for a living, Mr. Takvorian?" Might as well gather as much information as he could.

"I am an investment banker. I manage foreign investments for my countrymen in Turkey."

When the doors opened on the seventh floor, Takvorian hurried down the hall to his room and inserted the key card into the slot, calling out as he opened the door, "Nicky? Are you dressed?"

The Sniper unbuttoned his jacket and put his hand on the weapon holstered in the small of his back. Someone was in the room, and it wasn't Takvorian's wife.

Tense and alert, he followed the Armenian into a sitting room with plush blue carpeting. In front of a sofa upholstered in white leather, two empty wine glasses sat on a glass-topped coffee table.

Empty wine glasses? At this hour? Who else was in the room?

The bedroom door opened and a slender well-built black man with cafe-au-lait skin entered the sitting room, naked. His face was beautiful, large dark eyes, a sensual mouth.

Rent-boy, thought the Sniper, pulling out the Beretta with the attached suppressor.

The boy raised his hands, staring at him with terrified eyes.

He shot him in the forehead.

"No!" Takvorian screamed. "Why did you shoot him? You are not FBI. Who are you?"

"Is the flash drive in the attache case?"

All color drained from Takvorian's face. Sweat beaded his forehead. He put his hands to his mouth, his eyes darting everywhere, sweating profusely now.

"Is it in the attache case?"

Takvorian sighed, his shoulders sagging in defeat. "Yes."

"Who wants this information on the flash drive?"

"Many people."

"Like who?"

"Why should I tell you?" Takvorian said, his eyes full of dispair. "Even if I do, you will kill me."

He squeezed the trigger, two shots in rapid succession interrupting the quiet. Aram Takvorian collapsed on the blue carpet with a heavy thud, arms outstretched, head lolling to one side.

The shots had been muffled somewhat by the suppressor, but that didn't mean no one had heard them. Soon someone would call the desk, and security guards would investigate.

He opened the attache case. The only thing in it was a flash drive.

He shoved it into his jacket pocket, wondering what sort of the information the Armenian had on the Turkish official.

Information worth killing for apparently.

He squatted beside the body, careful to avoid the blood from the exit wound in Takvorian's head. He searched his pockets, found a wallet with credit cards, an International driver's license in Takvorian's name, a wad of cash, and a photograph of Aram and his wife.

A good-looking woman. Why did he need a rent-boy?

A fatal mistake. So much for avoiding collateral damage.

He put the wallet back and rose to his feet, tallying the rounds he'd fired. One for Rent-boy, two for the Armenian, one to the head, one to the heart. Twelve left in the magazine.

Lose count, you'd squeeze the trigger and hear the dreaded dead man's click. A fatal mistake if ever there was one.

He unscrewed the suppressor and put it his jacket pocket. The Beretta was a fine weapon, but heavy and bulky, difficult to conceal even without the attached suppressor. He picked up the spent cartridges before the spreading pool of blood reached them and looked around the room. He had touched nothing. No fingerprints to incriminate him. Or anything else for that matter.

Other than two corpses.

His pulse was steady, though a bit faster than usual. He hated close-combat kills. Close enough to smell the stench when the victim's bodily functions let go. Close enough to see the terror in their eyes and hear their pleading. He wanted a cigarette, but there was no time. He had to leave the hotel as fast as possible.

But what about the two men in the lobby? It seemed clear they were after the Armenian. Did they know which room he was in? He went to the door and pressed his ear against it. Heard nothing.

Holding the Beretta in his right hand, he took out a handkerchief with his right and cautiously eased open the door, just wide enough to peer into the corridor.

Phut.

He jerked back.

Heard another *phut.*

Bad news. Two bullets fired by a gun with a suppressor.

CHAPTER 16

9:30 AM

Having exchanged his dress blues for a polo shirt and a pair of slacks, Frank sat at his desk, relaxing with a Dunkin' Donuts iced coffee, cream no sugar, his reward after the sweltering heat at the presser. Kenyon and David had done the same, nursing their beverages of choice, an iced tea for David, hot coffee for Kenyon, who was eating a glazed doughnut.

"No feds on the platform for the presser," Frank said, "you notice?"

"Smart move," Kenyon said. "You know the feds, always want to take over. Smart not to take any questions, too, all those politicians standing in front of the platform, ready to rip him a new asshole."

"I'm glad he talked about Kimba Davis though," David said.

"Tugging on their heartstrings." Kenyon rolled his eyes. "I'm surprised the man didn't launch into an I've-Got-a-Dream speech."

Frank laughed, enjoying Kenyon's droll sense of humor, enjoying the camaraderie even more after yesterday's browbeating from Hicks.

Kenyon polished off the last of his doughnut and said, "The reward will get us a zillion tips, but eighty percent of them will be crackpots out for the money."

"At least we don't have to take the calls," Frank said. "But someone's gotta go to the task force meetings, and it's not gonna be me. Looks like you're it, Kenyon."

"Me?" Kenyon stared at him, aghast. "Why me? You're lead on the two homicides."

"If I go, he'll just look daggers at me, even if I keep my mouth shut."

Kenyon pointed at David, who shook his head and laughed. "Not me, pal. I'm supposed to catch the Shoplifter, remember?"

"Way to go, David!" Frank exclaimed, pumping his fist. "The point guard buries a three from the corner."

David grinned and drew a "one" in the air with his finger. "But the reward for the Sniper gave me an idea. I'm going to make a wanted poster with a photo of the shoplifter and post copies around the French Quarter."

"Yeah?" Kenyon said. "What picture you gonna use? Disabled old lady in a floppy hat? Girl in a Saints ball cap? Man, you might force her to invest in a whole new hat collection."

"Good idea though," Frank said. "Maybe you can get some stores to put up a reward. Not fifty grand, but you might get two or three thousand. Money talks."

"But getting them to put up the bucks won't be easy," David said.

"Talk to the owner of Rau's Antiques," Frank said. "Last I heard he was president of the Small Business Association, might ask his French Quarter buddies to put up some money."

His cellphone rang. He grabbed it and answered, "Renzi."

"I watched the press conference," Vobitch growled into his ear. "Hicks, slinging bullshit."

He winked at Kenyon and said into the phone, "What, you got nothing better to do than lie around in bed all day watching TV?"

"Last time I checked there weren't any naked dancing girls."

"Naked dancing girls?" Frank said, watching Kenyon crack up. "You feeling frisky?"

"Not frisky enough to jump one of the nurses. Hicks did one thing right though, talking about Kimba Davis. Make it personal for the media vultures, they might do a special on the victims."

"Hicks knows how to play the crowd but he's got no clue how to find the Sniper. Are you still set to go home tomorrow?"

"Hell yes. If they don't let me out of here, I'll shoot someone."

"Bad idea. I'll stop by tomorrow afternoon and fill you in on what's happening. Since you seem incapable of taking it easy like the docs keep telling you."

"Sounds good to me. I'll have Juliana fix dinner for you."

"No. Juliana's got enough to do. Behave yourself today and I'll see you tomorrow."

He closed his cellphone and said, "Vobitch is always good for a laugh."

"You got that right," Kenyon said, laughing. "Naked dancing girls? But I'm glad he's going home. Hospitals are no fun." Last year Kenyon had spent a week in the hospital after being shot.

"I'll drink to that," Frank said. He'd been there, done that, too. "But remember what I said about Hicks. He's doesn't have a plan for finding the Sniper, and the British Prime Minister is coming here on Friday. If he's the VIP target, how do we protect him?"

"Not your problem," Kenyon said. "Hicks is in charge of the task force."

"But I haven't told him about our VIP theory," Frank said. "And David Cameron arrives two days from now."

"Talk to the Super," Kenyon said. "Seriously. He's a good guy and he controls the budget. Tons of overtime on Fourth of July weekend, what's a few grand more to protect Cameron?"

"Okay," Frank said. "But we need a list of District-8 hotels so we can check to see if any male guests have been staying there since the Sniper shot the cabbie June fifteenth." He thought a moment. "No, since the first of June. In case he came here early to plan the hit."

———

The Sniper stood inside the half-open door holding the Beretta, his heart racing, fueled by the adrenaline flooding his veins. The two shots had narrowly missing him, slamming into the wooden door-jamb. Delivered by the two goons he'd seen in the lobby probably. Now they were on the seventh floor, gunning for Aram Takvorian, seeking whatever Intel he'd put on the flash drive.

Should he stay in the room or fight it out in the corridor?

He could wait them out, make them come to him, but that might take several minutes. If someone heard him shoot the rent-boy and Takvorian, hotel security guards might already be on their way to the seventh floor. The alternative wasn't much better. There was no cover in the corridor. To get to the elevators thirty yards away, he would have to kill two goons with silenced handguns and plenty of ammo. He had a Beretta with twelve rounds left.

Sweating profusely, he crouched by the half-open door, waiting. Listening. No telltale sounds of approaching footsteps, but the hall-way had thick carpeting.

A woman in the room next door solved his problem.

"What are you doing?" said a high-pitched female voice.

And moments later, "No! Wait! Don't shoo—"

A gunshot cut off her words.

He sprang into the hallway, arms extended, swung right and fired rapidly at what he judged to be chest height for the goons. *One, two, three, four, five, six, seven.*

The sound deafening inside the enclosed hallway. The suppressor was in his pocket.

No return fire.

The next few seconds passed in a blur as he eyeballed the corridor. One black-suited man down.

Momentarily frozen, a second gunman stood near a woman on the floor outside the door of the adjacent room.

Phut. The second man got off a wild shot, turned and ran for the elevators.

The Sniper fired three more rapid shots. One hit the gunman, but didn't put him down. Clutching his shoulder, the goon disappeared around the corner beside the elevators.

Damn it to bloody hell! If he'd had his rifle that goon would be dead too.

Two rounds left in the Beretta. Forget wasting them on the second goon. There might be others. And now that he'd fired ten rounds without the suppressor, all hell would break loose. No heads popping out of other doors along the hall yet, but he was certain people in their rooms were dialing up security on their phones.

The first gunman lay slumped against the wall, eyes closed. A ruptured artery sprayed crimson arcs along the wall and blood gushed from his mouth. He looked Slavic, a low sloping forehead, dark hair, an angular bony face. Russian, perhaps.

The handgun on the floor beside him confirmed his suspicions, a Soviet Makarov pistol with an interior suppressor for easy concealment, outfitted with a secondary suppressor.

The woman—a young Asian with a hole in her forehead—was dead, her black hair matted with blood.

Moving quickly, he searched the man, found his wallet and jammed it in his pocket. He'd examine it later. Soon the police would arrive and seal off the entrances. He had to get out now.

He sprinted to the elevators. A door to the left opened onto the stairs. A fire alarm was on the wall beside it. To avoid leaving prints, he used the sleeve of his jacket to pull the alarm.

An excruciating clang sounded, paining his ears. He jammed the Beretta into the holster at the small of his back and raced down the stairs. No worries about the wounded goon. He would be long gone, eager to escape from the hotel before police arrived.

Breathing hard, he took the stairs by leaps and bounds, whipping around the turns. Sixty seconds later, encountering no one, he reached the first floor. Panting, he leaned against the wall.

His next move would be risky. During his reconnaissance, he'd planned his escape route, but he hadn't counted on having to shoot his way past two armed men. Or a fire alarm.

He mopped his sweaty face on his sleeve. Loud voices filtered through the door to the lobby, hotel workers ordering frightened guests outside. That might work to his benefit. In the lobby he would be exposed and vulnerable.

Above him, footsteps sounded on the stairs. Satisfied that his breathing had returned to normal, he opened the door and walked down a short hall to the lobby. Hotel guests—some in bathrobes, others in disheveled clothing—stood in groups, all talking at once, raising their voices to be heard. Hotel employees in royal-blue uniforms, their names inscribed on gold nameplates, yelled at them to leave the hotel. Bellhops and doormen stood at the main entrance, waving away cab drivers carrying the luggage of arriving guests.

Despite the risk, he casually walked past the check-in desk to his right. Never display fear. In his business, fear could be fatal. His attire helped: a dark suit, white shirt and a boring beige tie, something a respectable businessman might wear. The suit jacket one size too big, to give extra room at the hips and shoulders, and his polished black shoes, cut high to the ankles, had soles with thick treads, the better to run in. His only distinguishing feature: horn-rimmed glasses to divert attention from his facial features.

Anyone who tried to describe him would find it difficult. He was a man in a suit, like dozens of other hotel guests. An ordinary man. Utterly forgettable.

He continued past other guests. A young mother struggling to control her toddler. Three portly men in golf shorts and T-shirts, unconcerned by the hubbub, chatting and laughing. A businessman in a dark suit walking toward the exit, shouting into his cellphone.

More guests entered the already crowded lobby. Some went directly outside. Others gathered in the tea room, looking anxious. Speaking in a loud voice, the manager told them fire alarms in hotels required all guests to exit the building, pointing at the doors that opened onto Canal Street.

But that wasn't how he was leaving.

It was barely ten minutes since he'd killed the Armenian. Less than five since he'd fired ten gunshots on the seventh floor.

Taking advantage of the chaos, he edged through the crowd milling around the lobby, making his way to the hotel lounge.

A hotel employee stood outside the door. "Sorry, sir. The lounge is closed."

"No problem," he said, gesturing down a short hallway. "I just need to use the restroom."

"Okay, but don't be long. The firemen will be here soon and they'll check to make sure everyone has left the building."

He didn't bother responding, just hurried down the hallway, walking quickly, the Beretta hidden beneath his jacket, visualizing the floor plan he had memorized last night.

Never enter a building without knowing how to walk out of it.

When he reached the restrooms, he turned. The employee outside the lounge was talking to someone else. A sign on the door opposite the restrooms said **Kitchen, Staff Only.** He pushed it open with his knuckles so as not to leave any prints.

The hotel workers' entrance was at the far end of the kitchen. He smelled eggs burning in a skillet on the stove, the odor of muffins baking in ovens. The kitchen staff had already fled, leaving the back door wedged open.

Sweating profusely, he took out the Beretta and crept past stainless steel refrigerators and wooden storage bins to the open door.

The goons who shot at him weren't spies or intelligence agents. They were assassins. Russian, he believed. He'd seen two, but if the Boss knew about the cop shooting and had decided to terminate his employment permanently, more goons might be waiting for him outside. He could not afford to discount this possibility.

He visualized the alley. The exit door swung outward to the left. Canal Street lay twenty yards to the right. If they were waiting to jump him, they would stand to the left of the door.

He flung open the door with enough force to stun anyone hiding behind it. The door banged against the side of the building.

No cry of distress.

Raising the Beretta, he stepped into the alley. No one was there.

So far so good. The alley was barely wide enough for a dump truck to pick up trash from the smelly containers against the wall.

He holstered his weapon and hurried toward Canal Street. The fire apparatus had arrived, two gigantic ladder trucks and three fire engines, sirens wailing. On this side of the neutral ground, southbound traffic was at a standstill, horns honking as a traffic cop directed them around the fire apparatus. On the other side of the neutral ground, northbound traffic was also stalled as drivers slowed down to gawk at the commotion.

A female patrol cop was coming his way, shooing people away from the hotel. He turned and walked in the other direction.

Three businessmen stood on the next corner, talking on cell-phones, their free hands covering their exposed ears. He took out his cellphone. When in Rome, blend in. Holding the phone to his ear, he pretended to talk to someone.

The person he wanted to talk to was Control.

Control had fed him a line of bullshit. Maybe the Armenian had put important information on the flash drive and maybe he hadn't. Control had given him outdated photos of Takvorian and his wife, and faulty Intel. Kill the Armenian in his room while the wife was out shopping. Get the flash drive and give it to Control.

Nothing about a fucking rent-boy.

Like the evil demon in *The Exorcist,* a more sinister possibility sprang to mind.

Control's assignment to kill Takvorian and get the flash drive was just an excuse to get him to the hotel.

So the goons could kill him.

CHAPTER 17

As Kenyon pulled his unmarked car to the curb on Canal Street, Frank jumped out and evaluated the chaotic scene. Ten minutes ago they'd gotten a call about multiple homicides at the Hotel Cavendish. Traffic on Canal Street was snarled in both directions, drivers gawking or leaning on their horns. Across the street, two ladder trucks and three fire engines stood in front of the seven-story hotel, sirens wailing, flanked by two ambulances and two patrol cars with flashing blues.

David and Kenyon joined him on the sidewalk. "Jesus," Kenyon said, "We got homicides and a fire?"

"I don't smell any smoke," Frank said. "Maybe the killer pulled the alarm as a distraction."

"Probably blocks away by now," David said, nodding in agreement.

"Let's get in there," Frank said. Dodging around stopped vehicles, they ran across Canal Street. On the opposite sidewalk, hotel guests in bathrobes, hastily donned clothes and business suits mingled with hotel workers, many covering their ears to block out the sirens.

A uniform guarding the entrance recognized Frank and said, "We've already secured the scene. Four dead on the seventh floor."

Like a bird dog on point, Frank charged into the hotel, hyper-alert. Light from ceiling chandeliers lit up the lobby and a nearby tea room with tables and chairs scattered in disarray. In front of the registration desk, the fire chief was talking to a visibly distraught gray-haired man in a royal blue uniform, the manager Frank assumed.

The chief waved them over. Nodding hello to Kenyon and David, he said to Frank, "We got a real mess here. My men need to make sure all the occupants are out of the building."

"Okay, but we've got multiple homicides on the seventh floor."

"So I heard. One of your uniforms is up there, guarding the scene."

Frank made some snap decisions. "Can you have your men clear the rest of the building first and call me before they go up to seven? I need to get a forensics team up there."

"Sure, Frank, no problem. No sprinklers going off, it's probably a false alarm."

To the manager, Frank said, "Homicide Detective Frank Renzi. These are my partners, Detectives Miller and Lee. Tell us what happened."

Clearly distressed, the manager took out a handkerchief and mopped sweat off his face. "This has never happened here before! Never! We have an excellent safety record—"

"I'm sure you do," Frank interrupted, "but we need information. *What happened?*"

The manager blinked. "Yes, sir. Someone on the seventh floor called security saying they heard gunshots. Two of my security guards were in the elevator when the fire alarm went off. They got off on five, walked up the stairs to seven and found ..." The manager shook his head and heaved a sigh. "They found two bodies in the hall and two more in Room 710."

"Okay," Frank said, "We need a list of occupants staying on the seventh floor."

"Just the occupants on seventh floor?"

"For now. Eventually we'll need a list of everyone who was in the hotel, including employees."

"Certainly, sir. I'll print one out for you." The manager hesitated, then said, "One of the dead people in 710 was here with his wife. My assistant is trying to reach her now."

"She wasn't in the room with her husband?"

The manager grimaced. "No. But someone else was." Mopping his sweaty face, he said, "One of the victims in the hall was staying in 709 with her parents, a Japanese couple. But they must have gone out before it happened. We're trying to locate them as well."

"Let us know when you do," Frank said. "We'll need to talk to them when they come back to the hotel. Can you get started on list of names? Seventh floor first, then all the others."

"Of course." The manager heaved a sigh. "I'm sorry, but this is incredibly distressing. That poor girl. She's just a teenager."

"You've been very helpful," Frank said. "Get started on that list."

As the manager went behind the registration desk, Frank said to David, "I need you to take charge down here while Kenyon and I go upstairs. Have the manager find you a room where you can isolate the seventh floor guests. When the fire chief clears the hotel for reentry, have the guests identify themselves and their room numbers as they come back inside."

"That might take a while," David said. "There must be sixty or seventy rooms."

"Have the manager help you," Kenyon said. "Give him something to do, it might calm him down."

"Can't be more than a dozen rooms on the seventh floor," Frank said. "Don't let them chit-chat with one another. Keep 'em quiet until you talk to them, one at a time."

"So they can't collaborate on what they heard," David said.

"Exactly," Frank said. "They'll be keyed up, so it might be tough. Have a patrol officer help you, and take good notes. Anything they heard or saw might be helpful."

"Better round up the hotel workers too," Kenyon said, "or they'll split. We'll come down and help you when we finish upstairs."

"Will do," David said, "but call my cell and tell me what you find on seven."

Kenyon rumbled a chuckle. "Got the curiosity bug like Vobitch."

"He'll go berserk when he hears about this," Frank said. Not only that, calling in a Terrorism Unit at the slightest hint of terrorism was all too common these days. Another nightmare. "Thanks for taking charge down here, David. We'll keep you posted."

Five minutes later, Frank and Kenyon stopped on the sixth floor landing to catch their breath. "Gotta be prints on the handrails," Kenyon said.

"No doubt. But our best bet will be any prints on the handrails to the seventh floor."

They pulled on latex gloves and continued up the stairs. The door to the seventh floor hall was open, guarded by a stocky patrol officer. Even here, the smell of death permeated the air.

"Did you go in any of the rooms?" Frank asked. Curiosity was always a factor, even with cops.

The patrolman shrugged and said, "Took a walk down the hall. Two doors were open, but I didn't go inside. The security guards might have, though."

"Okay," Frank said. "Nobody else gets onto this floor except firemen and the forensics team."

"You got it." The patrolman shook his head. "Man, you won't believe the bullet holes in there. Looks like a major shootout."

"Mum's the word," Kenyon warned. "Any loose talk could hinder our investigation."

They walked down the hall side-by-side, not speaking, comfortable working together as they had on so many homicides, scrutinizing everything: the carpeted floor, wallpapered walls, the doors and the ceiling. Frank pointed at five bullet holes in the wall. Kenyon nodded, scribbling on his notepad.

The first body was outside the door to Room 709, lying face-up on the blue-carpeting.

"The Japanese girl," Kenyon muttered. "One shot to the head."

"The door is wide open," Frank said. "Security guards might have checked the room."

"To see if anyone else was in there," Kenyon said. "Dead or alive."

Five feet beyond the girl, a large man in a dark business suit was sprawled on the floor, legs outstretched, his head and torso slumped against the wall. Swirls of blood spatter stained the wall beside him.

"Major arterial spray," Frank said. "Multiple gunshot wounds. Took one in the neck."

Kenyon pointed to the gun on the floor beside the man's hand. "You think he shot the girl?"

Frank backed away, studying the angles and the bullet holes in the wall. "Maybe. Or maybe there was more than one shooter out here. Let's check seven-ten."

They walked down the hall to Room 710 and stood outside the door. "Two slugs in the doorjamb," Frank said. "Another one in the wall beyond the door."

"The cop was right," Kenyon said. "Looks like the shootout at the OK Corral up here."

They stepped into the room and stopped short.

"What the hell is *this*?" Kenyon said.

"A dead man in a fancy suit and a naked black kid, also dead."

"No wonder the manager was freaking out. And the wife's out shopping? Kinky."

Frank nodded, scratching his head. "But how come the kid is naked and the guy's got a suit on?"

"He dialed up an escort service, watches the boy-toy get naked, and the killer interrupts them?"

"No way. There's two empty wine glasses on the table. Why would he open the door? Maybe they got interrupted, the guy in the suit went out to meet someone, told the kid he'd be right back."

"Got a call from someone he trusted," Kenyon said. "Went out to meet him, didn't expect to get popped when they came back here. But why come back here at all?"

Frank smiled tightly. "That's what they pay us the big bucks to find out. I better call for a forensics team and the coroner. Take a look around, see if you find anything."

He got on his cellphone, made the calls.

Just as he finished, Kenyon came back and said, "Nothing obvious in the bedroom. Bed still made, neat and tidy. The kid took his duds off in the the bathroom, left them in there."

"Something doesn't add up," Frank said. "Only weapon we've seen is the handgun with the suppressor beside the dead guy in the hall with multiple gunshot wounds. But the black kid took one in the forehead. Over and out."

"And the other guy takes one in the forehead and one in the chest, like a professional hitter, making sure he finished the job."

"Who was smart enough to take his weapon with him."

"So we got one or two shooters in the hall," Kenyon said, frowning now, "and another one in here?"

"Seems like it." Frank gestured at the man in the suit and the black kid. "Maybe they got shot first. The girl in the room next door hears the shots, opens her door to see what's going on ..."

"And the man in the hall shot her." Kenyon shook his head. "Damn shame."

Frank nodded. "She made a bad decision, but she wasn't the intended target. So who was? Ritzy hotel, plenty of rich guests ... if it was a robbery gone bad, why pick this guy?"

"And why two teams?" Kenyon said. "Seems like the shooters in the hall were after the killer in here. So he shot one of them and got away. But the other shooter in the hall got away, too."

"That sounds about right, unfortunately," Frank said. "Just what we need. A major shootout in a ritzy French Quarter hotel, and a sniper running around shooting people."

His cellphone rang. When he answered, Vobitch said, agitated, "I just saw a news bulletin on TV. What the fuck is going on?"

"Multiple homicides at the Hotel Cavendish. Four dead on the seventh floor."

———

He locked the door of his hotel room and leaned against it, his face sweaty, his heart racing faster than a horse crossing the finish line, his mind racing even faster. The shooters at the hotel were professionals with high-powered automatics, 9mm Makarovs equipped with suppressors, weapons often favored by Russians. Weapons designed to kill, even a person wearing body armor.

Only sheer luck had saved him. Otherwise he'd be dead.

He took off his jacket, tossed it on the bed and took the Beretta out of the holster at the back of his waist. Bloody hell! His hands were shaking. He set the Beretta on the bed, opened the top drawer of the bureau, took out a nip bottle of Stoli, unscrewed the cap and downed the vodka in two long gulps.

Never in his five years working for Zenith Intelligence had he experienced a life-threatening event like the one at the Hotel Cavendish. Danger, yes. Close encounters with death, no.

Those who worked for the Special Ops Unit did so for a reason. Some held grudges against their enemies; wet work gave them a sense of power. Others held political beliefs that predisposed them to killing without conscience. A few feared being outed and disgraced for their bizarre sexual preferences. The rest were mercenaries who killed for money. Like him.

He had grown up in poverty, his dad working ungodly hours, his mum scrimping to make ends meet. Long ago he had vowed never to be poor again. One day he would get out of this dirty business, and when he did, he intended to be rich.

During the war, the Army had seen to his basic needs. They had also turned him into a highly-skilled sniper. Bottom line, the Army had paid him to kill the enemy. He had transferred those skills to civilian life, working for Zenith Intelligence, and was well-paid for it.

The job entailed certain hazards, but he accepted this. Given an assignment, he took reasonable precautions to avoid unnecessary risks, but thoughts of his own mortality never entered his mind. His parents were dead, and he had no other relatives. He'd had his share of girlfriends, most recently the woman in Amsterdam, but he felt no emotional attachment to them. If a two-ton lorry ran him over, he'd be dead. End of story. He didn't believe in an afterlife.

He had no one to live for. Until now.

Fate had sent him to New Orleans.

Three days ago he'd found Win, his risk-taker soulmate, and discovered the exquisite delights of her company, in bed and out of it.

What if the Russians had delivered him into the deep dark chasm of death? His throat thickened. What if he never saw her again?

Unable to bear it, on the verge of tears, he took out his cellphone and dialed Win's number. After one ring, it went to voicemail.

"Hey, you know what to do. Later." Win's low-pitched voice.

He clicked off, massaged his eyes and pressed his fingers against his aching temples. If he kept thinking this way, it would be the death of him. No more negative thoughts.

He took his field glasses off the bureau and opened the window overlooking Canal Street. A blast of hot air hit him. Kneeling on the carpet, he stuck his head out the window, adjusted the knob and panned the glasses over the Hotel Cavendish, seven blocks south of him. Firetrucks had caused a massive traffic jam, and police were directing vehicles around them. The zoom lens gave him remarkably vivid magnification. He could even see the sweat on the cops' faces.

Someone rapped on the door.

Startled, he froze. Bloody hell! Had someone followed him here?

He scrambled to the bed, grabbed the Beretta and edged to the door. "Yes?" he called.

"Housekeeping," said a high-pitched female voice.

That didn't reassure him. For all he knew, a SWAT team could be out there, ready to breach the door and toss a flash-bang inside.

Aiming the Beretta at the door, center-mass height, he called, "Not now, I'm busy."

"Okay, I'll come back later. Sorry to bother you."

Sorry? How about thanks for living to see another day?

He heard the elevator doors open, then close. Only then did he lower the Beretta. He put it on the bed, picked up the field glasses and returned to the window.

On the sidewalk outside the hotel, a man in civilian clothes was talking to a fireman. He zoomed in on the man's face and recognized him. Renzi, the asshole detective who'd called him a coward.

If he had his rifle he'd blow him away with one shot. But that would be foolish. That would bring more heat from the cops, and he already had enough to worry about. Today's assignment had been a disaster. Just thinking about it infuriated him.

He took out his cellphone and dialed a number. When Control answered, he snapped. "Red sails in the sunset." The emergency code.

After a pause, Control said, "Do you think it will rain?" The correct response.

"One hour, the usual place," he said, and ended the call.

He took the flash drive out of his jacket pocket. He had no idea what was on it, but the Boss wanted it badly enough to have him kill the Armenian to get it. No way was he giving it to Control.

The flash drive was his insurance.

The two Russians at the hotel had tried to kill him, no doubt about that. The question was: Were they at the hotel to get the flash drive? Or had Control sent them there to kill him?

CHAPTER 18

She got out of the shower and wrapped herself in a bath towel. Last night she'd asked Peter to stay over, but he said he had work to do, so she'd slept late, didn't get up until almost eleven. She smiled at herself in the fogged-up mirror. Last night Peter seemed reluctant to leave, gazing at her with his sexy bedroom eyes. Then he'd kissed her—a chaste kiss, not one of their deep passionate ones—thanked her for helping him at the airport and zipped off on his Vespa.

Maybe he'd call her today. She was dying to see him.

She spiked her short dark hair with Ultra-Sport gel to make it stand up in tufts and blasted it with her hair dryer. Draping the towel over the shower rod, she put on a T-shirt and a pair of shorts, and went in the living room. A light on her cellphone was blinking.

Her heart sped up. No message, but she recognized the number. Peter had called her ten minutes ago.

When she called him back, he answered right away. "Win," he said.

"Hi, Peter, did you call me?"

"Yes."

She smiled and said, teasing him, "Wanna come over and give me a gun lesson?"

"No. Put on your TV."

Unnerved by his grim tone, she grabbed the clicker and turned on the TV. The screen blossomed to life, a local reporter doing a news bulletin outside the Hotel Cavendish. Her heart jolted. That was the hotel where the Armenian and his wife were staying!

"What happened?" she said.

"Someone shot at me."

"Jesus! Are you okay? Tell me what happened!"

"I must talk to my employer. Then I will come over and tell you about it."

"Are you hurt?" she asked, eyeing the headline on the TV screen. **Four dead at French Quarter hotel.**

"No. But it was … a close call."

"When will you be here? I'm worried about you, Peter."

A heavy sigh. "Thank you for that. I will come as soon as I can. This afternoon sometime."

"I'll be waiting." She put her cellphone on the coffee table and rubbed her arms. Four people dead at the hotel. Were the Armenian and his wife among them? But who shot at Peter?

She upped the volume, but the reporter, a ditsy blonde, just kept regurgitating the same garbage. The police weren't saying much, blah, blah, blah. She switched to another channel.

Another reporter, a man this time, said, "One of our sources tells us three men and a women were shot dead inside the Hotel Cavendish. It's owned and operated by a British conglomerate ..."

She muted the sound as the camera panned over the hotel and the chaotic scene on Canal Street, firetrucks, ambulances, cop cars.

And Peter had been in the thick of it.

Her stomach cramped as she ran in the kitchen, got a beer out of the fridge and ran back to the living room. A close call, Peter had said. What if someone had shot him?

Horrified by the thought, she sipped her beer. Peter would come over after he talked to his employer. But she didn't want to wait, she wanted to hold him in her arms right now.

———

11:30 AM

"I cannot believe it," Nicole Takvorian said, raking slender fingers through her light-brown, almost-blonde hair, exposing darker roots. "I go out shopping and someone—" Fresh tears filled her eyes.

Seated opposite her, Frank evaluated her demeanor. Suites at the Hotel Cavendish were expensive, but not too costly for Aram Takvorian apparently. Nicole was twenty years younger than her husband, slender and attractive in a pleated white skirt and a sleeveless red-silk blouse. Was she a trophy wife? Her distress seemed genuine, her dark eyes red-rimmed from crying, her face ghostly pale, as if every drop of blood had been sucked out of her.

The manager had let him use the hotel marketing office for the interview, a small windowless room with a computer desk, plush easy chairs grouped around an antique coffee table, and paintings of English hunting scenes on the walls. Kenyon and David were down the hall in two larger rooms, interviewing other guests and hotel workers.

"Aram was so kind to me," Nicole said, blinking back tears. "Ten years together and never a harsh word between us." She straightened in her chair and declared, "I want to see him!"

113

He'd already told her this wasn't possible. The coroner and the forensics unit were still in the room. So were the bodies, the naked man sprawled on the floor near Aram Takvorian.

Avoiding the word *morgue* which freaked people out, he said, "In a little while we'll take you to the coroner's office to identify him. Was he alone in the room when you left?"

"Yes."

"What time was that?"

"A little after nine, perhaps."

"Did your husband ever use an escort service?"

She stiffened and a muscle jumped in her jaw, her eyes darting around the room.

"We found another man's body in the room. Your husband was wearing a suit, but the other man had no clothes on." He wasn't going to sugar coat it.

With an audible gasp, she shrank back as though he'd hit her with a dead fish.

"Nicole, I'm sure you want us to find the person who murdered your husband. It's possible the other man has nothing to do with it. Then again, he might. You need to be honest with me. Did your husband ever use escort services?"

"They did it to blackmail him," she muttered.

"Why would anyone want to blackmail Aram Takvorian?"

Clenching her hands together, she pursed her lips and stared at the floor.

"Nicole," he said sternly. "Look at me."

She raised her head, gazing at him, her eyes fearful.

"Did your husband ever use an escort service?"

Adopting a defensive posture, she crossed her arms over her chest. "From time to time he would, yes. But Aram was always careful. Very discreet." She raised her chin defiantly. "I didn't mind. Such a small thing to make Aram happy. We had a good relationship. We loved each other!"

"Thank you for your honesty," he said. "It will help us identify the other man in the room."

She shook her head, wild-eyed. "But this is a catastrophe! What if they write about this in the newspapers? And talk about it on the tele-vision?"

"We won't discuss the specifics of what we found." But he knew it would get out eventually. Too many people knew about it. The hotel security guards, the coroner, the forensic techs, the patrol cop. Anything salacious, someone inevitably talked about it.

"Would you like some water?" he said. "I can get you some."

"No. I need …" A heavy sigh. "Something stronger."

"Wait here, I'll be right back." He went down the hall to the hotel lounge. Seeing no one, he went behind the bar, collected a brandy snifter, a bottle of Rémy Martin Cognac and a bottled water for himself. When he returned to the marketing office, Nicole was staring into space. Thinking of happier times, he hoped. Far better than seeing the horrors in the room on the seventh floor.

"I didn't get any ice," he said, setting the snifter and the bottle of cognac on the coffee table.

"I don't need ice. Thank you for being so kind, for understanding."

"No problem. I know this is difficult for you."

He poured two fingers of cognac into the snifter. Cupping it with her hands, she raised it to her mouth and took a large swallow.

"How did you meet Aram?" he asked. Personalize things, she might open up to him.

"We met at a resort in Nice, on the French coast. We hit it off right away." A faint smile. "Aram can be very charming."

"You're not Armenian then?"

"No. I am French. I grew up in a little town near Cannes, where they have the film festivals."

He sipped his bottled water. "Who would want to harm your husband?"

Nicole frowned. "Many people. The Turks hate Armenians."

"You lived in Turkey?"

"After we were married, yes. In Ankara."

"Why did you come to New Orleans? For a vacation?"

"No, not a vacation. We came here from New York. Aram said he had to talk to someone important."

Now they were getting somewhere. "Did he say who?"

"No. Just that he had to talk to someone." Nicole sipped her brandy.

"Did he tell you what it was about?"

115

"No." Her eyes glazed with tears. "And now he is dead. And I am here all by myself. I don't even have my belongings. They are upstairs in our room."

And the techs were going through them with a fine-toothed comb, Frank knew.

"Did Aram seem anxious about anything? In New York, or here?"

She drained the rest of her brandy and held out her glass.

He poured more brandy into the snifter, thinking, *The homicide detective plies the bereaved widow with brandy to make her talk.*

After a swallow of brandy she said, "Two days ago he went to a meeting in New York. When he came back he seemed angry."

"What sort of meeting?"

"I don't *know!*" she exclaimed. "A business meeting. Aram was an investment banker. He never talked about business with me. The next day we flew here."

"Why? Do you know people in New Orleans?"

"No. But to tell you the truth, Aram did seem … rather anxious."

"What about phone calls? Did anyone call him? Make an appointment with him?"

"Not that I know of." She heaved a sigh. "I'm sorry, Detective Renzi, I can't help you."

"Think carefully. Do you know of anyone who would want him dead? Business associates, perhaps? Or someone with a personal vendetta?"

"*Vendetta?*" Anger flared in her dark eyes. "How about an assassination? Hrant Dink, the editor of an Armenian newspaper, a powerful voice for the Armenian people, shot dead in broad daylight on a busy street in Istanbul in 2007. The assassin was paid by the government. The police caught him, but his trial was a joke! A national disgrace, Aram said. Dink's family got no justice. Dozens of journalists have been murdered in Turkey. Look it up. You will see this is true."

Impressed by her vehemence, he said, "I will. But your husband wasn't a journalist."

"No, but he knew many of them. And the Turkish government knew how passionate Aram was about winning justice for Armenians. Now that he is dead, I cannot return to Ankara." She shivered and rubbed her arms. "If I do, they will kill me, too."

"What will you do? Stay here? Do you have a visa?"

"Yes, but it is only good for two weeks. We did not plan to stay in America long."

"You need to talk to somebody—"

"Not at the Turkish embassy! Never. But I have a French passport. They have an embassy in New Orleans. Perhaps I will go there."

"Good idea," he said. "I'll get a detective friend of mine to help you. You'll like her." He knew Kelly would help. Maybe she could do the girl-talk routine and get more information. "The manager has given you a new room on the third floor."

"Without my belongings," Nicole lamented. "And my cellphone."

"Kelly will help you get whatever you need." He took out his card. "I'll need to talk with you again. But in the meantime, if you need anything, or think of anything helpful, call my cellphone. Anytime, day or night."

"This Kelly you speak about ... she is a detective?"

"Yes, Detective Kelly O'Neil. She's a great person. Think of her as your new best friend. Let's go up to your new room. I'll call Kelly on the room phone so you can talk to her."

CHAPTER 19

12:05 PM

The instant Control's butt hit the park bench beside him, the Sniper attacked. "Your Intel sucked! The Armenian's wife went shopping, but someone else was in the room."

Mopping sweat off his ferret face, Control managed to look anxious and angry at the same time. "I saw the television reports. What happened?"

"There was a rent-boy in the room, naked as a jaybird. I shot both of them."

"Did you get the flash drive?"

A red haze of fury glazed his eyes. "Is that all you care about? A fucking flash drive? When I tried to leave the room, two men shot at me. Were they yours?"

"No! Bloody hell, who were they?"

"I don't know." Actually, he did. He'd gone through the dead Russian's wallet, but found nothing useful. Nothing he planned to share with his idiot minder, anyway.

"You killed them?"

"One of them. I winged the other one, but he got away." His fury boiled over. "What if they'd killed me and the cops found my body? It's a British hotel. My cover won't hold up if they send Europol agents over here to investigate. They'll trace me to our employer."

Gazing at him through his thick eyeglasses, Control said, "But you escaped."

"Yes. By pulling the fire alarm."

An ice cream truck on the street behind the bench drove by, tooting a children's ditty through its speakers. *Three Blind Mice*. Ironic, given their discussion of the murders in the Hotel Cavendish.

"Did you get the flash drive?"

"Yes. What's on it?"

"I don't know."

"I want to talk to the Boss."

"No you don't. He's not happy that you shot the cop."

"He'll be happy that I killed the Armenian. The Client is Turkish, right?"

118

Control hesitated, then said, "Yes."

"Who's The Package?"

"I don't know!" Control exclaimed. "I told you that before! The Boss won't tell me. He said The Package will be here in a few days."

"A few days," he muttered. "How many? Two days, five?"

"When he tells me, you'll be the first to know. Give me the flash drive. The Boss wants me to call him as soon as I have it."

"You'll get the flash drive when I get my money after I finish the assignment."

Control flinched as though he'd struck him, staring at him, aghast.

Enjoying Control's obvious distress at this unexpected development, he thought, *Provided I don't kill you before I leave town.*

———

When she opened the door, Peter didn't even say hello, just strode past her into the living room, his jaw set, his expression grim. She threw her arms around him. "I've been so worried about you!"

He kissed her—not a quick peck, a long deliciously passionate kiss —his arms tight around her, as though he feared she might pull away.

Fat chance. Her body tingled. She wanted to know what happened, but if Peter wanted to take her to bed and fuck her brains out, she wouldn't complain.

He released her and caressed her face, gazing into her eyes. "This has been a horrible day."

Like she couldn't tell. His face was drawn and his eyes had a haunted look. "Want a beer?"

"Definitely." He smiled. "Now that I'm with my favorite woman."

Magical words worthy of her new description: Blitz-thrill.

She got two bottles of Becks out of her refrigerator and took them in the living room.

Peter patted the futon. "Sit here, beside me."

"Want to watch the news?"

"No," he said curtly. "They don't know what happened."

"Tell me," she said, gazing into his eyes.

He gulped some beer and set the bottle on her coffee table. "I had orders to get something from the Armenian, but when we went up to his room someone else was there."

"His wife?" Picturing the woman's pretty face.

"No. A male prostitute."

"Wow! That's kinky!" She drank some beer.

"I had to kill them." He raked his fingers through his dark hair. "I got what I needed, but when I tried to leave the room, two men shot at me."

"Jesus! Why? Who were they?"

"I don't know. My employer claims he doesn't know, either. But I don't trust him."

"Why?"

He waved a hand. "It's complicated. Too complicated to explain."

She put her arms around him. "But you got away. That's the important thing."

"Yes. Otherwise I'd never see you again. I'd be in jail. Or dead."

Shocked by his matter-of-fact statement, she climbed into his lap and gazed into his eyes. "I couldn't stand it if you were dead, Peter."

Without a word, he picked her up, carried her into the bedroom, set her down, pulled off her top and bra, and licked her breasts.

Electrical shocks coursed through her body. She didn't want him to stop, but his clothes were in the way. He stepped back, unbuttoned his shirt and took it off.

She ran her fingers over his chest hair. He pulled off her shorts and panties, threw her down on the bed and kissed her, his tongue exploring her mouth, his hands caressing her breasts. Standing on his knees, his cock fully erect, he pushed her thighs toward her chest.

Wild with excitement, she moaned his name, urging him on as he entered her. Time seemed to stand still. This was the way making love should be. Every touch of his lips, every flick of his tongue made her quiver. She thrust her hips upward, moaning as he pulled out and entered her again, an erotic rhythm, moving in and out of her in a relentless fury, eliciting a burst of pleasure so intense she thought she would explode.

He slid a hand under her butt to hold her in place. Another thrust sent her over the brink, and he buried himself deep inside her in an intense, shuddering climax.

Later, as they lay side-by-side, exhausted, she caressed his chest, running her fingers through his curly chest hair.

She'd never had sex like this in her life.

What if Peter wound up in jail? Or dead?

What would she do without him? Go back to her boring life, boosting stuff from ritzy stores? That was so yesterday. Now she had a handsome lover who was crazy about her.

Sure, his job was dangerous, but he knew how to survive. And he was madly in love with her. They were soulmates.

That's why he'd called her after his close call at the hotel this morning. For emotional support.

They were birds of a feather, and birds of a feather hang together. Given the proper encouragement—and she'd seen to that—they wind up in bed and have fucking fantastic sex. Sooner or later, Peter would make her his sniper partner. She just knew it.

———

9:10 PM

After the meeting, Frank asked Kelly and Kenyon to stay so he could get their take on how it went. To ensure that they didn't run into any other cops, Vobitch had reserved a room at the Poorhouse Pub for a birthday-party for T. Miller, AKA, Tanya, Kenyon's wife. No birthday cake, just a room with a table large enough to seat ten people. Seven of Vobitch's homicide detectives—Frank, Kenyon and David from D-8, two from District-5, two from District-1—plus three detectives from District-6, Kelly and two others.

Vobitch had insisted on picking up the tab for the burgers and beers. The detectives had chipped in to tip the waitress. The meeting had been productive, with lively discussions, the burgers and beer helping to build a sense of camaraderie.

"I'm glad we divvied up the male guests staying at the hotels since the first of June," Kenyon said. Pulling a face, he added, "Should only take two months to run 'em all down."

Kelly laughed. "Think positive, Kenyon. Only 106 names on the list, ten people to interview them? That's only about ten apiece."

"Still gonna take a shitload of time," Kenyon grumbled.

"I'll help you do the French Quarter hotels," Frank said.

Kenyon smiled. "Okay. Wanna split the task force meetings with me, too? It's fun watching the feds trying to outdo each other."

"Don't push your luck," Frank said. "What's up with the name? Operation Skyhawk?"

"Beats me," Kenyon said. "I thought it was a fighter plane, but Hicks claims it's some kind of bird."

"A predatory bird that hunts rodents," Kelly said. "I looked it up. I think Hicks is trying to suggest that the Sniper's a rat, and we're flying above him—"

"Gonna pounce on the motherfucker," Kenyon snapped. "The sooner the better."

"I'll drink to that," Frank said, raising his beer mug.

Kelly clinked her mug against his and said, "Why didn't you mention the shootout at the Cavendish?"

"I want to run it by Vobitch first. How are you getting along with Nicole Takvorian?"

"Okay so far. I took her shopping for clothes, but she's not talking much. I feel bad for her. She's terrified. Do you really think someone would try to kill her if she went home?"

"I don't know," he said. "No ID on the dead guy Kenyon and I found in the hall outside her room. I told the coroner to swab him for DNA. Maybe that will get us something."

"Crimestopper tips are useless," Kenyon said. "Lot of people looking for the reward on the Sniper, inventing stories." Making his eyes go wide, he said in an agitated falsetto, "I saw this big black guy, bigger than Shaq, walking around with a machine gun!"

Amused, Frank said, "You know how it is, Kenyon. The black guy is always the first to die."

"The one I liked best?" Kelly said, laughing. "The man disguised as a woman toting the AK-47. In broad daylight. On Canal Street."

"What about the Super?" Kenyon asked. "Did you tell him about the VIP theory?"

"Yes," Frank said. "It was touch and go until I said Hicks didn't seem receptive to my ideas about how to catch the Sniper. I'll give Sanders credit. When I told him we think the Sniper's actual target might be a VIP, the Super hardly blinked."

"Believe me," Kenyon said, "he's seen it all."

"Not quite. When I told him about Prime Minister Cameron, he looked like I squirted mustard on his hot fudge sundae. But he promised to beef up security on the July Fourth celebrations."

"He better assign some to the Hotel Cavendish," Kelly said, her eyes somber. "That's where Cameron is staying."

"Damn!" Kenyon exclaimed. "Are you serious?"

Kelly shrugged. "It's a British hotel. What did you expect?"

"No wonder the manager was flipping out," Frank said.

"You think the sniper kills and the shootings at the Cavendish are connected?" Kelly said.

"Beats the hell out of me. At this point, nothing would surprise me."

"You know," Kenyon said, "when I showed a picture of Aram Takvorian to one of the hotel busboys, he remembered seeing him in the tea room with another guy."

Frank's heart sped up. "Any description?"

"Yeah, a shitty one. The guy had on a dark suit and horn-rimmed glasses. I asked him was the guy short, tall, fat, thin, got nowhere. An average guy, the kid said."

"Men are useless with descriptions," Kelly said. "Women are much more observant, especially when it comes to guys. Talk to the tea room waitress. She might remember him."

CHAPTER 20

THURSDAY, June 30 – 12:15 PM

Still as a statue, he leaned against the trunk of an ancient oak, studying the house diagonally across the street. The T-shirt beneath his loose-fitting black windbreaker was soaked with sweat. He'd been here for two hours, sweltering in the relentless heat, the air thick with humidity.

Not much activity along this street, no pedestrians or dog-walkers, not many cars passing him. Control's car sat in the semi-circular crushed-white-stone driveway. He would have preferred to break in at night, but Control was afraid to go out after dark.

At noon, he'd made his obligatory check-in call. Control had nothing new to report. With any sort of luck, he would soon go out for his midday meal. Faint light shone through the curtains on the first floor. The windows were closed. He assumed the two-story Victorian had central air conditioning like other homes in the area, an upscale residential neighborhood with manicured lawns.

But he didn't plan to get in through a window. A set of lock picks was in his windbreaker pocket. His training at Zenith Intelligence had included detailed instructions on how to make clandestine entries, should that be necessary.

And this entry was essential. He needed Intel.

Some homes on the street probably had burglar alarms, but he didn't expect to find one in the gray-shingled Victorian across the street. If breached, the alarm would bring the police or a security agent from the alarm company, the last thing Control wanted.

At 12:38 the faint light behind the curtains disappeared. Excellent. Control must be getting hungry. Seconds later, he bustled out the front door in a beige-linen suit, got into his olive-green Volvo and drove toward the iron gate that barred entry to the property.

Hearing the Volvo's wheels crunch over the crushed white stones, the sniper flattened his back against the tree, waited for Control to lock the security gate and saw the Volvo drive off. At 12:42, he strolled across the street and walked along the eight-foot brick wall that protected the Victorian.

The spotlights mounted at intervals along the top were off. But the security cameras weren't. If someone else was in the safe house, they might be watching the monitors. A chilling thought. Once he started to doubt someone's honesty, eliminating suspicion was impossible. Control claimed to know nothing about the shooters at the Hotel Cavendish. But Control often lied.

How satisfying it would be to wrap his hands around that scrawny neck, give it a sharp twist and snap it like a chicken bone. But that could result in unintended consequences. The Boss might send someone worse over here to replace him. Better the devil you knew than the one you didn't.

He walked alongside the wall to the corner and turned right into the yard of the adjacent house. A fake decal on his windbreaker identified him as an electric company worker. Act like you belong and know where you're going, most people didn't bother you. Still, his palms dampened with sweat and a hard knot settled in his gut.

At the far corner of the wall, he turned right again. Getting over the wall was a danger point. Speed was the answer. Do it fast and hope no one was looking out the windows of the two-story white Colonial behind the Victorian. He sprinted twenty feet, leaped at the eight-foot wall, grasped the top with his hands, flung himself over it and landed with a perfect tuck-and-roll on the lawn.

He checked his watch. 12:47. Get in and get out before Control finished whatever the hell he was eating for lunch. A small porch with a wood railing led to the rear door. Another danger point. Anyone looking out a window on the second floor of the white Colonial would see him.

His pulse sped up as he mounted four wooden steps, took out an ultra-thin piece of flexible plastic and worked it between the doorjamb and the door. Ten seconds later the lock bolt was disabled. He took out the picks and got to work on the secondary lock. Aware of the passing minutes, he fished around, felt the tumblers engage and opened the door. Quietly stepping inside, he eased the door shut behind him and took out the Beretta.

His heart was beating abnormally fast. Not so long ago covert ops like this didn't bother him. Just another risk in a dangerous line of work. But that was when he had nothing to lose. Now he did.

He pictured Win at the airport in her sexy see-through blouse. Imagined kissing her breasts. Touching her hair. Kissing her slender neck. She had a certain stubborn quality, but her luminous brown eyes were irresistible. So was her mouth, her full lower lip begging to be sucked.

But this was no time for daydreams. *Get the Intel and get out!*

Inhaling the scent of cinnamon and coffee wafting from the pantry to his left, he flicked on the tactical light mounted under the barrel of the Beretta and moved it over the kitchen cabinets, the counter-tops and the appliances. The stove was spotless. Of course. Control was no chef. He barely knew how to use a coffeemaker.

Beside the sink, a fresh liter bottle of Jim Beam stood beside a wicker basket with rosy-red apples and a navel orange. Control eating healthy to make up for the copious quantities of booze he consumed.

Above him a floorboard creaked.

Fear stabbed him like an ice pick. Who was in the house?

A cold-eyed Russian with a 9mm Makarov pistol? Forget looking for Intel. If someone else was in the house he had to find them.

Raising his Beretta, he crept down a hallway toward the front door, checking each room he passed. A dining room with an oval table and ornate wooden chairs. A parlor with a red-velvet sofa, matching easy chairs, mahogany end tables, and a yellow-plastic bucket in one corner, guarding against any leaks from the stained ceiling above it.

He kept going. To his right, a library held a large desk and computer equipment. Control's office. A treasure trove to be explored after he cleared the house. He continued down the hall to the front door and swept the tactical light over the foyer. No mail on an antique sideboard that needed dusting.

Sweating profusely, he turned to a wide staircase with carved-wood balustrades. Treading carefully, keeping to the side of each step so the stairs wouldn't creak, he crept up to the second floor landing and stood with his back against the wall.

The silence unnerved him, raising the hairs on the back of his neck. Was someone up here waiting to kill him? Someone who'd seen him come inside?

Four doors along the hall were open, two on the right, two on the left. Clearing a staircase was bad enough; standing above him, a shooter would have a clear line of sight, no way to retreat without turning his back. Clearing four doorways by himself was far worse.

Positioned inside the room, a shooter could blow him away.

He advanced down the hallway, his heart pounding, his Beretta clenched in both hands.

But his fears were groundless. Three bedrooms showed no sign of use, awaiting others who needed to hide in a safe house. Control had claimed the largest bedroom, a neatly made king-sized bed, a bedside table with a reading lamp, a private bath, and a curtained window overlooking the yard outside the house.

Convinced no one was in the house, he hurried downstairs to Control's office. The blinds on a tall window were shut. He opened them and sunlight exploded into the room. He tilted the blinds to block the sun and shut off his tactical light.

Framed paintings of sun-dappled lighthouses and snow-covered mountains decorated three of the walnut-paneled walls. The remaining wall held floor-to-ceiling bookshelves. Two shelves held closed-circuit monitors displaying the yard around the house and the front gate. But there was no tape system. Excellent. His clandestine entry would not be seen by Control or anyone else.

Standing beside the window were a three-way printer-fax-copier, and a shredder, to eliminate paper trails.

The desk in the center of the room was neat and tidy, thanks to his OCD minder. No post-it notes, no desk calendar with names, dates and times. Nothing written on a yellow legal pad sitting on the green-felt blotter. In the bottom desk drawer he found hanging file folders, all of them empty. The drawer above it held yellow-sticky pads and boxes of ballpoint pens. On the desktop, a pen-and-pencil holder and a black stapler stood beside a Tiffany lamp.

A notepad sat beside a telephone. Like the legal pad, the top sheet was blank, but he could see indentations on it, as though Control had jotted notes talking to someone on the phone. He held it under the light but couldn't decipher the writing. Scarcely daring to hope, he checked the wastebasket beside the desk.

His heart almost burst with joy. A page from the notepad was in the wastebasket. Some angular doodles, a square and a rectangle then ... *Dry-Fart in London. Bitch in Berlin. Poodle in Paris. Mona Lisa. B-day.*

The Dry-Fart was probably the British Prime Minister. The Bitch in Berlin had to be Angela Merkel. The Poodle in Paris might be President Sarkozy, but who was Mona Lisa? He'd seen Leonardo da Vinci's *Mona Lisa* in the Louvre, but what was B-day? Birthday?

He checked his watch. 1:25. Time to get out.

Shoving the page in his pocket, he returned to the kitchen. Drawn to the pantry by the enticing aroma of coffee, he noticed a doorknob on the wood-paneled wall, a knob to open a secret door, he realized. He opened the door. Beyond it was a staircase. Noting the heavy-duty deadbolt on the inside of the door, he left it ajar and cautiously descended the stairs, the air damp and clammy against his skin.

At the bottom, he flicked a switch. A wire-caged bulb in the ceiling illuminated what appeared to be an interrogation room: a square metal table with a tape recorder on it, and three metal chairs. Beyond the table, a one-way mirror displayed an empty caged cell. The shelf beside the mirror held a polygraph, an electroshock machine, microphones, tape recorders, sterile syringes in plastic bags and ...

Bile rose in his throat. Were those blood stains on the cement floor? Jesus, did they torture people here?

Sickened, he raced upstairs, shut the door and stepped into the kitchen. And heard a key being inserted into a lock in the front door.

Control! His heart broke into a headlong gallop. He yanked open the back door and shut it behind him, breathing hard as he sprinted across the lawn toward the brick wall. With a flying leap, he grasped the top in both hands, rolled over the top and landed on the other side.

Spurred by the memory of the blood stains, he raced through the yard beside the white Colonial. His Vespa was parked outside a convenience store two blocks away. Another close call.

But if he couldn't figure out what the scrawls on the notepad meant, the risk he had taken would be all for naught.

———

Control set the container of Shrimp Creole leftovers on the sideboard in the foyer. A fine meal, but he hadn't eaten much of it. His stomach was too jittery, and his head throbbed with a dull ache. The memory of yesterday's meeting with the Sniper had kept him awake all night.

The bastard was impossible! Refusing to give him the flash drive.

His report about the men who'd shot at him was even more disturbing. Who else was after the flash drive?

He took the leftovers in the kitchen and put them in the refrigerator. A faint odor permeated the air, the nasty sour-sweat smell in men's locker rooms that he hated. He raised the top of the metal canister beside the sink where he kept the trash, bent down and sniffed. No stench of rotted food. Maybe he was imagining things.

But the two o'clock call he was expecting was no figment of his imagination. That was all too real. And terrifying.

He went to his office, removed his suit jacket, hung it on the wooden coat tree and turned to his desk. The red digits on his desk clock said 1:55. In five minutes the Boss would call.

Bloody hell! What was he going to tell him? *My helper got the flash drive but won't give it to me?*

Not bloody likely. Not if he valued his life.

He sat down at his desk and the telephone rang. It startled him so badly he clutched his chest, fearing his heart would explode. Staring at the phone, he mopped his face with a handkerchief.

After the third ring he picked up and said, "Yes?"

"I hope you are having a better day than I am," snarled the Boss.

"What's wrong?" he said, trying without success to keep his voice steady. Had the Boss seen news reports about the hotel shootings?

He picked up a pen, reached for his notepad and frowned. Strange. He always kept it lined up against the telephone . . .

"The fucking Poodle is what's wrong! He has too many problems. Riots outside his house. Disagreements with European leaders. And his wife is expecting." Control heard the Boss light a cigarette. "She doesn't want him to leave. He may not fly to New Orleans after all."

Control couldn't decide if this was good news or bad. "What if he doesn't?"

"Idiot! If he doesn't, we can't very well eliminate him, can we?"

He knew better than to answer. The Boss wasn't asking for his opinion.

"We may have to eliminate the Bitch in Berlin, instead. Did you get the flash drive?"

The dreaded question. Control clenched his hands to keep them from shaking, trying to decide how to answer.

"Yes. But there is a problem."

"Don't talk to me about problems! Did you get it or not?"

"Yes." Desperately hoping the Boss wouldn't ask if he'd checked to see what was on it.

"Good." Another drag on his cigarette, then a cough *ack ack ack.*

Taking advantage of the momentary silence, Control said, "My helper keeps asking when the Package will arrive."

More silence. He mopped sweat off his face, trying to decide if he should tell the Boss about the men who'd shot at the Sniper.

"Your *helper* didn't help us much by shooting that cop."

"That's what I told him. I said if he ever did that—"

"If the Poodle stays in Paris, we will no longer need your *helper*."

"What about his contract? We agreed to pay him—"

"You will terminate his contract when I tell you to. Understood?"

"Yes, sir." He heard a click and the line went dead.

Control mopped sweat from his forehead. *Terminate his contract.* He knew what that meant.

He didn't want to think about how he might do it.

CHAPTER 21

"I bet you'll be glad to sleep in your own bed tonight," Frank said.

"Damn right," Vobitch said, running a hand over his blue polo shirt and jeans. "Glad to dump the fucking johnny too, so my ass ain't waving in the wind for all to see."

Frank raised his hands in mock horror. "Stop! The image that conjures up is terrifying."

Usually they sat in the dining room to discuss cases, but Vobitch was seated on his leather recliner in the living room today. He looked good, his silvery hair neatly combed, his cheeks pink with color, though his face was gaunt.

"Juliana says I can only stay a half hour," he said. "We better get to work."

"She's worse than the nurses," Vobitch growled, "says I gotta take a ten minute walk around the house before she'll let me eat dinner. Tell me about the Sniper meeting and the hotel homicides. Christ, all hell breaks loose and I'm in a fucking hospital."

Frank spread his notes out on the coffee table between them. "Good meeting with the troops last night at the Poorhouse Pub. We're all on the same page. They report to me, I report to you."

Vobitch sipped some ice water. "So? You got any leads?"

"Nothing so far. The CrimeStopper and hotline tips are useless. Not surprising since we don't have a description of the Sniper, but at least people are paying attention."

"Money talks. You never know, something might shake out. Did you tell Hicks the Sniper might be gunning for a VIP?"

"No. He's pissed at me for talking to the media after the policewoman got shot, says I'm a loose cannon."

"Hicks is an asshole. He wants to be a hero, catch the Sniper and grab all the attention."

"Kenyon told me to talk to the Super on the QT, said he'd be more receptive than Hicks. This morning I did, right after I got some bad news from the NOPD Intelligence Unit. British Prime Minister David Cameron is coming here to participate in the July Fourth celebrations."

"There's a nightmare," Vobitch said, his slate-gray eyes somber. "All the shit that goes on in this town for the Fourth of July? Parades. Fireworks. Road races."

"Cameron flies in on Friday. He's scheduled to speak at a big event at the World War Two Museum on Sunday, July third. And Cameron will stay at the Hotel Cavendish while he's here."

Vobitch stared at him. "Are you shitting me? The hotel with the homicides?"

"I shit you not. I think we need to consider the possibility that they're related to the Sniper hits."

"Just what we need, another complication. How's Kimba Davis? Is she still in the hospital?"

The question didn't surprise him. Vobitch could be a grouch, but he had a big heart when it came to his troops, not just detectives, patrol officers too. And Kimba Davis had been patrolling District Eight when she got shot. "Still in the hospital, but she's better. Going home on Saturday."

"That's good news, at least. I'll go over and see her. What else you got going on the Sniper?"

"We're compiling a list of males who've been staying in hotels since the first of June, before the first Sniper hit. Every hotel in D-8 and the hotels in D-6 where he shot the runner. I figure we can inter-view them, see if anyone acts suspicious."

"Good move. The asshole's gotta sleep somewhere."

"True, but if he's got wheels, he could be staying anywhere. There are hundreds of hotels in the New Orleans area. It would take for-ever to check all of them."

"I've been thinking." Vobitch grimaced. "Plenty of time for that when you're in a hospital. He killed the cabdriver first. One shot, over and out. Same with the runner. But he shot Kimba Davis in the back. Maybe he went for a head shot and missed. Don't get me wrong, I'm damn glad he did, but maybe he's losing his touch."

"Think location. Maybe he shot her because she was there. Noth-ing personal."

"Nothing personal, my ass! He did it to get attention. Shoot a cop in the French Quarter, it's front page news, the lead story on TV. It scares off the tourists."

"In the beginning I figured him for a serial killer who gets his jol-lies by shooting people, but I searched the federal data bases for crimes with a similar MO and got zip. We've called a dozen big-city police departments to see if they had any similar cases recently and got nothing. Bottom line, we got no clue who the Sniper is, what he looks like or where he's staying."

"Focus on the targets."

"I already did, combed through their backgrounds and found nothing to connect them."

"The fucker wants attention. The taxi driver got shot outside a ritzy Canal Street hotel. That got massive publicity, so he shot the runner."

"I think he stalked her. She had a daily routine, went running at the same time every morning. He was waiting for her."

"Okay," Vobitch said. "But why there?"

"I don't know. When he shot the taxi driver and Kimba Davis, he had to be on a roof in the French Quarter, and now we got multiple homicides at the Hotel Cavendish."

"Gimme the gory details. Yesterday all you said was you had a dead man and a naked black kid in a room, and a dead man in the hall beside a dead Asian girl." Vobitch smiled thinly. "Not that we're giving that to the media vultures."

"I talked to Nicole Takvorian. The dead man in the hotel room was her husband."

"Hold on," Vobitch said, smiling as his wife entered the room. "Here's my dearest beloved, gonna crack the whip and make me go for a walk."

"That's right," Juliana said, bending down to give him a kiss, clearly happy to have her husband home. "I never owned a dog because I didn't want to walk one. But now I've got you."

"Woof woof," Vobitch said. "Give us ten minutes okay? Frank just got to the part about the dead guy and the naked boy-toy."

Juliana's eyes widened. "Sounds like a soap opera." Wagging a finger, she said, "Ten minutes, but no more. Dinner's waiting."

After she left the room, Vobitch said, "Tell me about the widow. That's an Armenian name."

"She's not Armenian, but her husband is. Aram Takvorian. They flew here from New York. She said he told her he had to talk to someone important. And I don't think it was the naked black kid."

Vobitch smiled tightly. "That's a good bet. She wouldn't tell you who he wanted to talk to?"

"She claimed she didn't know, and I believe her. She's distraught about the black kid. She's afraid the story will leak, and it probably will. Too many people knew about it. She's afraid to go home. They have a house in Ankara, but she's afraid the Turkish government will kill her."

"Not a big stretch. If Aram Takvorian came here to talk to someone important, maybe he knew something somebody didn't want him to talk about. If he swings both ways, and it appears that he did, maybe he knew some swingers in Ankara, dug up dirt on a closet-gay Turkish politician. The Turks hate the Armenians. You know about the Armenian genocide, right?"

Frank shook his head. "Not really."

"Remember how I told you my parents escaped the Russian pogroms against the Jews? The Armenian Genocide was a lot like what happened to them. Before World War I, two million Armenians were living in the Ottoman Empire." Vobitch gave him a sly look and a faint smile. "Now known as Turkey, in case you're geographically challenged. Over a million Armenians were deported in 1915. Hundreds of thousands of others were butchered. The rest died in concentration camps of starvation or disease."

"None of them survived?"

"Some of them did, but there were more massacres. Between 1915 and 1923, a million and a half Armenians died."

Embarrassed that he'd never heard of this, Frank said, "I've read about the Nazi war crimes and trials, and everybody knows about Hitler. Who gave the order to exterminate the Armenians?"

Vobitch shrugged. "SOS. Same old story. The political party in power. The Armenian Genocide is well documented, but even now a lot of Turks won't admit to it. Sort of like the Jewish Holocaust deniers. Most countries in the UN recognize it, but Turkey isn't one of them. Maybe Nicole Takvorian has a right to be worried."

"I'll keep that in mind next time I talk to her. After Kenyon and I worked the crime scene, we decided there were two sets of shooters. One in Takvorian's room, two others in the hall. I had the coroner swab the corpse in the hall for DNA, figured we could run it through some databases."

"Good, but if he's foreign you might not get anything. Whatever information Aram Takvorian had must have been damned important if two different shooters were after it."

Struck by a new idea, one that got his juices running, Frank said, "Maybe he knew who the Sniper's VIP target is."

Vobitch pursed his lips. "If he did, it sure as hell would be nice to know who."

"But he didn't tell anyone, not even his wife. I felt sorry for her. She doesn't know anyone here so I hooked her up with Kelly. She might get her to talk. You know, do the gal-pal thing. Even if Nicole doesn't know what Intel her husband had, she might say something to give us a hint."

"Smart move. Head on over to Kelly's house tonight and ask her." Vobitch flashed his evil grin. "You know, a little pillow talk after your amorous adventures."

Frank knew better than to respond to that. Five minutes later he left the house and got in his car, Vobitich's jibe ringing in his mind. Vobitch kept saying, "You and Kelly get along great, got that Italian heritage connection. Why don't you get married?"

When that happened, he'd blow him off with a smart-ass remark. "My calendar's booked." Or "I cry at weddings."

Knowing deep in his heart, when he was honest with himself what the real reason was. He was afraid that if they got married, it would screw things up. His first marriage had failed. He didn't want that to happen with Kelly. He cared about her too much.

Beyond the physical attraction and the cop-talk, they had a deep emotional bond. And he didn't want to lose it.

Truth be told, he really did cry at weddings, not that he went to many, but whenever he did, his eyes would tear up, thinking about his own wedding when he was a starry-eyed twenty-year-old, happy to be marrying Evelyn, the girl of his dreams. How thrilled he was when Maureen, his precious bundle of joy, arrived less than a year later.

How disappointed and hurt he'd been two months later when Evelyn wouldn't have sex with him.

At first he thought it was his fault. But after a few more attempts, he gave up and found solace elsewhere.

The beginning of the end of his marriage.

———

Paris, France 11:30 PM

Henri Bellest descended the red-carpeted staircase, hearing the chants of protesters outside the residence. *Les voyous racaille* his boss called them. The rabble. President Sarkozy could be ultra-charming for the TV cameras and with certain reporters. A writer for *Vanity Fair* had ranked Sarkozy one of the best dressed men in the world, just below David Beckham and Brad Pitt.

But they didn't work for him, didn't have to deal with him on a daily basis. Henri had been his personal assistant since 2006. Five long years and damn little appreciation.

Although he had to admit when his daughter fell ill last year, Sarkozy had surprised him, sending him to the hospital in a limousine and giving him extra time off until Olivia regained her health.

The French press delighted in taunting Sarkozy. It wasn't difficult. His thin-skinned boss was sensitive about many things. His short stature, five-foot-five allegedly, less when he was barefoot. His status as a thrice-married man, whose second wife had left him to marry another man. His wretched command of English.

A handsome man with curly dark hair, Sarkozy was well-educated, but his English was abysmal. When they traveled to English-speaking countries, Henri, who spoke fluent English, often served as his translator. For public events and meetings with heads of state, Sarkozy's official translator did the honors.

As Henri reached the ground floor, the chants outside seemed to grow louder. More virulent.

The Security Chief turned away from the window beside the door. Resplendent in a dark blue uniform decorated with ribbons and medals, he said, "What does he want?" Adding with a mischievous smile, "Wait. Could it be that the rabble outside is disturbing him?"

The Security Chief was as tall as Charles de Gaulle, six-foot-five, dwarfing Henri who was only five-foot-six, an inch taller than his boss. That was one reason why he was hired. Henri had dark hair and similar features. From a distance it was difficult to tell them apart. In fact he sometimes acted as a decoy, when Sarkozy didn't want the press hounding him. Henri had also been married and divorced.

Their primary difference: Sarkozy was fifty-six and president of France. Henry was thirty-six, and worked for *Groupe de sécurité de la présidence de la République* charged with protecting the president.

The chief gestured at the protesters. "Last night it was worse. They torched two cars and threw bricks at the fire brigade when they tried to douse the flames."

Henri nodded. These riots kept getting worse and worse. Two years ago, there had been 317 burned out cars and 240 arrests, almost double the numbers for the previous year, when many officers were injured, targeted by youths throwing fireworks and home-made Molotov cocktails.

"Imagine what it will be like on Bastille Day," Henri said.

A major holiday in France, the entire country celebrated the anniversary of July 14, 1789, when a mob of revolutionaries stormed the Bastille, a Parisian prison, resulting in the eventual overthrow of the French monarchy. Now, young men in bleak housing projects, many of them Muslim, saw Bastille Day as the perfect time to vent their anger about high unemployment rates and Sarkozy's "failure to integrate ethnic minorities."

"Don't remind me." The chief took out his cellphone and called the police.

When he ended the call, Henri said, "While I'm down here, he wants me to get him some hot chocolate and a hot babe."

The chief's eyes widened for an instant. Then he shook with laughter, clutching his ample belly. "Not getting any from Mona Lisa, eh?"

Mona Lisa was their code name for Sarkozy's wife. The president was Royal Flush. Sarkozy seemed pleased with it. A royal flush was the best poker hand one could hold, and "royal" implied an elevated imperial status.

"Getting a lot of flack from what I hear," Henri said. "I have coffee with Mona Lisa's maid every morning."

"When is she due?" the chief said. "Looks about ready to pop."

"October. She doesn't want to go to New Orleans. Doesn't want him to go either. Or so I hear."

"Better if he doesn't. Security will be a nightmare."

"But I'm looking forward to it. Hot jazz, great food, parades."

The chief frowned at him. "Do you know what the murder rate is in New Orleans?"

"No. Worse than Paris?"

"Much worse. Gangs run the city, I hear. American gun laws are a joke."

"Maybe," Henri said, "but I get the feeling Royal Flush would love to get out of Paris. It's not just these rabble riots. He's got problems with the auto workers. Renault signed a deal with Turkey to build their small cars there instead of in France. Say goodbye to a few billion euros."

"Say hello to Erdogan," the chief said. "Nobody hates Royal Flush more than Erdogan."

"Because he favors the new law recognizing the Armenian Genocide?"

The chief made his eyes go wide. "Genocide? What genocide? Erdogan says no such thing occurred in Turkey. If Armenians died, blame the Russians."

"Always a good choice," Henri said with an innocent smile. "Putin is to blame for global warming, isn't he? I better go get that hot chocolate or Royal Flush will flush me down the toilet."

"Good idea," said the chief. "Send the hot babe to me."

"*Mais non!*" Henri exclaimed in mock horror. "The hot babe is for me!"

CHAPTER 22

FRIDAY July 1 – 4:05 PM Louis Armstrong Airport

Frank stood near an exit door on the Departures level, gnawing his thumbnail. British Airways Flight 142 had landed right on time at 3:50 PM. Committed to his austerity plan, British Prime Minister David Cameron refused to use a private jet, though he and his security team had flown first class. The security team had whisked him off the plane and taken him to a secure holding room upstairs. Frank was in charge of the NOPD detail assigned to protect him.

Behind him, a dozen NOPD officers stood near the information desk. He didn't expect the Sniper to attack Cameron inside the terminal, but a three-story parking garage stood directly across from the terminal. At noon, two NOPD cops had begun stopping cars and questioning the drivers before they entered the parking garage. No reports of any suspicious males, so far.

It was bright and sunny today, a hot, humid Friday to kick off the Fourth of July weekend, air conditioners going full blast all over town. By this time, cars would already be backed up on the Causeway, workers heading for the cool comfort of their homes, north of Lake Pontchartrain.

Beyond the exit door, three NOPD vehicles idled at the curb, black SUVs with dark-tinted windows, waiting to take the PM to the Hotel Cavendish. Kenyon and David were stationed there, awaiting his arrival. Kelly was standing guard outside the terminal, sweltering in the heat, making sure no one was lurking near Cameron's caravan.

Despite the extra precautions, Frank felt uneasy. Even inside the air-conditioned terminal, his shirt was damp with sweat beneath his sports jacket. Security details were always a crap-shoot. Too many things could go wrong. He adjusted his earbud, awaiting word from Cameron's security team.

A blast of hot air hit him as Kelly came through the sliding door and said, "All clear outside. I got rid of the nicotine-fiends, told them to smoke outside another door."

"We should have posted cops inside the parking garage."

Kelly gave him a look. "Cameron's security men know how to do this. He's in a secure room. When he's ready to go, they'll alert you and bring him down in the elevator."

"Fine, but the danger point is getting him out the door and into the SUV. What if the Sniper figured out a way to avoid the cops outside the parking garage? If he got up to the roof, he'd have a clear shot at the PM."

"Calm down, Frank. Twenty seconds and they'll have him in the SUV."

Twenty seconds is plenty of time for the Sniper to shoot him. Frank popped a Tums to soak up the acid in his stomach. Kelly was right. He needed to calm down. Time to change the subject.

"You know anything about the Armenian genocide?" he asked.

"I vaguely remember hearing about it in my high school history class. Why?"

"When I went to see Vobitch yesterday, he told me about it. He thinks the dead Armenian must have had important information if two different shooters were after him."

"Like what?"

"I don't know. I'm hoping Nicole will tell you something."

"Last night I went to see her. She's afraid to go out, just stays in her room all the time."

"Vobitch says the Turks hate the Armenians and the feeling is mutual. Maybe the British PM isn't the target. Maybe the VIP is a Turk."

"But why would he come here? There's no Turkish Embassy in New Orleans."

"What if Aram Takvorian knew who the target was?"

Kelly's eyes widened. "You think?"

"I think anything's possible. Still no ID on the dead guy in the hall at the hotel. The coroner got a DNA sample, but Vobitch says if the guy's foreign—and he didn't look like your average American Joe to me—we might never identify him."

Kelly combed slender fingers through her short dark hair. "It does seem odd. Two out of three sniper hits in the French Quarter and four people get murdered in a French Quarter hotel."

He held up a hand as Cameron's security man spoke into his earbud. "Here they come," he said to Kelly. "Go on outside and make sure the area is clear."

Tense and alert, he watched the elevator. Surrounded by security men, David Cameron strode toward him, a tall handsome man in a pinstriped suit. At forty-five, his face was unlined, no gray in his thick dark hair. His wife had stayed in London, to be with their children, allegedly. In fact, Cameron's security team had insisted on it, unwilling to risk both lives if someone tried to kill her husband.

Frank nodded at Cameron's lead security man, who nodded back and kept walking. Fifteen seconds later, Cameron was inside one SUV with two of his security agents. The others jumped into the other two SUVs. Accompanied by motorcycles with lights flashing, the caravan pulled away from the curb and disappeared.

When Kelly came back in the terminal, Frank smiled and said, "Slick as a whistle, just like you said. Which means our work is done for the night. Wanna go see a movie?"

Smiling seductively, she said, using her sultry voice, "Only if it's playing in my bedroom and we're starring in it."

Man, he loved this woman.

"I think we should get started on that right now."

———

6:15 PM

"Why did you run away?" he said, gazing into the luminous brown eyes of his soulmate.

Playing footsie with him under the table, Win said, grinning at him, "Hit the road and see the world."

To take his mind off his problems, he'd taken her out for dinner, but not in New Orleans. Yesterday he'd seen her picture on a wanted poster in the French Quarter, fuzzy stills from a security video taken during one of her shoplifting forays. So he'd taken her for a ride on his Vespa to Jazz Seafood near the airport in Kenner, the drone of planes landing and taking off penetrating the window beside them.

"But you were only fifteen. That's much too young to go off on your own."

"No it isn't. Winona was making her first movie when she was only fifteen."

"Who's Winona?"

Win stopped running her bare foot up and down his leg. "Winona Ryder. She's my idol."

"The actress that played the screwed up girl in *Girl Interrupted*?" He cocked his head and smiled. "You look a bit like her. Especially your gorgeous brown eyes."

That got him a big smile. "You really think so? She's very pretty."

"Not as pretty as you." He forced down a bite of fried catfish. He couldn't wait to go back to Brussels and eat mussels steamed in white wine and garlic. And pommes frites with mayonnaise.

"She's a fabulous actress, but her career got sidetracked when she got busted for shoplifting. Did you hear about it?"

He frowned. "Is that what made you start shoplifting?"

"Sort of. Plus I hated school. So I saved some money, swiped two-hundred bucks from Mother's wallet, and bought a bus ticket to Hollywood. I wanted to see the store where Winona got busted."

"Your parents must have been frantic."

"After I got there I called Dad at the pharmacy and told him I was okay."

"What about your mother?"

Win drank some beer. "What about her? She didn't care. Mother never told me she loved me. Not even once."

Tossing off the words with a nonchalant shrug, but he could tell it bothered her.

"I still call Dad once or twice a year. He always says he misses me and wants me to come home. At least Dad loves me."

Dad isn't the only one. "What happened in Hollywood? What did you do for money?"

"I went to Saks Fifth Avenue in Beverly Hills where Winona got busted and swiped a bottle of perfume." Her eyes glowed with excitement. "What a kick! I can't tell you how thrilling it was."

Despite his worries, he had to smile. His sexy little soulmate got off on taking risks.

"I rented a room at a YWCA until I got good at shoplifting and learned how to fence the swag."

"In Hollywood?" He'd love to go there and visit a movie set, to see how they made films.

"Nah, I moved around a lot. Lots of malls in California, with fancy stores." She batted her eyelashes. "Then I met a guy and moved in with him, an aspiring actor, working as a waiter. He taught me how to drive. I had to call Dad and have him send me a birth certificate so I could get my license. But it's no good now. When I turned eighteen I changed my name to Win. No more Janis."

He drank some beer, annoyed by the music. No jazz at Jazz Seafood, just country music on the sound system, some old geezer whining about Lucille, who'd picked a fine time to leave him. Maybe he should ask the waitress to put on the Shostakovitch *Jazz Waltz*.

But she wouldn't know what he was talking about.

"And you never got caught?"

Win's triumphant expression morphed into a frown. "Only once, at a mall in San Diego. This fat security guard took me in the back room of the store, made me give him a blow job and let me go."

His hands clenched into fists. He wanted to find the bastard and rip off his balls.

"Too bad I didn't have a gun," Win said, her eyes blazing with fury. "I'd have waited till the store closed, followed the asshole to his car and put a bullet in his balls."

Astounded, he stared at her. Could his risk-taker soulmate read his mind? Reality slapped him in the face like a dead fish.

He couldn't afford to get emotionally involved with her. He had too many problems to solve. Getting paid to kill someone by a client whose identity he didn't know, controlled by a minder he didn't trust. Who might even be trying to kill him.

Last night he'd barely slept, lying in bed, parsing the words on Control's notepad. The Dry-Fart was the British PM, but David Cameron was already here, scheduled to celebrate Independence Day at the WW II Museum. Angela Merkel was the Bitch in Berlin, and Nicolas Sarkozy was the Poodle in Paris, but who the hell was Mona Lisa? And what did B-day mean? Birthday?

He'd looked up their birth dates on the Internet. Sarkozy was born in January, but Merkel's birthday was July 17, sixteen days from now.

Was she The Package? If not, who was?

Not knowing was maddening.

But he wasn't the only one with problems. He took out the wanted poster and showed it to Win.

"You better be careful or they'll catch you. I saw this in the French Quarter yesterday."

To his utter amazement, she beamed him a big smile.

"That settles it, Peter. No more shoplifting for me. You'll have to make me your sniper partner."

———

12:15 AM

Rosita stood in the recessed doorway facing the alley beside the Royale Hotel. It was late, but she needed a cigarette. If Mama caught her, she'd be in big trouble. She took out a Marlboro and stuck it in her mouth. Smoking made her feel grown up. She only smoked three or four a day, whenever she could find the time. She had not mastered it completely, but she was working on it. Soon she would be smoking half a pack a day, then a pack.

Imagining the horrified look on Mama's face if she found out her daughter was a smoker, she ducked back in the shadows and struck a match, puffing on the cigarette. Next year she would finish high school. Then she could give her nicotine habit the attention it deserved. And spend more time with her boyfriend. She'd met him at a youth group meeting one Sunday after Mass. He had a nice smile and wore tight shirts to show off his muscles. He was cute, too.

But not as cute as Peter. That was his first name. She'd found it in the register when Mama was away from the desk. His last name was long with many letters, impossible to pronounce. He'd been staying at the hotel several weeks, but she'd never talked to him.

When he talked to Mama, he spoke English without an accent, but he looked foreign. A world traveler perhaps, who liked sophisticated woman who smoked long, elegant cigarettes. Virginia Slims, not these Marlboros, which she'd stolen from one of the guest rooms.

A distant sound came to her from the far end of the alley. She exhaled, reflexively hiding the cigarette ember behind her. Something moved in the darkness. A trick of the light maybe. She was tired.

Who would be in the alley behind the Royale Hotel now, in the dead of night? Then she smiled. Was it the mysterious foreigner parking his Vespa in the alley?

She dropped the butt, stepped on it and stood there, waiting.

A minute passed. Maybe she had imagined it. It was just her wishful thinking, like Mama said. A fantasy-dream, like the movies she watched on TV.

The hotel owner allowed her and her sister and Mama to live in a small room on the first floor. Her father was hardly ever here, but he sent money to Mama every month. He picked strawberries in Texas in the summer, blueberries in Maine, and apples in Massachusetts in the fall. He was only two inches taller than she was, but very strong from all the hard work. Sometimes she couldn't remember what he looked like. But she was certain he wouldn't like it if he knew she was out here in the dead of night, smoking cigarettes.

Last year, she was a good girl, always behaving herself.

Last year she never would have smoked. But that was before she met Ramon and he took her her outside the church and taught her how to smoke and kissed her lips and pawed at her breasts, his manhood hard against her belly.

Her heart jolted at a distant sound. It wasn't a dream!

Peter was walking toward her, carrying the shiny black helmet he wore when he rode his Vespa.

Should she speak to him? Her English wasn't very good. If she spoke to him, he would know she was just an ignorant schoolgirl, the daughter of poverty-stricken immigrants.

Abandoning the idea, she opened the door and slipped inside.

Jamming the crumpled pack of cigarettes into her pocket, she sprayed Binaca in her mouth so Mama wouldn't smell smoke on her breath and tiptoed down the hall.

Why was Peter coming home so late, she wondered.

Did he have a girlfriend?

CHAPTER 23

SATURDAY July 2 – 11:05 AM

Frank set the photo of Aram Takvorian on the table in front of the waitress. "My colleague tells me you remember seeing this man in the tea room last Wednesday morning."

"Yes," said Bonnie, a stocky young woman with light brown hair, bright blue eyes and a friendly smile. "Because of his hair. White as the driven snow, it was. Very distinctive."

They were seated in the Hotel Cavendish marketing office, Frank's base of operations for his interviews. The manager had sent Bonnie to see him after she finished her shift in the tea room.

"But he didn't order anything," she said, "just sat down with the other man."

"What did the other man look like?"

Bonnie smiled. "A right handsome bloke he was, dark hair, hazel eyes. Wearing a splendid suit."

"Any idea how old he was?"

"Mmmm, somewhere in his thirties, I'd guess."

"Tall? Short?"

She hesitated. "He was sitting down when I served his tea. About as tall as you, maybe, but a bit huskier, broad shoulders. Not a Brit, though. Not from around here, either."

"What makes you say that?"

"He spoke American English well enough, but he looked …." Bonnie shrugged. "I don't know. Foreign somehow. His face had a certain look."

"Could you help us make a picture of him?"

Nodding enthusiastically, she said, "Like those TV shows when the coppers make a sketch of someone? I'd love to do that."

"Great," he said. "We've got someone who does that with a computer. I'll pick you up and take you to the station. But I need to call and find out when we can do it. It's a holiday weekend."

"I know," she said. "The fireworks last night were lovely."

"There'll be more tonight and Sunday, but the big show happens on Monday. Anything else you can tell me about the man you served in the tea room?"

"Well, he did seem … not nervous exactly. Uptight." Bonnie frowned. "Was he involved with the murders on the seventh floor? A pity if he was. He left a tenner for a four-dollar cuppa. That's a big tip, but I guess he was in a hurry. Didn't even wait for the bill."

In a hurry to take Aram Takvorian upstairs and kill him.

"Thanks, Bonnie. I'll call you later today or sometime tomorrow and tell you when we can have you work with our graphic artist. Have fun watching the fireworks."

After she left, he jotted notes in his spiral notebook. Six feet tall and husky, dark hair, hazel eyes, a man in a splendid suit who appeared foreign. Kelly was right. Women were far more observant than men, especially when it involved a handsome well-dressed man.

Maybe this was his lucky day. Next up, talk to Nicole Takvorian.

But when he went to the lobby, the manager button-holed him, frowning anxiously. "Detective Renzi, when will your blokes be done with the seventh floor? I need to get the contractors up there to renovate it as soon as possible."

"It shouldn't be much longer. I'll check with forensics and find out."

"Thank you, I'd appreciate it." The manager patted his brow with a handkerchief. "This whole thing has been a nightmare."

"Why? Are you getting a lot of cancellations?"

"No. Just the opposite. All the publicity has increased our bookings, but we're short on rooms. I had to book our seventh floor guests into other hotels. The Ritz let us have ten rooms, and the Marriott at Canal Place gave us another ten. But the bookings just keep coming. We can't let anyone stay on seven until we patch the bullet holes and replace the carpet."

The manager smiled for the first time. "The British PM and his entourage have taken all ten rooms on the sixth floor. Must be a dozen security men protecting him. Such a lovely man. I must admit it's rather exciting, having the PM stay here."

Provided someone doesn't try to kill him. "Bonnie was a big help. I need her to work with our graphic artist. Not at tea time," he hastened to add. "I don't want to leave you short handed."

"Thank you. She's our best waitress. We brought her over from our London hotel last year and she's been a joy. Everyone loves her."

"I need to talk to Nicole Takvorian. Is she still on the third floor?"

"Yes, but you'd best call first. She's a bit skittish."

Frank said he would. When he dialed her room on one of the hotel wall phones, she sounded more annoyed than skittish.

"Yes? What is it?"

"Hi Nicole. Detective Frank Renzi. I'm in the lobby. Okay if I come up and talk to you?"

"Of course. I'll be here."

Three minutes later, he tapped on her door and she let him in. She looked better than the last time he'd seen her. No bloodshot eyes, albeit with dark circles under them. No dark roots showing in her light brown hair. Wearing a blue silk dress with a short skirt today.

With practiced grace, she settled onto a two-cushion sofa with rose-colored upholstery and said, "Have you found the man who killed my husband?"

"Not yet, I'm afraid." He took a seat on a matching sofa, facing her over the low coffee table between them. "My boss told me about the Armenian Genocide. He said a lot of Turks still hate Armenians. Can you think of anyone specific who might have come here to kill him?"

"Of course! Erdogan's henchmen." Gazing at him, her eyes angry, she said, "I told you about the journalist they murdered in Istanbul. Assassinated in broad daylight!" She took a bottled water off the coffee table, handed it to him, then drank from her own.

He nodded his thanks and unscrewed the cap. "You said Aram knew a lot of journalists in Ankara. Maybe one of them dug up some dirt on Erdogan and gave it to him."

She sank back on the sofa and crossed her legs. Nice legs.

"Perhaps. But there are many criminals in the Turkish government. Erdogan is not the only one."

"What sort of criminals?"

"Shady financial deals. Assassinations. Political payoffs. Sex scandals." Nicole grimaced. "And all the while they pretend to be so pious. *Merde!*"

"If Aram had damaging information about someone, maybe he went to the *New York Times* to get publicity about it, and they blew him off."

An emphatic shake of her head. "No. Aram was not looking for publicity. He knew that would be dangerous."

"Okay. But if he had dirt on someone in the Turkish government, how would he use it?"

"To discredit the government. And Erdogan. He couldn't do that at home. The Turkish police wouldn't listen to him. The government-run newspapers wouldn't, either. He wanted to talk to someone in New York. The FBI, perhaps. Or the CIA."

Frank sipped some water, thinking it over. You didn't just dial up the CIA and make an appointment. Maybe Aram talked to an FBI agent in New York, got blown off, and decided to try a smaller FBI office, like the one in New Orleans. Frank made a mental note to find out if Aram had contacted them, or the FBI office in New York.

"I must go to the French consulate," Nicole said. "To see about my visa."

"Kelly can take you. But their offices are closed for the holiday, won't be open until Tuesday."

With a faint smile, she said, "You Americans, so enchanted with your Independence Day. So much celebration."

Frank laughed. "New Orleans is a celebration kind of town. The afternoon parades will go right past the hotel. And you'll be able to see the fireworks from here at night."

Her expression grew somber. "I don't like parades. In most countries, parades are just an excuse to show off their military might. Tanks and soldiers and big guns. Saber-rattling for the TV cameras. I got sick of watching what passes for news on television here and sent someone out to buy these." She took two newspapers off the coffee table and gave them to him, *Le Monde* in French, the *International Herald Tribune* in English.

A headline in the *Herald Tribune* caught his eye. **Erdogan slams French President over EU bid.**

"What's this about?" he said, tapping the article.

"Erdogan hates Sarkozy. For decades the Turkish government has been trying to get Turkey into the European Union. Sarkozy is against this." Nicole smiled. "So is Angela."

"Angela?"

"Angela Merkel, the German Chancellor. She and Sarkozy want to keep them out."

Frank's heart sped up. The president of France and the Chancellor of Germany. Two countries with embassies in New Orleans. "Would you mind if I borrowed these? Just for today."

Nicole waved a hand. "Keep them. I will send someone out to get more tomorrow."

"If you think of anything important, call my cellphone. I'll ask Kelly if she can take you to the French Embassy on Tuesday. Maybe you two can have dinner tonight."

"Kelly is a nice person, very ... *sympathique* with women's issues. But I like having dinner with a man." Smiling flirtatiously, she said, "Perhaps you and I can have dinner some night."

Amused, he stifled a smile. Kelly claimed that women were drawn to him because of his dark penetrating eyes and his equally dark aura. He was a cop, a man who took risks. Danger personified.

Was that why Nicole found Aram attractive? Because he courted danger?

"Thanks for the newspapers, Nicole. My French isn't great, so I might ask for a translation if I find anything interesting."

"I am happy to help you with this. But don't look for anything exciting in *Le Monde*. It is a very staid publication." Adding with a faint smile, "*Le Parisien* is much more ... spicy."

―――――

4:20 PM

After the darkness of the Prytania Theater, the sun was so bright it hurt her eyes. Peter wanted to see a movie, so they'd checked the listings and discovered they both loved crime thrillers. She wanted to see *The Tourist*. Johnny Depp was in it. When she was a teenager she thought he was the sexiest man alive.

But Johnny Depp didn't pick her up and carry her into her bedroom and rip off her clothes and put his cock inside her and fuck her brains out and make her come and come and come. Johnny Depp was a teen fantasy, probably wouldn't look at her twice.

And he wasn't a sniper like Peter.

When she told Peter she liked Johnny Depp, he seemed annoyed. "It's a stupid movie, and it's playing at Canal Place. We need to stay away from the French Quarter. Let's go see *The Town*."

She didn't want to argue so they hopped on Peter's Vespa and went to the theater on Prytania Street. He bought them a big bucket of popcorn and put his arm around her while they watched the movie. And smiled when she told him he looked like Ben Affleck.

Which he did, sort of.

But watching Ben Affleck didn't make her crotch wet like Peter.

As they walked along the sidewalk, hand in hand, she said "Want to go see where I play paintball?" Carlos had called her this morning to see if she was going, but she'd blown him off.

"You play paintball?" Peter said, gazing down at her with his sexy bedroom eyes.

"Most every Saturday. But not today. I'd rather spend time with you."

That got her a smile. "I'm hungry. Let's get a burger. There's a place near here. We can walk."

"Okay," she said. "I'm glad we saw *The Town,* but the ending was sort of sad. Do you think he ever saw his girlfriend again?"

Peter squeezed her hand and said, still smiling at her, "Definitely. When I leave here after my job is finished, maybe I'll take you with me."

Her heart thumped her ribs. Peter wanted her with him! He was in love with her! She wanted to jump for joy, but she had to be cool.

"What's the job? Will you be done soon?"

He took her to a sidewalk bench, sat her down and gazed into her eyes. "I can't talk about it. But when I'm done, I might take you to Brussels and show you the Mannequin Pis."

She threw her arms around him. "You make me so happy, Peter. Will we live in Brussels?"

His expression changed and his smile disappeared. Silently, he stared off into the distance. After a while, he said, "I'll take you to other cities, too. You'll love Paris, the most romantic city on the planet." He kissed her lips. "Lots of ritzy shops, I might even let you shoplift some swag."

"But I want to be a sniper like you. And be your partner." *And live with you in Brussels.*

He kissed her again. "Let's go get that burger."

CHAPTER 24

SUNDAY July 3 – 3:45 PM

Tense and hyper-alert, Frank paced the cavernous lobby of the Louisiana Memorial Pavilion inside the World War II Museum. Four stories high, the lobby held a stunning exhibit of WW II military might. Warplanes hung from steel girders, including a P-40 Warhawk, a P-51C Mustang and a huge B-17E Flying Fortress bomber dubbed "My Gal Sal." Below them, Frank passed Sherman tanks, amphibian jeeps, troop carriers and a Higgins Landing Craft, built by New Orleans's own Andrew Higgins, to ferry solders from their ships to the beaches on D-Day more than six decades ago.

Earlier he'd watched a parade of WW II veterans enter the auditorium, some in wheelchairs, hooked up to oxygen tanks; others walked slowly, using canes, all of them in their eighties at least, proudly wearing uniforms decorated with multi-colored ribbons and awards.

Now British Prime Minister David Cameron was speaking inside an auditorium adjacent to the foyer, an event to commemorate American and British collaboration during WW II.

Museum visitors had passed through metal detectors at the entrance. Outside, dozens of NOPD officers were regulating traffic. Others in plain clothes were inside, equipped with comm-packs like Frank. Kelly was down the hall, stationed at an emergency exit near the stage door to the auditorium. Earlier she had reported that Bulldog and his friends had entered the building. Code for David Cameron and his security detail.

The streets around the museum were one-way, and NOPD officers were stationed at each intersection to halt traffic, allowing Cameron and his security team to arrive and depart without encountering other vehicles. At no time would his caravan pass the parking garage a half block north on Magazine Street, a prime location for the Sniper, if he was gunning for Cameron.

When the ceremony ended, traffic would be halted on every street around the museum. Cameron and his security team would then leave through the emergency exit near the stage door, get in their vehicles and drive away.

The plan seemed foolproof, but Frank was all too aware that something could screw up the best laid plans. He'd seen it happen.

At this point he wasn't positive Cameron was the Sniper's VIP target, but there was no way to tell. Better to be prepared, than not.

He heard a smattering of applause and checked his watch. 3:55. Scheduled to end at four o'clock, the event was winding down. He spoke into his wrist mic, "Applause in the auditorium. Stay alert. Traffic patrol officers, be ready to stop all vehicles."

To begin the program, the combined Tulane and Loyola University bands had played the Star Spangled Banner, followed by "God Save the Queen," the British National Anthem. Now, they began playing "Stars and Stripes Forever," signaling the end of the program.

"Stars and Stripes." Kelly's voice in his earpiece. "Clear the traffic on all streets."

"Copy that," said a male voice, echoed by several others.

Frank signaled the NOPD cop stationed at the auditorium doors to keep them closed and headed for the emergency exit, trotting down a wide corridor. At the far end, Kelly stood beside the exit, her eyes fixed on the backstage door. As Frank reached her, the door opened and two British security men in suits came through the door, looked around and said, "Clear."

Wearing a broad smile, clearly pleased with the event, Prime Minister Cameron stepped through the door, followed by more security agents and the brassy sounds of the Sousa march.

"Don't go out yet," Frank said to the lead security man. "Let me check the area first."

Grim-faced and hard-eyed, the man said, "Do it."

He stepped outside onto a wide cement sidewalk. Momentarily blinded by the sun, he blinked, squinting at four SUVs idling at the curb twenty feet from the door, the only vehicles on Andrew Higgins way. The exit strategy called for Cameron's caravan to drive along Andrew Higgins Way to Camp Street and turn right. Their path cleared by NOPD police, the caravan would zoom up a ramp to the highway and take Cameron to the Hotel Cavendish.

Frank looked to his left. An NOPD patrol officer raised his hand, signaling to him that vehicles were stopped on Magazine Street. In his earpiece, the other traffic officers reported in.

"Traffic stopped on Camp."

"No traffic on Andrew Higgins Drive."

"Good to go," Frank said into his mic.

The emergency exit door opened and two of Cameron's security agents came outside.

Everything seemed fine, until Frank heard a strange buzzing noise. It sounded like a swarm of bees. He looked left, toward Magazine Street. An instant later a moped come around the corner.

The hairs on the nape of his neck prickled.

The traffic cop on the corner yelled, "Stop!"

But the moped kept coming.

The sound of the engine grew louder, a high-pitched whine. Now the sultry air seemed to crackle with the threat of danger.

He's going to kill Cameron, Frank thought.

Time seemed to stand still as his mind rapidly processed details. Small and compact, the moped's lime-green frame had a big headlight centered between the handlebars, and rear-view mirrors sprouted from it on either side. It wasn't going very fast, and the traffic cop was running behind it, trying to catch up.

The driver wore faded bluejeans, a black T-shirt and a shiny black helmet. A black face-guard hid most of the his face, but reddish stubble on his jaw indicated the driver was a man, a rather small one, but hunched over the handlebars with single-minded intensity, the faceless man seemed to know exactly what he was going to do.

His assessment took less than three seconds. *Do something or David Cameron will die.* "Abort, abort!" he yelled into his mic.

But Cameron and his team had already come out the door of the museum. Black-suited men standing outside the SUVs opened the passenger-side doors.

Frank pulled out the SIG P250 wedged in the small of his back, less than five inches long, weighing less than two pounds fully loaded, which it was.

The moped was only twenty yards away now, but the cop was chasing him, his eyes focused on the driver, his long legs pumping.

Shoot at the moped driver, I might hit the cop, Frank thought.

What happened next took only ten seconds, but it felt like an eternity. Aware the cop was chasing him, the driver glanced over his shoulder. The moped sideswiped a round two-foot-high cement pillar ten feet to Frank's left.

The driver lost control and the moped tipped over, dumping him onto the cement sidewalk, its tires whirling, its engine whining.

Undeterred, the driver jumped up and ran at Cameron, his mouth open exposing missing teeth, screaming, "You no-good fucker! Cancel my benefits and my health insurance!"

Someone yelled, "Gun!"

Cameron's security team pushed him down on the sidewalk and piled on top of him, shielding the PM with their bodies.

Frank charged at the driver, but the patrol cop reached him first and executed a flying tackle like an NFL lineman, knocking the driver to the ground. His head hit the pavement and his helmet flew off, exposing carrot-red hair.

Clenched in his right hand was a gun.

The gun went off, a loud bang. It was a wild shot that hit nothing.

Lying on his back, the driver screamed obscenities at the Prime Minister, still holding the gun.

"Drop the gun!" Frank shouted and jumped on him, but the agitated driver swung his arm and hit the traffic cop's face with the gun. The cop reeled back, momentarily losing his grip on the man.

Frank saw the would-be-assassin's finger go for the trigger.

Grasping his wrist with both hands, Frank twisted it and shouted, "Drop the gun, drop the gun!"

"Fuck you, arsehole!"

He bent back the man's wrist, twisted it hard and felt something snap. The man's fingers went limp and the gun fell to the cement.

"You broke my wrist, motherfucker!"

Breathing hard, Frank inhaled the stench of the man's body, vaguely aware of loud voices, shouts from Cameron's security team, and the blip of a police car siren. Beneath him, the shooter continued to fight, kicking his legs. Struggling to subdue him, Frank said to the patrol cop, "You got flex-ties? We need to button him up."

The cop pulled out plastic zip-ties and secured the man's wrists, but he kept kicking his legs. Frank grabbed his chin and said, "Stay still, asshole, or we'll knock you out."

Oddly the man quieted immediately. His eyes closed and his body went slack.

"Good job," he said to the patrol cop, whose face was ashen. "You took him down."

"Yeah, but you got the gun." Breathing hard, the cop shook his head. "Jesus, an assassin on a moped? What the fuck is that?"

They both started laughing, a nervous reaction to their heart-stopping fear moments ago.

Then a voice said, "Anybody hurt?"

Frank looked up. Kelly stood there, frowning at the shooter who lay still and quiet on the sidewalk.

"No," Frank said, gesturing at the patrol cop. "This guy took him down and I got the gun away from him and told him to shut the fuck up. Is Cameron okay?"

"He's fine," Kelly said. "They're already on the highway."

"Good. Let's get this asshole down to the District-Eight station so we can talk to him."

———

Paris, France – 11:20 PM

Standing at the window, dwarfed by the six-foot-six Security Chief, Henri regarded the mob of protesters outside the president's residence, their chants, though faint, penetrating the thick glass.

"Even on a Sunday they cannot be quiet!" Henri said.

"Sunday means nothing to these Muslims," said the Chief. "They said their prayers at the mosques on Friday." Grimacing, he said, "No car fires yet. Last night there were two."

"Did you see what Erdogan said about Sarkozy on EuroNews?"

"Nothing good, I imagine. He's worse than the lot outside," the chief said, gesturing at the protesters. "They throw rocks and Molotov cocktails. Erdogan makes anyone who disagrees with him disappear. What's he complaining about now?"

"Turkey's current attempt to join the European Union. Turkey's dream for a half century, or so Erdogan says. He also says the EU is a Christian club and its members are Islamophobic, especially President Sarkozy, who does everything in his power to keep them out."

"He's not the only one," said the Chief, frowning now. "What about the Armenians?"

"When the interviewer asked about the Turkish-Armenian protocols, Erdogan claimed that Turkey has fulfilled their obligations." Henri shrugged. "This means nothing, of course. Many Turks will never admit the Armenian genocide ever happened. Erdogan cannot control this."

"Perhaps not, but he is not a man to be trifled with." The Chief yawned. "Another late night tomorrow. Royal Flush may disagree with Washington on the Turkey-EU issue, but he loves the Americans. He will attend a fireworks display in their honor at the Eiffel Tower tomorrow."

"To celebrate the American Independence Day," Henri said. "And he has decided to visit New Orleans after all. Next Sunday they will hold a ceremony at the World War Two Museum, in honor of Bastille Day. The French Ambassador has invited him to stay at his residence."

Visibly irate, his cheeks reddening, the Chief said, "Why am I the last to know this? We have warned him not to go there, but his Royal-Flush-Highness marches to his own tune. Even his closest advisers tread carefully to avoid provoking his displeasure. Is Mona Lisa going?"

"No." Henri smiled. "Which means I might get a chance to see some of the sights. We fly there on Friday, fly back on Monday. I have already searched the Internet. I want to sample one of these beignets, little squares of fried dough covered with powdered sugar."

"You and your sweet tooth." The Security Chief wrinkled his nose in disdain. "What sort of wines do they have?"

"You'd be surprised. Some American wines are quite good and the food is outstanding. There is a fine restaurant in Jackson Square that serves Creole cuisine. Muriel's Restaurant. On the second floor, there is a séance room where a voodoo priestess used to do Tarot readings years ago."

Regarding him with somber eyes, the Chief said, "Get your Tarot reading before you leave, Henri, and forget sightseeing. The president has many enemies. Not all of them are in France."

CHAPTER 25

7: 20 PM

Frank pushed his plate aside and drank some coffee. Unlike his previous visits, he and Vobitch were seated at the dining room table, enjoying home-made apple pie and coffee, courtesy of Juliana. He had a million things to do, but he knew Vobitch hated being out of the loop. Not only that, he valued Vobitch's input. No sign of the Sniper, an assassination attempt on the British Prime Minister, he could use some strategic suggestions.

"Great pie," he said, nodding at Vobitch's plate, empty but for a few crumbs. "Did you take a walk before dinner?"

Vobitch iced him with a look. "I had to or Juliana said no pie." He sipped his coffee and said, "So who the hell is this guy at the museum, some nutcase?"

"Definitely. Swearing a blue streak, smelled like a pigsty, pretty much incoherent when we interviewed him, ranting at the PM for cutting his welfare benefits. Cameron's security chief told me Cameron instituted strict austerity measures last year, because of the financial crisis. He also said he checked with British Intelligence. They told him the guy's been in and out of institutions for years, some kind of mental illness."

"Off his meds," Vobitch said.

"Big time."

"What have you got so far?"

"Well, he's not the Sniper. William Wiggins, age 28, landed at the airport two hours after Prime Minister Cameron arrived Friday night, cleared Customs on a UK passport."

"Where did he go after he landed?"

"Good question. We checked the knapsack strapped to the moped, found his passport and a receipt for the moped but no credit cards, no evidence he checked into a hotel, no keys or key cards. But he managed to get a Glock 9mm somewhere, probably on the street. No extra ammo."

"Figured if he got close enough to the PM, he wouldn't need any."

"Seems like it. And no return plane ticket."

Vobitch pursed his lips. "Maybe this was a suicide-by-cop deal. Did he lawyer up?"

"No. Never even mentioned it. The Brits want to extradite him, fly him back to London. Both his parents are deceased, but he's got an older sister living in New Zealand. Two years ago she was appointed his legal guardian. They faxed her the papers, she signed them and faxed them back."

Vobitch made a dust-off motion with his hands. "No more Moped Killer."

"That's what the patrol cop called him, but it got me thinking. What if the Sniper uses a motor bike to get away?"

"Jesus Christ!" Vobitch said, staring at him. "Better than a car. Easy to maneuver."

"Exactly. Cameron will stay at the Hotel Cavendish until his security team takes him to the airport tomorrow for an early flight. If he was the Sniper's VIP target, the mission failed."

"I'm not convinced he was the target." Vobitch ran a hand over his mane of silvery hair. "You know what they said after Watergate. Follow the money. If two sets of killers were after the Armenian, dollars to donuts, he had something they wanted. Focus on the Armenian, Frank. The Sniper was after him."

"We're working on it." His cellphone rang. He checked the ID, waved a wait-a-minute finger at Vobitch and answered. "Hey Kenyon, you get anything?"

Kenyon's bass voice rumbled into his ear. "Not a helluva lot. When I showed the moped rental clerk the receipt, he remembered Wiggins, said he stank to high heaven. Wiggins paid cash for the rental, booked it for two days. Needless to say he never returned it, cuz it's in the NOPD evidence garage. I didn't mention what Wiggins was up to, but the clerk's no dummy. He'll see it on the news. I showed him the Sniper composite the waitress helped us with, asked if he'd been there to rent a bike. The clerk didn't recognize him, but there's at least a dozen places around here that rent them."

"Damn! We better check them, too, but not tonight. Thanks for doing the legwork. Go get some sleep. We'll figure it out tomorrow."

He shut his cellphone and said to Vobitch, "Kenyon talked to the clerk that rented him the moped. When he showed him our likeness of the Sniper, the clerk didn't recognize him, but there are a lot of other places that rent them."

"Christ, now we're looking for guys riding motor bikes?"

"Who looks like our picture of the Sniper, yeah," Frank said, frustrated that he didn't have more to tell him. "I'm in close contact with your D-5 and D-1 detectives, and Kelly's keeping me posted on what the D-6 detectives are doing. David's canvasing the hotels on Canal Street as we speak, checking out male guests who've been staying there since the first of June."

"Fine, but if he's got a motorbike—and now that you mention it, that seems like a good bet—you might be wasting your time. He could be anywhere." Vobitch drank some coffee. "Six days since he shot Kimba Davis. He could shoot someone else tomorrow."

Painfully aware that this was true, Frank felt a mounting sense of dread. Urgency trumped by helplessness. "The Super beefed up security for the Fourth of July events, but no way in hell can we stop him from getting on a roof somewhere."

Vobitch grimaced. "A security nightmare. A road race tomorrow plus three parades with dozens of floats. Hundreds of tall buildings border the parade routes and the road race. Shoot one of the runners or someone on a parade float, spectators scatter, he could pick off three or four more."

"And don't forget the fireworks, tonight and tomorrow. It will be dark, but every time one goes off the sky will light up like a thousand-watt flashbulb. Hundreds of spectators watching, most of them with kids? They'll be ducks in a shooting gallery."

Vobitch clenched his jaw, his eyes full of fury. "So will all the cops there to protect them. And we got no way to stop the motherfucker."

———

8:35 PM

Win held Peter's hand as they strolled through Woldenberg Park, happier than she'd ever been in her whole life. The park ran alongside the Mississippi River in the French Quarter from Canal Street to Saint Philip, ten blocks of open space with jogging paths. But no one was jogging now. After a spectacular sunset, the air remained hot and humid, the moon a yellow disc in the darkening sky. The park was jammed with a zillion people waiting for the fireworks to begin.

A lot of cops were here, too. Was this a kick or what! The cops were hunting for both of them, didn't have a clue how to find them.

When Peter insisted they wear a disguise, she'd suggested they go as hippies. Recalling pictures of Mother in her outfits from the '70s, she knew exactly what to do. She'd fashioned her long auburn wig into a ponytail for Peter to wear. She had on her blonde wig, the one that hung to her waist, a white sports bra that exposed her midriff, and an emerald green skirt that fell to her ankles.

Peter loved the sports bra. It gave him an excuse to caress her bare shoulders and kiss her midriff. She liked it too. The breeze off the river felt good against her bare skin. Peter was wearing bell-bottom jeans and a sleeveless vest, exposing his curly chest hair. To complete the hippie look, they wore chains around their necks with round peace signs dangling from them.

Before they went through the checkpoint to enter the park, Peter had told her to act like they were young lovers, maybe do some smooching right before they got to the cop. It worked like a charm. The cop had barely looked at them and waved them through.

She was dying for a cigarette, but Peter didn't like it when she smoked. He said it made her mouth taste awful.

To take her mind off it, she said, "This is so much fun, Peter. Let's swap stories. What was the most fun you ever had ..." She batted her eyes at him. "Before we had sex."

He leaned down to kiss her. "Before I had sex with you? Hmm, let me think about that." His dark eyebrows knit together in a frown. Then he smiled. "The parrot, I guess. After we moved to London, I wanted a pet. Mum said we couldn't afford a dog or a cat, but maybe I could have a bird. So she took me to a pet store, thinking I'd choose a canary or something, but they had this gorgeous African Gray parrot with big yellow eyes. After a bit of pleading on my part, Mum let me get it."

"Uh-huh," she said. "So what was the fun part? Feeding it?"

Peter laughed. "Hell no! Teaching him to curse! I'd heard all these naughty words when I hung out at my Dad's bike store. *Fucker. Bloody hell! Bollocks!* He learned those pretty quick, so I taught him whole phrases. *Bugger off twat-face. You sodding fucknugget. Fuckety Bye-bye.*"

She cracked up laughing, partly from the silly swears, partly from the gleeful look on Peter's face as he said them. "What did your Mum think when the parrot said fucknugget?"

"Yeah, well, at first she didn't like it, but after a bit she got to thinking it was funny, too. But when her flute students came, she made me put a towel over Guv's cage."

"Was that his name? Guv?"

"Right. Put a towel over his cage, Guv thought it was time to go to sleep."

"How long did you have him?"

"Several years. After I joined the Army, Mum took care of him for a while, but he got sick and died. Mum said he was pining for me." Peter shrugged. "I think it was just old age. Okay, now it's your turn. What was the most fun you ever had—"

"Before I had sex with you?" she said, hugging him close to kiss his bare chest.

Clearly pleased, he smiled and his hazel eyes lit up. "Keep saying things like that, I won't let you watch the fireworks, I'll take you home and put you to bed."

"Without my supper?" she said, teasing him.

He kissed her lips and said, "Tell me your story."

"When I was six Dad took me to an amusement park. It was summertime and Mother was away at one of her stupid peace-rallies. Dad took me on the roller coaster. I can still remember how big it was." She made her eyes go wide. "Bigger than your cock, even."

He shook his head. "Yeah, yeah, stop putting me on."

"When we went down the first hill, I almost wet my pants! Jesus, what a rush! But Dad put his arm around me and started laughing, and the next time I wasn't scared at all. Pretty soon I was getting a rush every time we climbed up the big steep hill."

Peter nodded. "The anticipation."

"Exactly! And then, zoom down the other side! It was so much fun. I coaxed Dad into taking me for two more rides. "

"You miss your Dad, don't you."

She heaved a sigh. "Sometimes. He's a great guy. You'd like him."

Peter didn't say anything, gazing at her, blank-faced. After a moment, he said, "There's a huge Ferris Wheel in London called the London Eye. It's on the South Bank of the Thames River. When we go there, I'll take you for a ride on it." Smiling at her now.

"I can't wait!" She pulled him close and kissed him. "When do we leave?"

His smile disappeared. "After I finish the job."

"You still don't know when it will be?"

His mouth quirked in annoyance. "No. My employer's giving me a hard time."

"Because I shot the policewoman?"

"No. There are other complications."

"Like what?"

"I told you. Someone shot at me." Frowning at her now.

"Okay," she said, and squeezed his hand. But her fabulous mood had turned to shit. Because of Peter, and his mercurial moods. One minute he seemed happy, an instant later he was gloomy and grim.

Trying to reassure herself, she thought, *It's because of the job.* Once he finished the job, they'd get on a plane and fly to Europe and live happily every after.

A dream she desperately wanted to come true.

After the movie the other day, he'd said he would take her to Brussels to see the Manikin Pis. But when she asked him if they would live in Brussels, he didn't answer, just stared off into the distance, like he was watching his own private movie.

A movie he didn't want to talk about.

She heard a faint pop, looked up at the sky and realized the fireworks had begun. Good. After the fireworks she'd take Peter back to her apartment, take him to bed and convince him that they were soulmates, like he said.

Think positive and your dreams will come true.

CHAPTER 26

MONDAY, July 4 – 2:30 PM

In no hurry to begin her chores, Rosita strolled down the alley alongside the Hotel Royale. It didn't seem fair that she had to work on a holiday. Her girlfriends were still at the mall. But later after she finished her work, Ramon was taking her to watch the fireworks tonight at Woldenberg Park. That would be fun.

Peter's Vespa wasn't parked in the alley today. Maybe he'd finished whatever he was doing here and checked out. Too bad.

Such an intriguing man: tall, dark-haired and mysterious.

Handsome, too. She loved his eyes.

What sort of work did he do? Something exciting, probably. Maybe he wrote stories for movies or TV shows. Plenty of ideas for that in New Orleans. Then again, he seemed standoffish. Maybe he was a spy or a terrorist. Or a serial killer! She'd seen shows about them on TV. But she was always imagining things.

That's what Mama said. "You imagine things, Rosita."

She opened the employee entrance door and went in the lobby. Her mother was behind the registration desk. Without looking up, Mama said, "Get busy with your housekeeping chores."

She rolled her eyes and pouted.

"Don't give me that look," Mama said, frowning at her.

Sulking, Rosita loaded the linen cart with clean towels and sheets and wheeled it to the elevator. It took forever to clean the rooms, more than two hours just to finish the rooms on the first three floors.

But the fifth floor would be easy. Only one room was occupied, and the man was never there in the daytime. She went in the room and tuned in a soap opera on the TV, glancing at it now and then as she changed the sheets.

In the bathroom, she replaced the used towels and restocked the miniature shampoos and soaps. She combed her long dark hair with her fingers. Almost done. In the bedroom, she ran a feather duster over the furniture and glanced at the television set. The girl in the soap opera was crying, silently, because the sound was muted. Her boyfriend took her by the shoulders and shook her.

Rosita clucked her tongue. Guys didn't understand women.

They were into sports, and rock and roll, and beer. And big tits, like Ramon.

She shut off the TV, wheeled the cart to the elevator and rode it up to the top floor. Only two rooms on Six needed cleaning. Then she could do as she pleased until dinner. A half pack of cigarettes was hidden beneath her mattress. Already feeling the urge to smoke, she went to room 602, where the intriguing mystery man had been staying for several weeks.

She rapped twice on the door. "Housekeeping," she called.

No response. Of course not. Peter wasn't there. His Vespa was gone. She let herself in with the passkey and smiled. He hadn't checked out. A black leather gym bag was in the corner near the desk. Peter had decided to stay for another day, at least.

The bed was unmade but neat, the coverlet pulled up over the bed-clothes and pillows. When she woke up in the morning, her sheets were always in a tangle. Her sister, who slept in the top bunk, often complained about her tossing and turning. But Peter seemed to sleep soundly. Either that or he was sleeping somewhere else.

With his girlfriend maybe. She changed the sheets and went in the bathroom. A bath towel hung from the metal rack beside the shower. She replaced it with a fresh one, then made a quick circuit of the bedroom, brandishing the feather duster. Ready to leave, she looked at the gym bag in the corner. Was he a writer? Or a spy?

She glanced around as if someone might be watching, moved quickly and stealthily to the bag, knelt beside it and reached for the zipper.

You shouldn't do this.

That's what she always thought when she went through a guest's luggage. Not that she did it often. But she'd done it once or twice be-fore, with guests she was far less curious about.

She opened the bag, mindful of how the contents were arranged, so he wouldn't know she'd been snooping. On top was a manila folder and a Canadian passport. She opened the passport. It belonged to Petra Mirotic. But the photo was of Peter, wearing glasses. Strange.

Below the manila folder were clothes, all of them black: several pairs of pants, T-shirts, and a sweatshirt. Below the sweatshirt some-thing glinted, something metallic. She reached for it.

And realized someone was standing behind her.

Peter had entered the room without a sound, looking at her now with cold eyes.

She rose to her feet, feeling lightheaded, her legs weak and wobbly.

"S-s-sorry," she stammered. "*La cucarachas* ... I try to make sure your bag ..."

He kept looking at her.

"But ees okay," she finished lamely. "I'll be going now."

She moved toward the door, clutching her chest, her heart pounding. Judging by the look in his eyes, she had the feeling this man, the mystery man who might be a spy or a terrorist or a serial killer, might hurt her. She hurried out the door and set off down the hall.

And remembered the cart.

She stopped and turned. The cart was still outside Peter's room.

He stood there, looking at her. Even from here she could see the anger in his eyes.

She went back to the room and mustered a sheepish smile. "Forgot my cart," she said.

He said nothing.

She turned the cart and pushed it down the hall, resisting the urge to glance over her shoulder. She could feel his eyes burning into her back. When she reached the elevator, she pushed the call button.

The doors seemed to take forever to open.

———

He watched the girl push the cart into the elevator. She was pretty —large dark eyes, long dark hair—and petite, barely five-two, with big tits. Even her maid uniform couldn't hide the grapefruit-sized bulges. But her simpering smile had not dispelled his anger.

He stepped back into the room, shut the door and rotated his neck in a circle to ease the tension in his neck and shoulders. Two deep breaths down to his diaphragm allowed him to think more clearly. She was just a teenager, doing a tedious job. She snooped as a matter of course, out of boredom. She suspected nothing.

But she had seen his face. What if she saw the composite the cops had put on TV and recognized him?

Had she seen the Canadian passport with his photograph and a different name in his bag? Over the course of many years, tens of thousands of blank passports had been reported stolen in Belgium.

In fact, they had been sold by civil servants on the take, some at the Belgian consulate in Strasbourg, France; others at the Belgian consulate in The Hague, Holland. His emergency passport was in his pocket, a Belgian passport with his likeness and real name.

He never went anywhere without it. But the passport wasn't his biggest concern. The girl had a passkey which meant she could come in his room whenever he was out.

He sat on the bed and massaged his eyes. *You should have killed her.*

But that would have set off red flags. The cops would pounce on a murder in another Canal Street hotel like hounds on a rabbit, no doubt about that.

Bollocks! How could this happen when he was so close to completing his assignment?

Last night he'd figured out what B-day meant. Not *birthday*, Bastille Day, the fourteenth of July, ten days from now. Which meant The Package had to be French President Nicolas Sarkozy.

Not that his fucking minder had told him this. Jesus! How long was he going to wait? Knowing the target's identity was one thing. Knowing when and where to kill him was crucial, essential Intel that he needed in order to prepare.

He sprawled out on the bed and started Shostakovitch's Fifth Symphony in his mind, a trick he'd learned from his mum. Listen to a piece of music enough times, it became a part of you, lying dormant in your mind until you called up the memory and got it going.

He felt the tension drain away. No cause for alarm. The girl was just a maid, a teenager who barely spoke English. After he checked out, she wouldn't give him another thought.

And he still had the flash drive. He didn't know what was on it, but it had to be important. Why else would Control have him kill the Armenian to get it? But he didn't trust his employers. That's why he'd kept the flash drive, to make sure they didn't double-cross him.

The Russians who'd shot at him inside the Hotel Cavendish were after the flash drive, too, but they didn't know where he was staying. Whenever he was out and about, he was careful to maintain situational awareness to make sure no one was following him.

He shut off the music in his mind and focused on the assignment. He felt certain Sarkozy was his target, but he needed to prepare. Sarkozy would come with an experienced security team. Bastille Day was ten days away. Soon his job would be over.

Will we live in Brussels? Visualizing the joyful expression on Win's face as she uttered the words filled him with guilt.

Last night after the fireworks he'd spent two glorious hours in bed with her. The sex kept getting better and better, more exquisite each time. He didn't want to think about leaving her. In fact, after the second time they made love, he had wrapped his arm around her, holding her close, debating with himself. She wanted them to be partners. A week ago the very idea seemed absurd, but last night, lying in bed with her, relaxed and happy, it was enormously appealing.

But that was then, this was now. In the cold light of day, alone in his hotel room, he knew the problems this would create. His employers wouldn't allow it; he would have to leave Win behind when he went on assignments; she would get bored ...

He sat up and flexed his shoulders.

Bottom line, it just wouldn't work. But one thing was certain: he had to find another place to stay, someplace his employers didn't know about. Not at Win's place. He didn't want to risk involving her, putting her in danger. After he finished the job, he'd collect his pay, hand over the flash drive and fly back to Europe.

Stealthy as a mouse approaching cheese in a mousetrap, guilt crept into his mind. He'd promised to take Win for a ride on the London Eye. Maybe he would. It didn't mean she was going to live with him. Why not celebrate for a few days with Win?

After a god-awful job like this, he deserved it.

————

6:15 PM

Control sat at the table in the breakfast nook, reading today's *Times-Picayune* as he snacked on the frozen pizza he'd cooked. He preferred to eat his main meal for lunch rather than go out at night.

He turned a page and got the shock of his life. There at the top was a color composite of the Sniper's face. Jesus, it looked just like him! Should he call and warn him?

No. The bugger was smart enough to monitor the news. Why ask for trouble? He was a cold-blooded killer, a force to be reckoned with, like a loaded gun aimed at your head. Trained as a sniper by the British Army, he had killed many men in Iraq. Since 2006, he had killed many others for Zenith Intelligence, usually with his sniper rifle, but not always.

On certain assignments, he'd killed people with his bare hands.

Control shuddered and pushed his pizza aside. The very thought of food made him queasy.

The trill of the telephone came from down the hall. Damn it to bloody hell! It had to be the Boss.

He hurried to his office and answered the call.

"The Package will arrive on Friday," said the Boss. "He intends to fly back to Paris on Monday."

Control didn't dare ask for a name. He heard the Boss light a cigarette and waited, picturing him seated at his desk, his brutish face a mask of vindictive cruelty.

"Do I need to tell you who it is?" In addition to his penchant for nicknames, the Boss loved to play guessing games.

His heart fluttered in his chest. He assumed the Package was French President Nickolas Sarkozy. Who else in Paris would warrant such an expensive operation?

He wiped his sweaty palms on his trousers. "The Poodle in Paris?"

"Good guess. He will stay at the French Consul's residence across the street from where your Helper shot the runner. Viktor will help us complete our mission."

"Viktor?" Control said, frowning. "Who is Viktor?"

He heard the Boss light a cigarette. "He knows how to handle these matters."

"What sort of matters?"

"Cleanup."

Control shuddered. He knew what that meant.

"On Sunday July 10, the Poodle will attend a Bastille Day celebration at the World War II Museum. After it is over he will return to the Consul's residence." *Ack-ack,* an explosive cough.

The Boss cleared his throat. "Tell your Helper to be in position on the roof where he shot the runner, so that he can kill him. Viktor will be nearby on another roof. Once Viktor is certain the Poodle is dead, he will terminate your Helper."

CHAPTER 27

TUESDAY July 5 – 12:10 PM

Relieved that his infernal daily telephone dance with Control was over, he pocketed his cellphone. Control had been more abrupt than usual. Maybe he was in a hurry to go out for lunch. That's where he was going, his emergency passport was in his pocket, plenty of cash in his wallet. What should he have, seafood or a steak?

Contemplating where to eat, he opened the door. Before he could step into the hallway, a hulking man in a dark suit put a meaty hand on his chest and shoved him into his room.

"Where is the flash drive?"

Instantly, he instinctively swung as hard as he could, a powerful right that slammed into the man's sloping forehead. That should have ended it, but the man didn't go down. His hand hurt like hell, but he punched him again, a solid right to the nose, and felt bone crunch. The man grunted and came at him like a wild animal, uttering a guttural sound, claw-like fingers going for his eyes.

Like a matador avoiding a bull intent on goring him, he dodged away. His attacker smiled, as if this were mere child's play.

"You want to be a hero? Don't bother. I'm just the errand boy. Where is the flash drive?"

Grammatically, his English was correct, but his accent was foreign, Russian, the sniper believed. He looked a lot like the killer at the Hotel Cavendish. Disillusioned by the corruption, lies and nepotism in their government, many Russians became contract killers.

He stepped back and his thighs bumped into the bed, nowhere to go, no room to maneuver, his .22 beyond reach inside his gym bag. But if he rolled across the bed …

The Russian exploded in a martial arts move, kicking the side of his head with a steel-reinforced shoe. Devastated by the blow, the Sniper fell to his knees, his head throbbing with pain, unable to think, barely able to see, his vision blurry, his skull on fire.

But he could not allow that to stop him.

The Russian had fists like anvils, wore killer shoes, and outweighed him by fifty pounds.

Put him down or he was dead.

His hand-to-hand combat skills kicked in. Forming his hand into a blade, he slammed it into the assassin's Achilles tendon, and before the Russian could react, he rolled across the bed to the other side and opened the gym bag. Ignoring the man's howl of pain, he grabbed the .22 and fired, once, twice, three times.

The Russian's eyes bulged, his mouth open but silent as he slowly toppled to the floor and landed with a heavy thud.

Panting, he stared at the Russian on the floor, his eyes closed, his mouth slack, one hand flung over his head like a man fast asleep. Except for the bright red blood pooling on the carpet beneath his rib cage.

Every nerve in his body was a four-alarm fire, screaming: *Get out before someone else arrives.*

He put the .22 in the gym bag and picked it up, comforted by the heft of it. Everything he needed was inside: other passports, credit cards and driver's licenses, packets of cash and extra ammo. He took his windbreaker out of the closet and put it on. Forget the rest, he'd buy new clothes.

Faint sounds came from the hall, distant voices. He ran to the door, the gym bag in his left hand, the .22 in his right. A quick glance told him no one was in the hallway. Yet.

He sprinted to the stairs at the other end of the hall. Twenty seconds later, encountering no one, he reached the first floor. No one behind the desk. He blew past it and went outside to the alley. No cars, no people, no sign of anyone reacting to the mayhem upstairs.

What would the maid do when she found the dead Russian in his room, he wondered.

His Vespa was in the storage unit, three blocks away. Forget that. Better to steal a car.

He left the alley, crossed Bienville and walked down Iberville, a one-way street toward the river, his back to any cars so no one would see his face. As he crossed Bourbon Street, litter crunched beneath his feet: windswept trash, crumpled leaflets, losing scratch tickets.

Raucous music blew through the door of a nearby bar. He had a sudden craving for a shot of vodka to steady his nerves. Ludicrous, of course. He couldn't afford to have someone notice him and give his description to the cops. Intent on putting as much distance as possible between him and the Hotel Royale, he kept walking toward Canal Place, head down, avoiding eye contact with any pedestrians.

Like the posh hotels and five-star restaurants, parking in the French Quarter was outrageously expensive. The Canal Place garage near the river was no exception. He climbed the stairs to Level Four and prowled the shadowy garage, waxed-and-polished BMWs and Mercedes parked beside dusty Fords and Buicks.

At last he found what he was looking for, a late model black Toyota Camry with a rental-car sticker on the bumper. It probably had a GPS tracking system, but he'd worry about that later. He jimmied open the driver side door and got into the Camry. Hot-wiring it would be a simple matter. He popped the ignition, used his utility knife to start the car, drove down the ramp to the exit booth and told the sleepy-eyed clerk he'd lost his ticket.

"Sorry, sir. I'll have to charge you for a whole day."

A scene from *Fargo* popped into his mind, Steve Buscemi shooting the parking attendant. But this wasn't a movie. This was life or death. Attract no attention. Make no fuss. He said nothing, paid cash and pulled forward when the gate swung up.

Ten minutes later he was driving past Audubon Park on St. Charles Avenue with the window open, the odor of ancient oaks draped with Spanish moss melding with the rental car's fake new-car smell.

Wearing mirrored sunglasses, he kept his eyes on the road, contemplating his narrow escape. All men felt fear. Even famous performers like Sir Richard Burton and David Bowie had stage fright. But they had learned to manage their fear, to act in spite of it.

So had he. No longer was his heart rate in the stratosphere. Thirty-one years old and still alive, thanks to his survival skills and his ability to focus on the immediate danger at hand.

But now he had another problem. He needed a place to hide.

Cruising the Garden District, he drove past sprawling high-priced homes with expensive cars in the driveways, the owners wealthy long-time residents or upwardly mobile professionals.

Not what he needed.

Ten minutes later he turned down a side street. Here the homes were less pretentious. A small two-story house caught his eye, white with blue shutters, and an attached garage. A tall cedar fence around the yard blocked the view from the adjacent house. Best of all, the shade were drawn on all the windows.

Maybe the owners were away on vacation.

He drove around the corner, parked at the curb and killed the engine. Retrieving his gym bag from the passenger foot-well, he left the Camry and walked around the corner to the house with the blue shutters. Across the street some boys were playing football in the front yard, their excited shouts carrying in the still air. Intent on their game, they paid no attention to him.

Adrenaline surged through his veins, elevating his heart rate as he walked along the cedar fence to the attached one-car garage. A window beside it was open an inch, to let in fresh air. In the backyard, a small concrete patio sported a round glass-topped table with a big green umbrella, and four chairs with green cushions.

He set his gym bag on the table, unzipped it and took out the .22. Some of his colleagues used larger guns—.44s or .357s—to feed their ego. They wanted to play Dirty Harry. He didn't. Small and quiet, a .22 did the job quite well at close range, very little mess, not much noise. Best of all, you could just put it in your pocket and walk away.

A small trash barrel stood near the house. He put the .22 in his jacket pocket, took the trash barrel to the open window beside the garage and used it as a step stool. With his utility knife, he pried off the window screen, raised the window, crawled inside and pulled the screen back into place.

His heart thumped his chest as he stood in the kitchen, listening, alert for any telltale sounds. Beside him on the refrigerator, snapshots displayed three generations of bright smiling faces, from toddlers to grandma, a small attractive woman with wavy dark hair.

Evelyn Parker, according to the AARP renewal notice on the counter. But where was she?

No lights on. No coffee pot in the coffeemaker. The house silent, no radio going, no TV sounds.

Maybe Grandma was away on vacation.

He crept down a long center hall toward the front door.

A woman's scream startled him.

He turned, his hand already on his weapon.

Frozen in the doorway of a bathroom, Grandma stared at him, then turned and ran toward the kitchen.

He sprinted down the hall and tackled her just as she grabbed the receiver of the phone on the kitchen wall. The receiver flew out of her hand.

1:32 PM

Frank put on latex gloves and stepped into the hotel room. Kenyon was downstairs questioning the desk clerk. Ten minutes ago she'd called 911, saying a maid had found a dead man on the sixth floor of the Hotel Royale on Canal Street. When they got there, the desk clerk, an agitated Hispanic woman, told them the dead man was-n't the man who was renting the room.

The corpse lay near the bed, bleeding onto the carpet, three gun-shot wounds in the chest. Dressed in a dark suit, he could have been the twin of the corpse in the hall at the Hotel Cavendish. Frank searched his pockets and found nothing. Just like the dead man at the Cavendish, and he didn't believe in coincidences.

He got on his cellphone and called David Lee. When he answered, Frank said, "When you checked the Hotel Royale on Canal Street, did you talk to all the targeted male guests?"

"Hold on." Ten seconds later David said, "No. I talked to two of them, got no red flags. But Peter Milovanovich wasn't in his room. Or if he was, he didn't answer the door. Why?"

"He's not answering it now either. Neither is the dead man on the floor of his room."

"Geez, you think Milovanovich is the Sniper?"

"Right now that looks like a good bet. Thanks, David. Talk to you later."

Kenyon came to the door and said, "I tried to talk to the maid, but she's hysterical, couldn't get zip out of her. What have we got here?"

"A corpse in a suit with no ID, like the one at the Cavendish. The man who rented this room was on David's watch list, but he wasn't here when David came to check."

"I'll be damned," Kenyon said. "The desk clerk gave me his name. Peter Milovanovich."

"Who might be the Sniper. Call dispatch and get the crime-scene techs and the coroner over here. I'll take a crack at the maid, see if I can get anything out of her."

Two minutes later, he was in the lobby, sitting beside the maid on a shabby couch with worn seat cushions. He'd told Kenyon to stay with the mother so he could talk to the maid alone. Rosita Rodriquez, age seventeen, gazing at him with large dark eyes, sniffling.

"It must have been a terrible," he said, "going in the room and finding a dead man." She nodded silently, her eyes welling with tears.

"But he wasn't the man who rented the room. Did you ever talk to Mr. Milovanovich? When you were cleaning his room, maybe?"

"No." A big sigh. "Well … one time he came back while I was cleaning his room."

Something flickered in her eyes. The girl knew something. He was sure of it. "What happened?"

"H-he came in and found me looking in his bag."

"What happened then? Did he threaten you?"

Rosita shook her head, staring at the floor. "No, but I was frightened. Will I get in trouble?"

"No, you won't get in trouble. What scared you?"

"His eyes were … so cold." Rosita gazed at him, her eyes fearful. "Like he wanted to kill me."

"What did you see in the bag?"

"A passport, Canadian, I think. With his picture, but a different name."

"We need to find out who killed the man in his room."

Her lips trembled. "Did Peter kill him?"

"I don't know. That's why we need you to help us. What else can you tell me?"

"H-he parks a black Vespa in the alley beside the hotel sometimes."

Frank wanted to kiss her. A black Vespa parked in the alley. He took out the color composite of the Sniper and showed it to her. "Does he look like this?"

Rosita shrank back, her eyes dark with fear. "*Sí*, just like that."

"Thank you, Rosita. You've been a big help. You can relax now."

As Rosita rushed to her mother, who put her arms around her, Frank waved Kenyon over and said, "Paydirt. Peter Milovanovich parks a black Vespa in the alley sometimes. Rosita ID'd him when I showed her the Sniper composite."

"Far out! Now we're cooking!" Kenyon exclaimed.

Frank nodded, but his heart wasn't in it.

It seemed clear that Peter Milovanovich had killed the man in the room upstairs, but if Milovanovich was the Sniper, he was long gone. And they had no idea where he was.

CHAPTER 28

She was strong for a woman her age, kicking him as they grappled on the floor. Panting, she rolled away and got her hand on the phone. Feeling her hot breath on his face, he slapped it away from her, but she scrabbled away and managed to get to her knees. He clamped a hand around her ankle, pulled hard and she fell to the floor, her breath coming in gasps, bleating a feeble call for help.

He slapped her face hard, stunning her, grabbed her by the arm, rolled her onto her back and straddled her. Still she fought him, scratching his neck, beating at him with her fists, arching her body to get him off. She opened her mouth to scream, but he put his hands around her throat and squeezed.

No sound escaped, thanks to the relentless pressure of his thumbs.

Contrary to what some people believed, strangling a human being to death required great strength, and it wasn't quick and easy. He squeezed harder, cursing Control, the man who'd driven him to this, the man who had no idea what it was like to kill someone up close and personal, hearing their pitiful screams.

Her face began to turn blue from lack of oxygen, eyes bulging with terror as she stared at him.

How terrible this must be for her, knowing there was no escape, no way out. He didn't want to kill her, but he couldn't allow her to call the police, or anyone else for that matter. Too many people were after him: the cops, the Russians, and, quite possibly, his employers.

Evelyn Parker had to die.

His hands began to cramp, but he gritted his teeth and kept squeezing her throat. Her struggles grew weaker. Finally her body went still, her mouth open, her tongue bulging out from her lips, no expression in her eyes now, only the pinpoint hemorrhages that came with death by strangulation.

He flexed his hands and his fingers, then massaged the aching muscles of his forearms. He hated close-kills, but now it was over.

Keep busy and don't think about it.

Breathing hard, he dragged her down the hall to the bathroom, removed her clothes, shoved her body into the linen closet and shut the door. Using a bottle of alcohol from the medicine cabinet, he wiped down the room. He didn't recall touching anything, but better to be sure. He gathered up her clothes and returned to the kitchen. A door beside the refrigerator led to a laundry room.

He loaded her clothes into the washing machine, stripped naked and added his clothes to the washer. He poured liquid detergent into a receptacle, added a half bottle of bleach, started the machine and went upstairs to her bedroom. In the closet he found a calf-length brown skirt and a medium-sized beige blouse and tossed them on the bed. In the bureau he found a pair of brown leggings, pulled them on, adjusted his privates and struggled into the brown skirt.

Tight, but it would have to do. Forget wearing a bra. He fashioned a pair of cotton socks into fake breasts, put on the blouse and stuck them inside. The blouse fit snugly enough to keep them in place as long as he didn't have to move much.

A wig stand with a blonde wig sat on top of the bureau. Strange. Did Grandma like to go out and hit a few bars as a blonde? Beside it was pair of sunglasses, large frames with tinted oval glass. Perfect. But what about shoes? He couldn't wear his own. They would instantly betray him. In the back of the closet, he found a pair of thigh-high winter boots, rubber-soled with a zipper along the side. He put them on. They pinched his toes but they would have to do.

He went into her bathroom and looked in the mirror, his head throbbing with fatigue. He'd barely slept for days. His face looked gaunt, the skin taut over his angular cheekbones, his hazel eyes looking out from sunken hollows. He opened a bottle of Evelyn's aspirin, shook four into his hand, dry-swallowed them and studied his face in the mirror. His thick black eyebrows had to go.

Using Evelyn's razor, he shaved them off and used her eyebrow pencil to give himself thin arching brows. He added brown eyeliner and a touch of mascara, then applied liquid foundation to conceal the marks on his throat where she'd scratched him. With a pair of manicure scissors, he chopped off most of his long dark hair and flushed it down the toilet. Then, using a fresh razor, he shaved the sides of his head, leaving the top long, a modified Mohawk.

If he had on his vintage army jacket and aviator sunglasses, he'd look like Robert De Niro in *Taxi Driver*, an Army veteran turned idealistic assassin.

He was ex-Army too, but he wasn't idealistic, he was a paid killer.

He put on the blonde wig and studied himself in the mirror. *Voila!* Now he was a woman. None of his enemies were looking for a blonde in a brown skirt and a beige blouse. He went downstairs. In the laundry room, the wash had finished spinning. He opened the tub, pulled out his own damp clothes, took them in the kitchen and stuffed them into a trash bag.

Holding the purse and the trash bag in his left hand, he grabbed Evelyn's car keys and went into the garage. Her car, a late-model white Ford, smelled like Lemon-Fresh. He backed out of the garage, used the clicker in the glove box to close the door and sped away.

With any kind of luck, no one would visit Evelyn for a day or two, and even if they did, they wouldn't look for her in a bathroom closet. Her car was gone and so was her purse. She could be out shopping or at a movie. It might be days before anyone found her. As long as he was careful he could use her car, but no speeding.

He checked his reflection in the rearview.

Now he was blonde law-abiding woman.

———

4:45 PM

Walking fast, Frank headed back to the D-8 station after an early dinner at Port of Call on Esplanade Avenue. Great burgers, but you had to get there early. When he left, a line people stood outside the door. Kenyon was eating take-out in the office, but after doing the paperwork on the Hotel Royale homicide, Frank had opted to go out and work off some pent-up energy.

Earlier when he'd called Vobitch to tell him about the latest homicide, Vobitch had said, "I'm getting those Jim Jones, drink-the-Kool-Aid type vibes. Seems like the Sniper is losing it, killing somebody in his own hotel room. But your hunch about the bike was right. Now we know he rides a black Vespa. You'll get him, Frank."

He sure as hell hoped so. But reality ruled his world. Bottom line: he had no idea where the Sniper was or how to find him.

Lengthening his stride, he turned right on Royal Street and walked past the Cornstalk Hotel. Built in 1816, the elegant three-story mansion had lacy ironwork on the balconies and a unique fence with iron corn-stalks and corn-husks in front.

A block later he passed an art gallery. One of David's wanted posters for the Shoplifter was posted in the window. Two grainy stills from security camera footage and big letters saying: **HAVE YOU SEEN THIS WOMAN?** $3,000 reward for information leading to the arrest of the Shoplifter.

But the Shoplifter was the last thing on his mind. He had too many other things to worry about. Multiple murders last Wednesday at the Hotel Cavendish, the Moped Killer's attack on the British PM at the World War II Museum on Sunday, and another homicide today at the Hotel Royale. Five days, five people dead. Plus the previous shootings: a cab driver and a female runner dead, a policewoman wounded.

His cellphone vibrated in his pocket. He pulled it out, checked the ID and answered. "Hey Tony, what's going on?"

"You're not gonna believe this. French President Nicolas Sarkozy is flying to New Orleans on Friday, a last-minute decision apparently. Word just came down to expect lots of overtime this weekend. And dig this. He's staying at the French Consul's residence on Prytania Street, in the same block where the Sniper shot the female runner."

"Christ! Sarkozy's the target."

"That's what I'm thinking," Tony said. "The Consul's residence is across the street."

"Thanks for the heads-up. Talk to you later."

He speed-dialed Kelly's number and she answered right away.

"Tony Coppola just called me," he said. "French President Nicolas Sarkozy is coming here on Friday."

"Whoa! You think he's the Sniper's VIP target?"

"Yes. I just worked a homicide at the Hotel Royale on Canal Street. The corpse was in a room that was rented by one of our male targets. Single, been here since the beginning of June. Peter Milovanovich. I'm pretty sure he's the Sniper."

Kelly gasped. "You've got his *name*?"

"A name? Yes, but he's long gone and I've got no idea where the hell he is."

———

Dark thunderclouds loomed in the sky as the Sniper drove north toward Lake Pontchartrain. A minute later the rain came, big fat drops at first, then a downpour, pounding the roof of Evelyn's Ford like hail, the windshield wipers working frantically, a sea of red brake lights ahead of him as cars slowed, the visibility just about zero due to the torrential rains.

But just as quickly, the weather changed. By the time he reached the lake, the rain had stopped and the sun was shining. He parked the car on Pontchartrain Boulevard. Off to his left, a magnificent rainbow arched over the vast lake, and several sailboats were bobbing along, their sails white against the blue-green water.

A postcard-picture scene that failed to ease his dark mood.

He went across the sidewalk to a vacant wooden bench and sat down. Evelyn's boots were killing his feet, his neck hurt where she'd scratched him, and so did his head where the Russian had kicked him.

But the physical discomfort was nothing compared to his emotional turmoil.

He studied the people in the park: a pasty-faced kid with a punk hairdo riding a bike, a young couple holding hands, an old man walking with a cane, white-haired grandparents with kids feeding bread to pigeons, women pushing babies in strollers. Ordinary people with their own little dramas, unaware that the man on the bench was the Sniper terrorizing the city.

A year ago—hell, *two weeks* ago—after besting a dangerous enemy like the Russian, he might have been tempted to stand up and shout, "I'm the Sniper, the best damn sniper in the world!" Not that he would have, but sometimes after conquering a seemingly insurmountable obstacle, his propensity for boastfulness escalated.

Not today. Today, he was staring into an abyss, populated by terrifying monsters like one of Goya's etchings, gargoyle faces with evil eyes, wormy skulls and castrated soldiers. *The Disasters of War.*

That's what he was, a wounded warrior, sitting on a park bench in a blonde wig, dressed like a woman, his balls and his cock trapped by skin-tight leggings. Emasculated.

A taxicab stopped on Pontchartrain Boulevard to drop off passengers and drove off. He watched it, thinking *Ghosts of the past.* The cab driver was the first to die. And since then, far too many others.

Too bad he couldn't shut off his mind.

Killing the Russian was self-defense—kill or be killed—but shooting the rent-boy wasn't. Since then he kept waking up at night, seeing the terror in the boy's eyes.

Would he have nightmares about Evelyn Parker? He pictured the snapshot on her refrigerator, her smiling grandchildren.

And he had murdered their grandmother.

What would Win think if he told her he'd strangled a woman with his bare hands? An innocent grandmother fighting for her life until the light went out of her eyes?

Control would call it collateral damage. Win would be horrified, gazing at him, her big brown eyes full of loathing and disgust.

No. He could never tell Win about Evelyn Parker.

He glanced at the lake, the calm waters, the clear blue sky and the rainbow. The air was warm, the sun beating down on him, but his insides were icy cold, colder than an Arctic iceberg.

What he desperately wanted right now was to ditch this fucking job, get out of here and take Win with him.

But he couldn't. His employers would never hire him again, nor would anyone else if the Boss put out the word to other firms like Zenith Intelligence. In fact, the Boss might even put out a contract on him. But right now he had to solve a more immediate problem.

Where would he sleep tonight? A hotel? Impossible. He was disguised as a blonde woman, but the moment he opened his mouth, they'd know he was a man. Sleep in Evelyn's Ford? No. The cops might find him. Stay at the safe house? Recalling the blood-stained basement floor, he shuddered. He had no desire to wind up in that basement to be tortured at length and then killed.

But as long as he had the flash drive the Boss wouldn't have someone kill him.

He took out his cellphone and dialed a number. When Control's prissy voice sounded in his ear, he said, "Code Red. Tonight, two in the dark, Red station." He ended the call before Control could utter a word. Control wouldn't like meeting him in the wee hours of the morning, but fuck Control.

He put the phone in his pocket, touched the flash drive and made a decision. Control had told him The Package would arrive soon. He was certain it was Nicolas Sarkozy. Security would be tight, but he had no doubts about his ability to complete the assignment. Then he would collect his pay and get out of here, with his soul-mate.

Yearning for Win and the emotional comfort he so desperately needed, he returned to the car. He didn't want to put her in danger by going to her apartment, but what choice did he have?

Twenty minutes later he rang her doorbell. When she spoke on the Intercom, he said, "It's me, buzz me in." Anticipating her reaction when she saw his disguise, he climbed the stairs.

She didn't disappoint him. She opened the door, took one look and burst out laughing.

He brushed past her and went in the living room.

"Peter," she said, gasping for breath between gales of laughter, "what the *hell* are you doing? Auditioning for a transvestite contest?"

For the first time all day, he smiled. "Yeah. Like it?"

She threw her arms around him. "I'll get used to it I guess. What's going on?"

He gave her a quick peck. After the excruciating events of the day, given the slightest provocation, he'd rip off her clothes and take her to bed. But he had things to tell her first.

"Someone tried to kill me at my hotel this afternoon."

Her eyes went wide with dismay. "Jesus, what happened?"

He pulled off the wig, ran his fingers through his Mohawk, sat on the futon and took off Evelyn's boots. "I put him down and split, but I can't go back there."

"You can stay here," Win said, adding with a faint smile, "I like the new hairstyle, but where did you dig up the gender-bender disguise?"

"It's complicated." He wasn't going to tell her about Evelyn. "Got any beer?"

"Coming right up," she said, and went in the kitchen.

He picked up her pack of Marlboros, took one out and lighted it. Her eyes widened when she came back with the beer and saw him smoking, but she didn't say anything. He drank some beer, puffed the cigarette and put it out in the ashtray. He hadn't smoked in years and it tasted awful. "I need to stay with you until I finish my job."

Her eyes lit up and she smiled, but before she could say anything, he said, "My life is in danger and so is yours." He took out the flash drive. "Hide this in the bedroom with your gun. If anything happens to me, take it and run. It's worth money so you can probably sell it."

For several seconds she stared at him wordlessly, her eyes welling with tears. Then, grasping his hands, she said, "Peter, I don't care about the money. I just want to be with you. Nothing's going to happen to you, okay? Promise me."

The Arctic iceberg inside him began to melt.

CHAPTER 29

WEDNESDAY July 6 – 8:00 AM – Paris

Henri watched his daughter zoom down the slide, beaming at him, thrilled to be playing in a park like other kids. Olivia was six years old, but small for her age and wise beyond her years. She looked like her mother: light brown hair, large dark eyes and prominent cheekbones. His ex-wife was a fashion designer. Yvette created elegant dresses for wealthy Parisians, when she wasn't out demonstrating for her political causes, President Sarkozy being one of her prime targets.

"Can I go again, Papa?" Olivia said, tugging at his hand, and his heartstrings.

During her first four years of life, she had been hospitalized countless times, an expense far beyond his means. Yvette's wealthy parents paid the doctor and hospital bills, as she had often reminded him during their frequent arguments. He adored Olivia, had been devastated when the doctors finally diagnosed the problem: Juvenile Idiopathic Arthritis.

"Not now, my love. I need to take you home so I can go to work."

"Maman says you work too much," Olivia said, slipping her tiny hand into his as they strolled down a gravel path lined with elm trees.

Maman says ... Henri clenched his teeth. Yvette said far too many things, chief among them—and a major cause of their divorce—was that he wasn't married to her, he was married to his job. And now that he was working for Sarkozy, her barbed comments were far worse.

He squeezed Olivia's hand. "In a few days I will go to America. To New Orleans where they celebrate Mardi Gras and Bastille Day just as we do. I'll bring you some Mardi Gras beads when I come home."

Olivia looked up at him, her dark eyes mischievous. "And beignets, with lots of sugar. I read about them online. Maman told me you were going to New Orleans. "

Henri laughed. "Okay, some beignets with lots of sugar, too."

Skipping along beside him, Olivia said, "Maman says it's dangerous there. Everyone has guns."

"No, it isn't. That is just your mother getting worried about nothing."

Olivia frowned. "But what if someone shot you, Papa? You would be so far away. I wouldn't be able to come to the hospital to visit you, like you always came to see me."

"Don't worry. No one is going to shoot me. I'm so proud of you for being smart enough to look things up on the Internet. Did you know that it is the middle of the night in New Orleans now?"

"Really?" Olivia frowned. "Do kids have to play on the slides in the dark?"

Henri laughed aloud. "*Mais, non.* New Orleans is in a different time zone. You can look it up online. And I don't want you worrying that someone will shoot Papa. Next week Papa is going to come home and bring you some beautiful Mardi Gras beads and some beignets with powdered sugar."

————

2:10 AM New Orleans

He stood in the darkness of an abandoned railway yard in a suburb of New Orleans, feeling the rage build inside him, churning his guts and his bowels. His innermost soul.

To calm himself, he pictured Win's face when she saw his disguise, recalling her laugh, and the delights of making love to her.

Face-to-face meetings with his minder were dangerous, to be avoided whenever possible, but he had things to say that could not be conveyed in a coded phone call. Still, no matter how many times he did it, a tense knot invaded his stomach.

Fifty yards to his left, a dead-end street was quiet, no cars, no dogs barking, no kids riding bikes. A jagged flash of lightning split the jet-black sky, casting bright light over the rail yard, followed by a gust of wind and a sharp crack of thunder.

He'd been here for an hour. Five minutes ago he'd seen Control arrive, and moments later his coded signal. Still, he waited to make sure no other footsteps were audible. Satisfied that they were alone, he flicked his lighter and quickly shut it to snuff out the flame.

When he stepped out of the shadows, Control emerged from behind an abandoned maintenance hut and hurried toward him, his expression angry. Before Control could speak, he attacked. "Someone came to my hotel room today and tried to kill me. A Russian bigger than a fucking tank, looking for the flash drive. Was he yours?"

"No! I told you to give me the flash drive—"

"And I made it clear that you'll get it when the job is finished."

"Did you kill him?"

"Of course, or I wouldn't be here. But I can't stay at that hotel. I don't know how the Russian found me, but there may be others."

"You can stay at the safe house."

When hell freezes over. "I have a place to say."

"Where?" Control said, frowning, peering at him through his thick spectacles.

"None of your fucking business. When does the Package arrive?" He was certain it was the French president, but he needed to know when and where the hit would be.

Another flash of lightening, the deep rumble of thunder, then a spatter of raindrops.

"The Boss called me last night. French President Nicolas Sarkozy, code name Poodle, will fly here on Friday. He intends to fly back to Paris on Monday." Control narrowed his eyes and spoke in a stern voice. "This we must not allow to happen."

"Fine. Tell me where he'll be and I'll take him out."

"He will attend a Bastille Day celebration at the World War II Museum on Sunday. We know there will be extra security for this event, but Poodle will be staying at the French Consul's residence on Prytania Street in the same block where you shot the runner—"

"So *that's* why you sent me there. You knew all along—"

"No, I didn't!" Control exclaimed. "The Boss told me put you on that roof."

So I could kill an innocent civilian. "When do I hit him?"

Control gave him a sheet of paper. "Here are the details of his flight and the address of the Consul's residence. The museum event on Sunday will end at seven PM. After a photo-op, Poodle will get in a vehicle with his security men and proceed to the residence. When he leaves the vehicle to enter the residence, you take him out."

"What's to say there won't be heavy security at the Consul's residence? The cops know I shot someone near there."

Control avoided his gaze, frowning as though he was debating with himself. At last he said, "The Boss is sending another shooter. In case you miss."

Stunned, he said, "What?? The fucking asshole doesn't think I can do the job?"

"Calm down," Control said. "The Buyer is paying a huge sum of money to eliminate this man. If we do not finish the job, The Buyer won't pay. That is why the Boss insisted on sending another shooter."

Take him out. Eliminate him. Finish the job. His prissy minder couldn't bear to utter the word *kill*.

Through a red haze of fury, he eyed Control's scrawny neck, flexing his fingers, recalling how he'd killed the woman in the Garden District no more than twelve hours ago. Wrap his hands around Control's neck, give it a twist and the asshole would be dead.

But that would cause problems. At this point, the Boss was probably edgier than a bitch in heat. Why make waves when he was so close to finishing the job? Take the money and run.

"Who's the other shooter?"

Control's right eyelid twitched spasmodically. "I don't know. The Boss didn't say."

He was certain Control was lying, equally certain that no amount of browbeating would make him reveal more information. But no matter. He had his insurance.

"Next time you talk to the Boss, remind him that I have the flash drive, which I will deliver to you *after* I get paid. And if you're smart, you'll keep me informed about the security arrangements for the Poodle." Without another word, he turned and stalked away.

———

4:45 AM

Frank woke up in a cold sweat, jolted awake by a nightmare, a faceless corpse with scrawny arms reaching out to him, its mouth open in a silent scream. The red digits on his alarm clock said 4:45. Forget getting back to sleep. He got out of bed and put on his running suit. When he left his condo a thunderstorm was rolling across the city, bolts of lightning sharp against the leaden sky, then loud thunderclaps, storm-whipped winds lashing the branches of trees.

Soon it would rain, but he didn't care. He'd always felt wired on the street at night, even when he was a cop in Boston. Prowling the French Quarter alone was dangerous, but the night had an energy, an electricity he couldn't resist.

A few writers and artists still lived in the Quarter, and wealthy professionals paid big bucks for refurbished condos. Most of the rest were street people: transvestites, homeless junkies and winos, eking out a subsistence-level life, panhandling tourists who strolled Bourbon and Royal streets, snapping photographs like visitors at the zoo.

He jogged past a dark alley, inhaling the cool, dank smell, his feet pounding the pavement. A flash of lightning lit up the street like a flashbulb, followed by deep rolling thunder. He ducked into the doorway of a darkened store, frustration festering inside him.

He'd worked his ass off on the Sniper case, had spent countless hours and expended an enormous amount of energy, with damn little to show for it. Multiple homicides at the Hotel Cavendish a week ago, the waitress's description of the Sniper, and a corpse with no ID in the hall. Another corpse with no ID at the Hotel Royale today, and Rosita's tip about the Vespa. Hell, he even had a name.

But the Sniper had disappeared like a puff of smoke.

Every day in America a criminal crossed the line and an innocent person died. Then it became a battle of wills: Cops versus killers. Frank wanted justice for the Sniper's victims: the cab driver, the female runner and the wounded policewoman, the Armenian and his boy toy and the Japanese tourist.

Not an eye for an eye maybe, but if it came to that ...

He banished the thought. Flirt with the edge, the desire for justice could suck you under faster than a stormy riptide at a sandy New England beach. Then he'd be no better than the killers.

He left the alley and jogged through Jackson Square. Three hours from now the magnificent St. Louis Cathedral would be drenched in sunlight, its soaring white spires gleaming in the morning sun as face-painters, fortune tellers and sidewalk artists plied their trade in Jackson Square. He would be sitting in the D-8 homicide office, trying to figure out how to catch the fucking Sniper.

His cellphone vibrated in his pocket. Knowing any call at this hour was bad news, he pulled it out, answered.

"Frank," Detective Roger Vance said, agitated, "I'm at a homicide scene in the Garden District. A woman asked for a wellness check on her mother, said she'd called five times but Mom didn't answer. A patrol officer went to the house and found the mother's body stuffed in a bathroom closet. But here's the weird thing. The daughter checked to see if any valuables were stolen. She said her mother's blonde wig was missing. The mom used it during her chemotherapy treatments when she lost her hair."

Frank felt a creepy-crawly sensation on his neck as a movie scene flashed in his mind. The assassin in *The Day of the Jackal*, preparing his disguise in order to kill French President Charles de Gaulle.

And French president Nicolas Sarkozy was coming here on Friday.

"What about her car?" Frank asked.

"Not in the garage. Her car keys and purse are missing too."

"It might be the Sniper."

"That's what I'm thinking," Vance said. "I already put out a BOLO on the car, a white 2010 Ford Focus."

"Great. I'll be there in twenty minutes."

Frank turned and ran toward his condo, thinking: *Vobitch will never believe this.*

Vobitch thought they were looking for a man riding a black Vespa.

Now they were looking for a man in a blonde wig driving a white Ford Focus.

CHAPTER 30

Bleary-eyed from lack of sleep, Frank entered NOPD Headquarters and rode the elevator to the top floor. Three hours ago at the Garden District homicide scene, he and Roger Vance had decided this warranted a meeting with the NOPD Superintendent. And Deputy Superintendent Wendell Hicks, unfortunately, since he was in charge of Operation Skyhawk. But no one else would be there.

When Frank entered the Superintendent's office, Raul Sanders, an imposing six-foot-six man with ebony skin, greeted him with a smile. Unlike Wendell Hicks, seated in a visitor chair facing the Super's desk, stone-faced. Despite his rank and title, Frank couldn't muster any respect for the man.

The chair beside Hicks was conspicuously vacant. Roger Vance sat one chair over. No flies on Vance. An experienced detective in his mid-forties, Vance had pale blue eyes, a world-weary demeanor and a weather-beaten face. In his spare time—when he had any—Vance was a sailor.

"You look beat, Frank. Have some coffee." Raul Sanders gestured at a tray on his desk with a pot of coffee, white Styrofoam cups and a plate of pastries, the rich aroma of coffee filling the air.

"Thanks, I will." He poured himself a cup and took the vacant chair beside Vance. Which meant he had to sit beside Wendell Hicks for an hour. Not good. He warned himself to stay cool.

Sanders looked at him expectantly. "You got me out of bed early, Frank, but I'm happy to hear you and Roger have new information about the Sniper. I want to hear the details before we release them to the task force. Let's walk it through from the beginning. You're lead on the first one, Frank. Refresh my memory on the timeline."

"Gladly. It's always good to look at the big picture." He opened his notepad to the one-page summary he'd written. "The Sniper shot the cab driver on Canal Street on June 18. Six days later on June 24, he shot the female runner on Prytania Street in D-6." He gestured at Vance. "That's Roger's territory, so he's lead on that case, but we've been collaborating ever since."

Beside him, Vance nodded and sipped his coffee.

"Three days later on June 27, the Sniper shot Kimba Davis, the mounted policewoman."

"Damn shame," said the Superintendent, grimacing. "Thank the Lord, she survived."

A brief silence followed as they contemplated the darker scenario. A dead policewoman.

"At that point," Sanders said, "I put Wendell in charge of Operation Skyhawk. The media attention demanded it, not to mention the folks at the tourist bureau and local businesses. And I have to say, I was concerned that the Sniper might be targeting police."

"We all were," Vance said. "These days every cop in the city puts on a uniform to go to work, doesn't know if they'll make it home at night."

"Fortunately, he hasn't," Frank said. "But two days later on June 29, Aram Takvorian was murdered at the Hotel Cavendish on Canal Street. Detective Kenyon Miller and I found a corpse in the hall near Takvorian's room. No ID on him. No wallet, nothing."

"What about prints?" the Super asked.

"We ran them through the usual data bases and got nothing. My boss, Detective Lieutenant Vobitch, says if he's a foreigner we may never identify him. Same with the DNA sample."

Hicks ran a hand over his shaven pate and said, "Keep trying. You might get something. We get plenty of foreign visitors. Check with TSA at the airport."

"We will, especially after what happened yesterday. But I don't want to get ahead of myself. There were other victims at the Hotel Cavendish, collateral damage if you will. A male prostitute in Takvorian's room, whom we've since identified as Rasheed Brown. No close relatives, no friends or associates who could tell us anything, and since Rasheed is dead, we can't ask him about the shooter. The other victim was a Japanese teenager on holiday with her parents, staying in the room beside Takvorian's. We think she heard shots and opened her door, and the man in the hall shot her."

"What makes you think the Sniper was involved?" Hicks asked. "It seems like a totally different scenario. No rifle, multiple victims ..."

"Two things," Frank said. "These Sniper attacks might be a prelude to something bigger. The real target might be a visiting VIP."

"That's a big leap," Hicks said, frowning at him. "We had a sniper in New Orleans back in the seventies but he wasn't after a VIP, he was shooting at cops."

"I'm aware of that case," Frank said. "But that guy had a grudge against cops. In our case, the first two sniper victims had no connection to one another, no enemies. No connection to the wounded policewoman, either."

"And the other reason?" said Superintendent Sanders.

"The Takvorians came here from New York. Nicole, the widow, said Aram told her he had to talk to someone important. Unfortunately, he didn't say who or why. From the ballistics report we know two different guns were involved. One killed Takvorian and Rasheed Brown. The Japanese woman was shot with a different weapon. We recovered a Russian-made semi-automatic in the hall. Which means two sets of shooters were gunning for Aram Takvorian. We believe he had important information that other people wanted."

"Like what?" Hicks snapped impatiently. "I still don't see the connection to the Sniper."

"We don't know and I'm not sure it matters. A Hotel Cavendish waitress told me Takvorian met a man in the tea room right before he was murdered and gave me a description of him. I think he killed Takvorian, but someone pulled a fire alarm and the killers got away during the chaos. The only other lead, if you want to call it that, came from Nicole Takvorian. She says the Turks hate the Armenians. She's convinced the Turkish government had him killed."

"That's hearsay," Hicks said. "It would never hold up in court. Why do the Turks hate Armenians?"

"Because of the Armenian genocide in Turkey back in 1915," Frank said. "Which many Turks refuse to acknowledge, even now."

Clearly unimpressed, Hicks shook his head, but before he could say anything else, Roger Vance said, "The composite the waitress helped us draw up was very helpful. Before that we had no idea what he looked like. About six feet tall, right Frank? Dark hair, good-looking, wearing a suit?"

"That's what she said." Turning to Hicks, Frank said, "How many tips are we getting?"

"Hundreds, none of them useful so far. But there was an assassination attempt on Prime Minister Cameron on July 1, when Frank was in charge of security at the World War II Museum."

Inwardly fuming, Frank maintained a blank expression, thinking: *You prick. Making it sound like it was my fault.* Apparently Vance thought so too, nudging his knee.

"An unsuccessful attempt and clearly not the Sniper," said Superintendent Sanders. "The man was mentally ill. Should have been in a hospital."

"Maybe," Hicks said, "but I will be supervising security at any VIP events from now on."

"Good," Frank said, blank-faced. "That will free me up to work on the Sniper case." And felt Vance double-tap his knee. "That summarizes the Sniper timeline. Until yesterday."

Nodding eagerly, the Superintendent said, "You got a break."

"Two actually," Frank said. "At one o'clock we got a 9-11 call saying a maid at the Hotel Royale on Canal Street found a dead man in one of the rooms. I went there immediately. The dead man could have been the twin of the corpse in the hall at the Hotel Cavendish, a large foreign-looking man in a suit, no ID." Addressing Superintendent Sanders, he said, "I should explain that by then we had developed a list of potential Sniper suspects, single male guests staying at hotels in the French Quarter and the Garden District, starting from June 1, prior to the first Sniper kill."

"Good thinking," the Super said, nodding. "Go on."

"I called my colleague, Detective David Lee, to see if he'd checked any guests at the Hotel Royale. He had, but one man didn't answer the door. Peter Milovanovic. The corpse was in his room, but the maid said it wasn't Milovanovic. She'd had previous interactions with him. When I showed her our Sniper composite, she said it was definitely Milovanovic. She also said he sometimes parks a black Vespa in the alley alongside the hotel."

"Excellent!" said the Super, his face wreathed in a smile. "So we know where he's staying, and we know he rides a Vespa."

"True, but I doubt he'll go back there." Frank gestured at Vance. "I'll let Roger tell you what happened next."

Vance cleared his throat and said, "Twelve hours later, I caught a homicide in the Garden District. Evelyn Parker, 62, lived by herself. A patrol officer did a wellness check for her daughter, found the mother's body in a closet. It was a professional hit, no doubt about it. The killer wiped everything with alcohol, washed the victim's clothes. We found them in the washer, still damp. No trash in the trash bin.

But here's the important part. The daughter said when her mother lost her hair during chemo treatments last year, she wore a wig. And her blonde wig was missing. That's when I called Frank."

"Twelve hours after the murder at the Hotel Royale," Frank said, "Roger and I figured it was the Sniper, maybe took the wig to use as a disguise."

"The victim's car, car keys and purse were missing," Vance said. "So I put out a BOLO on her car, a white Ford Focus. No sign of it yet, but my patrol officers found a Toyota Camry one block away with the ignition popped. We ran the plate and found out the car was reported stolen that day. It was parked in the Canal Place garage."

"Good work!" the Superintendent said to Vance. "After he killed the man in his hotel room, he went to the garage, stole the car, went looking for a place to hide, and Evelyn Parker had the misfortune to be home."

"And the President of France is arriving on Friday," Frank said.

The Superintendent frowned, tapping his pen on his notepad. "If the Sniper is planning to shoot a VIP, President Sarkozy would make a fine target. Damn it, we need to catch the bastard!"

"Cover the airport, train and bus stations." Hicks said.

"Why?" Frank said. "He's not leaving. He's gunning for President Sarkozy. And our composite is no good if he's using a disguise."

"A sniper in a blonde wig, dressed as a woman?" Hicks said sarcastically. "I don't think so."

"He might use it to get past security," Vance said. "Ditch the disguise, go up to his sniper's nest and get ready to shoot."

"Sarkozy will be doing an event to celebrate Bastille Day at the World War II Museum on Sunday," Frank said. "We need to beef up security there—"

"I'll handle that," Hicks cut in, glowering at him.

"Fine, but Sarkozy and his entourage will be staying at the French Consul General's residence on Prytania Street, the same block where the Sniper shot the female runner."

"Damn!" said the Superintendent. "Frank and Roger have built a convincing case. At this point, that doesn't seem like a coincidence."

"How far can he shoot from?" Hicks asked. "With a reasonable certainty of hitting his target?"

"Pretty far," Roger Vance said. "I read where some military snipers in Iraq shot people more than a mile away."

"Lord help us," said the Superintendent. "Okay, send me a list of all the tall buildings within a mile of those two locations. What else?"

"We need to secure a perimeter around both locations," Frank said. "Check the IDs of people near the French Consul's residence."

"And set up metal detectors at the museum," Vance said. "The Sniper might be setting it up so we'd think he's going to use a rifle, go after Sarkozy with a handgun or a knife."

"Nonsense," Hicks said, shaking his head. "If the Sniper intends to assassinate Sarkozy, and I'm not convinced about that, he won't use a knife or a handgun."

Grim-faced, the Superintendent waved a hand, ending the discussion. "That's enough for now. These suggestions will require many police officers, reams of overtime and cost a shitload of money. But that's my problem. I'll talk to the Mayor and the City Council President." Focusing on Frank and Roger, he said, "Thank you for your efforts. Excellent work, but I want to know about any new developments right away. Call me directly."

Not telling them to go through Deputy Superintendent Wendell Hicks, Frank noticed.

Sanders skewered him with a look, his dark eyes intent. "No one is going to assassinate the President of France in New Orleans. Not on my watch."

CHAPTER 31

THURSDAY July 7 – 12:30 PM

Hunched over his desk, his head throbbing with a fierce ache, Control doodled on his notepad, trying to figure out what to tell the Boss about his meeting with the Sniper. When he got back to the safe house at the ungodly hour of 2:30 AM, he hadn't slept a wink, just belted down some Jim Beam, collapsed on his bed and stared at the ceiling. Meeting the bastard in that creepy railroad yard was bad enough. The murderous expression in his eyes was far worse.

Stabbing pains assaulted his temples. The Boss would be angry about the Russian, apoplectic when he told him the Sniper wouldn't give up the flash drive until he got paid for the job.

It was time for lunch, but the very idea of food sickened him.

The clang of the doorbell startled him. How could anyone ring the bell? The gate was locked.

He hurried to the front door and put his eye to the peephole. A strange-looking man in a black sweatshirt and dark trousers raised his fist and thumped on the door. "Open up! Boss sent me."

His hands trembled as he unlocked the deadbolt. When he opened the door, the man pushed past him, set two large canvas bags on the floor in the hall and turned to face him. By his estimate the man was only four inches taller than he was, five-foot-eight perhaps, but he had muscular arms and a massive chest. Thick dark hair swept back from his low forehead fell to his shoulders. His eyes were black, boring into him now, his face expressionless.

"How did you get through the gate?"

"Easy. I climb over. You are Control?" Spoken in a monotone, no inflection.

"Yes. The Boss told me you were coming, but not when you would arrive. You are Viktor?"

"Yes. I stay here until job is finished."

Control shuddered. Jesus! The Cleaner was going to stay *here?*

"Show me where I sleep."

Obeying his command, Control took him upstairs to one of the bedrooms. Viktor put the two black canvas bags on the bed. "Show me kitchen."

He took him downstairs, feeling the man's eyes on his neck every step of the way. "There's not much in the refrigerator, but you're welcome to whatever strikes your fancy."

Trying to appear friendly, he smiled.

"Good. I will eat now." No smile from the Cleaner.

Control hurried out of the kitchen, his heart beating his ribs in a frenzy of terror. The Boss had sent Viktor here to make sure Sarkozy was dead and terminate the Sniper.

For all he knew, Viktor had orders to terminate him, too.

It would be easy enough. Sneak into his bedroom some night and it would be lights out. Forever.

3:35 PM

Viktor circled the vast space inside the WW II Museum, dressed in a polo shirt and jeans to blend in with other visitors. He paid no attention to them, gazing at the tanks and armored vehicles with American flags and stars painted on them. French President Nicolas Sarkozy would attend a ceremony here Sunday afternoon. To celebrate Bastille Day, whatever that was.

Boss was right. Control had no balls, a little man with a flabby gut and thick eyeglasses, gaping at him when he gave him a disposable cellphone, and his orders. "Stand outside the museum on Sunday during the ceremony. Call me when people begin to leave the museum. Call me again when Poodle and his protectors leave."

Boss had taught him everything, had chosen him out of all the other boys in the Budapest Metro station. Viktor ran his fingers through his hair. He loved the silky feel of it. At the orphanage in Romania, the attendants shaved everyone's head. His mother had left him there when he was six months old. Or so he'd been told. He had no memory of her. His earliest memory was being in a cage with other naked children, stinking of shit and piss. Many died of starvation or disease before they could crawl or walk. To survive, he had stolen food from the smaller ones.

His eyes widened as he studied the planes suspended from the ceiling by thick steel cables. One of the planes had his number on it!

Romanian orphans had no names, just numbers, assigned to them when they were brought to the orphanage. His was 2428.

Twenty-eight years ago, but he still remembered it.

He studied the plane with the number. Perhaps this was a good-luck sign, telling him that his mission would succeed. But why put warplanes inside a building? Not that it mattered.

On Sunday, all the warplanes in the world would not save Sarkozy.

Just as no one had come to save him in the orphanage. Over the years, he stole food from weaker children and often beat them. The attendants made him do it. Viktor clenched his fists, remembering the other things they made him do. Worse things. Things that made him want to escape. When he was ten, he did.

Living on the street was dangerous, almost as bad as the orphanage. Stunted by malnutrition, he was small for his age, but he'd used his fists and his wits to survive. By the time he was fifteen, he had grown stronger and smarter. And ruthless.

That's why Boss had chosen him thirteen years ago in the Budapest Metro station. "Want a job?" Boss had said.

"What is job?"

"I pay you to do things for me."

Recalling what they'd made him do in the orphanage, he said, "No fucky. I bite off your cock."

"No fucky," Boss said. "I pay you to beat up people." So he had gone to London with Boss, who had chosen him because he'd seen him beat up another boy and steal his food and the coins in his pocket. "You were fearless," Boss had said.

When his English was good enough, Boss let him choose a name. He chose Viktor. He liked the sound of it for one thing. Hard and explosive, like a gun. He liked its meaning even more. Victorious.

Which was exactly what he had intended to be when Boss put him to work.

Continuing his walk around the lobby, Viktor came to the exit door and went outside.

When Sarkozy landed at the airport tomorrow, he would be there to check out his protectors. On Saturday he would return to the museum after it closed for the night and see what sort of security measures the police had put in place. And prepare his distraction.

He noticed a flock of pigeons, drinking water from a puddle in the gutter. As he drew closer, most of them flew away, but one remained. The brave one, Viktor thought.

Unlike the man at the safe house with the thick eyeglasses and the smell of fear about him. A man not to be trusted.

In fact, he trusted no one, but he needed Control's help to complete his work. That could be a problem. When he returned to the safe house, he would show the man with no balls exactly what would happen if he screwed up.

———

9:30 PM

Win paced her living room, smoking one cigarette after another. If Peter was here, he'd tell her to stop. But he wasn't here, he was out doing whatever it was he did.

She was thrilled to have him living here. Just being around him was exciting. Okay, she knew he killed people for money. He'd told her that. But two days ago, a man had tried to kill him. That's why he couldn't stay at his hotel. He hadn't told her where it was, but she assumed it was the Hotel Royale on Canal Street. A news bulletin on TV said the police were investigating a murder there.

Peter said he'd killed the man, left the hotel and dressed up in that silly Mrs. Doubtfire-in-a-blonde-wig disguise.

But he wouldn't tell her where he got it. She was glad he escaped, but sometimes when he sat beside her on the futon, silently thinking, a deadly stillness came over him. When that happened, she didn't dare ask what he was thinking, didn't even dare to look him in the eye, fearing it might trigger the violence that lurked within him.

Her hands trembled as she snubbed out the cigarette in the butt-filled ashtray. She hated not knowing where he was, but earlier when she asked where he was going, he gave her that look, the look that frightened her. She didn't understand it. Most of the time he was so gentle with her, stroking her face after they made love, asking about her childhood, telling her to reconcile with her mother.

Where was he? What was he doing? What if he didn't come back?

That night at the park before the fireworks, they had shared their favorite memories: Peter's hilarious tale about his pet parrot and her story about how thrilling her first roller coaster ride was. Peter had promised to take her for a ride on a big Ferris wheel in London.

But what if he didn't? What if she never saw him again?

Tears misted her eyes. What if he finished his job here—whatever the hell it was, he wouldn't tell her—took the money and went back to Belgium without her?

———

11:45 PM

Frank lay beside Kelly, lost in thought. Usually after they made love, he felt relaxed and happy. But not tonight. Not even making love to Kelly could quell the feeling of dread inside him.

French President Nicolas Sarkozy would arrive on Friday, two days from now, and he had no clue where the Sniper was or how to catch him. Two days to stop a presidential assassination.

Kelly opened her eyes and looked at him. "You're worried about Sarkozy," she said.

He leaned down and kissed her. "I need a beer. Want one?"

"No, but I'll share some of yours."

He went in her kitchen, took a bottle of Becks out of the refrigerator, popped the cap and took a long swallow. As she so often did, Kelly had unerringly zeroed in on his mood.

Sometimes when he hadn't seen her for a day or two, she'd call him after she got in bed and they'd talk about their day. Grousing about some aggravation at work or just joking around, laughing about some trivial event, comfortable with each other, like a married couple.

But Kelly was in no hurry to get married again, either. She'd lost at love too. One Saturday night her off-duty patrol-cop husband stops to help a disabled motorist and a ten-ton truck hits him, over and out. He'd never forget the night she told him about it. No tears, no whining, no self-pity.

The night he started to fall in love with her.

One night two years later, he brought one of his favorite CDs to her house: the Blood Sweat and Tears "Greatest Hits Album." When he put it on, Kelly gazed at him, her eyes stricken. "Frank, turn it off. Please." It turned out that was Terry's favorite album. She'd been listening to it when she got the call the night that he died.

Sometimes music soothed the savage beast.

Other times it brought back memories too painful to bear.

When he returned to the bedroom, Kelly was sitting up with a pillow behind her back, leaning against the headboard. "Are you going to the airport tomorrow?" she said.

"No. Hicks is handling security there. Let him take the heat if something goes wrong." He handed her the bottle of Becks and joined her on the bed, propping a pillow behind his back.

"No more random shootings, at least." Kelly sipped some beer and gave the bottle back to him. "Ten days since the last one."

"Vobitch says to focus on the Takvorian murder. I'm certain the Sniper killed him, but we don't know why. And he ran into complications. Someone else was gunning for him at the hotel."

"Or gunning for Aram Takvorian. Maybe the Sniper just got in the way."

Frank swigged some beer. "But why kill Takvorian? And why two different shooters? Nicole said he came here to talk to someone important. I feel like I'm missing something."

"Maybe two different shooters are gunning for the VIP."

"Maybe. But how do we know that Sarkozy is the target?"

"If not Sarkozy, who?" Kelly said. "The creep that tried to kill Prime Minister Cameron at the World War Two Museum wasn't the Sniper, but Sarkozy will be doing an event there on Sunday."

"One thing is certain. The dead man at the Hotel Royale was on the same team as the dead man in the Hotel Cavendish hallway. Two foreign-looking men, no ID on them, nothing in the usual DNA databases. Who the hell are they?"

"At least we've got the Sniper's name. Peter Milovanovic."

"If that's his real name, which I doubt. The maid saw another passport in his room with a different name and told me he rides a black Vespa. But if we assume he murdered the woman in the Garden District, we might be looking for a man in a blonde wig, driving the woman's white Ford Focus, which we still haven't located. Where the hell is he? He won't go back to the Hotel Royale, but he's gotta sleep somewhere. What if he's got a helper?"

Kelly stared at him. "Whoa! You think there's another sniper?"

"Not exactly. I've been reading up on military snipers. Most of them work in pairs. One's the shooter, the other's the spotter. Maybe the spotter rented a room somewhere else. Maybe that's where the Sniper is right now. Hell, maybe Sarkozy isn't even the VIP target."

"Go with your gut, Frank. Sarkozy is the target. And I think you're forgetting something." Kelly pulled him closer and kissed him. "If the Sniper's been here since early June, maybe he got horny and found himself a girlfriend. Maybe he's sleeping at her place."

"Jesus," Frank groaned. "That's just what we need. A horny Sniper hiding out with a woman."

CHAPTER 32

FRIDAY July 8 – 3:00 PM

Viktor took a taxi to the airport and paid the driver in cash. No rental car, Boss had told him. This would require a credit card and leave a paper trail. He'd paid cash to rent a motorbike, but he knew security would be tight at the airport. A motorbike might attract attention. A taxi would not.

Wearing jeans and a polo shirt, he strolled into Concourse D where international passengers arrived. Boss had told him Sarkozy's private jet would arrive at 3:30. Security was already in place, armed police in uniform patrolling the concourse, some with sniffer dogs.

Not wanting to draw their attention, he bought a newspaper, went to a nearby Smoothie King and ordered a Smoothie. Pineapple and strawberry, his favorite flavors. He sat at a table outside the shop, positioning himself so he could watch Sarkozy and his protectors come up the ramp into the terminal. Would a convoy of cars be awaiting him? How many security men would be with him?

He sucked on the straw, savoring the Smoothie, recalling the constant hunger of his childhood, the yearning for attention, the sexual abuse inflicted upon him. Sarkozy had suffered none of these things. Boss had told him all about this man, not that he cared. His targets meant nothing to him, but Sarkozy had enjoyed a life of privilege.

Last week, seated in Boss's living room in London—just as he had thirteen years ago, dazzled by the plush furnishings and the big-screen TV—he had listened as Boss told him about Sarkozy.

His father, a Hungarian aristocrat, came to Paris in 1948, made a fortune in advertising and married a French woman. But after Nicolas arrived in 1955, he paid scant attention to him and left the family when Nicolas was five. Sarkozy's maternal grandfather became his father-substitute. Not until he died in 1972, did Nicolas and his brothers learn of their mother's Jewish heritage.

Viktor studied the photograph beside the article on the front page of the newspaper: Sarkozy, smiling at him, a powerful, important man coming to New Orleans to speak at the WW II museum. At least Sarkozy knew who his father was, a wealthy important man.

His father was a nobody. His mother was a whore.

But Sarkozy did so badly in school his family sent him to a private Catholic school. Viktor was not impressed. He had never attended school. Boss was the only teacher he needed. Boss had taught him how to speak proper English, what to wear in different situations, and all the math he needed to know: wind speed calculations, distance to the target and so forth.

He finished his Smoothie and checked the time: 3:20. Sarkozy would land in ten minutes.

A mediocre student, Sarkozy managed to obtain his diploma in 1973 and went on to college, earning two law degrees. He enrolled in the Paris Institute for Political Studies, but failed to graduate due to his poor command of English, Boss said. Still, Sarkozy managed to pass the French bar exam and became an Advocat specializing in business and family law.

Viktor straightened alertly, aware that a policeman was approaching him. He pretended to read the newspaper and forced himself to relax, keeping his breathing slow and even. This he had learned at the orphanage. Never show fear. Others could smell it, just as he had smelled fear on the orphans he stole food from, crusts of bread and bits of meat.

The policeman passed his table and continued toward the glass exit doors. Viktor's heart sped up as four black SUVs with tinted windows pulled to the curb. Sarkozy's security vehicles had arrived. He checked his watch: 3:22. His flight must have landed early. Boss had told him an important person like Sarkozy would be taken through Customs quickly.

Other people in the terminal turned to look as two dozen policemen formed two lines facing outward, standing shoulder-to-shoulder to create a human funnel that Sarkozy and his protectors would pass through. Viktor tucked the newspaper under his arm and strolled toward the crowd of spectators. In situations like this, his short stature was an advantage. A five-foot-seven man in a blue polo shirt could hide behind a taller man and look over his shoulder.

And there he was! President Nicolas Sarkozy in a fancy pin-striped suit, surrounded by taller men with grim faces. Viktor sneered as he watched him. Sarkozy was only five-foot-five, two inches shorter than he was, and rather sensitive about it, Boss said.

"Vive la France!" shouted a voice.

Viktor turned. A media crowd had gathered near the exit doors: reporters, photographers and TV cameramen with helpers equipped with bright lights. A flashbulb went off, startling two policemen, but Sarkozy kept going, urged on by his protectors who rushed him out the door, across the cement sidewalk and into one of the black SUVs.

A disciplined operation, Viktor thought. Sarkozy's security team was good. But not good enough to thwart him.

He watched three more men in dark suits walk toward the door, men with hard eyes and bulges under their suits. But no women. Sarkozy's wife was not with him. Boss had told him about her, too. The third of Sarkozy's wives was pregnant, awaiting their first child.

A child that would not be dropped off at an orphanage like a piece of garbage.

————

6:25 PM

Frank parked outside the French Consul General's residence on Prytania Street, went to the door and rang the bell. Above him on a gleaming white flag pole, the French Tricolor—three vertical stripes of red, white and blue—flapped in the breeze. The door was opened by a man in a black suit—the standard uniform of security agents the world over—who eyed him suspiciously.

He stepped inside and flashed his badge. "Homicide Detective Frank Renzi. I need to talk to President Sarkozy's security chief."

The short, dark-haired man—five-foot-five tops—frowned. "You 'ave an appointment?"

"No, but this is urgent. I need to talk to him."

"Wait here." The man went to a door, opened it and disappeared.

A young woman at the reception desk smiled at him. "Bonjour, Monsieur. Please have a seat."

Weary from lack of sleep, Frank settled onto an antique settee with gold upholstery. On the opposite wall, a gold pendulum inside a grandfather's clock swung back and forth, ticking off the time.

A half hour ago, he'd called Superintendent Sanders to give him an update. "No forensic evidence at the Garden District homicide, but after the Sniper shot the man at the Hotel Royale, he left in a hurry. The forensics team collected DNA from a toothbrush in the bathroom. I put a rush on it, got the results this morning."

"And?" Sanders said eagerly. "What did you find?"

"Nothing in the federal database, so I called Interpol and asked them to run it through theirs. They were happy to oblige. The Hotel Cavendish is British property and they want to solve the murders there. An hour later, they called back. Peter Gibbs served in the UK Army from 1998 to 2006. Not only that, he was a trained *sniper,* served in Iraq during the 2003 Gulf War. But that's all they could give me. No records on Peter Gibbs after October 2007."

The Superintendent groaned. "Damn! We get one step closer and hit a stone wall. You think he's a paid assassin?"

"I think it's a good bet. This morning a sharp-eyed patrol officer spotted the murdered woman's Ford on Esplanade Avenue in the French Quarter. No telling where he went from there. I don't want Sarkozy staying at the Consul's residence on Prytania Street where the runner got shot. Is it okay with you if I talk to his security chief and ask him to house Sarkozy somewhere else?"

"I admit the location is worrisome," the Super had said. "Talk to him, Frank, but don't ruffle any feathers." A deep chuckle. "We don't want to cause an international incident."

Frank checked the grandfather clock. 6:45. Where the hell was the security chief? He didn't want to ruffle feathers, but he didn't want the Sniper to kill President Sarkozy, either.

Footsteps sounded on the polished-wood floor. An older man with gray hair entered the foyer, accompanied by a younger man, both wearing dark suits. The younger man looked amazingly similar to photographs he'd seen of Nicolas Sarkozy. He rose from the settee as they approached him.

The older man said, his expression frosty, "I am Andre Delacroix, chief security agent for President Sarkozy during his stay here." Gesturing to the younger man, he said, "This is Henri Bellest, a member of my team. What is this urgent matter you bring to me?"

"Since the middle of June, a sniper has shot several people in New Orleans. Two weeks ago he shot a woman on Prytania Street, right here in this block."

Delacroix frowned. "We 'ave heard about this, but not that he shot someone near here."

"We think these shootings are a smokescreen."

Seemingly mystified, Delacroix turned to Bellest, who looked at Frank and said, "A deception?"

"Yes. We believe he intends to kill President Sarkozy. The NOPD Superintendent and I want you to consider housing President Sarkozy somewhere else."

"Not possible," Delacroix said emphatically. "The French Consul has invited us to stay here."

"Please, hear me out. Last Sunday a man tried and failed to assassinate British Prime Minister David Cameron at the World War II Museum. He wasn't the Sniper, but we have reason to believe the Sniper may try to assassinate President Sarkozy."

"We know about this attack on Cameron." The security chief raised his chin imperiously. "We will make sure nothing 'appens to President Sarkozy when he speaks there on Sunday. What makes you think this sniper will try to kill President Sarkozy?"

Frank clenched his jaw, aggravated by Delacroix's dismissive attitude. "He's ex-military, a trained sniper for the British Army. We don't know where he is and we can't guarantee that we'll find him before Sunday. The manager at the Hotel Cavendish has reserved an entire floor for President Sarkozy and his security team. It's a fine hotel, very secure. I strongly urge you to have President Sarkozy stay there during his visit."

Delacroix smiled faintly and said to Bellest, "Do you think the cuisine at this hotel will be comparable to what we enjoy here at the French Consul's residence?"

"I'm sure the hotel has fine accommodations," Bellest said diplomatically. "But British cooking cannot be compared to French cuisine."

"Exactly so," Delacroix said. "Thank you, Detective Renzi. I will discuss your concerns with President Sarkozy. Now I must return to my room to prepare for the fine dinner the French Consul's chef is preparing for us."

After his boss left the room, Henri Bellest said, "I am a big fan of your beautiful city, Detective Renzi. Can you tell me please where to hear some hot jazz?"

Frank smiled. "Glad to hear you're a jazz fan. So am I. Go to Snug Harbor on Frenchman Street. I'm not sure who's playing, but I know you'll enjoy it. They serve great food, too." He hesitated, then said, "Will President Sarkozy be with you?"

"No," Henri said, his eyes aglow with excitement. "Tomorrow night I will have some time for myself to see the sights. I must get some beignets for my daughter." Like a proud papa, he smiled. "She's only six but she's very smart. She read about them on the Internet. Olivia has a sweet tooth."

Warming to the man, Frank said, "I hear you on that. My daughter is a lot older than Olivia, but she loves beignets, too. Get them at Cafe du Monde in Jackson Square. And make sure you take a taxi to and from Snug Harbor. To be safe."

"Thank you for your kind suggestions." Bellest hesitated, his eyes somber now. "Do you really think this sniper intends to kill President Sarkozy?"

"Yes, unfortunately. But dozens of police officers will be stationed at the museum." Frank took out two of his cards. "Give one to your boss and ask him to call me if anything changes. Try to convince him to stay at the Hotel Cavendish, Henri. It's a fine hotel, very elegant, and he'll be safe there."

Looking dubious, Henri said, "I will try, but President Sarkozy can be … very obstinate."

———

11:30 PM

Lurking behind a tree, the Sniper studied the safe house across the street. The neighborhood was quiet at this hour: no dog-walkers, no late-night joggers, no passing cars. After the sun went down, a few residents had come out for a stroll, enjoying the cooler air.

Control was not among them. He never left the house after dark if he could avoid it.

Beyond his hiding place, streetlights illuminated the sidewalks. The only light visible inside the safe house was on the second floor. Control's bedroom. What was he doing? Drinking whiskey to fortify himself, awaiting last minute orders from the Boss?

This morning Win had woken him, eager to have sex, but he had resisted her seductions. From now on his rifle was his mistress.

The Boss had sent another shooter here. A backup man to make sure Sarkozy was dead, according to Control. What an insult!

Infuriated, he clenched his fists, flexing them spasmodically. This was *his* assignment. When Sarkozy left his vehicle to enter the French Consul's residence on Prytania Street, he would shoot Sarkozy and he did not intend to miss. *One shot, one kill.*

No way would he allow some fucking backup man to kill Sarkozy.

That's why he was monitoring the safe house. *Know your enemy.*

He'd been here since four o'clock, having assumed the backup man would monitor Sarkozy's arrival at the airport and return to the safe house. But he hadn't. No one had entered or left the house. Where was Backup Man and what was he doing? Scoping out the French Consul's residence on Prytania Street from whatever rooftop the Boss had assigned to him?

Motion caught his eye. A man came around a corner to his left and strode down the opposite sidewalk.

Still as a statue, he studied the man. He had a foreign look about him, not like the Russians who'd tried to kill him, but his face had a brutish quality, like many who grew up under totalitarian dictatorships: Bulgarian or Romanian perhaps.

A short man with powerful arms and legs, dressed in a black running suit, carrying a large canvas bag. His weapons bag. Like many short men, he compensated for his size by wielding a big gun.

He stopped at the gate outside the safe house, punched in a code and the gate swung open. He hurried to the front door and disappeared inside.

The Sniper relaxed, breathing easier. Backup Man was no match for him. He had executed every assignment the Boss had ever given him perfectly, killing each target with one shot. This job would be no different. He was the best sniper in the London Special Ops office, maybe the best sniper Zenith Intelligence had anywhere, period.

He pictured Win, lying beside him in bed this morning, gazing at him with her big brown eyes as she stroked his cock. After he killed Sarkozy and collected his hard-earned pay, he would put her on his Ducati, get on a plane, take her to his hideout in Brussels and make love to her every day for a week.

Then he would take her for a ride on the London Eye, the biggest Ferris wheel in the world.

He smiled, imagining the excitement in her luminous brown eyes.

What a delight it would be, living in Europe with Win. Forever.

CHAPTER 33

SATURDAY July 9 – 9:10 AM

He stood in the shadows deep inside an alley, his eyes fixed on Nicolas Sarkozy.

Last night he'd slipped out of Win's apartment with his sniper gear at midnight and went to the rooftop on Prytania Street near the French Consul's residence. No cops flagging people down, asking for their ID and questioning them yet, but on Sunday there would be.

He'd spent a sleepless night on the roof, nodding off only to be jolted awake by nightmarish images of bloody corpses with dead eyes. At dawn, he watched the sun come up, a faint pink glow in the east, the sky streaked with purple. At 8:30, Sarkozy left the residence and got into one of two black SUVs out front. In a panic, he'd grabbed his gear and made a mad dash to his Vespa. He hated to use it, but what choice did he have? He had to stay mobile in case Sarkozy went somewhere.

To a posh health club six blocks away on St. Charles Avenue as it turned out.

He raised his rifle and peered through the sniper scope. At the rear of the club was a large oval outdoor running track with four lanes. Sarkozy and his security men were the only runners. Sarkozy didn't have to worry about security. Others were paid to do this. But there he was in the cross-hairs, a man with powerful enemies, jogging along, oblivious to his vulnerability.

Four men surrounded him, each man an inch or two taller than Sarkozy and dressed in similar attire, dark running suits with red pin-stripes down the legs. A common tactic used by security agents. Create five targets, not one. Five sets of arms and legs swinging in unison, five men jogging along at the same pace, presenting slightly different targets. A sniper's nightmare.

And this narrow alley was a piss-poor shooting position. In Iraq he'd shot through violent sand storms, driving rain, even glass windshields while seated or standing in a moving vehicle. Day or night, he had killed men from distances greater than a thousand yards.

But in Iraq, the police weren't after him and a color composite of his face wasn't playing on prime time TV. In Iraq, at least he knew who his enemies were.

208

Here, his enemies were different, some of them obvious, others not. The police. The Russians. His employers. And a backup man who wanted the money that rightfully belonged to him.

But if Sarkozy died today, Backup Man wouldn't get it.

Sarkozy and his security team rounded the curve on the short end of the oval track and jogged down the long side opposite his hiding place. He zoomed in with the scope, centering on Sarkozy's head. He was an inch and a half shorter than his protectors, no doubt about it.

He inhaled the scent of gun oil, felt the silky-smooth stock nestled against his cheek. This was what he lived for. Nothing else mattered. Acquire the target and shoot to kill.

He set his finger on the trigger. Even at the relatively short distance of 200 meters, the flight of a 7.62 round built up tremendous kinetic energy. When it hit the target the result was devastating.

Two seconds passed.

He squeezed the trigger.

The suppressed round was quiet, but not totally silent, loud enough to send a flock of pigeons beside the track into the air, wings flapping, cooing at the sudden disturbance.

Sarkozy kept going, oblivious. Alert to any unusual sound, his protectors pushed him to the ground. Two fell on top of him, shielding his body with their own. The other two agents drew their weapons, their eyes searching the area to find the shooter.

None of them noticed the dead pigeon on the ground.

Before they could figure out where the shot came from, he ran to the other end of the alley and ducked around the corner. Despite the temptation, at the last second he had decided not to shoot Sarkozy. Better to stick with his plan and perform the test.

A test that told him Sarkozy's security agents were well-prepared.

Sharp. Alert. Active. But that wouldn't save him on Sunday.

One shot was all he would need.

_____

12:15 PM

Seated opposite Vobitch at the dining room table, Frank massaged his temples, fighting the headache lurking behind his eyes.

"You look like shit," Vobitch said. "Worse than me after I got out of the hospital."

Irritated, he snapped, "I forgot to put on my *Dancing With the Stars* makeup."

"Okay, I know you're working overtime, but at least you're not out of the loop like me. Any news on the Sniper?"

"No. Kelly thinks he's got a girlfriend, might be hiding at her place."

Vobitch gave him his evil smile. "Never discount the sex angle. A man's got his needs."

"He's also got a sniper rifle and I'm afraid he's going to shoot Sarkozy. I talked to Sarkozy's security chief yesterday, but he blew me off." Frank shrugged. "Politely, of course."

"Even after you told him about the Sniper?"

"Yes. He said his security team is perfectly capable of protecting Sarkozy. It's a territorial thing. You know how that goes. Believe it or not, at the meeting with the Superintendent on Wednesday, Wendell Hicks actually posed a good question. How far away can a sniper be and still hit a target? Roger Vance said he's heard about snipers hitting targets almost two miles away."

Vobitch stared at him, disbelief written large on his face. "Two *miles?*"

"Correct. No way can we cover every building within a two mile radius with a direct line of sight on the museum. Or the French Consul's house on Prytania Street, for that matter."

"What's the plan at the museum?" Vobitch asked.

"The Super stationed an NOPD communication van near the entrance, staffed around the clock as of eight this morning. They'll have direct communication with every NOPD officer in the area, and the CCTV monitors will access feeds from security cameras near the museum." Frank spread his hands in frustration. "What else can we do? It's a fucking crap shoot."

"Maybe the Sniper won't even try to shoot him at the museum. Maybe he'll wait till Sarkozy goes back to the place on Prytania Street, shoot him there."

"We'll have security patrols near the Consul's residence."

"Better check the roofs of all the buildings along the street."

"That too," Frank said. "Every available NOPD cop will be working on Sunday." His cellphone rang. He checked the ID and said, "I better take this."

When he answered, Andre Delacroix, Sarkozy's security chief, said, "Allo, Detective Renzi. I 'ave talked with President Sarkozy about your concerns. He refuses to stay at the Hotel Cavendish, but I have drawn up an alternate plan for the museum. Plan B, as you Americans call it. Sometimes President Sarkozy uses a decoy to avoid the media. If something should 'appen at the museum, my team will rush President Sarkozy out to the security vehicles and take him to the Hotel Cavendish. The decoy will leave the museum through a different door and another team will drive him to the residence. "

"I'm glad you're got an alternate plan. Who's the decoy?"

"The man you met when you were here yesterday. Henri Bellest."

Dismayed, Frank pictured the diminutive security agent with the six-year-old daughter. Last night Henri had called to thank him after he left Snug Harbor. "The jazz was fantastic and so was my dinner," Henri had said. "As you suggested I have purchased some packets of beignet mix at Cafe du Monde. When I get home, I will make some for Olivia and put lots of powdered sugar on them."

But if something went wrong at the museum, Henri would be a stand-in for Sarkozy.

"Thank you for calling me, Mr. Delacroix. Let's hope nothing happens at the museum, but if it does, take good care of Henri."

"But of course," Delacroix said. "We value him highly. *Au revoir,* Detective Renzi."

Frank closed the phone and said to Vobitch, "Sarkozy's security chief set up Plan B in case anything happens at the museum."

"You don't seem too happy about it," Vobitch said.

"I'm not. I met another security man at the Consul's residence. Henri Bellest is a dead-ringer for Sarkozy. They use him as a decoy when Sarkozy wants to go somewhere without drawing attention. If something happens at the museum and they drive Henri to the Consul's residence on Prytania Street, the Sniper will assume he's Sarkozy and shoot him."

———

11:45 PM

Under the cover of darkness, the moon shrouded by thick clouds, Viktor worked his way toward the large white van with the NOPD emblem on the side, darting quickly from one position to the next, waiting a full minute after each move.

His entire outfit was black, including the balaclava that hid his face, and the knapsack with his equipment. He had blackened any visible patches of skin with charcoal. But he hated open spaces, and the area around the museum entrance near the van offered little cover.

Twelve minutes later he reached the van that served as the NOPD command post. He set his knapsack on the ground and reviewed what Boss had told him on the phone last night. "Your goal is to disable the command post, draw other officers to the museum and create confusion. Try to avoid killing civilians. We want them to leave the museum and go around the corner to watch the photo op when Sarkozy leaves the building. Can you do that, Viktor?"

"Yes, Boss. You can count on me," he'd said.

He became aware of voices drifting through a small screened window near the back of the trailer. He crept to the window and peered through it at an angle. Two men in police uniforms sat at a small metal table, smoking cigarettes, talking in low voices. A pack of Camels and two Glock semiautomatic pistols sat on the table beside a detailed map of the area around the museum.

Cigarette smoke curled through the open window. Viktor had to clench his teeth to keep himself from coughing. These cops were worse than Boss, who smoked one cigarette after another, and told Viktor never to start smoking.

"You think these sniper shootings are random?" said one man, sucking on his cigarette.

"You want random?" said the other, an older man with pock-marked skin. "In the war I saw guys die for no reason, shot out of the blue, sometimes by their own men. I heard them screaming, no hope of getting to a field hospital in time." He snubbed his Camel out in the ashtray. "And I'll tell you this. They don't scream to God. Don't scream for Daddy, either. They scream for Mama, cuz they know Mama loved them more than anyone else ever could. More than God, even. If there is one."

Viktor thought about this. If he was dying, who would he scream for? Not his mother, certainly. And not for this god that people talked about. He would scream for no one, he decided. He was only twenty-eight and he didn't intend to die for a long time.

And now it was time to get to work. He opened his knapsack and carefully removed the IED, made sure the C-4 explosives were in place, and tucked the cellphone into the cloth pouch beside them.

He couldn't use a timer. The event at the museum would not end until twenty hours from now, maybe more. Boss said these events often ran longer than expected. That's why he needed Control to tell him when people began leaving.

But Control was not to be trusted. Boss said you could tell who a person was by what he threw away.

In the kitchen trash at the safe house, he had found a can of men's deodorant, a big empty bottle of Jim Beam, several empty Heineken bottles, a crumpled pack of English Opals and a plastic bag full of cigarette butts.

Sweet-smelling Control needed liquor and cigarettes to give him courage. But Viktor had no doubt that the prissy little man would obey his orders. Yesterday he had backhanded him across the face with his fist, snapping his head to one side. Blood spattered the wallpaper in his bedroom, a cascade of drops that ran down the wall.

"Please," said the man with no balls. "Please don't hit me again. What do you want from me?"

Relishing the fear in his voice, the man no doubt imagining what else he might do to him, Viktor had said, "Do your job. Be at the museum on Sunday and follow my orders."

Now, focused on his task, he clutched the IED to his belly and slid underneath the trailer. Using pre-cut lengths of thin wire, he secured the IED to one of the struts that held the rear wheel of the command post van in place, the wheel farthest from the entrance.

Satisfied that he had fulfilled Boss's wishes, he slid out from beneath the trailer and left the area as silently as he had come.

A black figure disappearing into the mist, seen by no one.

CHAPTER 34

SUNDAY July 10 – 5:05 AM

Frank slipped inside the foyer of the four-story building opposite Linda Seeling's apartment. It was still dark outside, but a ceiling light illuminated eight mailboxes on the wall, two units for each floor.

In his experience, the twilight-zone hour before dawn was the best time to serve an arrest warrant. Or capture a killer.

For weeks, he'd spent most of his waking hours focused on the Sniper, which included researching the mindset of military snipers. They were meticulous and patient, and they got off on risk. For some reason, jumping out of aircraft and getting shot at by other snipers excited them.

Peter Gibbs had fought in the Gulf War, a sniper trained to locate and kill the enemy, skills he could use as a paid assassin, likely more than once by now. Over time, criminals learned what to avoid, altering and improving their MO with each repetition.

At this point, Frank felt like he knew the Sniper well enough to anticipate what he might do in certain situations. Listening for telltale sounds above him, he crept up to the second floor. Every cop in town was looking for the Sniper, but no one had seen him. No surprise there. The Sniper knew they were after him. A full-color composite of his face was running on the local television newscasts.

He'd never laid eyes on the man, but his gut was telling him the Sniper intended to shoot President Sarkozy from the same roof where he'd shot Linda Seeling. Thanks to widespread media reports about Sarkozy's visit, the Sniper had to know the French Consul General was hosting him at his residence. The Sniper would expect extensive precautions to be taken to protect Sarkozy, including security sweeps near the Consul's residence today.

Why not go up to the roof early and hide?

Last Friday Andre Delacroix had brushed off his warning about the Sniper, saying his men were perfectly capable of protecting President Sarkozy. So why set up Plan-B? Had something happened since Friday to make him change his mind?

If so, Delacroix hadn't told him about it.

215

That's what had kept him awake most of the night. If something went wrong at the museum, Henri would be the stand-in for Sarkozy. French security agents would drive him to the Consul's residence. The Sniper would assume Henri was Sarkozy and shoot him.

On the third floor, the building seemed eerily quiet, no residents up before dawn, sipping coffee and planning their Sunday. Was the Sniper on the roof? Or was this a waste of time?

David Lee had spent the night at the Hotel Cavendish, prepared to supervise the emergency arrival of President Sarkozy if necessary. He was probably still asleep, but Vobitch was an early riser, having his first cup of coffee right about now, pissed that he had to monitor things from home on his police radio. Frank had promised to keep in touch via cellphone. If he used his radio, too many people would overhear, including Wendell Hicks, who was in charge of security at the World War II Museum.

When Frank got to the fourth floor, he took out his SIG. A surge of adrenaline upped his heart rate as he crept down the hall to the stairs that led to the roof. He hadn't told anyone he was coming here, not even Kelly. Push came to shove, his motto was FTR: Fuck the Rules. Besides, if he got into a shootout with the Sniper, it would be on the roof. No innocent civilians in the line of fire.

Gripping the SIG in his right hand, he put his left hand on the door knob, conscious of his heart thudding against his ribs.

If the Sniper was on the roof, he'd be armed, but Frank had no intention of shouting a warning. The Sniper was a stone-cold killer. If he saw a weapon in the Sniper's hand, he'd shoot the fucker.

He flung open the door, sidestepped away from the doorway and dropped to a crouch, extending the SIG in front of him with both hands, aimed at the part of the roof overlooking Prytania Street.

Silence. Nothing moving in the shadowy darkness.

No Sniper along the parapet overlooking Prytania.

Alert for any sudden movement, eyes darting everywhere, Frank circled the ten-foot-square shed that housed the air-conditioning unit, springing around each corner, ready to shoot anything that moved.

No Sniper. And nowhere else for him to hide.

Still, the back of his neck prickled as he walked the perimeter of the roof, sniffing the air like a wolf tracking its prey. No tripod, no rifle, nothing to indicate the Sniper would shoot Sarkozy from here, but he could almost smell the bastard.

The Sniper had been here recently, he was certain of it.

Soon, NOPD cops would park cruisers at both ends of the block to prevent vehicle access. In a few hours, he and Kenyon would be at the World War II Museum, along with dozens of NOPD uniforms. Two senior officers would be inside the communications van, monitoring security cameras in the area. Other NOPD officers, including Kelly O'Neil and Roger Vance, would stand outside the Consul's residence to protect Sarkozy and his security team when they got in their vehicles to drive to the museum.

And even more worrisome, when they returned from the ceremony. If the Sniper was on the roof, waiting to shoot Sarkozy, Kelly would be in the line of fire.

After a final look around, he returned to the door that opened onto the roof. Maybe his concerns were groundless, a product of his over-active imagination.

But where the hell was the Sniper?

———

5:15 AM

He sat on the woman's couch, watching a movie. Turner Classics had a great lineup. Earlier he'd watched Kubrick's *2001, a Space Odyssey*. He loved the opening music, *Also Sprach Zarathustra* by Richard Strauss. Too bad he had to keep the volume low. Now he was watching *Bonnie and Clyde,* with the sound muted. He'd seen it before, the two lovers dying in a slow-motion hail of bullets from FBI agents. Sad. Maybe he wouldn't watch the end.

The bag with his sniper gear sat on the carpet by his feet, and his Beretta lay on the couch beside him. The woman was tied up in the bathroom, her ankles and wrists bound with tape. He'd stuffed a sock in her mouth and taped it shut to keep her quiet.

He drank some bottled water, went to the window, raised one slat of the Venetian blinds and looked down at Prytania Street. The building where the runner used to live was across the street. The Consul's residence was two buildings down to his left. Sarkozy was probably sound asleep, but his protectors might not be, more than likely worrying about what had happened yesterday.

After he shot the pigeon, he'd eaten a big breakfast at a diner four blocks away. No one took any notice of him. Then he came back here, but not to the roof. He waited under the stairwell. At noon, he heard footsteps on the stairs, descending one flight, then another. After hearing the front door open and close, he crept up to the second floor. Sounds leaked out from under the doors of those apartments.

He continued to the third floor. Hearing no TV sounds or voices, he tapped the door of the flat overlooking Prytania Street, ready to jump anyone who opened the door. No one did. Using his lock pics, he opened the door and crept from room to room.

Finding no one, he went back to the kitchen. An electric bill addressed to a woman was on the counter. If she was married or had a boyfriend, he might have a problem. But she didn't.

Or so she'd said when she came home at six-thirty.

He studied the street below him. An NOPD cop came around a corner and walked past the Consul's residence. He lowered the slat and backed away from the window. He'd shut off the lights in the woman's apartment, but why take chances?

When he'd jumped her, the woman didn't put up much of a fight. His face was hidden by a balaclava but she could see the Beretta in his hand. He said he wouldn't hurt her as long as she didn't make a fuss. When he asked if she lived alone, she hesitated. "Don't lie," he said. "I saw the electric bill. Does anyone else live here?"

She shook her head mutely, her blue eyes leaking tears, a dumpy older woman with gray hair. "Expecting any visitors tonight?"

Another head-shake. He didn't want to kill her. He'd already killed too many innocent civilians, so he tied her up in the bathroom. Every half hour he checked on her, removed the gag and gave her a sip of water. At midnight, he'd helped himself to one of the frozen dinners in her refrigerator, careful to wear gloves and clean up after himself.

Leave no evidence.

Now he was in full Special-Ops mode. Fifteen hours from now he would shoot Sarkozy and escape during the chaos that would inevitably ensue. He returned to the couch.

Damn! There it was, the big shootout scene, Bonnie and Clyde cut down by the fucking FBI agents.

The cops would never take him. He'd rather die than go to jail. Spend the rest of his life behind bars? Forget it.

After his midnight snack, he'd called Win and told her not to wait up for him. When she asked where he was, he'd said, "Next time I see you, my job will be finished."

"Be careful, Peter. The cops are looking for you."

"If anything happens to me, take the flash drive and run. It's worth money."

"Don't say that!" Win exclaimed. "I don't care about the money. I care about you."

"Don't worry," he'd said. "After tomorrow, we'll be together for a long time."

But thinking about it now in the darkness of the woman's flat, he wasn't so sure. Would they live happily-ever-after in Europe together? With all his heart, he wanted this to be true. But given the importance of his target and the extensive efforts to protect him, it might not be.

He glanced at the TV. Disgusting! The FBI agents were celebrating over the bullet-riddled bodies of the two lovers.

Thrill-seeking Bonnie and Clyde would never rob another bank.

What quirk of fate had caused this particular movie to be on tonight of all nights?

Would he live to see another day? He wasn't worried about the Russians. They'd found his hotel on Canal Street, but they knew nothing about his sniper's nest on Prytania Street. He didn't know why they wanted the flash drive, but it didn't seem to be have anything to do with Sarkozy.

But another man was gunning for Sarkozy too, sent here by the Boss, who might have told Backup Man which roof he'd be on when he shot Sarkozy.

He would take some precautions when he went to the roof.

Always be vigilant. Trust no one.

———

5:45 AM

Viktor sat up and rubbed his eyes, woken by the ding of his wristwatch alarm. Above him in the darkness, a ceiling fan whirled, cooling his naked body. Boss had rented the apartment for him, but told him to stay at the safe house after he arrived to make sure Control followed orders. The timid little man with the thick eyeglasses and the naked fear in his eyes.

Last night after planting his surprise at the World War II Museum, Viktor had come here for the first time. After securing the door, he called Boss on his disposable cellphone, told him he'd placed the device as instructed and was now in the apartment.

"Good work," Boss had said. "I shall be watching the news after it blows the NOPD communication van to smithereens. The whole world will be watching. The cops will think it's a terrorist attack and rush our target back to the location near you."

Taking care to reveal no specific details.

Viktor arched his back to ease his cramped muscles. No furniture in the apartment, so he'd slept on the floor. But he'd slept in worse places. A straw pallet infested with bugs in the orphanage. The Metro station in Belgrade, stinking of garbage and overrun by rats.

No rats or roaches here. No food either. The electricity was on, but Boss had warned him not to turn on any lights. He opened one of his canvas bags and took out a peanut-butter protein bar.

A Kalashnikov with a five-inch butt-stock was in the other bag, the perfect weapon for this job, easy to hide and easy to carry, with an effective range of 350 meters. His target would be much closer. Armed with a specialized 40-round magazine, set on semi-automatic, the Kalashnikov could fire 40 rounds a minute. In short bursts, a hailstorm of 100 rounds a minute.

Savoring the protein bar, he went to the window. The blinds were shut, but dim light from the streetlamps leaked around them. He eased back one edge of the blind and looked out. In an hour the sun would be up, but now the street was dark, except for the streetlights. One of them stood in front of the Consul's residence down the street to his right.

He finished the protein bar and peeked out the other side of the window. The NOPD police had parked a squad car at the end of the block to prevent cars from entering this block. Boss had told him to expect heavy security. To Viktor, it seemed like Boss spent all day and half the night on his computer, preparing for this job.

Last night, Boss had told him that after the ceremony at the museum ended, Sarkozy would do a photo-op outside for the media. He wouldn't, of course. By then, the IED would have ripped the NOPD communication van apart. Sarkozy's protectors would rush him into a vehicle and bring him to the Consul's residence.

Viktor would be waiting. One 40-round burst from his Kalashnikov would kill Sarkozy and anyone near him. Others would rush to their aid. During the confusion, he would go to the roof of the building down the street and complete his assignment.

No loose ends, Boss had said.

CHAPTER 35

4:45 PM

Anticipating an overflow crowd, WWII Museum officials had placed two huge speakers on either side of the entrance to allow those unable to get inside to hear the ceremony. Beside them, on tall flagpoles, French and American flags flapped in the breeze.

People were in a festive mood, singing along as French songs celebrating Bastille Day boomed through the speakers. Sweating profusely, Frank mingled with the crowd. Despite the setting sun, the air was still hot and humid. That wasn't why he was sweating. He was looking for the Sniper, one man in a vast sea of humanity.

Lots of little kids in the crowd, waving tiny American flags in one hand, the French Tricolor in the other. Some people wore red-white-and-blue outfits; others wore Mardi Gras colors, purple-green-and-gold. Tall men in Saint's ball caps and black-and-gold T-shirts avoided his gaze when he scrutinized their faces.

Forty yards to his left inside the NOPD communications van, two officers were monitoring feeds from nearby security cameras. Officials had closed the museum early so their staff could evacuate the building. Five minutes ago, Deputy Superintendent Wendell Hicks had reported over the NOPD radio channels: *All clear in the museum.*

Hicks had ordered composites of the Sniper posted on doors of the buildings along Prytania Street. Frank didn't like it. This would alert the Sniper that they'd be looking for him on the roof. But maybe he wasn't on the roof, maybe he was here, wearing a disguise.

A good-looking blonde walked past him, not the Sniper in a wig, but it seemed like blondes were everywhere.

He noticed a tall rugged-looking soldier in fatigues. The man saw him and hurried away. Even though Frank had on a blue polo shirt and black slacks, the guy had made him as a cop. Frank followed him.

The soldier turned and gave him the finger. Not the Sniper.

A minute ago the entry doors had opened, but the line waiting to enter the museum kept growing. Inside, everyone had to pass through a metal detector, then a bag search. This slowed things down, but most people were used to it. This was standard procedure to enter the 'Dome and the Little 'Dome for sporting events and concerts that were held there.

The T-shirt vendors and face-painters down the street had cleaned up today. Many in the crowd wore T-shirts imprinted with *Vive La France!* and half the kids had red-white-and-blue painted faces.

But Frank wasn't worried about kids. He was worried about a tall well-built man with dark hair or a man dressed as a women in a blonde wig, acting suspicious.

Kenyon strolled up to him, his eyes roving over the crowd. "Looks like a police convention, more uniforms here than at roll-call before a shift change. He'd be a fool to try anything here."

"Maybe, but there must be two thousand people here."

"Well, you can forget the black guys. He can't fake that."

"Okay, but that leaves at least eight hundred guys, how the hell do we spot him?"

"He'll be the one shooting at Sarkozy," Kenyon said.

Frank gave him a look. "Not funny." He scanned the skyline to the south, then to the west, dozens of tall buildings visible in the hazy sky. "I hope he's not on a roof."

"Me too," Kenyon said. "Gives me the creeps, knowing he's got a scope and a rifle powerful enough to shoot a target two miles away. You talk to Vobitch?"

"Fifteen minutes ago on my cellphone."

"I bet he's ripshit, gotta stay home, out of the action."

"That pretty much sums it up." His radio crackled. Frank took it off his belt, no bigger than his cellphone, but narrower and thicker. Heard Hicks say, "Attention all units. All clear on the observation posts. Stay alert. They'll be here in ten minutes. Out."

Kenyon looked at him, his dark eyes somber. "Good to know the rooftops on Prytania Street are clear. Kelly's there, right?"

"Yes." Another worry. Kelly had been shot while on duty once before. He didn't want it to happen again.

"What I hear, Hicks refused to stay in the communications van," Kenyon said, "commandeered a room on the second floor of the museum. Seems like he's got a handle on things though."

"Maybe, but the worst is yet to come. Get Sarkozy here, get him into the museum and get him back to the Consul's residence."

Kenyon mopped sweat from his forehead. "Man, I'll be glad when this is over."

Frank nodded. "You and me and every other NOPD cop."

5:28 PM

She opened another beer and sat on the futon, puffing a cigarette. It aggravated her headache but she couldn't help it. After Peter's phone call last night, she hadn't slept a wink. She was thrilled when he said he would finish his job today, but then he said if anything happened to him she should take the flash drive and run.

Just thinking about it made her stomach cramp.

"Don't worry," he'd said. "After tomorrow, we'll be together for a long time." But his voice sounded odd, no inflection, no excitement, just a matter-of-fact statement.

Forget sleeping after that. She'd crawled out of bed and got on the Internet. She hadn't boosted anything for ages. She found a Royal Street store she'd never hit before, one that sold leather accessories. She picked out a black leather handbag with brass studs and went in the bedroom to figure out which disguise to use. She had settled on her Perky Teenager outfit, her long brown wig with the ponytail …

Something flashed on the TV screen. Damn! The news was on.

She grabbed the remote and upped the volume. On one of the local channels, an anchorwoman was talking about some guy who'd just been elected to Congress. But the crawl line at the bottom of the screen caught her eye: *Celebrate Bastille Day with French President Sarkozy*

Goosebumps rose on her arms. The president of France was in New Orleans? Holy shit! Was that Peter's target?

She muted the sound, snubbed out her cigarette and drank some Becks. She should have paid more attention to the news, but she was so happy to have Peter staying here, she'd spent most of her time fixing meals and talking to Peter.

A wide shot of the crowd outside the WWII Museum filled the screen, smiling people waving flags and swaying back and forth. But dozens of police officers were there too.

"Security is extra tight at the WWII Museum today," said the newswoman. "French President Nicolas Sarkozy and the French Consul General are here to celebrate Bastille Day, honoring the historic connection between France and New Orleans. Tomorrow President Sarkozy will fly back to Paris, to participate in Bastille Day celebrations there."

No he won't. Peter's going to shoot him. And then what would happen?

She moaned, recalling the video clip she'd seen on the History Channel. Jack Ruby shooting Lee Harvey Oswald, JFK's assassin, in the basement of a Dallas police station.

Tears filled her eyes. What if that happened to Peter? Then she'd be all alone.

She opened the drawer of the end table and took out a joint. She lapped the end, lit up and dragged deep, holding the smoke in her lungs, like she did when she got depressed thinking about Mother, the frown of disapproval, the down-turned lips, the hard stare in her eyes. If she fell off her bike and skinned her knee, Mother just slapped a Band-Aid on it and told her to go outside and play.

No I-love-you's from Mother. The only people Mother loved were anti-war protesters and Janis Joplin. And Dad, maybe.

Buzzed by the joint, she leaned back against the futon. Dreamy-eyed optimism blossomed inside her like a holiday balloon. Every-thing was going to be fine. Peter would finish his job, take her to Eu-rope and they would live happily ever after, just like he said.

6:15 PM

Control stood outside the museum behind a crowd of spectators listening to the music blasting through the speakers. Viktor had told him not to go inside, ordering him around like some kind of lackey.

He touched his bruised cheek where the bastard had punched him. His eyelid fluttered, a spasm of anxiety. He couldn't decide who he feared most, the Boss or Viktor, the thug with the dead eyes and the toneless voice and the vicious fists.

The infernal music on the speakers ended and the crowd cheered. Good. The program was about to begin. Music from five to six-thirty, speeches until seven. But a Sousa march started up. *Stars and Stripes Forever*. Everyone knew that one. Blood hell, why couldn't they get on with it?

He couldn't wait for this job to be over. Tomorrow he would fly to London. Catch up on sleep during the seven hour flight, get through Customs, take a taxi home and celebrate with a stiff drink.

The cellphone in his pocket vibrated, a text from Viktor: *Call me*

Holding a hand over one ear to block out the music, he punched in the number.

"What is happening?" Viktor said.

"The program is running late. They haven't even begun the speeches yet."

"Call me when it is over." A click sounded in his ear.

He put the cellphone in his pocket and studied the NOPD cops standing behind the crowd, at least a dozen by his count. Off to his left, thirty yards away, a white NOPD van bigger than a camping trailer stood near the building. The officer in charge of security was probably in there.

Control smiled. The cops were afraid someone might shoot Sarkozy at the museum. But nothing was going to happen here.

The real action would be at the Consul's residence.

———

6:35 PM

Henri stood in the wings at the right side of the stage. The loud music was giving him a headache. His boss, Andre Delacroix, was in a secure room down the hall with President Sarkozy and the French Consul General. When the music finished, he would go tell them it was time for the speeches. And after the speeches, what?

His heart fluttered inside his chest.

Yesterday someone had shot a pigeon during Sarkozy's morning jog. He wasn't there but another agent told him about it. When they found the pigeon, Sarkozy yelled at them, saying they'd pushed him to the ground for nothing. Some kid shooting at pigeons, he'd said.

But last night Delacroix had held a meeting to set up an emergency plan. If anything happened at the museum, Delacroix and his team would take Sarkozy to the Hotel Cavendish. Henri would be the decoy. Four other security agents would put him in a caravan and drive him to the Consul's residence.

Henri rubbed his icy hands together. Detective Renzi had warned of a possible assassination attempt. A sniper had recently shot a woman near the residence. Last night after the meeting, he had called his ex-wife. Midnight in New Orleans, already eight o'clock Sunday morning in Paris. When Yvette answered, he asked to speak to Olivia.

"She's in her room getting dressed. We're going to my parents' house for Sunday dinner."

"Just put her on, Yvette. It will only take a minute."

"All right," Yvette said, clearly annoyed. "Hold on."

And then Olivia's sweet little voice said, "Hello, Papa. How do you like New Orleans?"

"Not as much as I like hearing your voice. Yesterday I got you some beignets."

"Thank you, Papa. I knew you would. When will you be home?"

"On Monday, but it will be late. I might not see you until Tuesday."

"I'll be waiting, Papa. I love you."

"I love you, too, Olivia. See you soon."

Then he'd tried to sleep, but dark thoughts intruded. The chants of protesters outside the residence in Paris, and the Chief of Security's words. *Sarkozy has many enemies. Not all of them are in France.*

The music stopped and thunderous applause came from the audience. Time for the speeches.

Last Friday when he asked Detective Renzi about a possible attack, Renzi had told him not to worry, many police officers would be on duty. Delacrox's alternate plan worried him, but his job was to protect President Sarkozy and he intended to do it.

He threw back his shoulders and marched down the hall, thinking positive thoughts. An hour from now he and President Sarkozy would be safely inside the Consul's residence, preparing to fly home tomorrow. Recalling the treats he'd bought for Olivia, Henri smiled.

Tuesday morning he would make her a big batch of beignets, with lots of powdered sugar.

CHAPTER 36

7:20 PM

Viktor ate every bit of the apple, crunching the seeds and the core with his teeth. He would have preferred another peanut butter protein bar, but Boss had told him a proper diet included fruits and vegetables, which would keep him healthy and strong.

But they didn't make him grow any taller.

Before Boss took him to London, he had never seen an apple, much less eaten one. No fruits or vegetables in the orphanage, just wormy bread and thin gruel.

The room was dark, except for the fading light seeping through the open window. He raised his head and sniffed. Someone was cooking hamburgers. He stood at the window, inhaling the tantalizing odor. His stomach gurgled. No hamburgers for him tonight, but after he returned to London, he could eat all the hamburgers he wanted.

Far off to his right, the setting sun was a faint pink glow. Soon the only light would come from street lamps below him and the bright lights outside the French Consul's residence.

His weapon lay on the floor, armed with a 40-round magazine. Set on semi-automatic, the Kalashnikov could fire all 40 rounds in sixty seconds. Two spare magazines were in the canvas bag, but he doubted that he would need them. Sarkozy and his protectors would be 100 meters away at most. How could he miss?

He picked up his weapon and stroked the smooth plastic stock, recalling the day ten years ago when Boss had explained the math. Traveling at a velocity of 2,350 feet per second, the 7.62x39mm rounds would turn his target into … Viktor smiled. … hamburger.

His cellphone rang, a sharp sound in the darkness. He snatched it and answered. "Yes?"

"The ceremony is over," Control said. "People are leaving the museum."

"What about the others? You said there was big crowd outside."

"Most of them have left."

"Good. Go to the NOPD trailer and stand near the side window."

"Why? There are cops inside. I need to go—"

"Shut up!" The skin on his scalp prickled, just as it had at the orphanage when they came with the razor, knowing they would shave his head, knowing he was powerless to stop them.

"Do it. Now. Tell me when you are there." He waited, running his fingers through his thick dark hair, the silky feel of it soothing him, calming him.

"I'm near the window," Control whispered. "What do you want me to do?"

"Wait there until I call you," he said and ended the call. Boss had told him to leave no loose ends, including the timid little man with the thick eyeglasses and fearful eyes.

He rolled up his shirtsleeve. Unwilling to rely on his memory for this crucial detail but unwilling to write it down on paper, he'd used a black marker to print the number of the cellphone that would trigger the IED on his forearm. He could not afford to make mistakes. Boss had devised the perfect plan and had chosen him to carry it out.

He punched the number into the phone.

———

7:29 PM

Stunned by the concussion blast, Frank fell to his knees. Assaulted by flying debris, he covered his head with both arms. Moments later, realizing he had sustained no major injuries, he rose to his feet, trying to make sense of it. What the hell was this? A terrorist attack?

Ten feet away a man called to him, but Frank barely heard him, partially deafened by the explosion. All around him, people lay on the ground, crying out for loved ones, high-pitched screams of anguish. A man scooped up his little girl and ran toward the parking lot across the street. People exiting the museum scattered, frantically running toward their cars in various parking lots or the parking garage. Others just stood there, stupefied.

He got on his radio and said, "Explosion outside the WWII Museum with multiple casualties. We need ambulances right now!" Then he ran to the man with the chest wound ten yards away.

A middle-aged woman ran up to him. "I'm a nurse. Let me help." She wrapped a plastic bag around her hand and jammed it against the wound. The man screamed in pain. An ambulance stationed in the parking lot across the street slowly drove toward them, maneuvering to avoid the crumpled bodies on the ground.

Frank waved his arms and shouted, "Over here!"

Everywhere he looked people were screaming in pain. Others were using their cellphones, but not to call for help. The idiots were taking pictures with their smartphones. Across the street, two television crews were setting up, getting ready to broadcast live from the scene.

He clenched his jaw. The 24-hour news cycle never stopped, an unrelenting maw begging to be fed.

When he turned to see where the blast had come from, he felt like someone had punched him in the gut. Fifty yards to his left, the NOPD communications van was engulfed in flames, acrid black smoke billowing from the windows.

Aware that two NOPD officers had been inside, he sprinted toward the van, but intense heat from the blazing inferno stopped him twenty yards away. A charred body lay beside the van, almost decapitated by flying debris, the top of the skull gone.

Circling the van, he found two uniformed officers tending to a pair of teenagers on the ground beyond the van. Even here the heat was intense. One officer saw him and said, "I called dispatch, told them to send more squad cars and ambulances."

"Did anyone get out of the trailer?" he asked, dreading the answer.

"Not that I saw," said the other cop, his sweaty face smudged with soot. "Christ, nobody could survive in there. Had to be a bomb."

"A bomb," Frank muttered, only now beginning to comprehend what had happened. A bomb was the last thing they'd been worried about. Where was Sarkozy? And Henri?

He turned and ran toward the museum entrance. Halfway there Kenyon grabbed him. "Frank, are you okay? Your face is bleeding."

"I'm fine, got cut by flying debris. What the hell is this? A terrorist attack or …"

"Or a diversion to distract us while the Sniper picks off Sarkozy."

"I better go check on him. Delacroix set up Plan-B in case of an emergency, and if this isn't an emergency, I don't know what is."

"Do it," Kenyon said. "I'll stay here, do what I can to help."

Frank sprinted toward the side entrance where Sarkozy had been scheduled to do the photo-op. Two firetrucks and three ambulances roared past him, sirens wailing. Ahead of him, he saw Delacroix and his team shove someone in a suit into an SUV with its nose pointed at Magazine Street. As soon as the doors closed, two motorcycles and the NOPD cruiser ahead of it took off, and the SUV followed.

Beyond them, another cruiser blocked the intersection at Magazine Street. When the caravan passed it, that cruiser fell in behind them, flanked by two more motorcycles, and the caravan disappeared.

Vehicles leaving the parking garage clogged the street, panicked visitors desperate to escape any new danger, whatever it might be. Drivers on side streets leaned on their horns, yelling epithets through open windows, undeterred by the acrid smoke that filled the air.

But traffic jams weren't his main concern. He got on his cellphone and called Andre Delacroix. The line was busy, so he called Henri. But his phone was busy too. Cursing in frustration, he ran back to Kenyon, who was helping an EMT tend to a bleeding man.

Taking him aside, Frank said, "A French security team just put someone in an SUV and drove off with an NOPD escort, but I couldn't tell if it was Sarkozy or Henri."

Kenyon grimaced. "We got one helluva a mess here, Frank. Any word on the guys in the NOPD van?"

"It doesn't look good. Where the hell is Wendell Hicks? Anything on the radio channels?"

"No. Dispatch put out a Code Blue to clear the channels for emergency calls." Kenyon mopped sweat off his face. "Damn, it's fucking chaos out here. I better go find Hicks."

"Do it," Frank said. "I'm going to Prytania Street. My car's in the lot across the street."

Dodging an ambulance, he ran across the street. In the parking lot, two bodies lay on the ground, their faces covered with bloody towels. A medic in an orange jumpsuit knelt by an injured man, pulled a syringe from his kit-bag, uncapped it and injected it into the man's arm. Nearby, an older man with a gaping chest wound lay beside an overturned wheelchair, his face ashen. The man was huge, had to weigh 300 pounds at least. Two EMTs rolled him onto a plastic tarp and loaded him into the last ambulance. Another medic and a civilian helped a bleeding woman into an SUV.

Incredibly, even here idiots were taking pictures with smartphones.

Frank wanted to slap them. Soon they'd be uploading them to Facebook. Others would share them, the posts would go viral and bingo: worldwide footage of the disaster at the World War II Museum in New Orleans.

———

Security Agent Emile La Place wiped sweat from his brow. Day or night, New Orleans was hot and humid, worse than the Amazon jungle he believed, though he'd never been there. If he were wearing Kevlar body armor like the close-detail agents it would be worse.

But he was too tall for that detail—six inches taller than President Sarkozy—and too old, fifty-four.

Even after two decades with the *Service de la Protection* (SDLP), a unit of the French National Police responsible for protecting French and foreign dignitaries, the wires from the communications kit to his wrist mic still irritated him. The ear fob was worse, jammed into his ear like a wad of gum.

During those decades he had stood outside countless buildings, guarding countless VIPs, studying the expressions of bystanders. Faces didn't lie. He could read a face as well as he could shoot a gun. But the constant stress had left him with an ulcer and deep wrinkles on his forehead, not to mention the ruination of his marriage.

Two years ago, his job became even more stressful. He was reassigned to *Groupe de sécurité de la présidence de la République* (GSPR) responsible for protecting the President of France. Whenever Sarkozy traveled, Emile stood outside his hotel to prevent anyone from harming him, scanning the crowds to make sure nobody shot him.

His boss, Andre Delacroix, feared that might happen here. Emile didn't speak fluent English like Henri Bellest, but he understood it well enough to read a newspaper. New Orleans had one of the highest murder rates of any city in America. Last month the NOPD had run a buy-back program, paying people to turn in their guns, no questions asked. They had collected almost six hundred.

Merde! Six hundred guns!

The agitated voice of Andre Delacroix sounded in his ear fob. "There has been an explosion at the museum. We are executing Plan B. Stay alert at the Cottage. My instructions will follow."

Alarmed, Emile slipped his hand inside his suit and touched the pistol in his shoulder holster. The Cottage was code for the Consul's residence. NOPD police cars were parked at both ends of the block to prevent vehicles from entering, and several police officers stood guard outside the residence, but Delacroix had been adamant last night. NOPD officers were only backup. French security agents were responsible for Sarkozy.

Or in the case of Plan B, Henri Bellest.

Emile took out a tin of Tagamet pills and dry swallowed two of them. Soon three vehicles would arrive, two police cars and a black SUV, bearing Henri and four French security agents, who would take Henri into the residence. His job was to make sure no one shot them.

———

Lying prone on the roof, the Sniper heard distant sirens. Far off to his left, a red glow lit up the sky. Fearing it was coming from the WWII Museum, he grabbed his night-vision field glasses. He couldn't see the museum from this angle, but a major fire appeared to be raging somewhere near it, a large plume of smoke rising into the air.

Jesus, did someone try to kill Sarkozy at the museum?

Unnerved, he put down the field glasses and looked at the Consul's residence diagonally across the street to his left. A woman with short dark hair stood outside the entrance, talking on a cellphone. No uniform, but he was certain she was a cop. She trotted over to a French security agent and spoke to him. Then she turned and pointed.

He ducked down below the two-foot cement wall that lined the perimeter of the roof. Fuck! She was telling the security agent to check the roof of this building. He took out his Beretta, ran to the access door, wedged it open and raced down the stairs. He paused on the fourth floor, listening, his heart a machine-gun inside his chest.

Hearing nothing, he ran down to the apartment on the third floor, went inside and hurried to the bathroom. The woman looked at him.

He aimed the Beretta at her. "One sound and you're dead."

She nodded, her eyes wide with fear.

He shut the bathroom door, ran back to the hall and heard footsteps on the stairs below him. He opened the door wider and stood behind it, flattening his back against the wall.

Thirty seconds later, the French security agent burst into the apartment, arms extended, gripping a handgun in both hands.

With a violent chopping motion, he slammed the Beretta down on the man's wrists. The agent yelped and dropped his weapon. He slammed the edge of his hand into the agent's throat, knocking him to the floor.

Should he kill him or tie him up like the woman?

But this man was no innocent civilian. If he managed to free himself, he would contact his colleagues and tell them someone had attacked him.

Clutching his throat, the security agent, an older man with gray hair and deep wrinkles on his forehead, gazed at him, a silent plea unmistakable in his bloodshot brown eyes. *Don't kill me.*

For an instant, he wondered how the man had come to be a security agent. But no matter. His life was about to end. Steeling himself, the Sniper shot him in the eye with the silenced Beretta.

Eventually, the man's colleagues would look for him, but if someone had tried to assassinate Sarkozy at the museum, their top priority would be to bring Sarkozy to the Consul's residence.

If he was still alive.

As the Sniper dragged the agent's body deeper into the living room he noticed an earbud in the man's ear, and wires from a communications pack to a wrist mic. Working quickly, he located the comm-pack inside the man's jacket. He unhooked the wires and thrust the earbud, the comm-pack and the wrist mic into his pocket.

What could have been a disaster might turn out to be a goldmine.

He left the woman's apartment and raced back to his sniper's nest on the roof.

CHAPTER 37

Kneeling at the open window, Viktor trained his night-vision field glasses on the area near the museum. Almost two miles away, but he could see a red glow, and a cloud of black smoke was visible in the gray sky. Using his thumb, he increased the magnification. It took him a few seconds to locate the NOPD communication van.

His heart surged, beating a tattoo against his ribs.

Orange-red flames danced over the NOPD van and black smoke gushed from one window. Beneath it, a body lay on the ground. He couldn't see who it was, but he assumed it was Control. The man with no balls had obeyed his orders. Good. No loose ends.

No firemen spraying water at the flames, but he heard faint sirens in the distance, fire engines and cops rushing to the museum just as Boss had predicted. Adding to the chaos, traffic was at a standstill as people tried to escape in their cars, and two firetrucks were approaching the museum followed by three ambulances with flashing lights.

Boss had invented the perfect plan. Use a bomb to create chaos at the museum and divert attention from the actual target site. When the bomb went off, the French security team would put Sarkozy into a vehicle and rush him back to the Consul's residence.

He put down the field glasses and studied the street below him. To his left, two cops in uniform stood beside the cruiser with flashing lights blocking the intersection. To his right, diagonally across the street, other cops were placing waist-high metal barriers on the sidewalk in front of the residence.

Viktor shook his head. Did they think someone was going to attack Sarkozy with a knife or shoot him with a handgun?

These cops were idiots, ignoring the possibility that the biggest danger to Sarkozy might come from above.

A man with a sniper rifle on a nearby roof and another man with a far more lethal weapon.

Viktor picked up the Kalashnikov with the 40-round magazine.

Not that he would need that many to kill Sarkozy.

Cursing the sea of red brake lights in front of him, Frank clenched his jaw, his gut churning with acid. The Consul's residence was only two miles from the museum, but it might as well be two hundred. Magazine Street was gridlocked. Forget lights and sirens, the cars had nowhere to go.

Traffic was bad enough, but communication was impossible. He wanted Delacroix to abort Plan-B and take Henri to the hotel, but each time he called Delacrox's cellphone, he got a busy signal. The same with Henri. He'd called Kelly twice, but both times it went straight to voicemail.

That worried him. She had to know about the explosion by now.

His cellphone vibrated. Hoping it was Kelly, he answered.

"What the fuck happened at the museum?" Vobitch said. "I can't get jackshit on my radio."

"A bomb blew up the NOPD communications van. It's chaos over there, multiple casualties."

"A *bomb*? What the fuck is that? You think it's terrorists?"

"No. I think it's a diversion so the Sniper can shoot Sarkozy at the Consul's residence. But I can't reach Delacroix to warn him."

"I thought Hicks said they cleared all the roofs on that block."

"He did, but that was hours ago, before Sarkozy left for the museum. What if he got up there later? I'm in my car on Magazine Street heading for the residence, but traffic is gridlocked."

"Want me to send a Rapid Response Unit to the Consul's residence?"

"They'll never get there in time."

"Maybe," Vobitch said, "but I'll send one anyway."

"Okay, thanks. I need to call Kelly." He ended the call and dialed Kelly's number, but it went straight to voicemail. Jesus, where the hell was she? If the Sniper shot Henri, Kelly would know it was the Sniper and go after him, and the Sniper would shoot her, too.

Vivid memories of the night a drug-dealer shot her played in his mind. Racing to the hospital, finding her hooked up to machines, her eyes closed, her face pale. Seeing the energetic, volatile woman he loved lying there as still as a corpse. The doctor told him if the slug had hit her an inch or two to the left, she'd be dead.

He'd called her father, a Chicago cop, and told him she'd been shot. A volatile Italian like Kelly, her father said, "I'm on the next plane. Stay with her! Don't leave her until I get there." So he had, dozing in the chair beside her bed until her father had arrived.

Kelly had survived that shooting, but every day was a crap-shoot for cops. A lot of them wound up dead, and he wasn't going to let that happen to Kelly. He couldn't imagine life without her. Never seeing those sea-green eyes again, eyes that spoke to him more eloquently than words ever could.

Hoping the tires would withstand the impact, he wrenched the wheel and bulled his way over the curb onto the neutral ground, sped to the next intersection and cranked his lights and siren.

The driver in the left lane gave him a dirty look, but Frank ignored him, cut in front of his car and bleeped his siren at the driver in the right-hand lane. Startled, the woman stared at him as he blew past her onto the cross street. Only a few cars on the side street.

He bleeped his siren and they slowly moved out of the way. At the next intersection he turned left onto Prytania and hit another logjam. Blocks ahead of him, he saw flashing blue lights. Henri, in an SUV escorted by motorcycles and two NOPD cruisers, but it looked like they weren't moving either.

Another bleep of his siren and cars inched out of the way. But time was the enemy. His gut told him the Sniper was on the roof.

If he didn't get there fast, Henri would die. And so might Kelly.

———

Crouched on the roof, the Sniper waited for an update on the earbud. A minute ago, the man in charge of Sarkozy's security team had said, "There has been an explosion at the museum. We are executing the emergency plan. Stay alert and wait for my instructions."

Speaking French, of course. That didn't bother him—he spoke fluent French—but the explosion at the museum bothered him a lot. Was Sarkozy dead or alive?

Shrouded in darkness, he pressed the rifle against his cheek, impatient, ready to finish the job. Diagonally across the street to his left, the lights were still on outside the Consul's residence.

Would they leave them on? That would make his job easier.

"Poodle is safe," said the voice in his ear. "Puppy is on his way to the residence."

Poodle is safe. The Sniper let out a sigh of relief. Sarkozy was alive. But who was Puppy?

Before he had time to think about this, the voice said, "Traffic is a problem, but he should be there in ten minutes. He will exit the vehicle on the curbside. It should take no more than ten seconds to get him into the building."

"Ten seconds?" said a different voice. "No media?"

"No. They are at the museum. Wait for my instructions."

Hearing sirens in the distance, the Sniper peered through the scope and adjusted the reticle, centering on the front door of the residence. Sarkozy had been scheduled to do a photo-op at the museum, so he assumed Sarkozy would be wearing body armor.

Only a head shot would be guaranteed lethal.

Having observed the quick reaction of Sarkozy's security team on Saturday, he knew he would get only one shot. Recalling the Minnesota Fats line in *The Hustler*, he smiled. *The money shot.*

He'd made plenty of money shots in Iraq. During his final mission, his spotter had given him the target's location. "Fourth floor of the building, third window from the left." He zoomed in on the window, saw the muzzle of a rifle and spoke into his mic, "Cross-hairs on target, setting sun behind me, no optics reflection. Good to go." And he'd blown the target away.

The voice in his ear jolted him back to the here and now. "The motorcade is approaching." The security chief feeding him Intel, not realizing his worst enemy was listening.

He leaned forward over the parapet to check the street below him. In the distance he saw flashing blue lights. Sarkozy's caravan. But three blocks behind it was another car with flashing blue lights.

That could be a problem.

A voice spoke in his ear, another security agent with a deep gravelly voice. "What about his adoring fans? Poodle has a lot of fans."

"The police officers at the residence will clear a path to the door to make sure no one can get near him. Stay alert when he exits the car. Focus on the bystanders. Out."

The Sniper took a deep breath to steady his heartbeat. Soon his target would be here. This was what he lived for. But his reputation was on the line, not to mention his job. No margin of error in a shot like this. No margin of error at all.

One shot was all he would get to kill Sarkozy.

———

Frank punched Henri's number into his cellphone. Still busy. Damn it to hell! Traffic on Prytania Street was at a standstill. Ahead of him, he saw the NOPD cruiser blocking the intersection pull out of the way to let Henri's caravan pass. But that was three blocks away.

Any minute now Henri would get out of the SUV and walk to the front door of the Consul's residence. Then anything could happen.

What if Kelly was standing there? He dialed her number again. It went to voicemail. He listened to the message, savoring every syllable.

"Hi, I can't take your call right now, but please leave a message."

After the beep sounded, he breathed, "Kelly." And stopped. What could he say? *If something happens to you, I won't be able to stand it?*

He pulled to the curb and left a message, his voice urgent.

"Kelly, stay away from Henri. I'm three blocks away. If something happens, don't do anything until I get there."

Then he jumped out of the car and started running as hard as he ever had in his life.

A cop at the corner tried to flag him down, but Frank flashed his badge and kept running, his feet pounding the pavement. Pedestrians kept getting in his way, people out for a stroll, enjoying the balmy weather before starting their work week. Jesus, didn't they watch TV? Didn't they know about the bomb at the museum?

Breathing hard, he kept running. Now he was two hundred yards away from the residence, two football fields away. He set his jaw and ran faster, knowing in his heart that he'd never get there in time. Any second now Henri would leave the SUV and the Sniper would shoot him. And Kelly might be next.

———

Viktor watched the NOPD police car pull out of the way. Beyond it, two police cars with howling sirens and flashing blue lights waited, escorted by a pair of motorcycles in front and behind them.

The important vehicle was between the two police cars, a large black SUV with tinted windows.

He gripped the Kalashnikov, his heart thrumming his chest. Inside the black SUV was French President Nicolas Sarkozy, the self-important man who had enjoyed a life of privilege.

But that life would end tonight.

When Sarkozy left the SUV, his protectors would rush him into the residence through the front door. His hosts had provided the perfect setting for Sarkozy's final steps, bright lights above the door, beside it two French flags fluttering lazily in the breeze.

Viktor focused on the SUV as it slowly approached the residence, his heart beating in a slow easy rhythm. The woman in Paris who was expecting Sarkozy's child was about to become a widow. Would she drop the child off at an orphanage? Of course not. Sarkozy was rich.

But all the money in the world would not save him tonight.

A minute from now the SUV would stop, and Sarkozy's protectors would rush him toward the residence.

He curled his finger around the trigger.

Counted down the seconds. Fifty-nine ... Fifty-eight ...

———

Gripping his rifle, the Sniper set his eye to the scope. On the reticle, thin vertical and horizontal lines met in a cross. The intersection was centered on the door of the Consul's residence, bathed in bright light. To the right, two flagpoles displayed the French Tricolor.

Pleased, he released a silent breath. The preparation was done. The range, elevation and wind adjustments calculated. He had zeroed the scope at sixty-three inches up from the pavement, an inch less than Sarkozy's five-foot-four height.

A security agent would get out of the SUV and open the back door to allow the president to step onto the sidewalk. Then the other three agents would surround Sarkozy and rush him toward door of the residence.

But one slug from his L39A1 Enfield rifle would enter Sarkozy's head just above his ear and rip off the top of his skull.

One of the greatest assassinations in American history. This one would be written up in all the history books, along with the assassinations of JFK, RFK and MLK.

But their killers had been caught. He wouldn't be.

Below him, the sirens went silent. The SUV stopped and all four doors opened. The security agents exited first, four men in dark blue uniforms, their eyes darting everywhere, alert for danger.

They were good. But good wouldn't cut it today.

Today, Sarkozy was going to die.

Two words in his earbud. "Sixty seconds."

Adrenaline coursed through him, every nerve in his body humming like a high-tension wire, a feeling like no other. This was the moment he lived for. Time to execute the money shot.

Some British Special Ops commanders wished their snipers "good luck." But luck had nothing to do with it.

He drew in a breath and scanned the area near the front door.

Several women had gathered on the sidewalk. They appeared to be Sarkozy fans, but plenty of people hated Sarkozy. Still, these women wore sleeveless tops and summer shorts with no place to conceal a weapon. Moreover, metal police barriers held them back, revealing the path Sarkozy would take.

Even at ground level this was a major security breach. To a trained sniper in an elevated position, it was like a lighted runway at an airport, delineating the path the target would take.

Seconds from now this job would be over. Then his life with Win could begin in earnest.

Sarkozy stepped onto the sidewalk, a handsome man with dark curly hair. The Sniper set his finger on the trigger, eyes glued to the target. *You are a dead man.*

But something felt wrong. What was it?

He studied the target, calibrating the man with his eye, comparing him with the man he had watched on Saturday.

Unlike the man jogging around the outdoor running track, the man in the suit with the curly brown hair was as tall as his protectors.

He took his finger off the trigger.

Was that really Sarkozy, or someone posing as Sarkozy?

CHAPTER 38

Viktor watched the police caravan stop in front of the residence and got into a zone of concentration. That's what Boss called it. Focus on every detail, Boss said, it could be important. Viktor had done this many times. Boss was right. Each time his senses grew sharper and time seemed to slow down.

The air was calm now, no smell of hamburgers drifting through the window to distract him. The bright lights above the door of the residence were still on, but the red-white-and-blue French flags beside the door were drooping now, almost as if they knew what was about to happen.

The black SUV that had driven Nicolas Sarkozy here from the museum had dark-tinted windows, idling at the curb now, its headlights on, like the two police cars, one in front, one behind. The officers remained inside, waiting for instructions perhaps.

Viktor set the Kalashnikov on automatic. One pull of the trigger and a burst of 7.62x39mm rounds would leave the muzzle at tremendous speed, destroying human bone and tissue. It would be an easy shot. The door of the residence was only one hundred meters away.

But Sarkozy was still inside the SUV with his protectors.

What were they waiting for?

Troubled by the delay, he stroked his hair with his right hand. The soothing feel of thick hair beneath his fingers calmed him.

The doors on both sides of the SUV slowly opened. His heart sped up, thrumming his chest. The moment he had been waiting for.

He slipped his finger inside the trigger guard.

One by one, Sarkozy's protectors climbed out and planted their feet on the ground, four men in dark blue jackets with bright brass buttons. The men were short, no more than five-foot-six by his estimate. The two agents on the curbside of the SUV extended their hands and helped Sarkozy out of the SUV. The privileged man who had no doubt eaten plenty of fruits and vegetables as a child.

But they hadn't made Sarkozy any taller, either.

Voices on the street below distracted him. Several women darted into the street and approached the SUV. Two cops jumped out of the police car behind the SUV and shooed them away, women tarted up

241

like London streetwalkers, glossy lips and painted eyes. Like fans at a pop music concert, they ran to the sidewalk and stood behind the metal barriers with their cellphones, calling out to him, "President Sarkozy! Look over here so I can take your picture."

Viktor clenched his teeth. These foolish women could be a problem. Shoot cops or security agents if necessary, Boss had said, but try not to kill civilians.

Sarkozy's protectors grasped his arms and rushed him toward the front door, the well-lit door that allowed Viktor to acquire his target. He lined up the shot. Hit the center of mass, Boss had said, the sweet-spot in the center of the torso.

He pulled the trigger, raking his target with a five-second burst. The loud reports hurt his ears, but he maintained his focus. Sarkozy and two of his protectors were down, but he had to be sure. Sarkozy might be wearing body armor. Centering on Sarkozy's head, he raked him with another long burst and saw his head explode.

Elated, Viktor pumped his fist. No doubt this time. Never again would Nicholas Sarkozy give another speech. Or eat another apple.

His ears were ringing, but even so he could hear shrieks from the women, then moans as they stared at Sarkozy and two of his protectors, lying on the ground in a puddle of blood. His other protectors ran to their fallen comrades. Two police officers, the man and the woman in civilian clothes, rushed over and joined them.

The rest of the cops weren't looking to see where the shot came from, they were yelling at the women, telling them to run away.

Viktor set his weapon on the floor. The muzzle was still hot due to the many rounds he'd fired.

Focused on his next task, he stripped off his black shirt and trousers, stuffed them into his canvas bag and took out a long-sleeved plaid shirt and a pair of worn jeans. He pulled on the jeans, then the shirt, fastened the buttons on the front, and checked his weapon.

The muzzle was cooler now, cool enough to hide inside the trash bag he'd brought. Modified for just such a necessity, from the tip of the muzzle to the end of the cut-off stock the Kalashnikov was only twenty-four inches long.

He grabbed his canvas bag, picked up the trash bag and ran to the door. Here was a danger point. Other residents would have heard the gunshots. He cautiously opened the door.

A bearded young man and a slender woman in shorts and a tank top rushed past him.

"What's up?" he called, a convenient phrase Boss had taught him.

"Someone shot President Sarkozy," the woman yelled, rushing by without looking at him.

He heard voices and footsteps on the stairs below him, other residents running outside, adding to the confusion. The cops would be too busy with crowd control to look for him. All he had to do was make his way to the building four doors away and finish the job.

No loose ends, Boss had said. Including the man with the sniper rifle.

———

When the automatic gunfire sounded, the Sniper froze, unable to grasp what was happening. He couldn't move, couldn't breathe. It was as if an atomic bomb had gone off, sucking the wind out of him, delivering a mushroom cloud of disbelief.

But what he saw across the street wasn't a World War II documentary about Hiroshima. The man he was supposed to kill lay dead on the sidewalk. Before he had a chance to pull the trigger.

It had taken only fifteen seconds, but it seemed like the longest fifteen seconds of his life. His heart hammered his chest as he replayed it in his mind, like a movie.

When the first rounds hit him, Sarkozy fell to the ground. Seconds later, the second volley blew his head off. Now Sarkozy lay near the door as till as a stone, surrounded by a widening pool of blood.

Overcome with fury, he clenched his fists. What a disaster!

After all the time and energy he had wasted preparing for this moment, endless hours of planning, killing innocent civilians. The new assignment to kill the Armenian, a task that had put him in grave danger. The Russians had tried to kill him twice, necessitating perilous escapes, infuriating meetings with Control, and the death of another innocent civilian.

Despite all this, he had soldiered on, committed to executing the assignment they'd given him, the most difficult of his career, one that would cement his reputation as their top sniper.

Now his crowning achievement had been snatched away like windblown confetti at a wedding party. Because he had waited, questioning why Sarkozy seemed to be as tall as his protectors, debating whether it was really him. Wasting precious seconds, which allowed someone else kill Sarkozy.

The assignment they'd sent him here to do was over.

Or was it?

In the beginning, the plan was simple. Make the cops think a sniper was randomly shooting innocent civilians, when the actual plan was to assassinate a VIP.

But that was a bait-and-switch, and he was the dupe.

The real plan: Have him play a deranged sniper killing civilians to make sure the cops were hunting him, and bring in another shooter. Control claimed the man who'd mowed Sarkozy down less than a minute ago with a machine gun was his backup.

His fury boiled over, rocketing his heart rate and inflaming his cheeks. The cocksuckers had fed him a line of bullshit!

Control was the messenger but the Boss was the mastermind, creating a Byzantine labyrinth of deceptions. Have him shoot the runner from a roof near the Consul's residence. Withhold Intel about The Package until the last minute. Have Backup Man plant a bomb at the WWII Museum to divert attention from the residence.

Have Control send *him* to his rooftop sniper perch and tell him to shoot Sarkozy, knowing all along the *other* man would shoot first.

He clenched his fists. They had set him up as the patsy, so Backup Man could escape.

In fact there was a distinct possibility that Backup Man wasn't finished. Maybe he had another assignment. Kill the Sniper.

He heard sirens approaching. Galvanized into action, he broke down his equipment and stowed it in his gym bag. Any second now the cops might come up here looking for him.

His first impulse was to leave the building as fast as possible. He had already planned his escape route.

But one false move could be fatal.

If the Boss intended to have Backup Man kill him, he would have told the man with the machine gun where to find him.

Which meant Backup Man might get here before the cops did.

Planning his next move, the Sniper checked his Beretta to make sure to make sure the safety was off.

———

Frank was one block away when he heard the shots. Not just one, a volley of rapid-fire reports. They had to have come from the Consul's residence. Time had run out and he was two hundred yards away, an eternity if there was a live shooter.

With that many shots fired, there had to be casualties.

A sick feeling of dread mushroomed inside him. Where was Kelly?

He took out his SIG and sprinted toward the residence. People saw him coming, saw the gun and got out of his away. But as he ran closer people running in the opposite direction slowed him down. A woman in a white halter top ran toward him, screeching wordlessly, her mouth open, her eyes wide with terror. He realized the red dots on her white top were blood. And then she was gone.

"Police," he shouted, shoving people out of the way, thinking, *Please let Kelly be safe*. Not praying exactly, he hadn't prayed since his first communion, but he couldn't imagine life without Kelly. Seeing her again in his mind after she got shot before, lying in that hospital bed, silent and still, hooked up to machines.

Time crawled by in micro-seconds, his senses heightened by the adrenaline coursing through his body. High-pitched screams, the flashing blue lights of squad cars reflected in windows, the bitter taste of fear inside his mouth. Not fear for his own safety.

For Henri. And Kelly.

When he reached the end of the block, an NOPD cruiser was parked sideways across Prytania Street, engine idling, lights flashing. No cops inside, anyone could jump inside and take off.

But the worst lay ahead.

Cops shouting orders and shrieks from stampeding bystanders, trying to get out of harm's way. The chaos that gunfire and sudden violent death inevitably brought. On the left side of the street, the black SUV that had brought Henri to the residence stood at the curb, sandwiched between two NOPD cruisers with flashing lights.

All four doors of the SUV were open. So were the doors of the cruisers. No one inside them.

Frank clenched his jaw, recalling his Sicilian grandfather years ago, furious over some real or imagined slight, putting the Sicilian curse on a man who'd insulted him. The Malocchio. The dreaded Evil Eye.

That's what he wanted to do. Put the Malocchio on the man who'd fired the machine gun.

He jumped over a metal barrier and ran along the sidewalk, fearing what he might find, his eyes darting here, there and everywhere, searching for Kelly.

Outside the door to the residence, metal barriers stood on the sidewalk to protect Henri Bellest—posing as President Sarkozy—from bystanders. But it was all too clear that no further protection was necessary. Illuminated by bright lights above the door, two French security agents and several NOPD officers stood near three bodies on the sidewalk. Two wore the uniforms of French security agents. The third wore a business suit. Henri.

Blood pooled on the sidewalk beneath their bodies. Beyond them, gunshot holes crisscrossed the door to the residence.

He spotted a patrol officer tending to a woman lying in the street. Jesus was it Kelly? His heart pounded as he drew closer. But the woman had long reddish hair. Not Kelly.

Frantic now, he whirled and studied the building across the street, the one he had entered early this morning, looking for the Sniper. Kelly knew that was the rooftop the Sniper had used to shoot the runner. Was she up there now, trying to catch him?

He bolted across the street, pushing his way through a crowd of onlookers that spilled off the sidewalk.

Someone grabbed his arm. Startled, he turned.

Kelly stood there with an anguished look on her face, her eyes glazed with tears. Overcome with relief, he grabbed her and pulled her close, oblivious to the nearby screams and cops shouting orders and sirens. Nothing else mattered.

She clung to him, her face buried into his neck. Inhaling her familiar scent, he rubbed her back, felt her chest heave in a silent sob. His throat thickened. He couldn't imagine the horror she had witnessed.

She raised her head, gazing at him as she brushed tears from the sea-green eyes he loved so much. "He shot him, Frank. The fucker mowed him down with a machine gun."

He didn't want to let go of her, but he had a job to do. Kelly was alive, but Henri Bellest, the man who loved jazz, the man with the six-year-old daughter, was dead. His joyous relief that Kelly was safe was tinged deep sorrow and regret. And guilt.

All along he'd been convinced the assassination would happen here, and he had failed to prevent it. Prytania Street was lined with beautiful trees, elegant homes and upscale apartment buildings, not a place you'd expect to encounter an assassin, much less two of them.

He brushed tears from Kelly's cheeks and kissed her. "The Sniper didn't kill Henri. A machine gun doesn't fit his MO. There were two shooters and I'm going to get them."

Her eyes got that steely look that he knew so well. "Okay, but I'm going with you."

"No," he said. "I need you to stay here." Well, not exactly. What he needed was for her to stay out of harm's way so he could go find the motherfucker that murdered Henri. "Vobitch is sending a Rapid Response team, should be here any minute. I need you to tell them where to go."

She opened her mouth to protest, but he cupped her face in his hands and kissed her. "Kelly. Do you know how worried about you I was? Check your voicemail. I can handle this."

———

Viktor edged along the crowded sidewalk, everyone talking loud to be heard above the din of police sirens and the whoop-whoop of ambulances. A woman bumped into him, tears dripping from her eyes. He kept going, edging through the mob of people trying to see what had happened across the street. He didn't bother to look.

The only important thing had already happened.

He had killed Sarkozy.

Ahead of him, a young couple was leaving his target's building. Recalling the photo Boss had given him, Viktor studied their faces. The man didn't match the photo.

A woman in shorts came out and held the door open for him.

"What's going on?" he said, but she didn't answer.

He heard footsteps on the stairs above him. He ran his right hand over the trash bag, located the trigger guard and set his finger on it. If he saw the sniper …

But the footsteps belonged to a woman. She frowned at him and hurried out the door.

Now the building was silent. He crept up to the second floor. Seeing no one, he went up another flight. Boss had told him the entrance to the roof was on the fourth floor at the end of the hall.

On the fourth floor landing, he stopped and listened.

Hearing nothing, seeing no one, he hurried down the hall to a narrow staircase. He set the canvas bag on the floor, pulled the Kalashnikov out of the trash bag and checked the magazine. At least twenty rounds left. That should be plenty.

Gripping the Kalashnikov with both hands, he crept up the stairs.

The door at the top was slightly ajar. Perfect.

CHAPTER 39

The Sniper knelt on the asphalt beside the shed with the AC unit. The access door to the roof was twenty feet away. He'd left the door ajar, not wide enough to allow anyone to see him, just two tantalizing inches. In the end he had decided to make his stand here.

Backup Man wasn't his only problem. He could hear the wail of sirens, police cars bringing more cops, but others might have already entered the building. Here, he had the upper hand. If he left the roof, they might ambush him on the stairs.

The screams of people fleeing the area were fading, but shouts from the cops on Prytania Street were clearly audible. It was twilight now, the light fading, but the air remained hot and humid, his shirt drenched with sweat, a rank odor rising from his armpits.

He'd left the gym bag with his sniper equipment near the parapet that overlooked the street. Whoever came through the door would see that first, a momentary distraction that might give him an extra second or two. In a situation like this, every second was precious.

The door to the roof opened wider, but silently, no shouted orders from police telling him to drop his weapon. Gripping the Beretta in both hands, he took a deep breath and set his finger on the trigger.

Would a tactical squad of cops burst through the door, guns drawn? If they did, he was done for. He might kill one or two, but sooner or later he'd run out of ammo.

If the man with the machine gun came through the door, his chances were better, but he knew what the weapon could do.

He'd never used one on a job, but when he was in the Army he'd practiced with one. Set on full auto, it sprayed a rapid volley of high-powered ammo, certain to kill anyone in its path. But he also knew what one well-placed round from a Beretta could do.

He let out the breath he'd taken, drew another and focused on the door, waiting. Patience, patience.

A short dark-haired man stepped onto the roof, holding a Kalash-nikov in both hands.

He squeezed the trigger. Stunned, the man froze. He didn't scream, but a shocked expression twisted his mouth, followed by a grimace of pain. Excruciating pain, the Sniper assumed.

One shot to the head would have killed him, but that would have been too easy. He wanted the motherfucker to suffer, so he'd shot him in the groin. The man slowly sank to his knees, his lips drawn back in a silent snarl. But he kept his grip on the Kalashnikov, his eyes focused on the Sniper, eyes full of hate.

For an instant, they stared at each other, motionless. Until the Sniper sprang to his feet, took aim and pulled the trigger.

The man's head jerked back as a small hole appeared in the center of his forehead. He slowly toppled sideways, but some involuntary synapse deep inside his brain sent a message to his trigger finger, enough to spray another volley of slugs. When he landed on the asphalt, the Kalashnikov fell from his hands and the volley stopped.

But not before several slugs ripped into the Sniper's legs.

The shock blew him backwards. He landed on the asphalt on his butt. Gritting his teeth to fight the pain, he stared at his thighs. Bright red blood was seeping through multiple holes in his pant legs, his life-blood leaking onto the asphalt.

No hopping on a plane to Europe now.

No living-happily-ever-after with Win.

His luck had run out. He had killed his enemy but in the end Backup Man had defeated him. What a cruel quirk of fate.

Maybe it was preordained, part of his family heritage. Fleeing persecution in Yugoslavia, Mum and Dad had settled in Brussels, the city of his birth. Five years later, they obtained fake documents with English-sounding names, which helped get them into the UK. In London, he was Peter Gibbs, his father repairing bikes and motorcycles, his mum giving flute lessons.

A spasm of pain radiated from his thighs into his groin. Maybe he should end it now before the pain got worse. One shot from the Beretta, over and out. A deep sadness welled up inside him.

What would happen to Win, his beloved soul-mate? The woman he had always yearned for and finally found. *Will we live in Brussels?* she'd asked, her luminous brown eyes aglow with excitement.

He'd never even told her he loved her. Would he have told her on the Sky-Eye when their chairs stopped at the top? Shouting it out to the whole city, the whole world? *I love you, Win!*

That would have been a kick. Too bad it wasn't going to happen.

Poor Win. She hated her mother, had run away to escape her unhappy home life, saying she didn't have a normal childhood.

But what about his childhood? On the surface it seemed normal enough. His mum and dad loved him and worked hard to take care of him, but was it normal to change names and pretend to be someone else, Mum having no friends, reading him bedtime stories about murder and monsters.

After he joined the Army, his mates became his family, and he'd found his true calling, embracing his job as a sniper, excelling at it. But while he was killing the enemy in Iraq, Dad died, leaving Mum all alone. Then he'd changed his name again.

His employers at Zenith Intelligence thought he was Peter Milovanovic, but on her deathbed Mum had given him the key to a safe deposit box in Brussels. His original birth certificate was still there: Peter Dragic, his dad's surname, his mum's favorite given name. Inside the box were thousand of dollars in cash, money he'd saved for when he got out of the paid-assassin business.

But forget Brussels. He was going nowhere. Unless he wound up in the La-la-land in the sky. That brought a smile to his lips.

Maybe Mum was up there. They could read dark stories together. *It was the best of times ... it was the worst of times.*

He clenched his teeth. The pain was worse, that's for sure. His legs ached, bleeding profusely, the pain invading his gut now, the blood loss making him dizzy and weak. Defenseless.

And his rifle was thirty yards away.

That's what he needed. A goal to keep him focused.

He got down on his belly and hitched himself across the roof with his elbows, his eyes focused on the gym bag.

———

When Frank got to the second floor landing, he heard a gunshot, then another, followed by a volley of shots from an automatic weapon. He charged down the hall and ran up to the third floor. Seeing no one, he kept going.

No activity on the fourth floor, either, but at the far end of the hall beside the stairs to the roof a black canvas bag sat on the floor.

Gripping the SIG in both hands, he ran to the staircase. Above him, the door to the roof was wide open. An adrenaline rush hit him as he climbed the stairs. He stopped just inside the door, the familiar odor of spent gunpowder filling his nostrils.

Ten feet away, visible in the fading light, a man lay on the asphalt in a pool of blood, his right arm flung out to one side. Near his hand a Kalashnikov lay on the asphalt.

Beyond the dead man, a trail of blood led from the AC storage unit to the parapet overlooking Prytania Street. A man sat with his back against the parapet, his legs extended. Beside him, the muzzle of a rifle poked out of a gym bag. The hackles rose on Frank's neck.

He was face-to-face with the Sniper, but the Sniper wasn't dead. He had a gun in his hands, aimed directly at him.

Shoot him or not? Two men with their fingers on the trigger, it could go either way.

He blocked out the distant shouts below them, the intermittent flashes of blue light from the cruisers, and focused on the Sniper, a trained marksman twenty yards away. Not likely to miss at that range, and Frank wasn't wearing a ballistic vest.

One shot and he'd be dead.

The Sniper was wounded, blood pooling on the asphalt under his legs, but a wounded killer with his back to the wall had nothing to lose. Still, Frank wanted answers.

He took ten slow, deliberate steps forward and stopped at the edge of storage unit near the blood trail.

"Don't come any closer or I'll shoot you," the Sniper said.

"Put the gun down. You need medical attention. I'll call an ambulance."

The Sniper smiled, more of a grimace than a smile. "No. They'll take me to a hospital, fix me up and you'll throw me in jail. Put the fucking gun down or I'll shoot you."

Frank believed him. His eyes were cold and unforgiving. Merciless.

On the other hand, it seemed like he wanted to talk. Frank had en-countered that before, a cornered killer knowing his life of crime was over, eager to justify himself.

Let him talk, Frank thought. He's lost a lot of blood. Sooner or later, he'll pass out.

Holding his left hand in the air, Frank set the SIG on the asphalt with his right hand.

"You're the cop who called me a coward, right?"

"Why'd you kill the Armenian?"

"Just following orders."

"Whose orders? Who do you work for?"

The Sniper squinted at him. "You're Detective Renzi, right?"

"Right. NOPD Homicide. Who do you work for?"

"On the news you called me a coward. You think you're so brave? Come one step closer and I'll shoot your fucking balls off. That's what I did to the guy behind you."

Don't take the bait, keep asking questions.

"Who was the dead man in your room at the Hotel Royale?"

"You're the detective. You figure it out."

Score one for the Sniper. "Why was he after you? What was he looking for?"

"Fuck you, Renzi. I'm not telling you anything."

"Peter Milovanovic was the name on the register. What's your real name? Peter Gibbs?"

The Sniper's eyes widened slightly, but he said nothing.

"The maid told me about you. Seems like she had a crush on you."

"I should have killed her, but I didn't." The Sniper raised his weapon and aimed it at Frank's heart.

———

The pain was worse now. His whole body felt cold and clammy. In a quick motion, he wiped sweat off his face with one hand, then gripped the Beretta in both hands. If Renzi came one step closer he'd shoot him.

"Who's the dead guy with the machine gun?" Renzi said.

"He shot Sarkozy, the French president." Thinking: But Backup Man with his fucking machine gun wouldn't get the glory or the money. He'd seen to that.

"No he didn't. He shot a decoy."

The words hit him like a hand grenade. Fuck! He was right all along, had seen it with his own eyes. The man posing as Sarkozy was just as tall as the security agents. Backup Man had shot the wrong man! Not that it mattered now. The Boss would be livid, but screw that motherfucker.

"Who's the man with the machine gun?" Renzi asked again.

"They double-crossed me. They said he was my backup, but he wasn't. He was a Cleaner, like Harvey Keitel in—" He clenched his teeth, the pain radiating into his chest now.

"*Reservoir Dogs?*" Renzi said.

"No, not that one. You like movies, Detective Renzi?"

The cop gazed at him, his dark eyes venomous. "Only if the bad guys die in the end. Why did you shoot the policewoman?"

"I didn't." The words came out before he could stop them. Damn! He couldn't tell Renzi what really happened. He had to protect Win. A sharp pang of regret swept over him. If things had worked out the way he wanted, two days from now they'd be in Europe.

Unfortunately, that wasn't going to happen. He was dying.

But he wasn't going to die like Bonnie and Clyde. He wasn't going to jail either. He was going to die right here on this roof.

"I didn't want to kill her." He tried to think of something else to say, but a wave of dizziness hit him. He sagged back against the parapet, the pain sapping his strength. The Beretta felt heavy, too heavy to hold, slipping out of his hand. The cop was saying something, but he couldn't hear him or see him, a red haze filming his eyes.

Time to let go. Time to go see Mum.

———

Frank saw the Sniper's eyes close, saw the weapon fall from his hands as his body went limp.

He ran to him, kicked the Beretta aside and held a finger to the Sniper's neck. He felt a pulse, but it was weak and thready. It would be easy to let him bleed out. Why save him and get bogged down in a judicial system that all too often failed to put killers in jail?

He felt no compassion for the man. The Sniper was a cold-blooded killer, who'd showed no mercy for his victims, killing innocent civilians. But he had more or less admitted that someone was paying him, and Frank wanted to know who.

He took off his belt and used it to fashion a tourniquet around the Sniper's right thigh above the gunshot wounds. He needed one for the other leg too, so he took off his shirt, then his T-shirt and tore it into thin strips. A lousy tourniquet but it would have to do.

He fastened it around the Sniper's left leg, pulled it tight and rose to his feet.

Using his cellphone, he called Dispatch, gave them the address and told them to send an ambulance and a crime scene unit.

Then he called Kelly.

"Frank!" she exclaimed. "Are you okay? I heard gunshots."

"I'm fine. Is Sarkozy safe?"

"Yes. I called David and he said Sarkozy and his security team are already in their rooms at the Hotel Cavendish. What happened up there?"

"The shooter with the machine gun is dead. The Sniper shot him, but the guy got off a few rounds and hit the Sniper in both legs. He's unconscious, lost a lot of blood, but I'm hoping the EMTs can save him. I've got a lot of questions for him. Talk to you later."

He shut his cellphone, but when he turned and looked at the Sniper he knew he would get no more information.

The Sniper's eyes were wide open, staring at the sky, covered with the opaque milky-white film of death.

CHAPTER 40

MONDAY, July 11 – 10:30 AM

She stood at the bathroom mirror, applying makeup to her eyes, mascara then eye shadow, a useless attempt to hide the fact that she'd been crying. And really, why bother?

She had no friends, and her lover was dead.

Tears blurred her vision. She gripped the sink with both hands, recalling what the newswoman on TV had said early this morning. On the roof of a Prytania Street building, police had found the two men believed to be responsible for the explosion at the WWII Museum and the attempted assassination of French President Nicolas Sarkozy. Both men were dead. The woman didn't say who they were, but Win knew right away one of them was Peter.

She spoke the words aloud. "Peter is dead."

That made it worse. She couldn't bear it, the grief sapping her strength, leaving her weak and helpless. She knew she was crying, but it felt like she was on some faraway planet, watching herself sink into a dark pit of despair. Without Peter.

Numb, chilled to the bone, she pulled her silk robe on over her bra and panties and went into her bedroom. Her suitcase lay open on the bed, full of clothes. Peter had told her what to do if something happened to him. She bit her lip, fighting back tears.

If something happened to him. Words that broke her heart, telling her what to do if someone killed him. Take the flash drive and run.

Two loud raps on her apartment door startled her. For an instant, she fantasized that Peter was knocking on her door. But no matter how badly she wanted this to be true, the rational part of her mind told her it wasn't going to happen.

The rapping continued, loud and insistent.

Who was banging on her door? Fearing it might draw unwanted attention from her neighbors, she belted the robe around her waist, went in the living room and stood by the coffee table, eyeing the door. What if it was the police?

But how would they connect her to Peter?

Just thinking his name brought fresh tears to her eyes.

Two loud thumps hit the door. "Open up or we break down the door."

Her heart drummed a jagged tattoo against her ribs. She hurried to the door and worked the locks with trembling fingers. She put her hand on the doorknob, swallowed hard and opened it.

Two men in dark suits stood in the hallway. One was big. The other was bigger. He put his hand on the door, shoved it open and pushed past her. The other man grabbed her arm with one hand and dragged her into the living room. His other hand held a gun, big and black and shiny. The sight of it sent a ripple of fear down her neck.

Her mouth went dry and her stomach lurched. Two huge men with hard eyes were inside her apartment. Who were they? Not cops, that's for sure. Fearing she might vomit, she clutched her belly. "What do you want?" she asked, her voice thin and plaintive. A pitiful sound. Hating herself for showing weakness, she gritted her teeth.

"The flash drive," said the biggest man, the giant, six-foot-six at least, his eyes dark and menacing. "We know you have it."

How did they know she had it? That thought immediately followed by another. Peter said it was valuable. Maybe she could bargain with them, get some money, give them the flash drive, and they'd go away and leave her alone. She dug her nails into her sweat-soaked palms.

"Where is the flash drive?" His voice skittered over her skin like palmetto bugs. Deep and menacing, with a foreign accent.

The air left her lungs with a swoosh. She wanted to kill the mother-fucker, running his eyes over her body as though he could see through her silk robe. She clenched her jaw, willing herself to be strong, her lungs screaming for air.

She had to stay strong or she would die.

The other man aimed the gun at her head. "Give it to us or we will kill you."

She blocked out the words and watched his lips move, cruel lips. If she thought about the words, it was all over. She had to do some-thing. Say something to appease them. "Please. Don't shoot me."

Desperately trying to figure out how to get to the snub-nosed re-volver inside her bureau drawer next to the flash drive.

"Your boyfriend is dead. There is no one else to protect you," he said, his voice flat and hard.

Her guts turned to liquid. He knew about Peter. Had they followed him here? But really, what difference did it make? He knew she had what he wanted. Too frightened to look at him, she gazed at the bottle of Alien on her bookcase, hoping it would give her courage.

"The flash drive is in my bedroom. Wait here while I go get it."

The giant smiled, baring his teeth. The two in front were gold. He took the remote off the coffee table and turned on her TV. A local channel came on, the one she'd watched earlier that had delivered the devastating news. A game show was on now.

Using the remote, the giant raised the volume, louder and louder, the sound blaring into the room. He tossed the remote on the futon, grabbed her arm and bent her wrist back, snapping it like a twig.

She let out a shriek of pain. He slapped her face, silencing her.

"Take us to it. Now."

All rational thought fled, the pain consuming her like a raging fire, her eyes welling with tears. She moaned wordlessly as painful memories flitted through her mind, all the terrible things she had said and done, not just the shoplifting, the pain she'd caused Dad and, she had to admit, Mother. Peter had urged her to reconcile with her mother.

But she hadn't and now it was too late. The giant was dragging her into the bedroom, the man with the gun following them.

The sound from her TV wasn't as loud here, but she could hear raucous laughter from the game show audience, almost as though they were mocking her. *You've been a bad girl and you're going to pay for it.*

The man let go of her arm and she fell to her knees, clutching her broken wrist to her belly, watching him study her suitcase on the bed.

The giant with the gold teeth smiled at her. "Going somewhere?"

Don't think about the pain. Placate them.

She licked her lips and forced a seductive smile. "How about if I do you a favor?" she said in her low sexy voice. "A favor for both of you. I won't tell anyone, not even the cops."

His eyes met hers and drifted away, his face a blank mask, his only reaction a tightening of the muscles around the eyes. Then, without warning, he clubbed the side of her head with his fist.

She collapsed on the carpet, clutching her knees to her chest. The other man kicked her back.

Through a red haze of pain, she cried out.

At least she thought she did, but maybe she didn't. The pain was so bad she couldn't think, could only whimper, "The flash drive is in my bureau."

One by one, the man with the gold teeth opened the drawers, pawing through the contents. He opened the bottom drawer and said to the other man, "Shoot her in the eye."

"No!" she screamed. "No!"

She heard a loud bang, felt an instant of pain, then nothing.

The man with the gold teeth pocketed the flash drive. Speaking in Russian, he said, "The treacherous bitch had a gun. But we got what we came for."

"It might have been fun to fuck her," said the other man, also in Russian.

"We have no time for that. Our flight leaves in three hours. We must go to the airport."

———

12:15 PM

Frank left Headquarters and got in his car, still shaken by yesterday's disaster. The national news media were calling it **Massacre at the Museum**. The international media focused on the failed assassination: **Sharpshooter Fails to Kill Sarkozy**.

But no headlines for the men who had died protecting him. This morning Sarkozy had flown to Paris. Tomorrow Andre Delacroix would fly there with caskets bearing the bodies of three French security agents, one of them Henri Bellest.

After his rooftop encounter with the Sniper, Frank had set aside his grief and anger, focusing on work. By midnight Prytania Street was as quiet as a graveyard. The forensics unit was processing multiple crime scenes, the only lights visible along the street. Then Andre Delacroix called him, clearly distraught. He had spoken to Henri's ex-wife, a conversation he termed "very difficult." He also said one of his agents was missing, could Frank look for him?

Kelly recalled seeing the agent enter the building with the Sniper's nest. They found the agent's body in a third floor apartment. Then, hearing muffled cries, they discovered a woman in the bathroom, bound and gagged. After they cut her loose, she sobbed, "He said if I made any noise he'd kill me!" They'd called an ambulance which had taken her to the hospital.

Frank yawned and massaged his eyes. Ten hours later, he still hadn't slept. Superintendent Sanders had ordered every NOPD officer who'd worked the bombing and the Prytania Street shootings to come to Headquarters this morning.

No rest for the weary, not after a disaster like this.

Seated in the large conference room, they got the casualty report. Five people had died at the museum: two NOPD officers in the communication van, a man near the van, and an elderly woman who suffered a fatal heart attack. Somber-faced, Sanders said, "The other two victims were teenagers, members of the Lycee Francais de la Nouvelle-Orleans band who played at the ceremony."

After a moment of silence to honor the deceased victims, Sanders reported that sixty-one others had been injured, the youngest age six, the oldest seventy-two. Their injuries ranged from third-degree burns to broken bones, lacerations and bruises.

Then they got down to business. Who was responsible?

They had already identified the Sniper as Peter Gibbs, who'd used a variety of aliases. Inside the canvas bag near the stairs to the roof, Frank had found a British passport issued to Viktor Smith and a disposable cellphone. The bomb squad had found charred pieces of a cellphone under the trailer. After determining the number written on Viktor's forearm was the number assigned to that phone, they concluded that Viktor had used the cellphones to set off the explosion.

Many questions remained, but later this week Superintendent Saunders would hold a task force meeting to discuss what else needed to be done.

Frank yawned and checked the time: 12:30 in New Orleans, 7:30 PM in Paris. He keyed the number Delacroix had given him into his cellphone. The call he'd been dreading. When a woman answered, he identified himself and asked if she was Yvette. She was.

After he conveyed his condolences, Yvette said, "Sarkozy is safe because Henri put his life on the line to protect him."

Frank agreed, but didn't say so. He asked to speak to Olivia.

A minute later a voice said, "Allo, Monsieur Frank. My English is not too good."

"It's better than my French." Steeling himself, fighting his emotions, he said, "I spent some time with your father, Olivia. He told me you were very smart. He was very proud of you."

"Papa called me yesterday before—" A soft sigh. "Before Maman took me to Grandmere's house. He said you were a nice man and made a joke about your name. Because it sounds like franc, the money we use to buy things. Papa liked you. He said you told him about a wonderful place to listen to music."

A lump formed in his throat. He swallowed hard, fighting back tears. "Your father was a brave man, Olivia. He loved you very much, more than you could ever imagine. He asked me where to get some beignet mix so he could make some for you."

"With lots of powdered sugar?"

"With lots of powdered sugar, he was very clear about that."

After a short silence, Olivia said, "Were you there when the bad man shot Papa?"

Frank clenched his jaw. "No. Some brave men tried to protect him. They couldn't, but here's the important thing. Your father was think-ing about you when it happened. Always remember that."

"I will, Monsieur Frank. I could never forget Papa."

Yvette came on the line and said, "I need to take Olivia to my par-ents' house now."

Frank thanked her and ended the call. The saddest call he'd made in a long time, maybe ever.

He yawned again, a reminder that he hadn't slept for thirty-nine hours. Maybe he'd take a quick nap before he interviewed the woman he and Kelly had liberated from her bathroom.

His cellphone rang, Kenyon calling him. "What's up Kenyon?"

"Homicide on Dauphine Street in the French Quarter. You better get over here."

"Please don't tell me we've got multiple victims." Thinking, in New Orleans, crime never sleeps. Killers did their dirty deeds regardless of massacres and assassinations.

"No, just one. But it's the shoplifter, looks like she might be the Sniper's girlfriend."

All thoughts of sleep forgotten, Frank got there in record time.

Inside a third floor apartment, Kenyon was waiting in the living room, pumped up and eager to talk. "Her neighbors called the man-ager, said the TV had been blasting for hours. He knocked on the door, got no answer, opened it with his key and found her body in the bedroom. He shut off the TV and called 911."

"How do you know she's the shoplifter?"

Kenyon pointed at a bookcase. "That's the bottle of Alien she stole last month. The gun's in the bedroom, a peashooter .22, but here's the best part." With gloved hands, Kenyon took a cellphone off the coffee table and thumbed a button. "Took a selfie with her boyfriend. The Sniper, right?"

The photograph took his breath away. A smiling young woman with short dark hair and big brown eyes cheek-to-cheek with a handsome man with dark hair and hazel eyes, smiling for the camera.

"No doubt in my mind. Show me the body."

The woman lay on her back in the bedroom. Her robe had fallen open to expose her bra and panties. The carpet beneath her head was stained with dark coagulated blood. Her face didn't look like the face in the selfie photo. Her lips were pulled back in a grimace and a gunshot entry wound had obliterated her right eye.

"Whoever killed her was looking for something," Kenyon said, gesturing at a bureau. "All the drawers open, contents messed up."

"Looks like a professional hit to me," Frank said. "See her wrist? Looks like it's broken."

"Damn! You think they tortured her?"

"Yes. Vobitch kept telling me to solve the Takvorian homicide and he was right. I was focused on the Sniper, but he wasn't the only one gunning for Takvorian. Remember the dead man with no ID at the Hotel Cavendish? And his look-alike twin in the Sniper's room at the Hotel Royale?"

Kenyon nodded. "Foreign-looking, no hits in the usual fingerprint and DNA data bases. We found a Russian-made pistol at the Hotel Cavendish and Viktor Smith used a Kalashnikov to kill Henri and the security agents. You think they were Russians?"

"Maybe. We thought they wanted to shut Takvorian up before he could talk to anyone, but maybe he had something tangible, documents or a thumb drive or something. Maybe the Sniper took whatever it was and gave it to his shoplifter-girlfriend."

"Looks like they found it," Kenyon said. "Then they killed her."

Too exhausted to think, Frank said, "Thanks for the heads-up, but I've gotta crash.

Kenyon clapped him on the shoulder. "Go catch some winks, partner. I'll handle the scene here, get as much info as I can, meet you in the office tomorrow and we'll figure it out."

CHAPTER 41

Five days later SATURDAY – July 16 – 4:15 PM

Frank started a Clark Terry CD on the stereo in Kelly's living room and went in her kitchen. He seldom had time to cook. Why not enjoy it? Have a beer and listen to jazz while he fixed dinner. He had a key to Kelly's house but rarely used it. Usually she was home, but she was working today. He'd taken the day off.

Yesterday Kenyon had found him in the office, sound asleep at his desk, woke him up and sent him home. "Take tomorrow off, Frank. David and I can handle things."

This morning he'd slept late, didn't get up until ten. His condo was a mess so he did some housekeeping, went out to buy groceries and drove to Kelly's house, figuring he'd cook dinner and surprise her. Salmon teriyaki on the grill, the same dinner he'd cooked the first time he came here four years ago.

A magical day, the first time they made love.

Today would also be a celebration. Despite his heart-wrenching fear that Kelly would die outside the Consul's residence, she was alive and so was he.

He took a ceramic dish out of the refrigerator, spread minced garlic over two salmon fillets and fixed the marinade: teriyaki sauce, a squirt of lemon and a splash of OJ. He dripped some on his finger and tasted it. Excellent, tangy with a hint of sweetness. He poured half of it over the salmon, put the dish in the refrigerator and sat down at the table with a bottle of Heineken.

Inevitably, details of the investigation intruded.

After the shootout, they found the apartment the machine-gunner had used. The window overlooking Prytania Street was still open, a crumpled peanut butter protein bar wrapper on the floor below it. The manager said the apartment had been vacant for two months. Frank called the real estate agent who told him a man had called two weeks earlier asking about the apartment. When she asked if he'd like to see it, he said he'd get back to her. Last Friday the man had called again and asked if he could see the apartment on Sunday. She said she was busy Sunday, but she could show it to him Saturday. He declined. He didn't leave his name, but the woman said he sounded British.

On Wednesday, the British Embassy had identified the man who died near the NOPD van. Harold Wilson had been staying in a house near Lafayette Park since the first of June. The date got Frank's attention and so did the address. On Tuesday, a raging fire had reduced the two-story Victorian to rubble. The fire marshal told him someone had doused each room with gasoline, which intensified the flames, causing the entire building to collapse into the basement.

Frank didn't think this was a coincidence. Three men with British passports figured in the investigation, all of them dead. He opened his notepad and studied the list: Peter Gibbs, the Sniper; Viktor Smith, the man with the Kalashnikov; Harold Wilson, killed by the bomb blast at the museum.

The British Embassy had given him the phone number of Wilson's employer. When he called the London office of Zenith Intelligence to ask about Harold Wilson, a woman took his name and number and said she'd have Wilson's boss call him. But he hadn't. Yesterday, he'd called again and got the same runaround.

He heard a car door slam and smiled. Kelly was home. A minute later she sauntered into the kitchen. Even in her work outfit—a steel-gray pantsuit, white blouse and high heels—she looked ravishing. She'd look even better after dinner, in her birthday suit.

She leaned down and kissed him. "Hey, Frank. You look rested. No bags under your eyes."

He wagged a finger at her. "Be nice. I'm cooking your favorite dinner. Salmon teriyaki on the grill."

She clapped a hand to her forehead in mock horror. "What was I thinking? Forget what I said about the bags under your eyes, you look sexy as hell in that pullover."

Amused, he said, "That kind of flattery will get you ... a beer. Heineken or Coors Light?"

"A Heineken would be good."

"Have a seat and I'll get it. Gotta take care of my working-woman lover." He took a Heineken out of the refrigerator, brought it to the table and sat down opposite her. "How was your day?"

"Not bad. No frantic calls from women getting beaten up by their asshole lovers. After a week out of the Dom-V unit, I spent the day catching up on paperwork. How's the investigation going? Roger Vance has been keeping me in the loop with emails, but I'm sure you've got stories to tell."

"Yeah. It's been a long week. I talked to Olivia on Monday."

"That must have been tough," Kelly said, her eyes somber.

He drank some Heineken, wishing he hadn't mentioned it, the memory of his conversation with Olivia bringing back the brooding melancholy funk he'd been mired in since the bombing and the shootings on Prytania Street. "Heartbreaking. I said her father loved her very much and told her he was thinking about her when it happened. Which may or may not be true."

Kelly squeezed his hand. "You did what you could, Frank. No one could have predicted that a bomb would go off at the museum."

"Maybe. But that doesn't make it any easier."

"Thanks to you Sarkozy is alive."

"No," he snapped. "Sarkozy's alive because Henri took the bullets intended for him."

In the silence, the sound of Clark Terry's jazz trumpet drifted into the kitchen, an upbeat solo on Satin Doll, which didn't jibe with his continuing sense of regret and guilt when he thought about Henri.

"Did you talk to the woman we found in that apartment?" Kelly finally said.

"Yes. The Sniper was hiding in her apartment when she came home Saturday night. He tied her up and hid in her apartment, which explains how he avoided the security sweeps."

"I'm surprised he didn't kill her."

"He killed plenty of others. He'd have killed *you* if you got in his way." He chugged some beer. "Nicole Takvorian called yesterday, asked me to come see her. She had something to show me."

"And what would that be, her sexy legs? She's after you, Frank. The widow is hot to trot."

Frank laughed. Trust Kelly to lighten things up. "Maybe, but I'm not interested. She showed me an article in Thursday's *International Herald Tribune,* saying Turkey's Finance Minister had been forced to resign because of shady financial dealings and other improprieties. Another article quoted President Sarkozy saying he was adamantly opposed to allowing Turkey into the European Union."

"So? She should be happy. The Armenians don't want Turkey to get into the EU, right?"

"Yes. More to the point, Nicole said everyone in the Armenian community knew the Finance Minister was a crook, including her husband. She's convinced Turkish Prime Minister Erdogan paid someone to kill him."

"You think he had proof?" Kelly asked, twirling a lock of dark hair around her finger.

"No doubt in my mind. You were right, Kelly. The Sniper had a girlfriend. The shoplifter."

"Whoa! Are you serious? I heard about it on the news, but all it said was the female shoplifter who'd been stealing from French Quarter stores had been murdered."

"She was renting an apartment on Dauphine Street. On Monday someone killed her there. Kenyon caught the squeal, called me right away after he got there. Plenty of evidence that she was the shoplifter *and* the Sniper's girlfriend. She took a selfie of them with her smartphone."

"Get out!" Kelly said. "This I gotta see!"

"Hold on, there's more. Whoever killed the shoplifter tortured her first, broke her wrist, kicked her in the kidneys. They were looking for something, documents or more likely a thumb drive, incriminating information that Aram dug up on the Turkish Finance Minister."

Kelly drank some beer. "Evidence to back up whatever he was going say to whoever."

"Exactly. They tossed her bureau, no telling what they found, but I think Aram saved the evidence on a thumb drive, figuring it might prevent Turkey from getting into the EU."

"But if someone paid the Sniper to kill Takvorian and take the thumb drive, how did the dirt wind up on the front page of a newspaper?"

"Excellent question, Detective O'Neil. Let's assume someone paid the Sniper to kill Takvorian and take the evidence so they could bury the dirt Aram dug up on the Turkish Finance Minister. But maybe someone else wanted to *publicize* it, to force the Finance Minister to resign and diminish Turkey's chances of getting into the EU."

"The people who killed the shoplifter."

"Exactly. Kenyon and I checked with TSA to see if any foreigners flew out of New Orleans after she was murdered. Monday afternoon at four o'clock, two Russians boarded a Delta flight to Minneapolis. Illya and Alexei Kuryakin. The gate agent remembered them because Illya had two gold teeth. In Minneapolis they got on a Delta flight bound for Amsterdam. From there a KLM flight took them to Moscow." Frank drank some beer. "Which proves nothing, of course. And we have no concrete evidence to request their extradition."

"Two months ago," Kelly said, "we thought we had a sniper shooting people at random, but it turned into a jigsaw puzzle with a thousand pieces. I need a shower. See you in a bit."

"Okay," he deadpanned. "Don't bother getting dressed. A towel would be fine."

She arched an eyebrow. "Not so fast, Renzi. You promised me a great dinner. Go start the grill."

After she left the kitchen, he scrubbed two baking potatoes and put them in the oven, but it was too early to fire up the gas grill. He opened another Heineken and sat down at the table, ruminating about the jigsaw puzzle with a thousand pieces. Too many pieces were missing, and when the alphabet soup agencies figured out they were dealing with an international conspiracy, the NOPD would be out of the loop and he might never find out who was really responsible. He hated that.

Just because the shooters were dead didn't mean the case was closed. Not in his mind.

But if he didn't stop grinding on it, it would ruin his celebration with Kelly.

He went in the living room and put on another CD, Blue Bossa, with jazz pianist McCoy Tyner and trumpeter Claudio Roditi. Music to banish the savage beast and elevate his mood.

Ten minutes later Kelly entered the kitchen dressed in shorts and a halter top.

"You're way sexier than Nicole," he said. "How hungry are you?"

"Frank, you promised me salmon Teriyaki on the grill, baked potatoes—"

He silenced her with a kiss and pulled her onto his lap. "True, but the potatoes will take time to cook. Plenty of time for us to neck for awhile, before I fire up the grill."

She put her arms around his neck. "Is this a prelude to a quickie before dinner?"

"Sounds good to me." But then his cellphone rang. He reached over to shut it off, but noticed the call was from London. "Sorry, Kelly, I gotta take this."

"Tease," she whispered, making a face as she climbed off his lap and sat in her chair.

He put his cellphone on speaker and answered. "Detective Renzi."

"Adam Smith," said a deep gravely voice, "Zenith Intelligence. I got a message to call you."

Another fake name, Frank thought. Even he knew Adam Smith was a famous economist.

"I need some information about Harold Wilson. I understand he worked for you. He was killed in an explosion here last Sunday. He'd been here for several weeks."

"Yes. Harry was on holiday. I guess he was in the wrong place at the wrong time."

He locked eyes with Kelly. "Four days ago the house where he was staying burned down."

"Really? I don't know anything about that."

Kelly shook her head, scribbled on his notepad, *Fake name. Harold Wilson was British PM years ago.*

Frank nodded at her. "How about Viktor Smith? Does he work for you?"

"Viktor? No. Years ago I adopted him. He was one of those Romanian orphans, emotionally damaged. I tried to help him, but he could be … unpredictable."

"Unpredictable enough to kill the President of France?"

Silence. Then an explosive cough, *ack-ack-ack.* "What makes you say that?"

"Last Sunday he tried to kill President Sarkozy."

"But Sarkozy was speaking in Paris yesterday."

"True, but Viktor shot three of his security agents. We believe his real target was Sarkozy. Did you know he was in New Orleans?"

"No, but Viktor hated Sarkozy. Two weeks ago when we watched a BBC documentary about him, Viktor became very angry. Sarkozy is a man of privilege, he said, raised by wealthy parents. Viktor never knew his parents. He grew up in filthy conditions in an orphanage."

Frank clenched his jaw. The man was feeding him a sob story. "Did Peter Gibbs work for you?"

"No."

"How about Peter Milovanovic. And Peter Mirotic."

"Never heard of those blokes. Who are they?"

Bullshit. "I need the personnel files for Harold Wilson. How soon can you send them?"

"I'll send them tomorrow. Before he went on holiday, Harry was working on an important project. Unfortunately, the project was not completed. His client won't be pleased, but I shall assign another man to it."

"What sort of project was it?"

"One of our typical projects, gathering intelligence about a business our client was interested in. That's what we do at Zenith Intelligence, collect data about corporations, run the numbers through a computer program and send a report to the client."

What a crock of shit. Aloud, he said, "If I were you, Mr. Smith, I'd put my best man on the project. I hear Turkish Prime Minister Erdogan doesn't take failure very well."

Big silence on the other end. Then, "I have to take another call. Good day, Detective Renzi."

"Fucking asshole!" Frank jumped up and stomped around the kitchen. "I'd like to punch his lights out. Zenith Intelligence, my ass! How about Assassins For Hire. That prick was running the Sniper. Viktor too, probably."

"Let it go, Frank. I know you're distraught about Henri, but Sarkozy is safe. The Sniper is dead. We know Viktor planted the bomb at the museum and shot Henri, but Viktor's dead, too."

"Viktor and the Sniper were expendable hitmen, paid by that asshole on the phone probably, but whoever ordered the hit will get off. And so will the men who killed the shoplifter."

Kelly got up from the table and wrapped her arms around him. "You know what the problem is, Frank? We've got too many clothes on."

That stopped him, a stark reminder that solving homicides wasn't the only important thing in his life. He had a marvelous daughter whom he adored, a father who was dear to his heart, a boss who backed him when the chips were down, and a marvelous woman who understood him.

Gazing into her sea-green eyes, eyes that told him more than words ever could, he said, "Thank you for reminding me what's important. Last Sunday when I heard the gunshots, I wasn't worried about Henri. I was worried about you." He traced a finger down her cheek. "Terrified that you might be dead and what would I do without you."

"I know," she whispered. "I listened to your message on my voice-mail. I worried about you too, when you went after the Sniper. But we're alive. That's the important thing. So let's celebrate."

He kissed her, a long lingering kiss. "You're right. We've got too many clothes on. I need to feel your skin against mine. But that's only part of it. You know that, don't you?"

"Frank," she said, her eyes smiling at him. "If that's all it was, you wouldn't be here."

He kissed her lips, soft and pliant beneath his, feeling her heartbeat against his chest.

Dinner was going to have to wait. He had a feeling that once they got in bed, they were going to be there for a while.

The End

ABOUT THE AUTHOR

In her travels, Susan Fleet has worn many hats: trumpeter, college professor and music historian. While teaching at Brown University and Berklee College of Music, she discovered her dark side and began killing people. Fictionally, of course!

In 2001 she moved to New Orleans, the setting for her award-winning thrillers featuring NOPD Homicide Detective Frank Renzi. The Premier Book Awards named *Absolution,* the first book in the series, Best Mystery-Suspense-Thriller of 2009. Feathered Quill Book Awards named *Natalie's Revenge* Best Mystery-Thriller of 2014.

Although she still plays her trumpet every day, Susan spends most of her time dreaming up new ways to terrify her readers. She now divides her time between Boston and New Orleans, the setting of her Frank Renzi crime thrillers. You can read more about Susan, her novels and her multifaceted career on her website: http://www.susanfleet.com/

Susan says . . . If you'd like an email alert when my next book comes out, sign up at http://eepurl.com/ExkX9 ... I promise never to share your email. If you enjoyed reading *Sniper,* please consider posting a review on the Amazon site where you purchased it. Believe it or not, authors depend upon reader reviews like yours to spread the word about their books, and I would love to know what you thought of it!

Crime fiction by Susan Fleet

ABSOLUTION

DIVA

NATALIE'S REVENGE

JACKPOT

NATALIE'S ART

MISSING

NATALIE'S DILEMMA

SNIPER

Praise for Susan Fleet's non-fiction

Women Who Dared: Maud Powell and Edna White

At a time when most women stayed home to raise children, violinist Maud Powell and trumpeter Edna White traveled the world, thrilling millions with their performances.

"Fleet is an expert on female musicians who deserve wider recognition in the history of jazz and classical music." — Matt Morrell, Jazz at WGBH, Boston, MA

"Fleet's heroines were successful, artistic performers, attracting and enriching broad audiences." — Howard Mandel, music critic, *Billboard*

"Getting to know Edna White [inspired] Susan Fleet to learn about other talented yet forgotten women instrumentalists. This book will add to the important history of female musicians of the past." — Grady Harp, Vine Reviewer, Amazon

DARK DEEDS: Volume 1 and Volume 2

True crime cases about serial killers, stalkers and domestic homicides.

"Well researched and well written. The inner world of these killers is vividly and psychologically portrayed." — Arthur Smukler, MD, author and psychiatrist

"I found this book enlightening and frightening at same time. Susan Fleet is an awesome writer!! — Amazon reader

"Well written, well researched true crime shorts. While many were familiar to me as an avid true crime fan, even the ones I knew about were written in a fresh and informative manner." — Amazon reader

ACKNOWLEDGMENTS

Writing Sniper was quite an adventure! In the process, I learned a lot about snipers, shoplifters and international assassination plots. Two books were especially helpful: *Sniper One, On Scope and Under Siege with a Sniper Team in Iraq*, by Sgt. Dan Mills, and *The Steal, a Cultural History of Shoplifting*, by Rachel Shteir.

Although the names of certain known individuals appear in the novel, they exist in fictional situations and events that are the product of my imagination. David Cameron is no longer the UK Prime Minister, and Nicolas Sarkozy is no longer the president of France. However, I consulted articles published by various news sources about both men, which are readily available on the Internet. Much has been written about the plight of Romanian orphans who lived in the abysmal conditions in orphanages. However, Viktor and Henri Bellest are fictional characters.

Thanks to my beta readers for their insightful comments on the final draft. My deepest thanks to John Amaral, who proofread the manuscript and offered many editorial suggestions which greatly improved the book. His advice on firearms, weapons terminology and ammunition were invaluable.

Many thanks to NOPD Detective Armando Asaro, who generously took the time to listen to my story scenario and answer my questions about NOPD police procedures and protocols. However, all events and actions in *Sniper* are fictional. In some instances I have taken a certain amount of dramatic license. Any errors or inaccuracies are mine alone.

And finally, a huge thank-you to all my readers! Without you, all my work would be in vain. I enjoy getting emails about my books from all over the world and always answer them. I'd love to hear from you. Email me at susan@susanfleet.com